FEBRUARY 2020

# RUDYARD KIPLING'S

EST.
1865

# JUST SO
# COMICS

## TALES OF THE WORLD'S
## WILDEST BEASTS

CAPSTONE

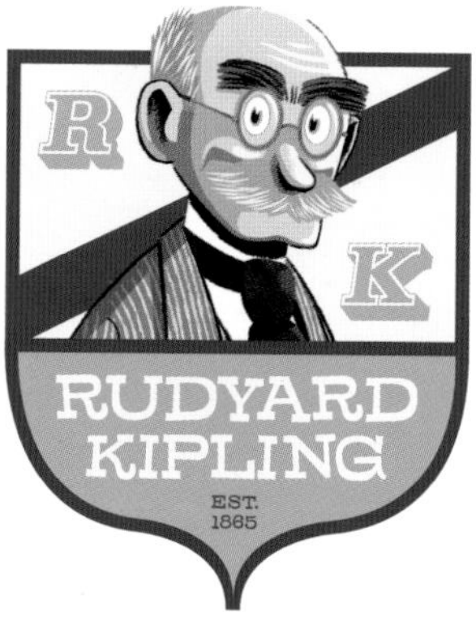
R
K
RUDYARD KIPLING
EST. 1865

# TO OUR READERS

The animal world has long been a place of intrigue. Countless mysteries surround its magnificent creatures. For years, humankind has wondered how animals came to look and act the way they do.

Finally, the questions have been answered. Famed author and worldwide explorer Rudyard Kipling has traveled the globe, searching for the greatest of beasts. He's witnessed and recorded animal behaviors unlike anything seen before. And now we are sharing his findings with the world.

Let Kipling be your guide as you journey into jungles, grasslands, and deserts. Use his invaluable research to unravel the mysteries yourself. It is an exciting time for animal lovers. Thanks to Kipling, we can all be a part of it.

Sincerely,
The Editors

# SECTIONS

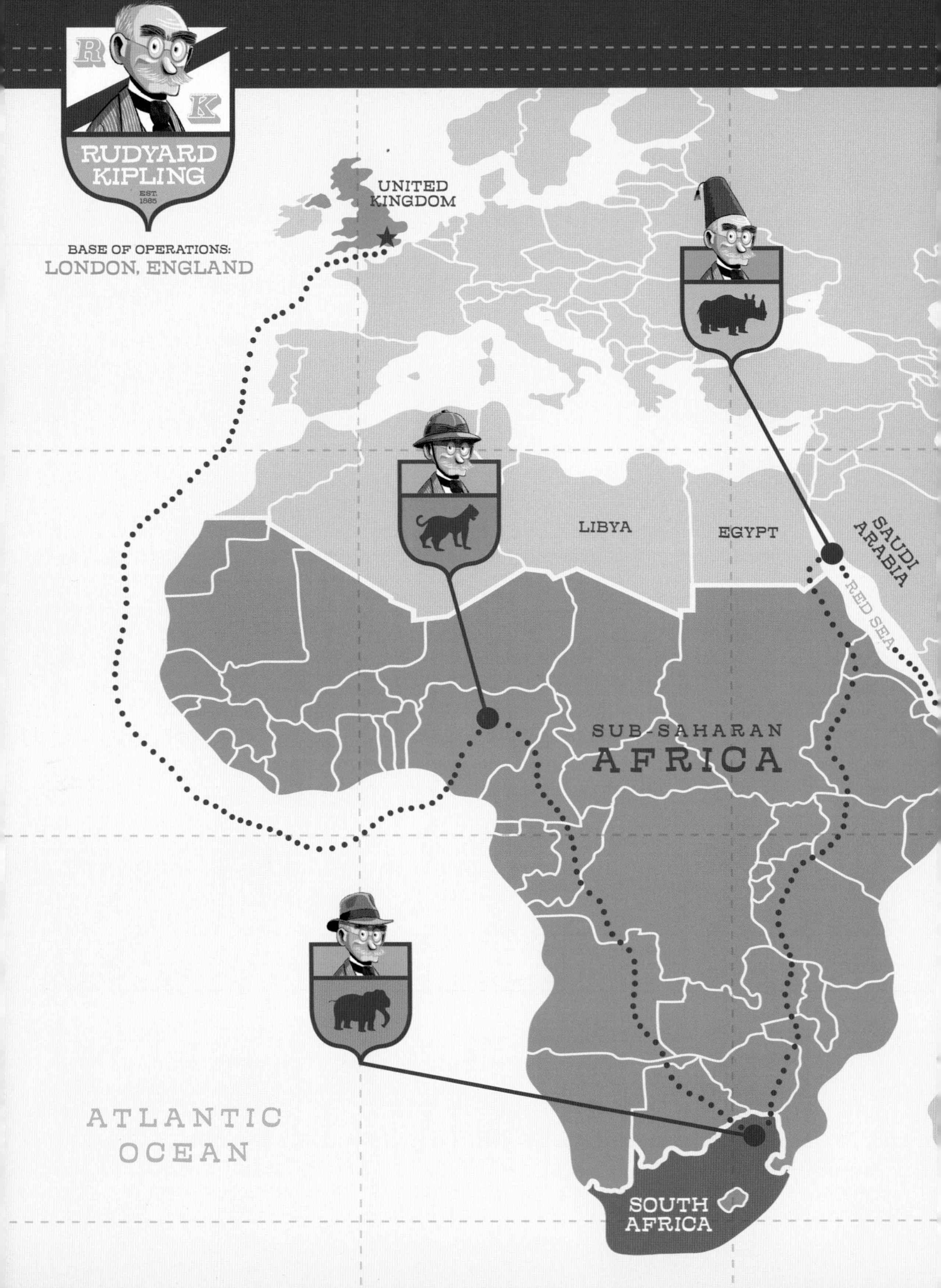
R
K
RUDYARD KIPLING
EST. 1885
BASE OF OPERATIONS:
LONDON, ENGLAND
UNITED KINGDOM
LIBYA
EGYPT
SAUDI ARABIA
RED SEA
SUB-SAHARAN
AFRICA
ATLANTIC OCEAN
SOUTH AFRICA

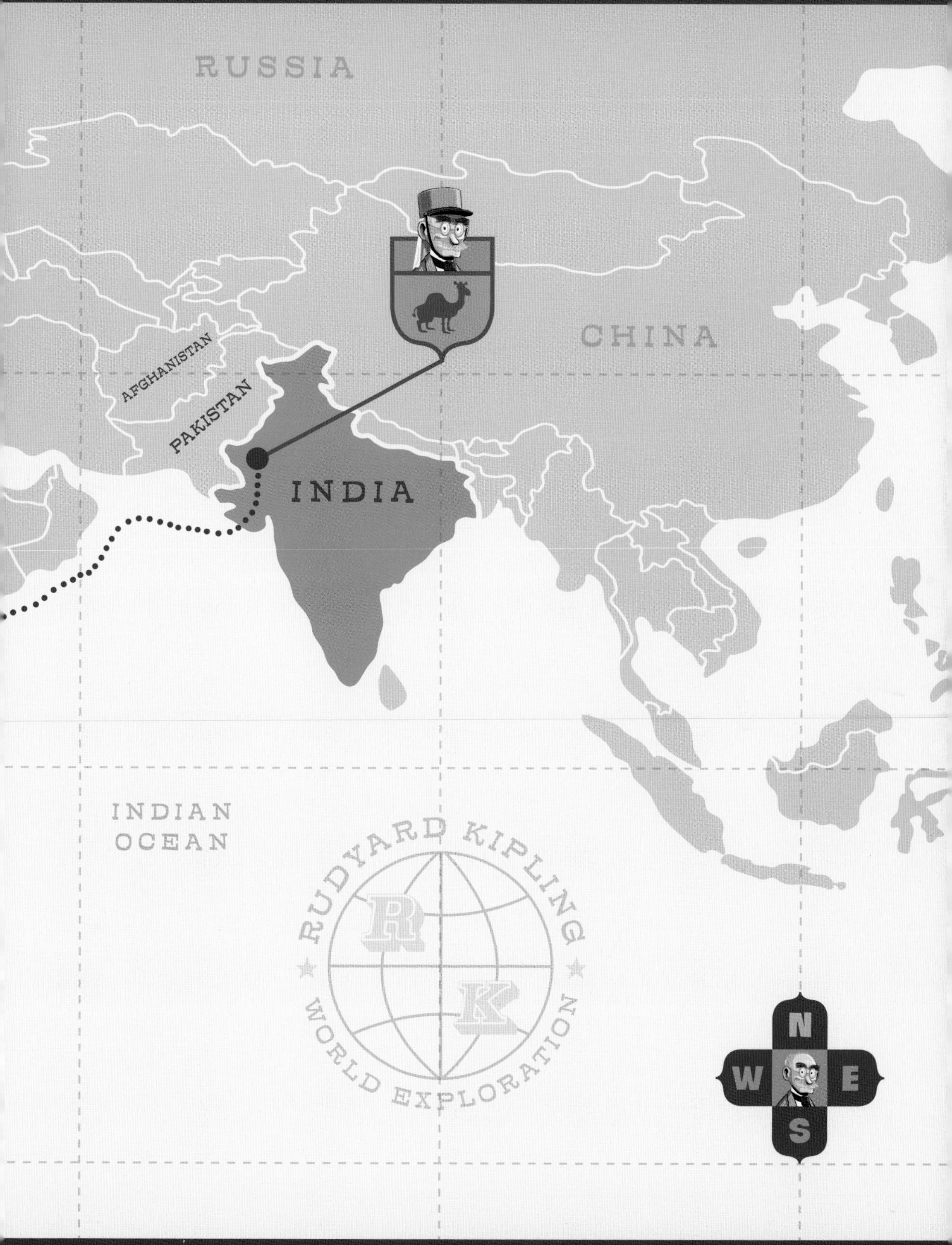

RUSSIA
CHINA
AFGHANISTAN
PAKISTAN
INDIA
INDIAN OCEAN
RUDYARD KIPLING
R K
WORLD EXPLORATION
N
W
E
S

# RUDYARD KIPLING

EST. 1885

# HOW THE LEOPARD GOT HIS SPOTS

as retold by

## SEAN TULIEN
TEAM WRITER

# RESEARCH

SPECIMEN:
SAND-SHADED LEOPARD
(Fig. A)

HABITAT: Sub-Saharan Africa (Fig. B)
HUNTING PARTNER: The Ethiopian (Fig. C)
PREY: Zebra (Fig. D); Kudu (Fig. E);
　　　Giraffe (Fig. F)

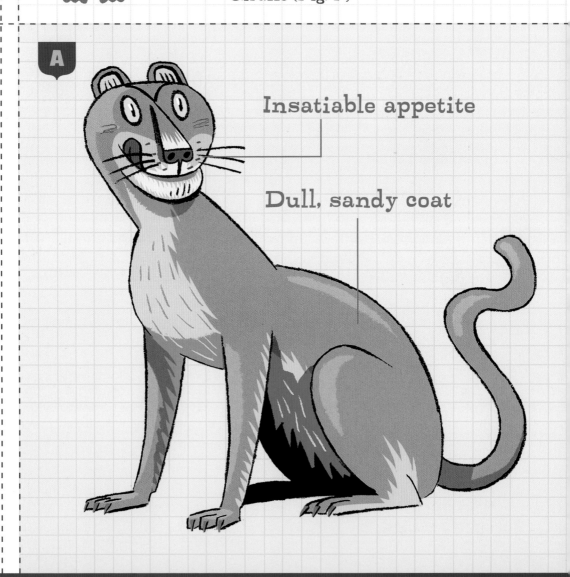

**A**

Insatiable appetite

Dull, sandy coat

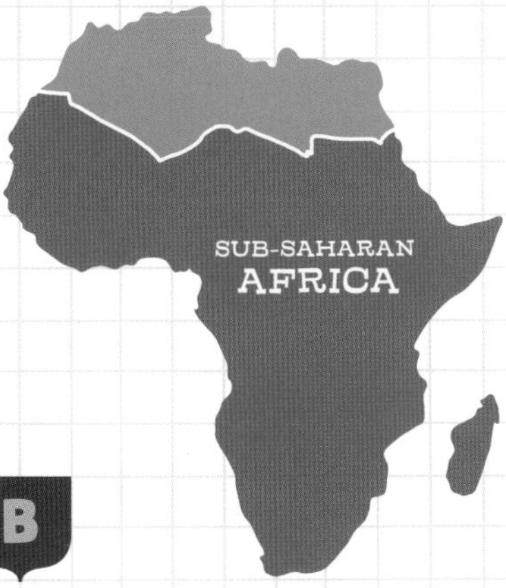
SUB-SAHARAN
AFRICA

B

C

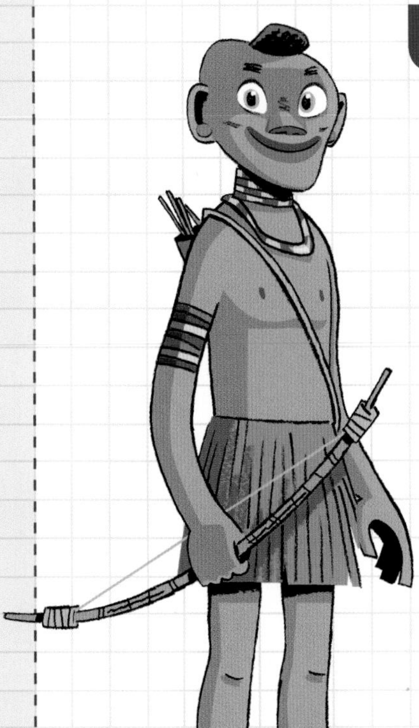

D

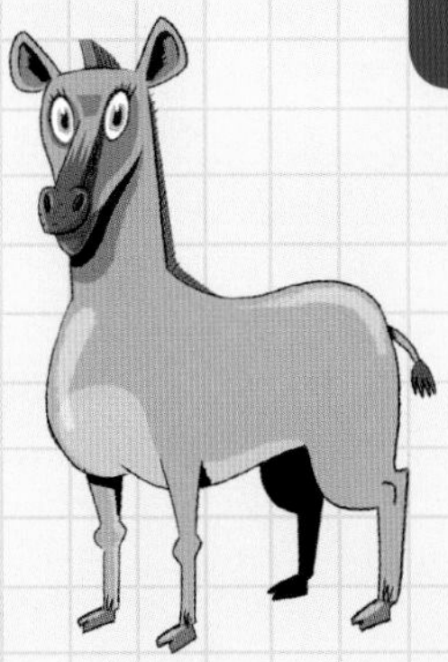

E

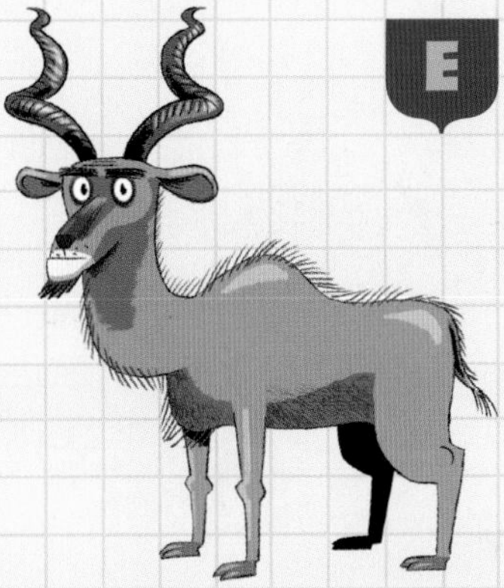

F

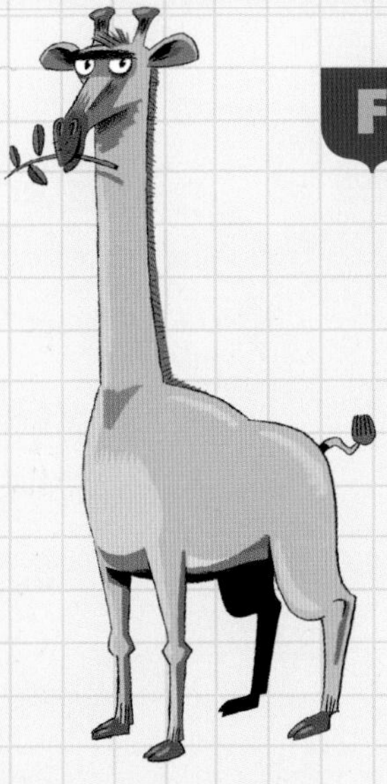

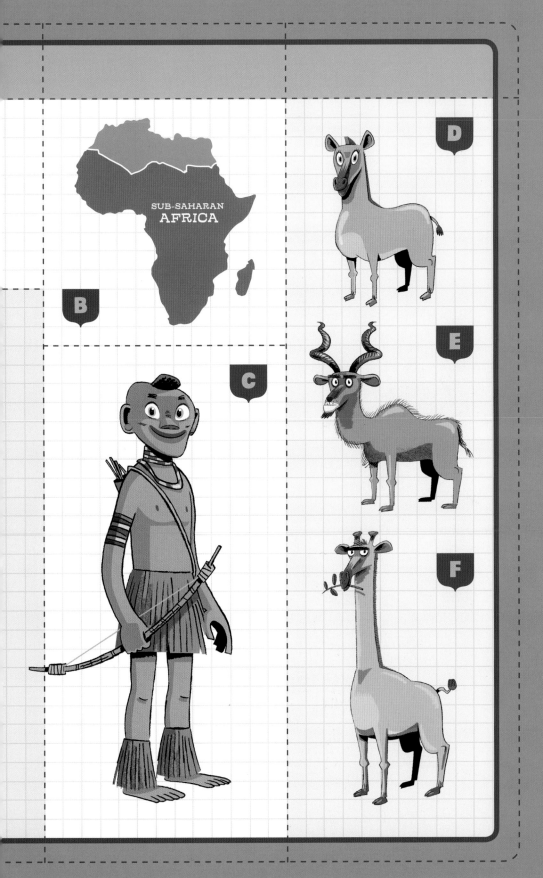

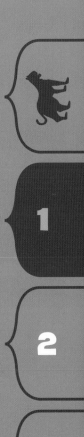

# KIPLING'S OBSERVATION

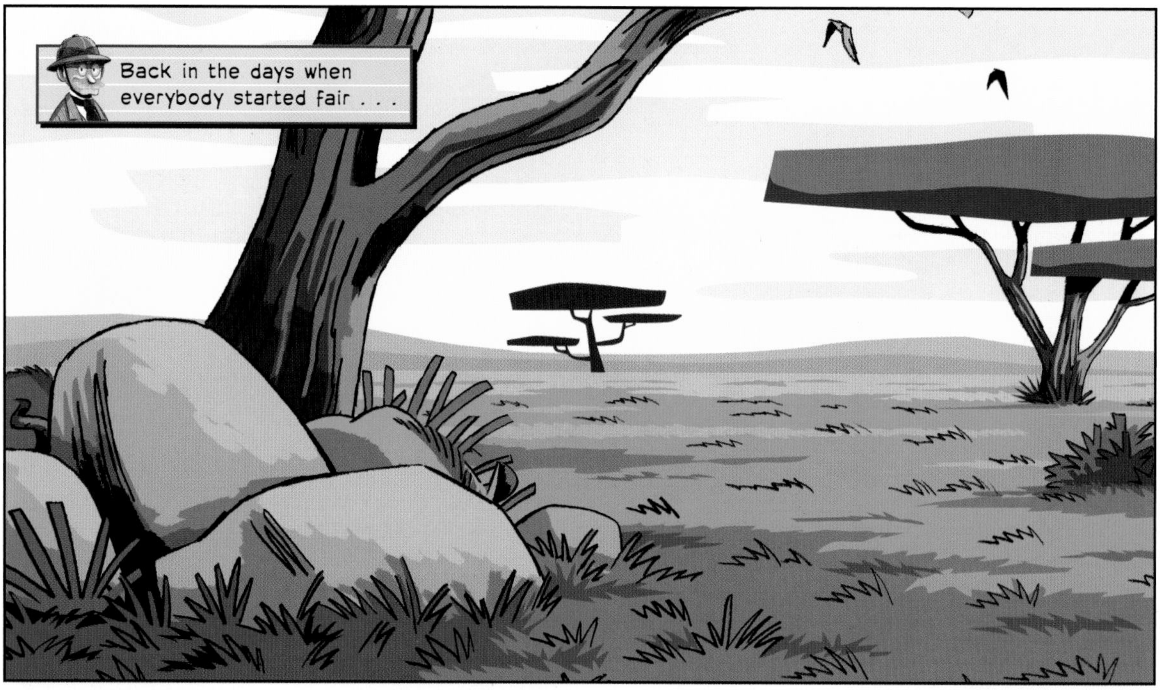
Back in the days when everybody started fair . . .

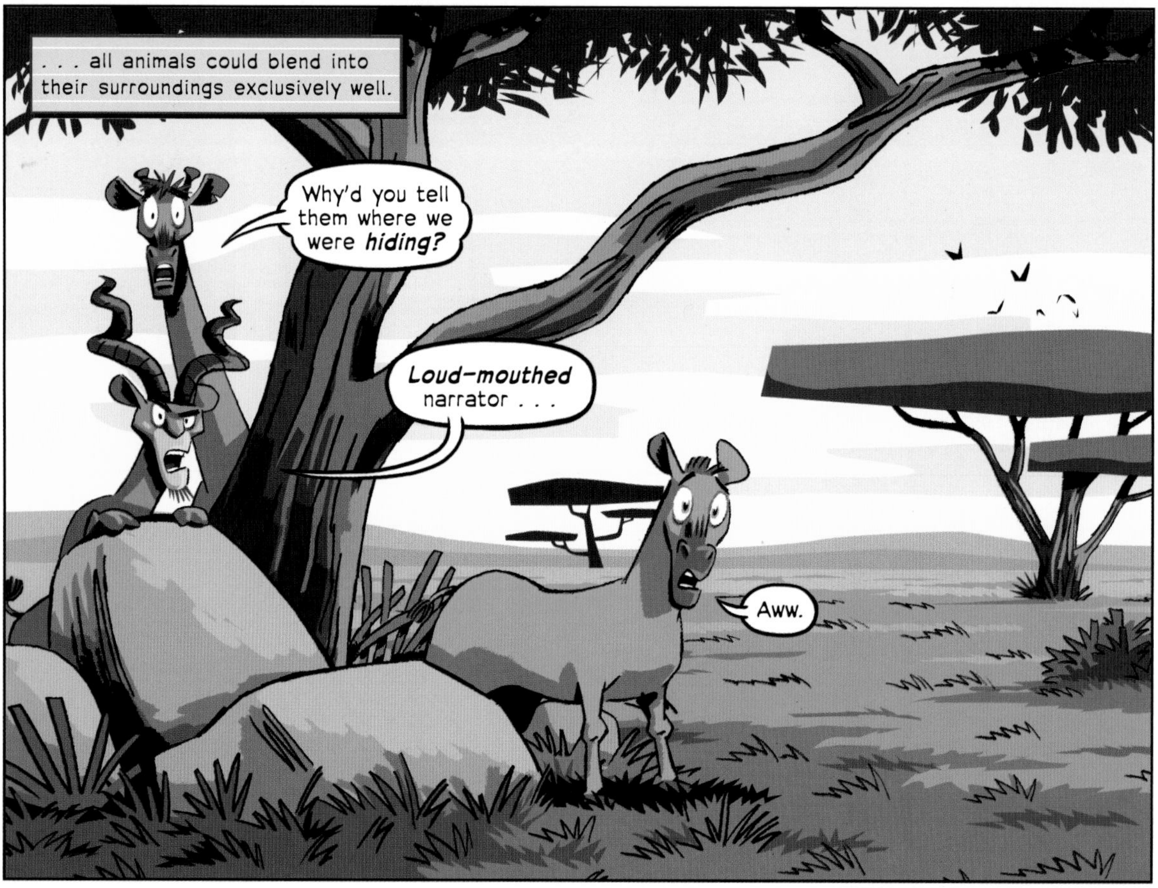
. . . all animals could blend into their surroundings exclusively well.
Why'd you tell them where we were *hiding?*
***Loud-mouthed*** narrator . . .
Aww.

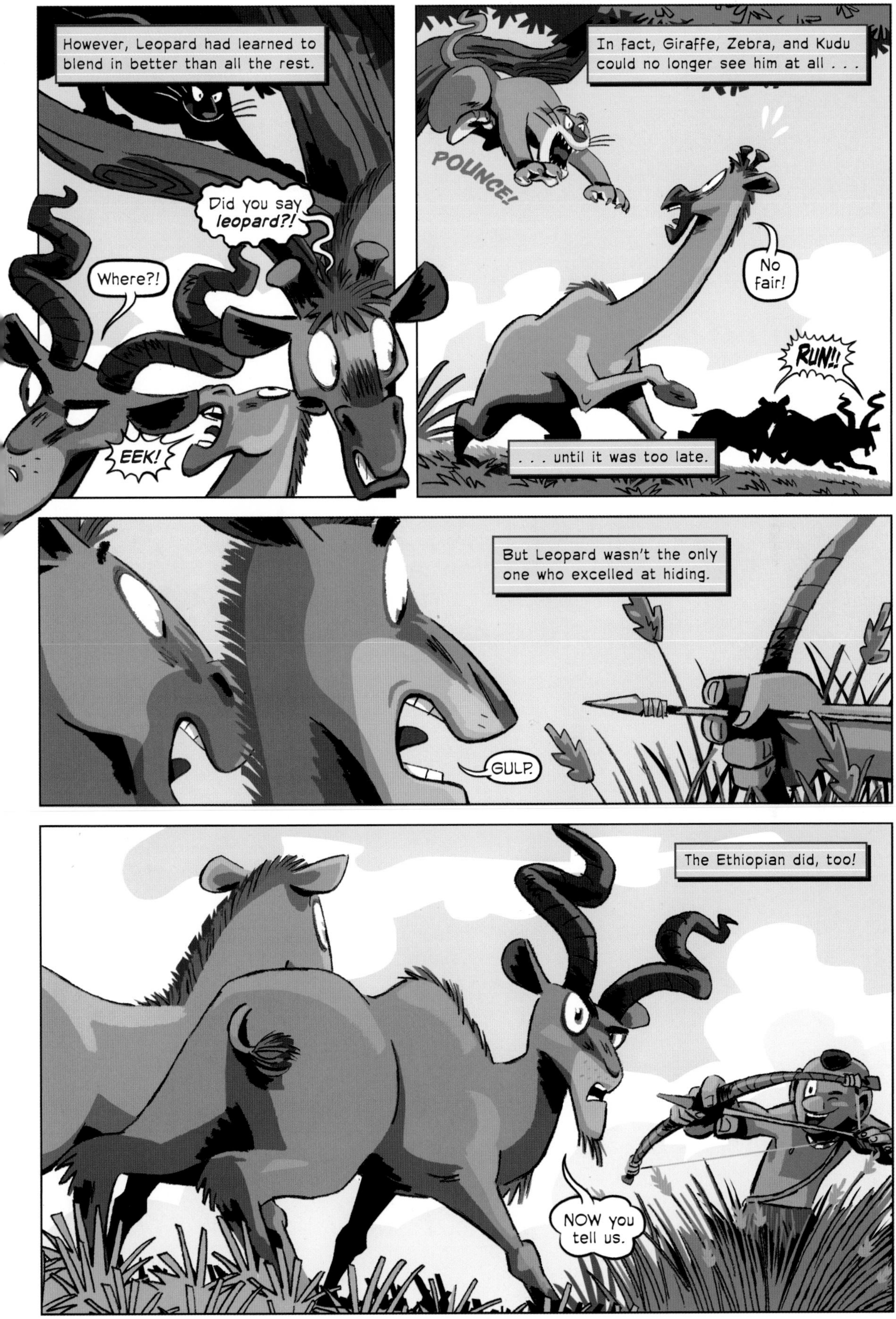
However, Leopard had learned to blend in better than all the rest.
Did you say *leopard?!*
Where?!
EEK!
In fact, Giraffe, Zebra, and Kudu could no longer see him at all . . .
POUNCE!
No fair!
RUN!!
. . . until it was too late.
But Leopard wasn't the only one who excelled at hiding.
GULP.
The Ethiopian did, too!
NOW you tell us.

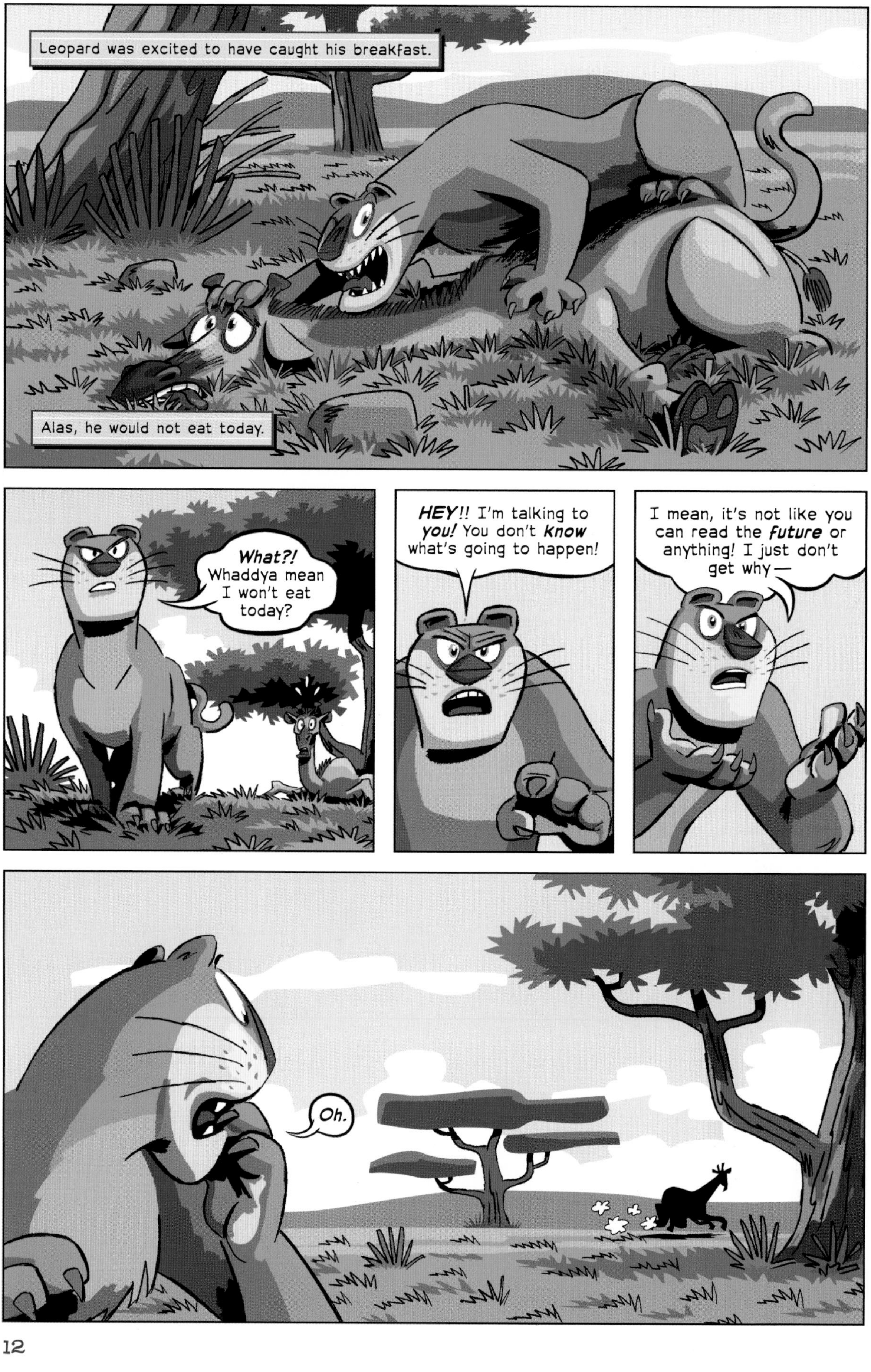
Leopard was excited to have caught his breakfast.
Alas, he would not eat today.
What?! Whaddya mean I won't eat today?
HEY!! I'm talking to you! You don't know what's going to happen!
I mean, it's not like you can read the future or anything! I just don't get why—
Oh.

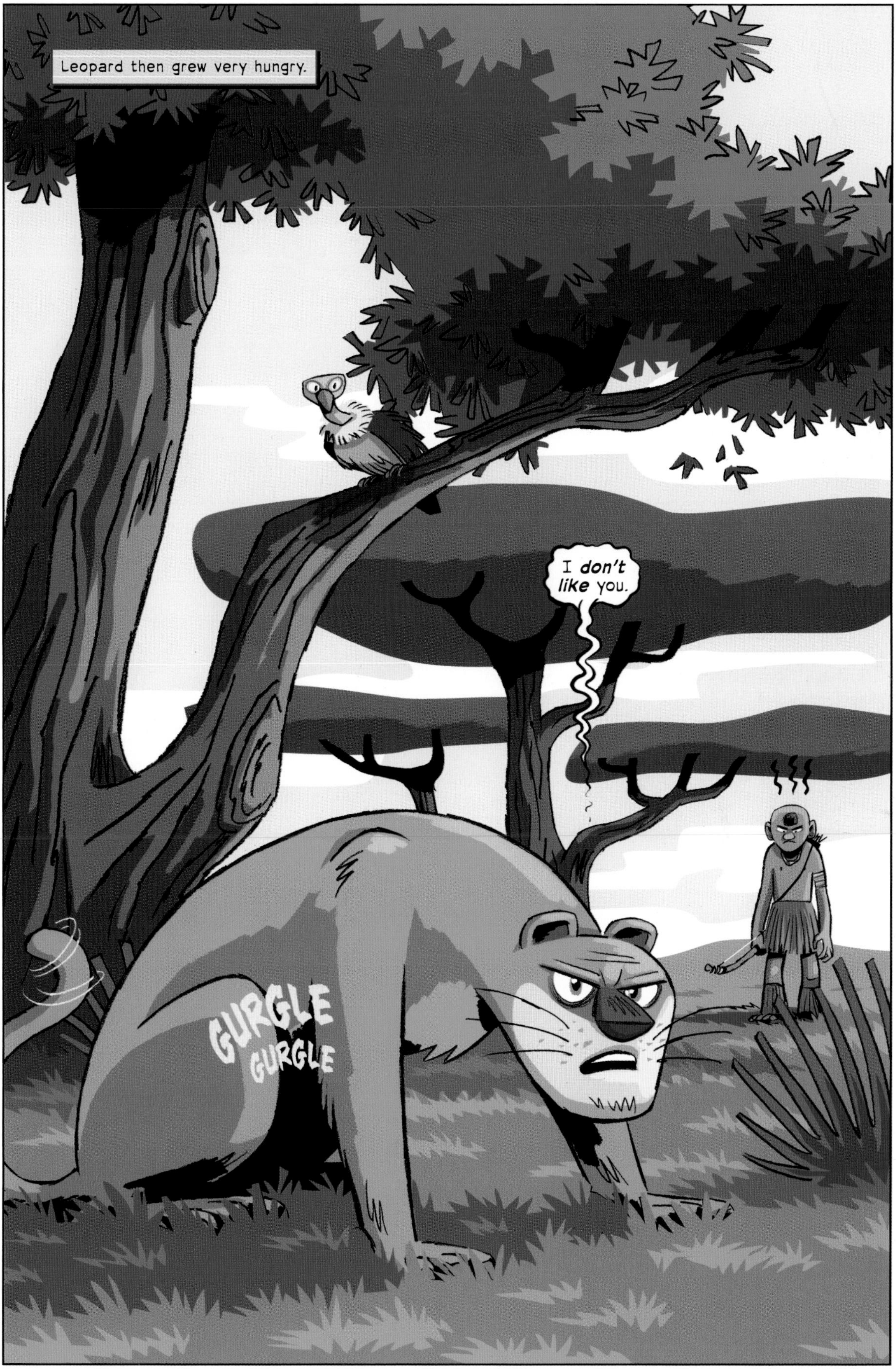
Leopard then grew very hungry.
I don't like you.
GURGLE
GURGLE

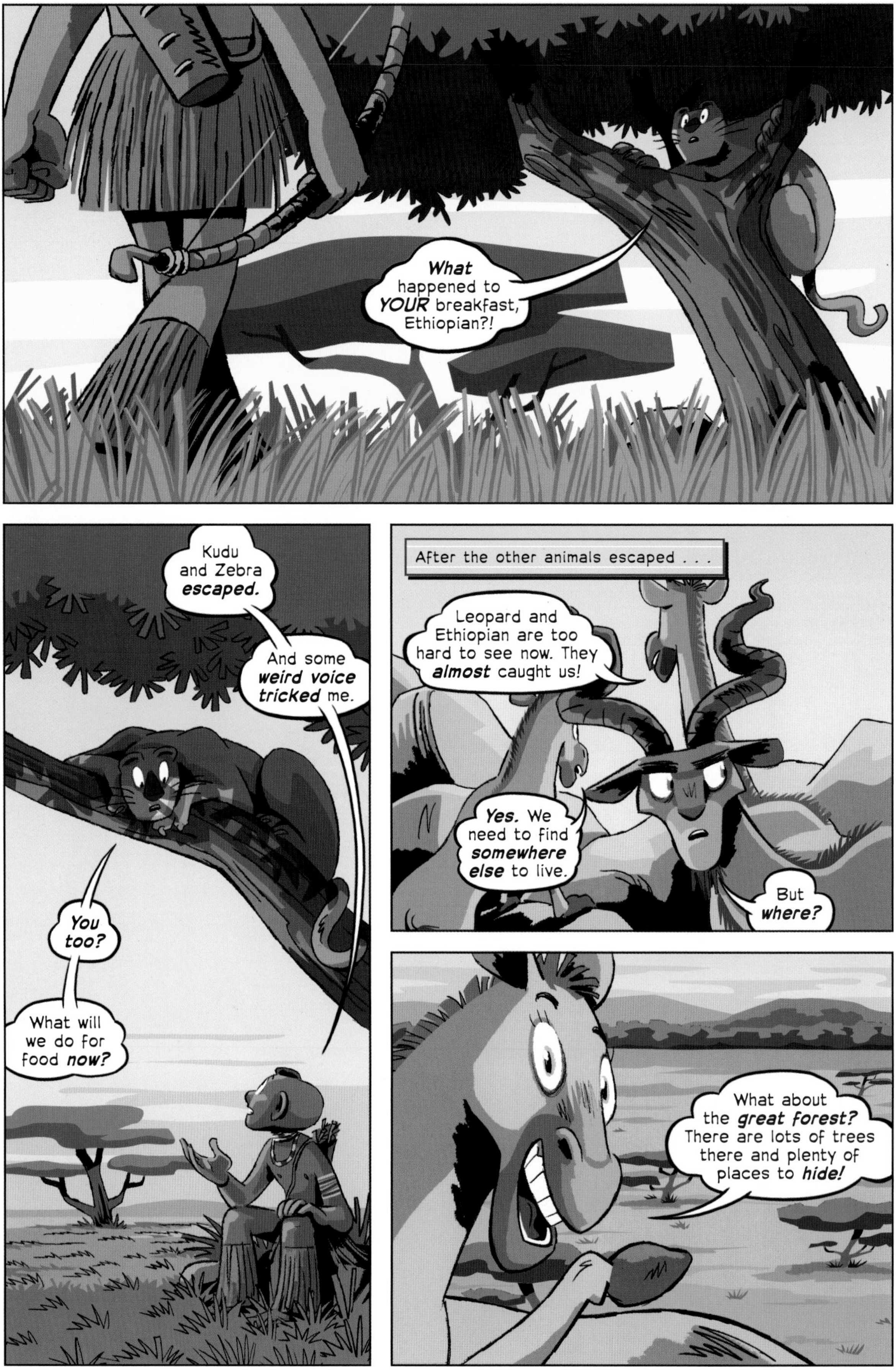

What happened to YOUR breakfast, Ethiopian?!
Kudu and Zebra escaped.
And some weird voice tricked me.
You too?
What will we do for food now?
After the other animals escaped . . .
Leopard and Ethiopian are too hard to see now. They almost caught us!
Yes. We need to find somewhere else to live.
But where?
What about the great forest? There are lots of trees there and plenty of places to hide!

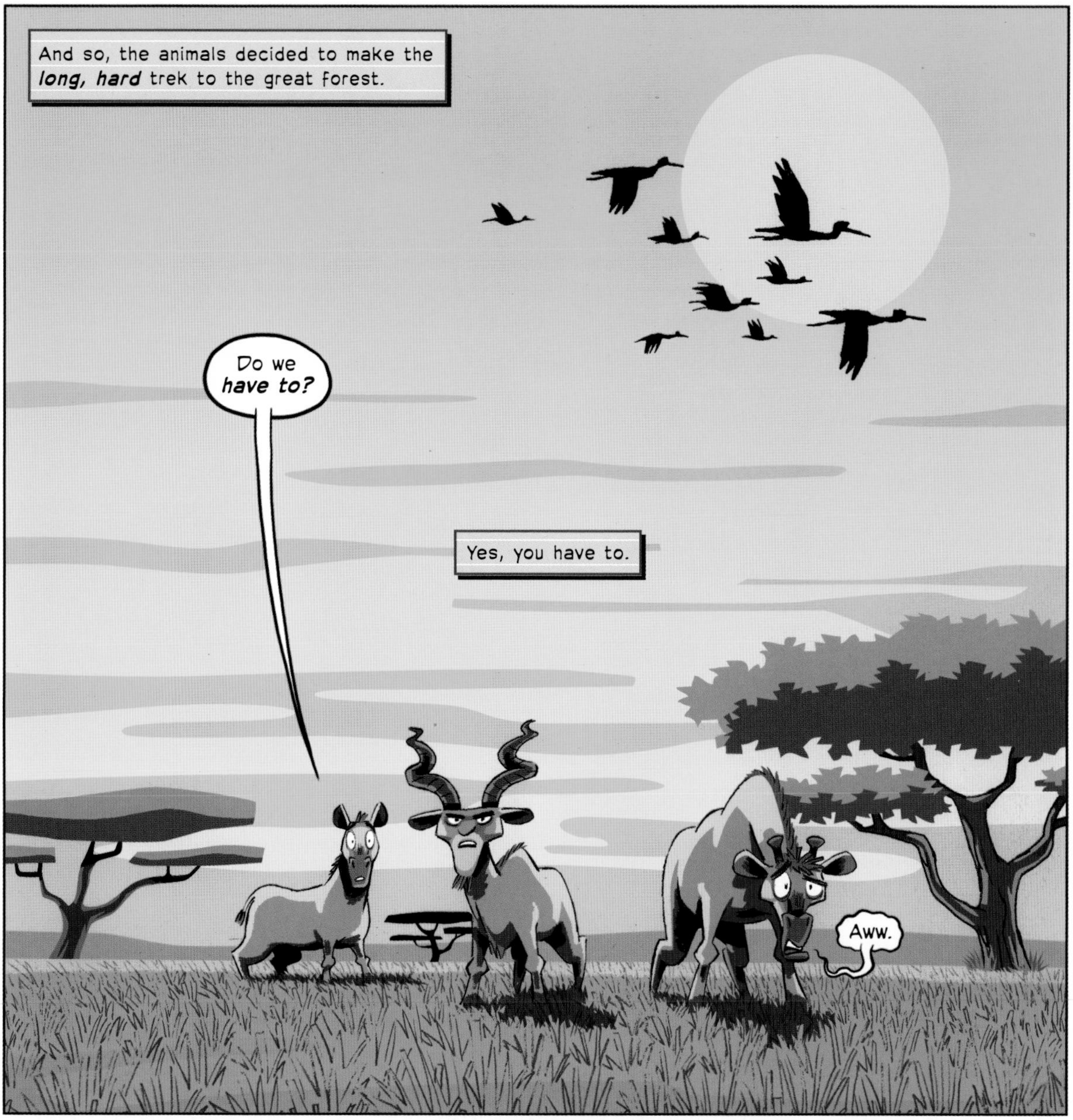
And so, the animals decided to make the ***long, hard*** trek to the great forest.
Do we ***have to?***
Yes, you have to.
Aww.

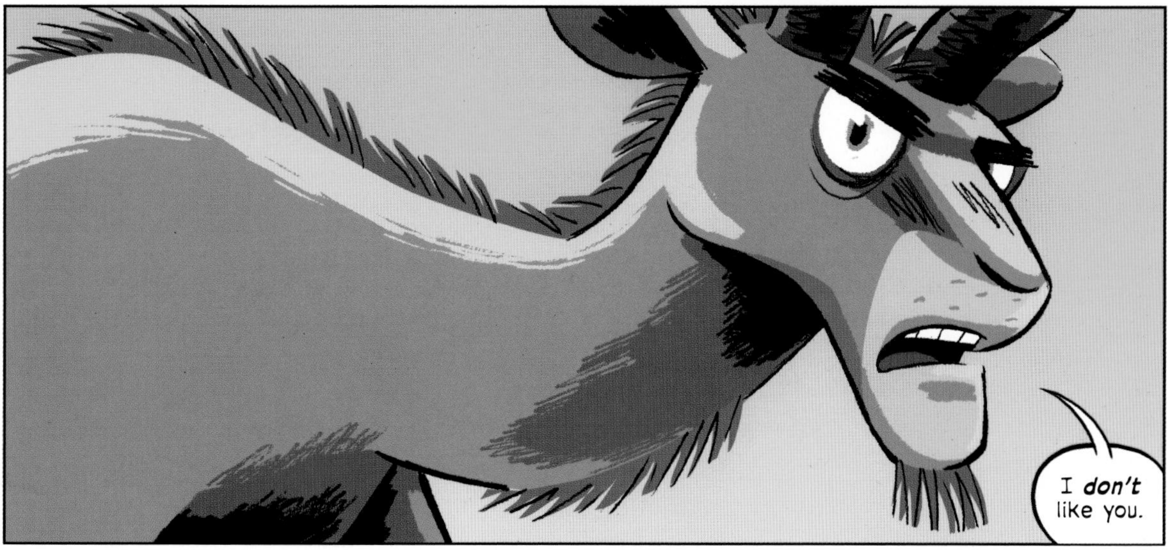
I ***don't*** like you.

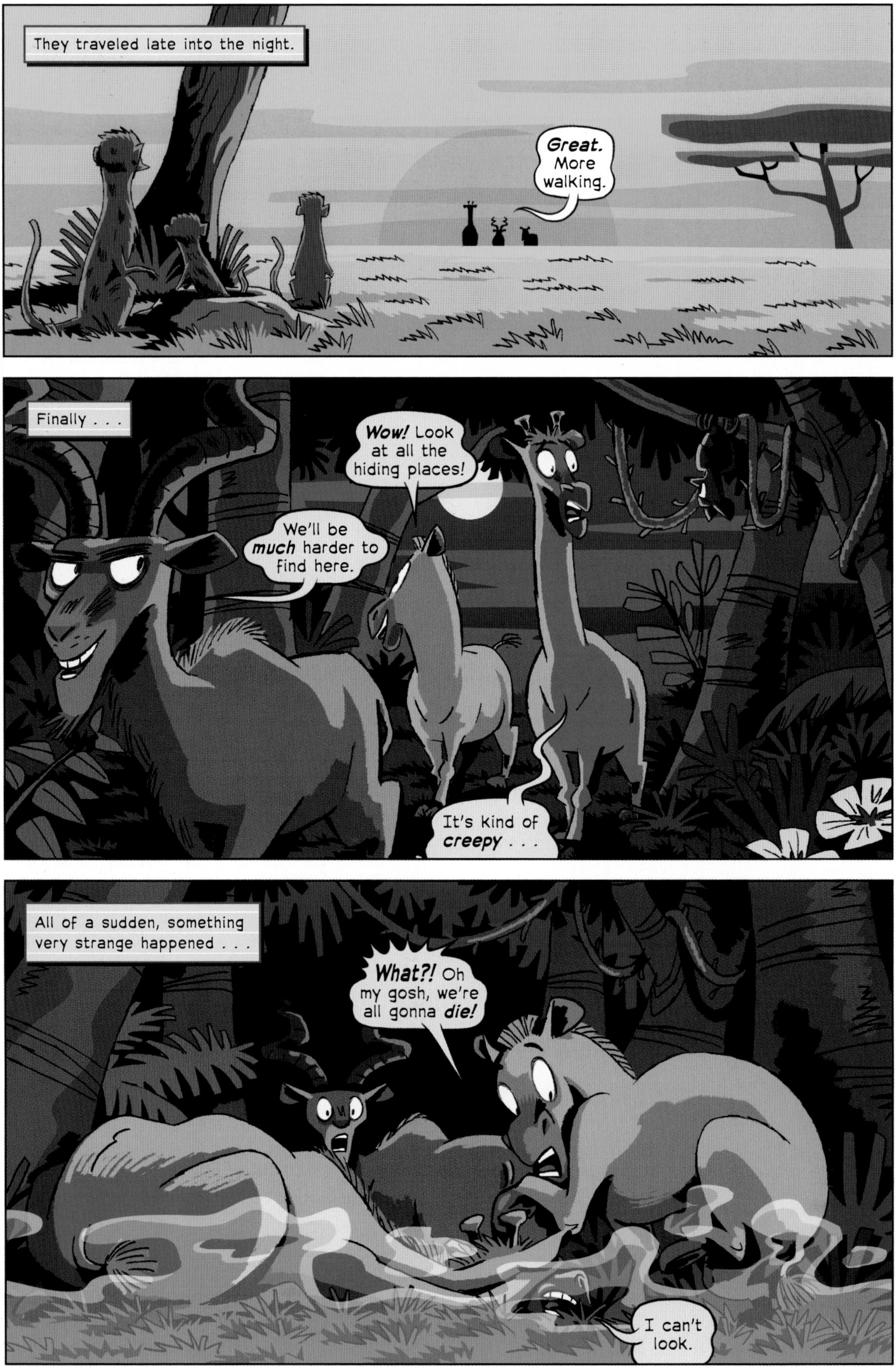
They traveled late into the night.
Great. More walking.
Finally . . .
Wow! Look at all the hiding places!
We'll be much harder to find here.
It's kind of creepy . . .
All of a sudden, something very strange happened . . .
What?! Oh my gosh, we're all gonna die!
I can't look.

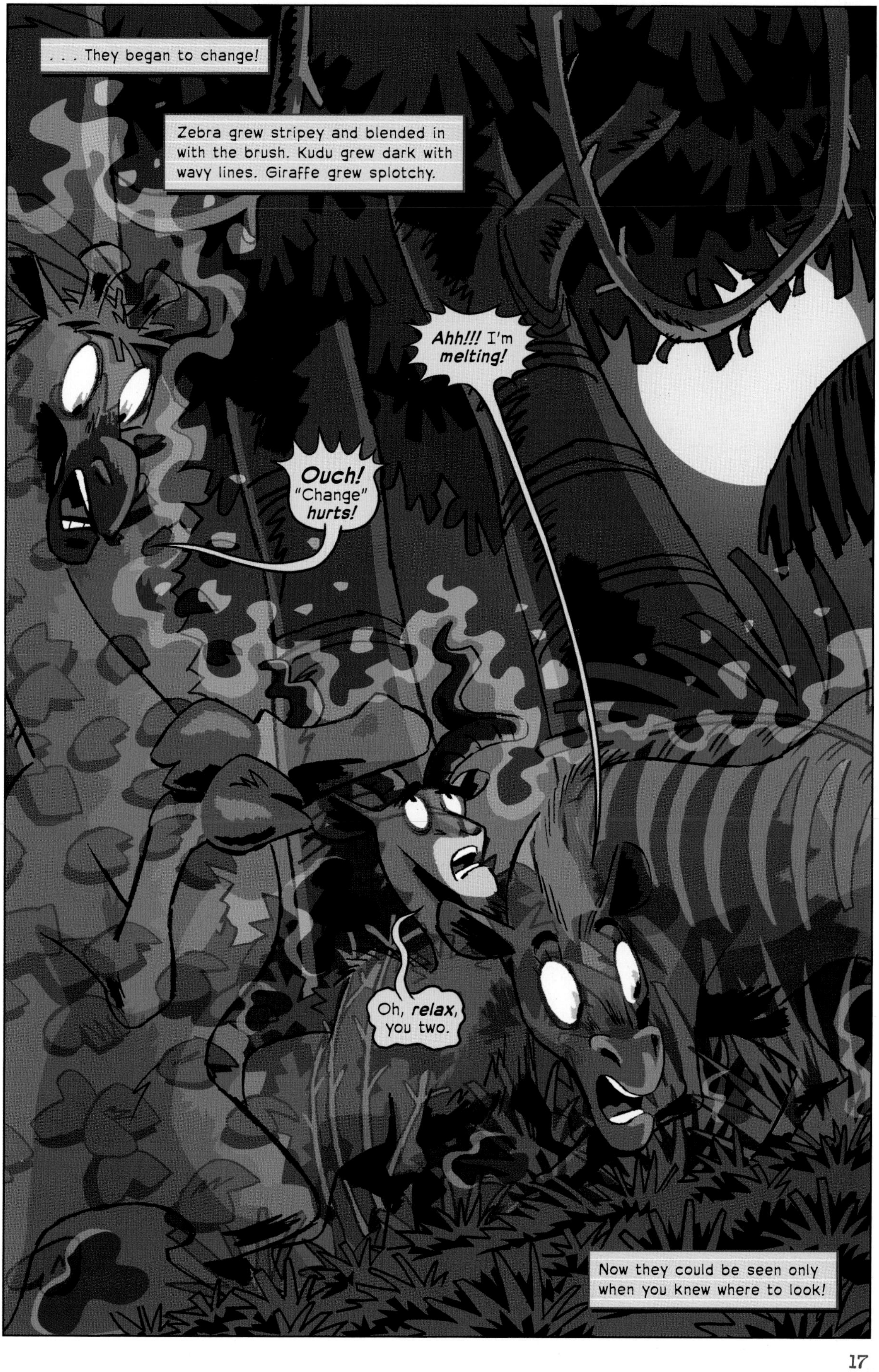
. . . They began to change!
Zebra grew stripey and blended in with the brush. Kudu grew dark with wavy lines. Giraffe grew splotchy.
Ahh!!! I'm melting!
Ouch! "Change" hurts!
Oh, relax, you two.
Now they could be seen only when you knew where to look!

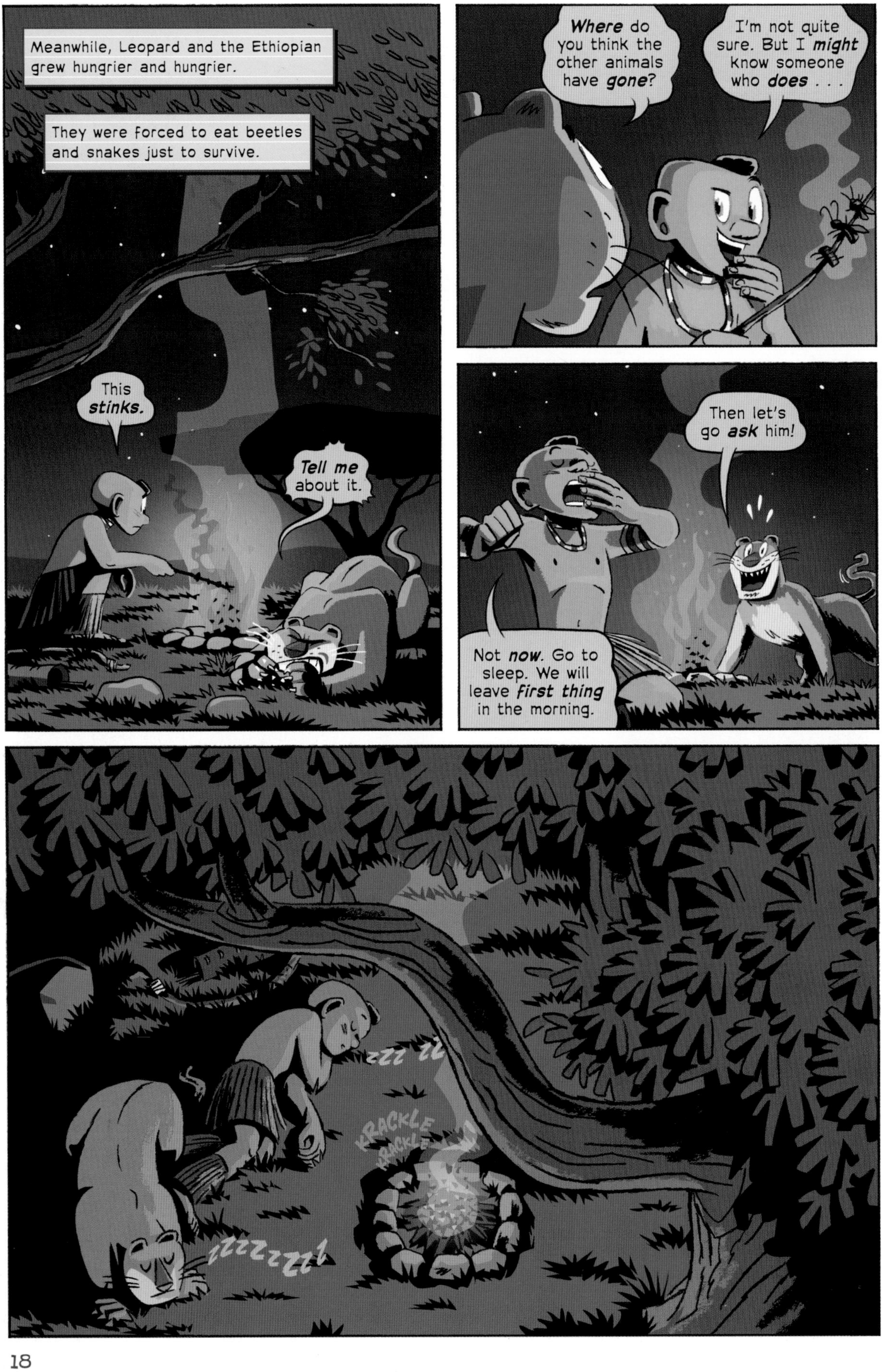
Meanwhile, Leopard and the Ethiopian grew hungrier and hungrier.
They were forced to eat beetles and snakes just to survive.
This stinks.
Tell me about it.
Where do you think the other animals have gone?
I'm not quite sure. But I might know someone who does . . .
Then let's go ask him!
Not now. Go to sleep. We will leave first thing in the morning.
ZZZ ZZ
KRACKLE
KRACKLE
ZZZZZZZZ

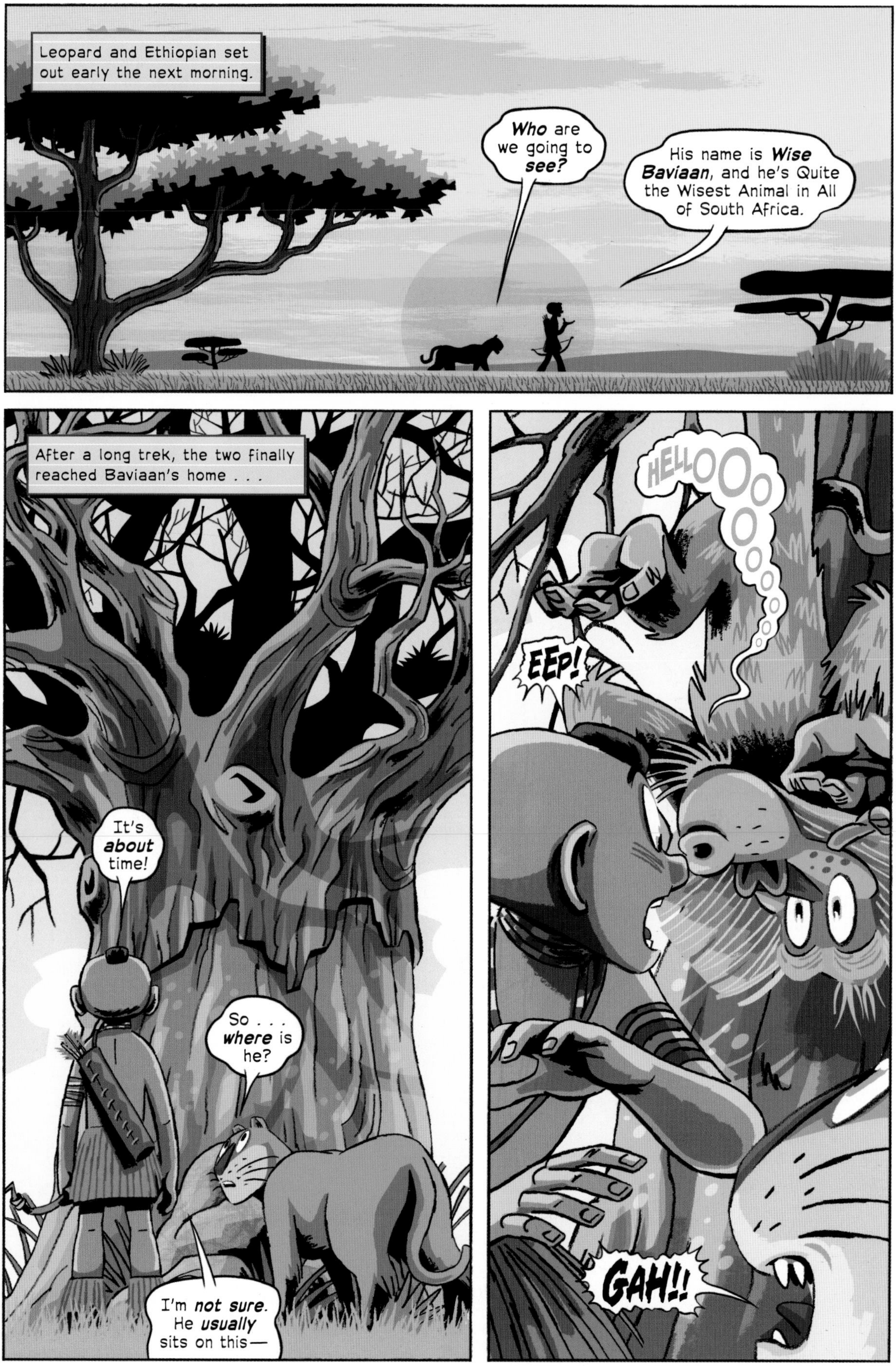
Leopard and Ethiopian set out early the next morning.
Who are we going to see?
His name is Wise Baviaan, and he's Quite the Wisest Animal in All of South Africa.
After a long trek, the two finally reached Baviaan's home . . .
It's about time!
So . . . where is he?
I'm not sure. He usually sits on this—
HELLOOOOOOOO
EEp!
GAH!!

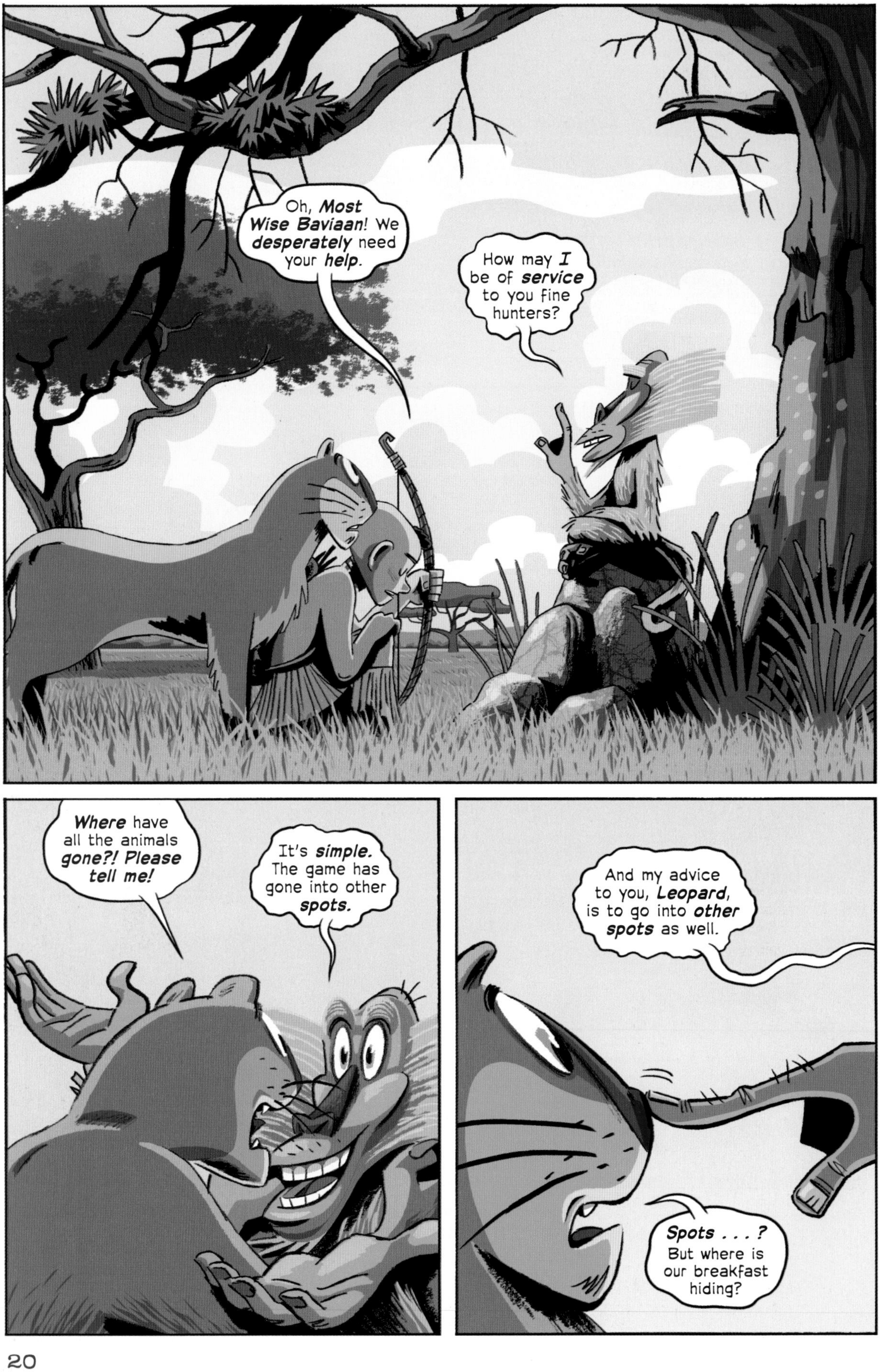
Oh, Most Wise Baviaan! We desperately need your help.
How may I be of service to you fine hunters?
Where have all the animals gone?! Please tell me!
It's simple. The game has gone into other spots.
And my advice to you, Leopard, is to go into other spots as well.
Spots . . . ? But where is our breakfast hiding?

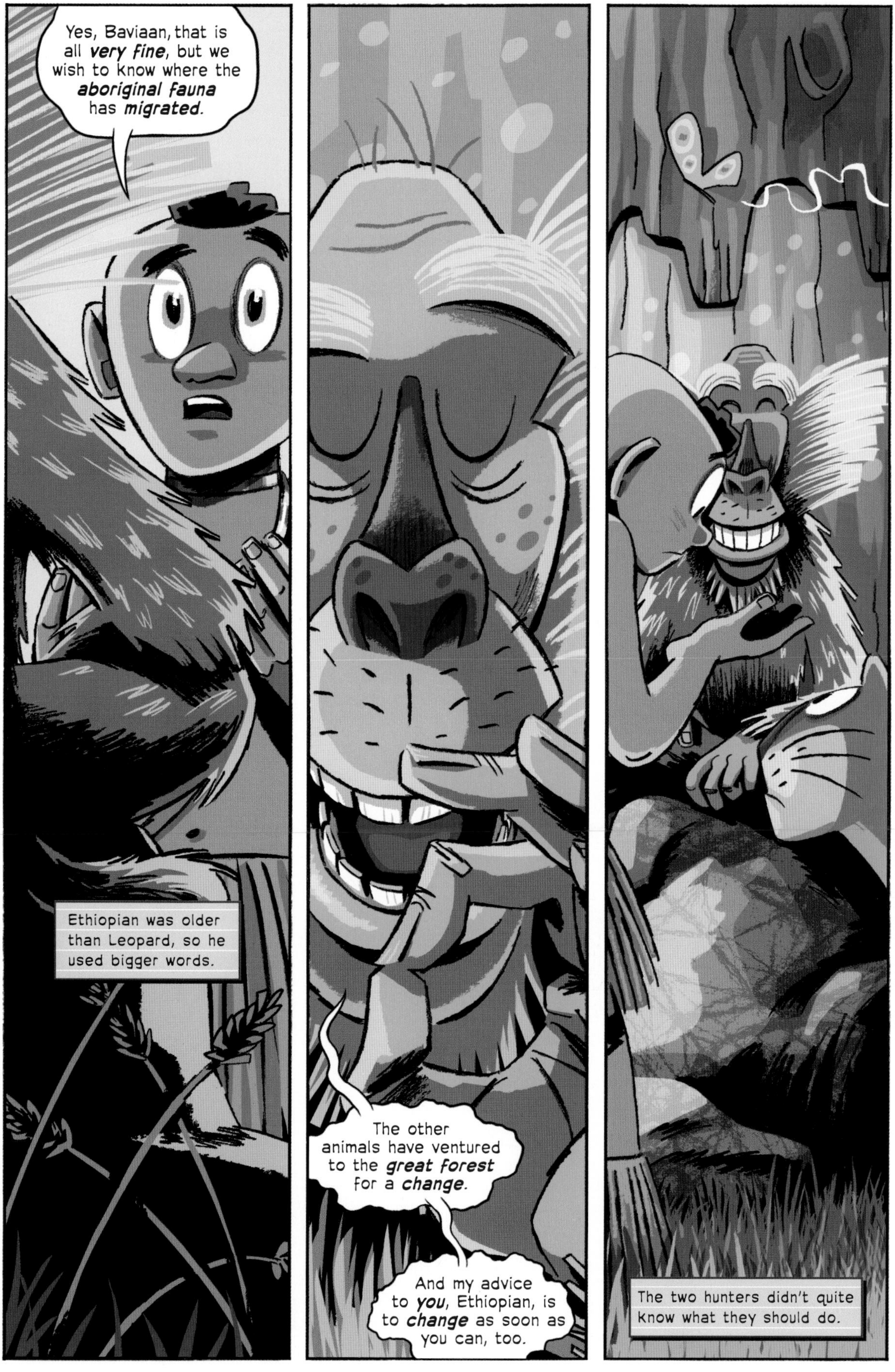
Yes, Baviaan, that is all *very fine*, but we wish to know where the *aboriginal fauna* has *migrated*.
Ethiopian was older than Leopard, so he used bigger words.
The other animals have ventured to the *great forest* for a *change*.
And my advice to *you*, Ethiopian, is to *change* as soon as you can, too.
The two hunters didn't quite know what they should do.

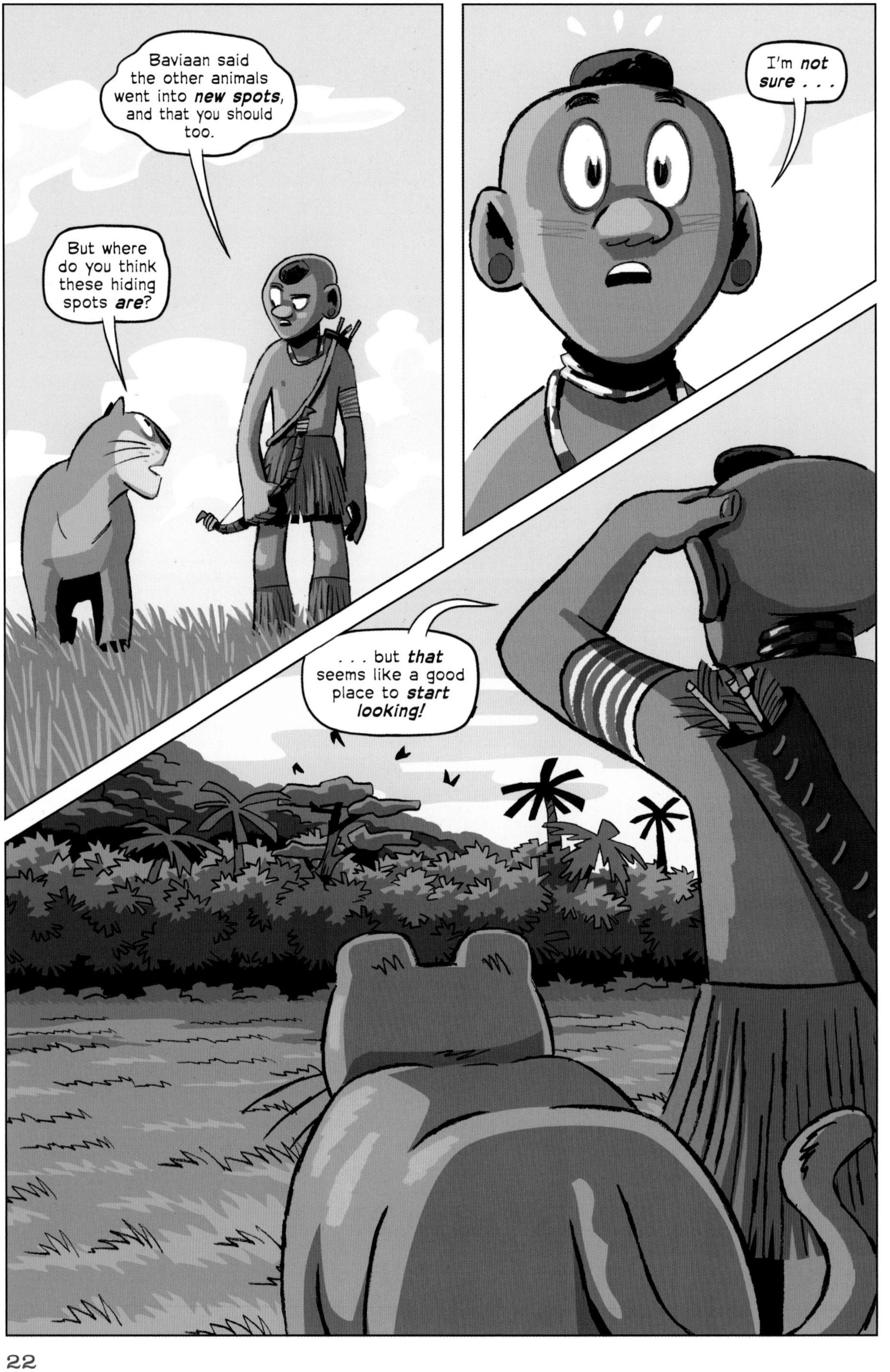
Baviaan said the other animals went into *new spots*, and that you should too.
But where do you think these hiding spots *are*?
I'm *not sure . . .*
. . . but *that* seems like a good place to *start looking!*

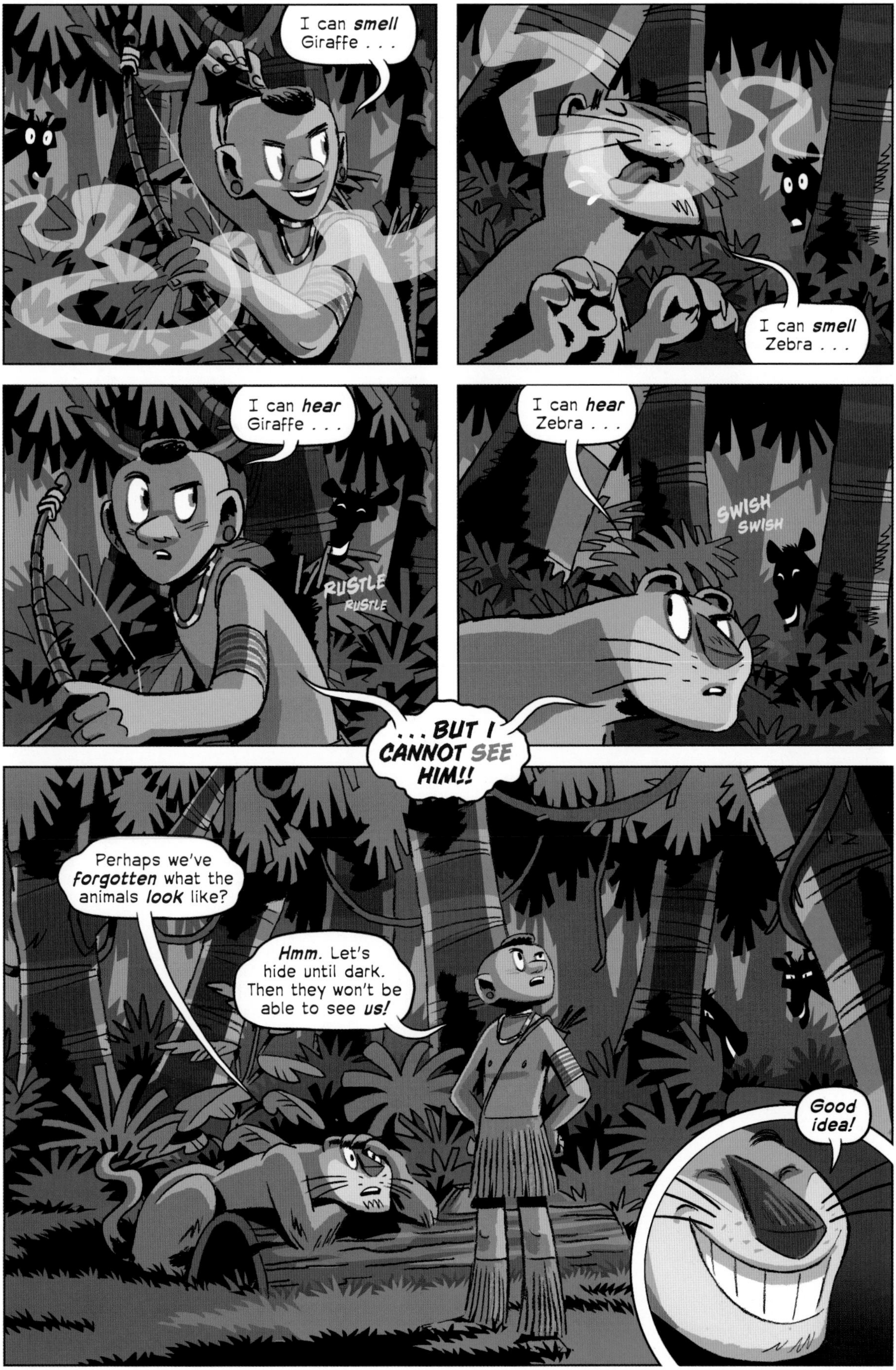

I can *smell* Giraffe . . .
I can *smell* Zebra . . .
I can *hear* Giraffe . . .
RUSTLE
RUSTLE
I can *hear* Zebra . . .
SWISH
SWISH
. . . BUT I CANNOT SEE HIM!!
Perhaps we've *forgotten* what the animals *look* like?
*Hmm*. Let's hide until dark. Then they won't be able to see *us!*
*Good idea!*

The cloudy skies hid the forest from the moonlight, giving the hunters the perfect opportunity to stalk their prey.

*"Hunters?"* Hey — that's *us*, Ethiopian!

*Finally* he gives us some *good* news!

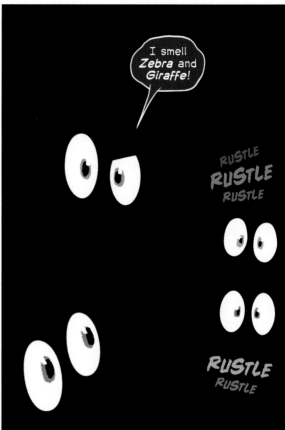

I smell *Zebra* and *Giraffe!*

RUSTLE RUSTLE RUSTLE

RUSTLE RUSTLE

*Pounce* on them!

Hi-YA!!!

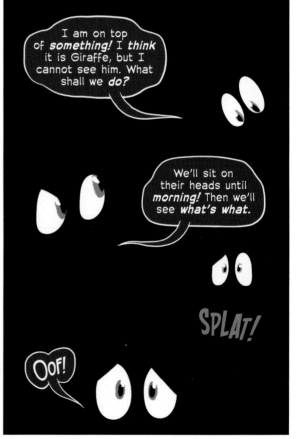

I am on top of *something!* I *think* it is Giraffe, but I cannot see him. What shall we *do?*

We'll sit on their heads until *morning!* Then we'll see *what's what.*

SPLAT!

Oof!

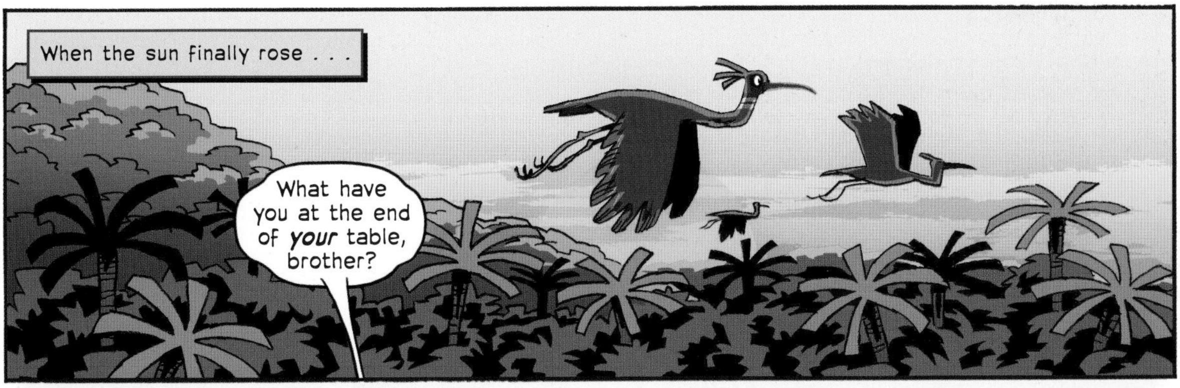
When the sun finally rose . . .
What have you at the end of *your* table, brother?

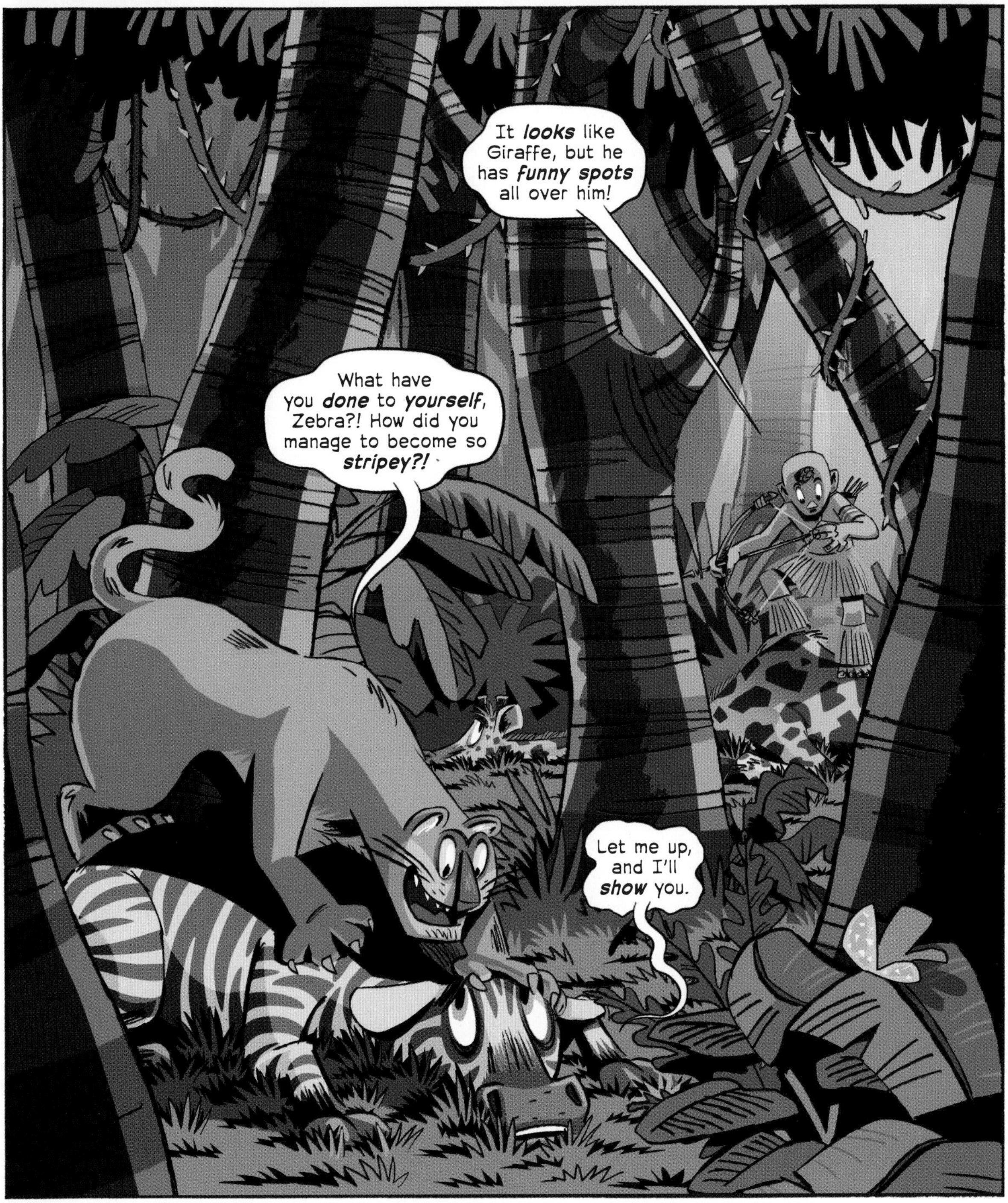
It *looks* like Giraffe, but he has *funny spots* all over him!
What have you *done* to *yourself*, Zebra?! How did you manage to become so *stripey?!*
Let me up, and I'll *show* you.

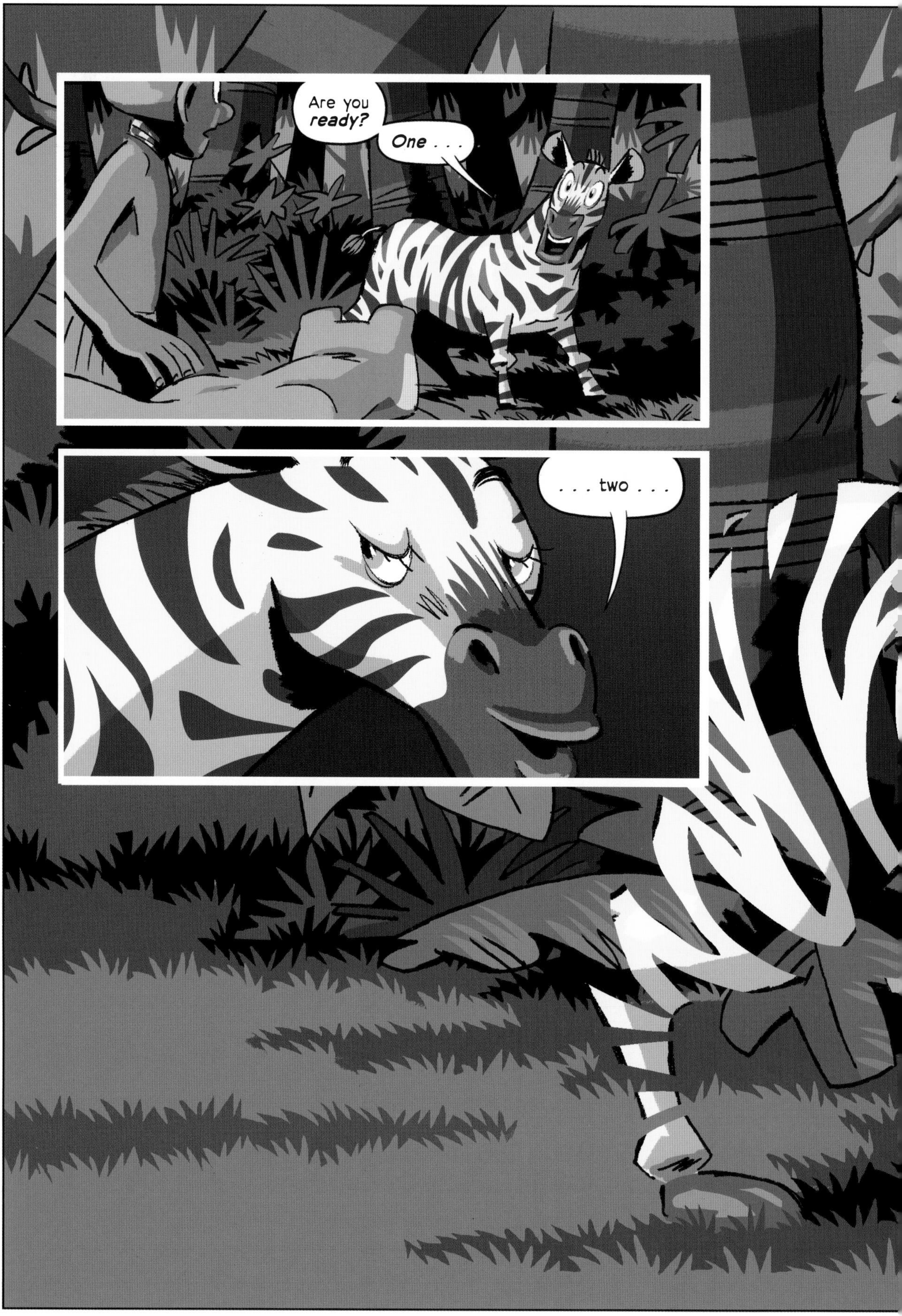
Are you *ready?*
*One . . .*
. . . two . . .

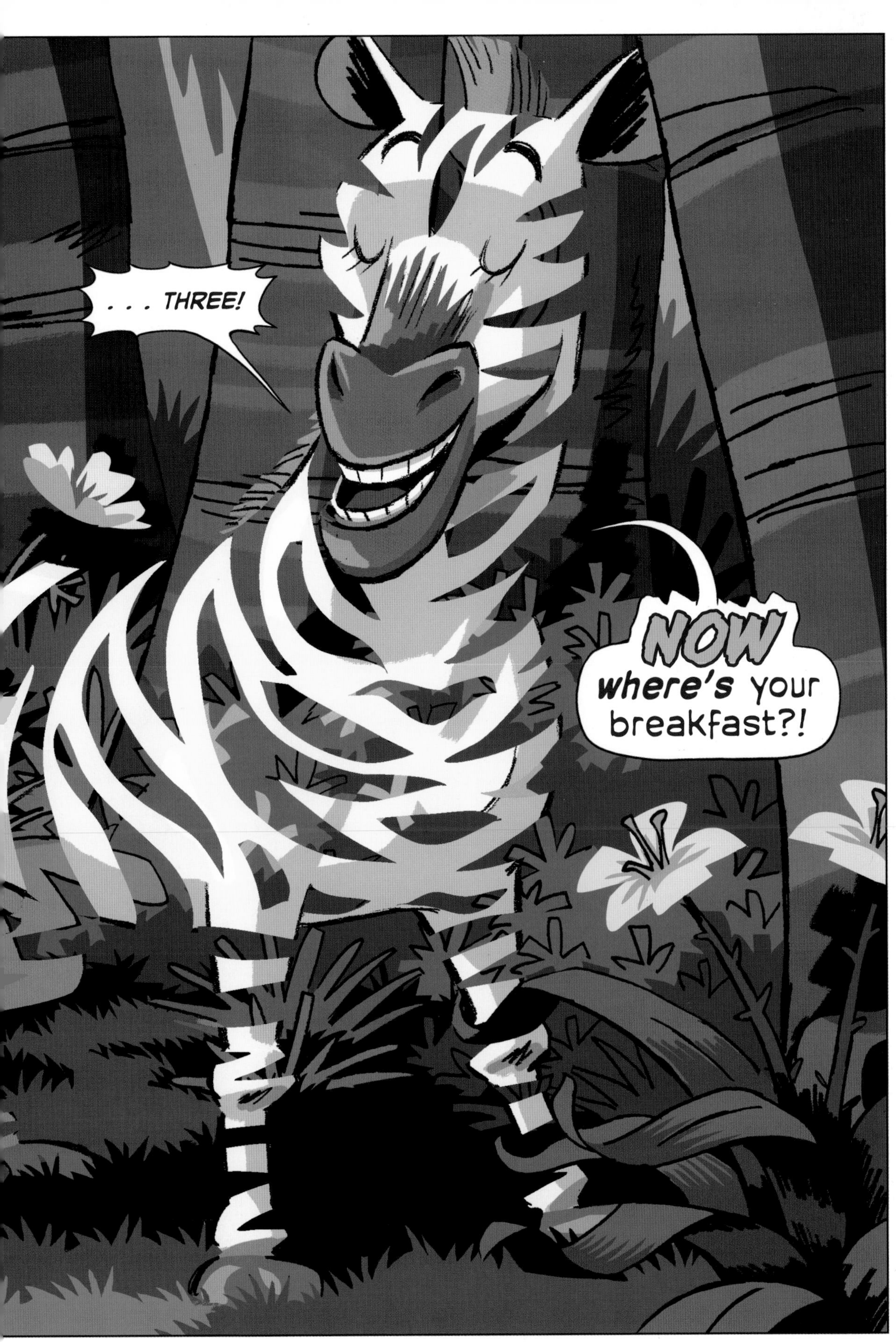
. . . THREE!
NOW where's your breakfast?!

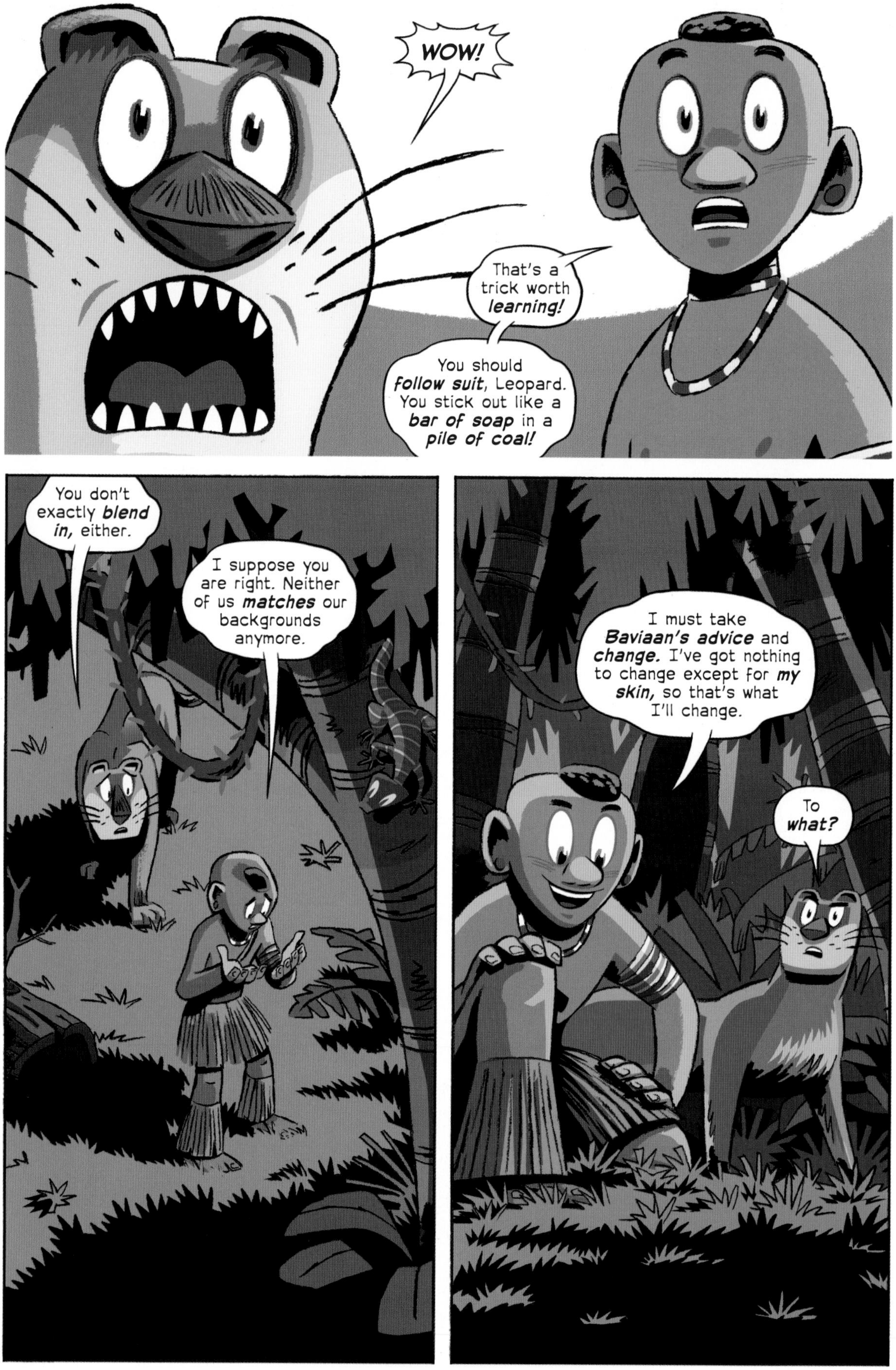
WOW!
That's a trick worth learning!
You should follow suit, Leopard. You stick out like a bar of soap in a pile of coal!
You don't exactly blend in, either.
I suppose you are right. Neither of us matches our backgrounds anymore.
I must take Baviaan's advice and change. I've got nothing to change except for my skin, so that's what I'll change.
To what?

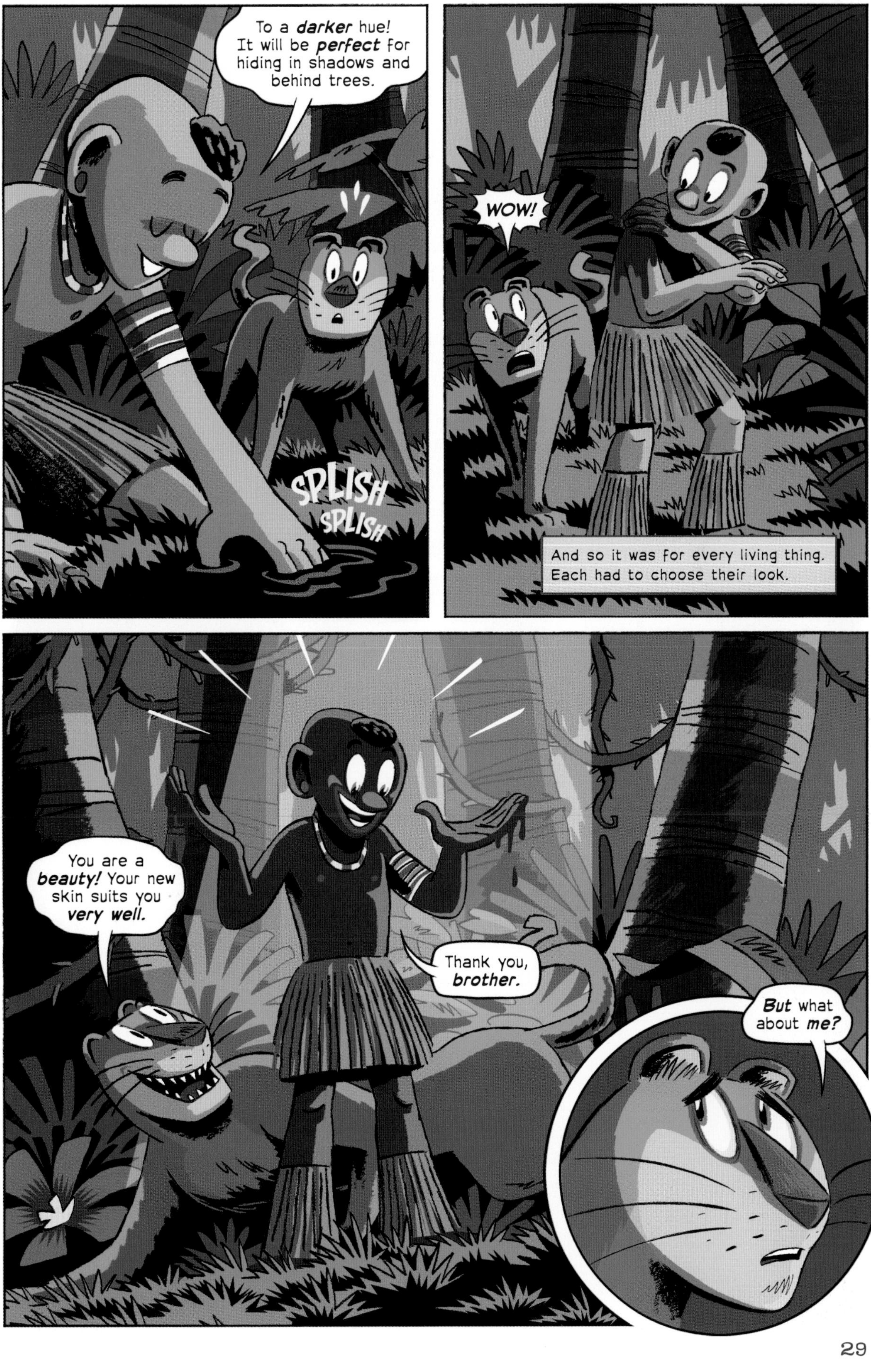

To a darker hue! It will be perfect for hiding in shadows and behind trees.
SPLISH SPLISH
WOW!
And so it was for every living thing. Each had to choose their look.
You are a beauty! Your new skin suits you very well.
Thank you, brother.
But what about me?

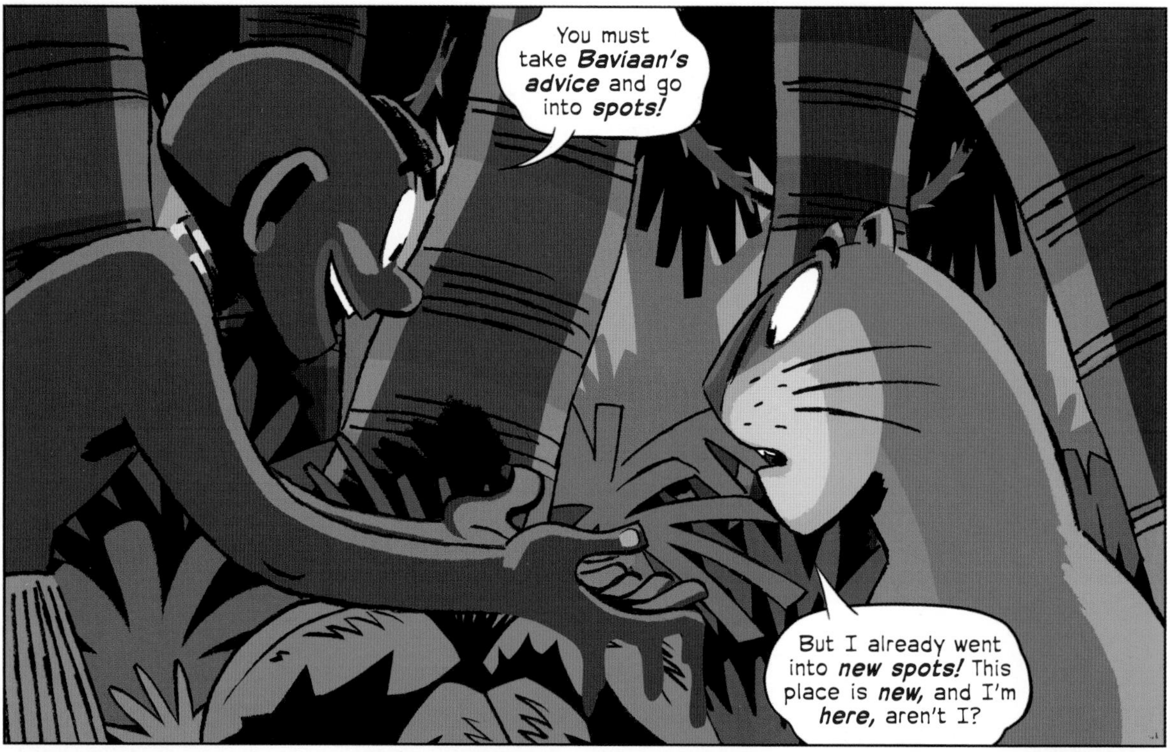
You must take Baviaan's advice and go into spots!
But I already went into new spots! This place is new, and I'm here, aren't I?

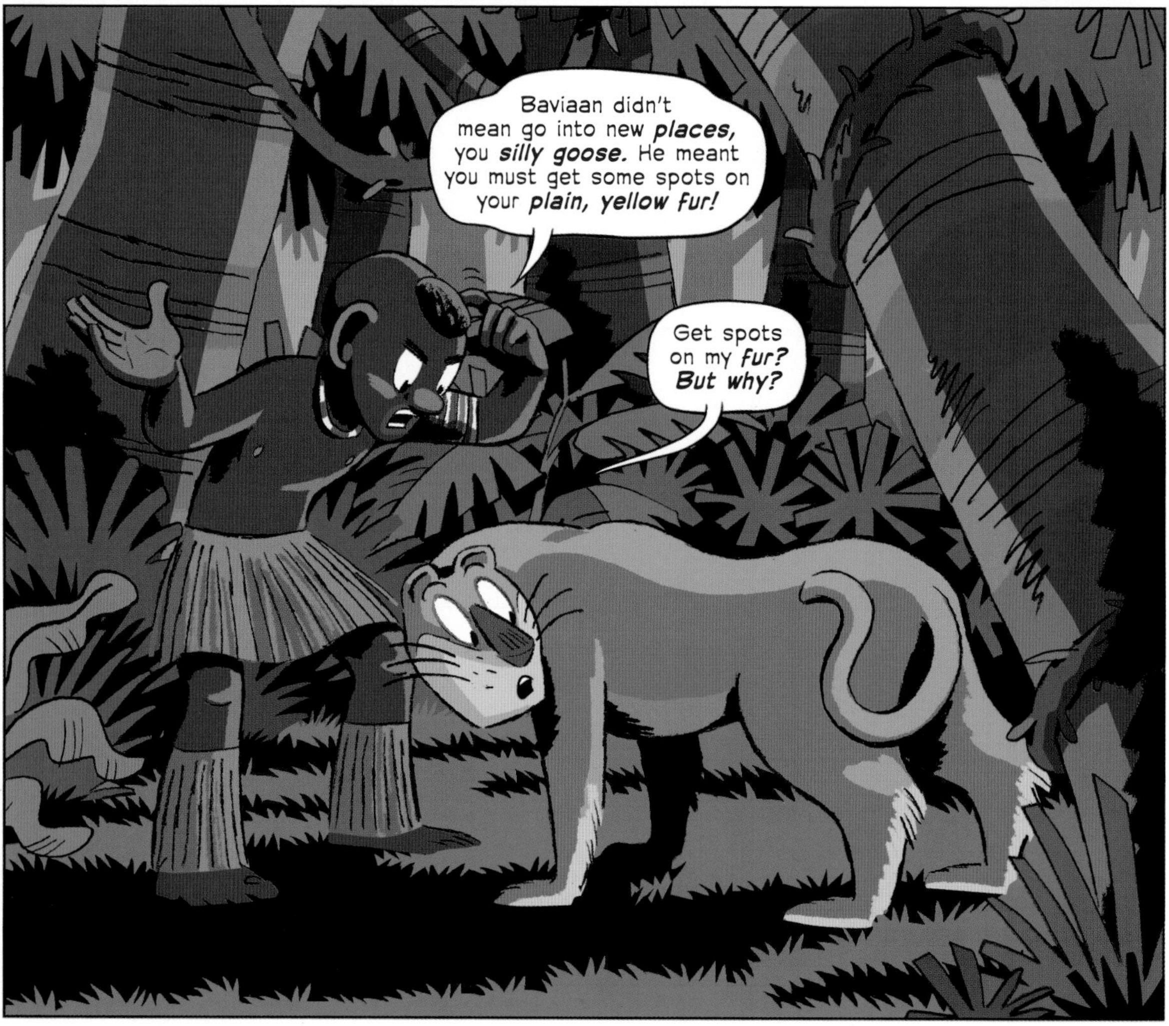
Baviaan didn't mean go into new places, you silly goose. He meant you must get some spots on your plain, yellow fur!
Get spots on my fur? But why?

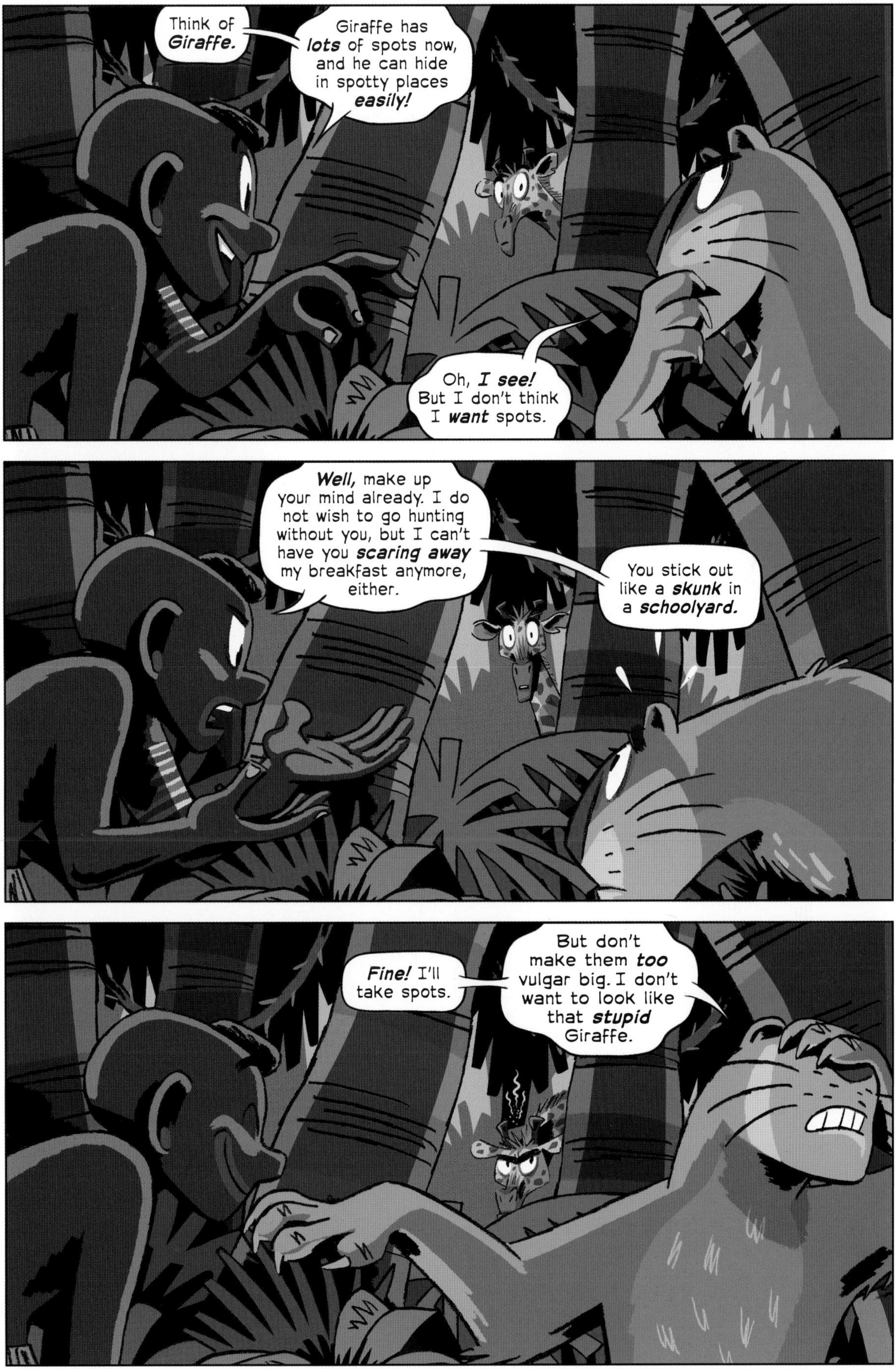
Think of *Giraffe.*
Giraffe has *lots* of spots now, and he can hide in spotty places *easily!*
Oh, *I see!* But I don't think I *want* spots.
*Well,* make up your mind already. I do not wish to go hunting without you, but I can't have you *scaring away* my breakfast anymore, either.
You stick out like a *skunk* in a *schoolyard.*
*Fine!* I'll take spots.
But don't make them *too* vulgar big. I don't want to look like that *stupid* Giraffe.

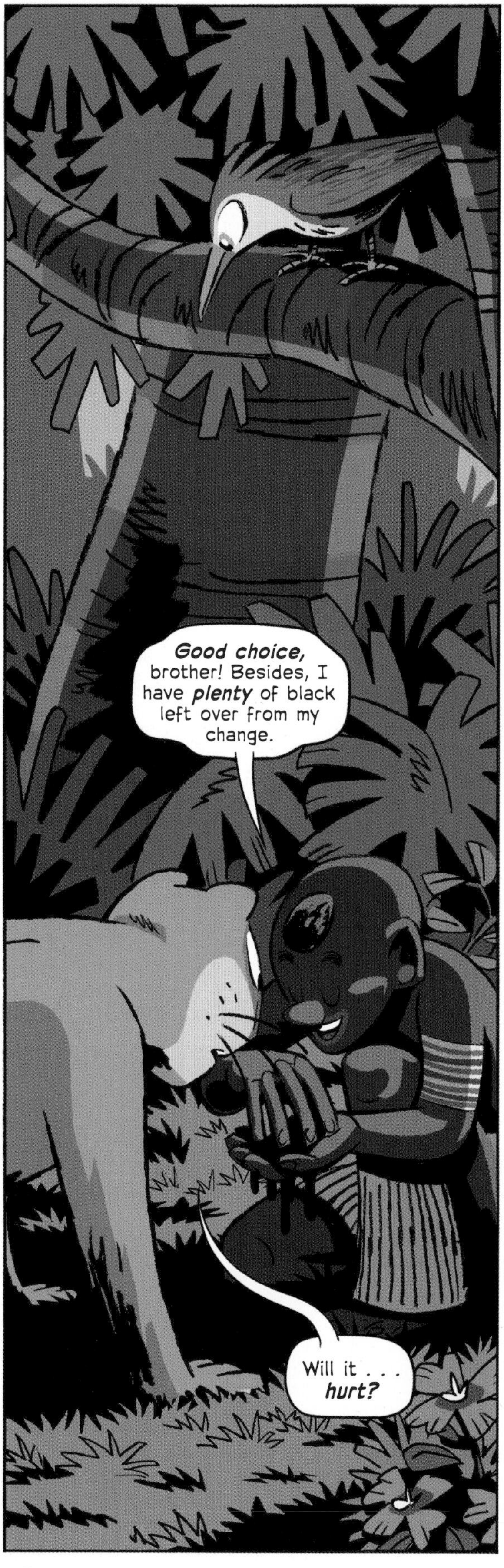
*Good choice,* brother! Besides, I have *plenty* of black left over from my change.
Will it . . . *hurt?*

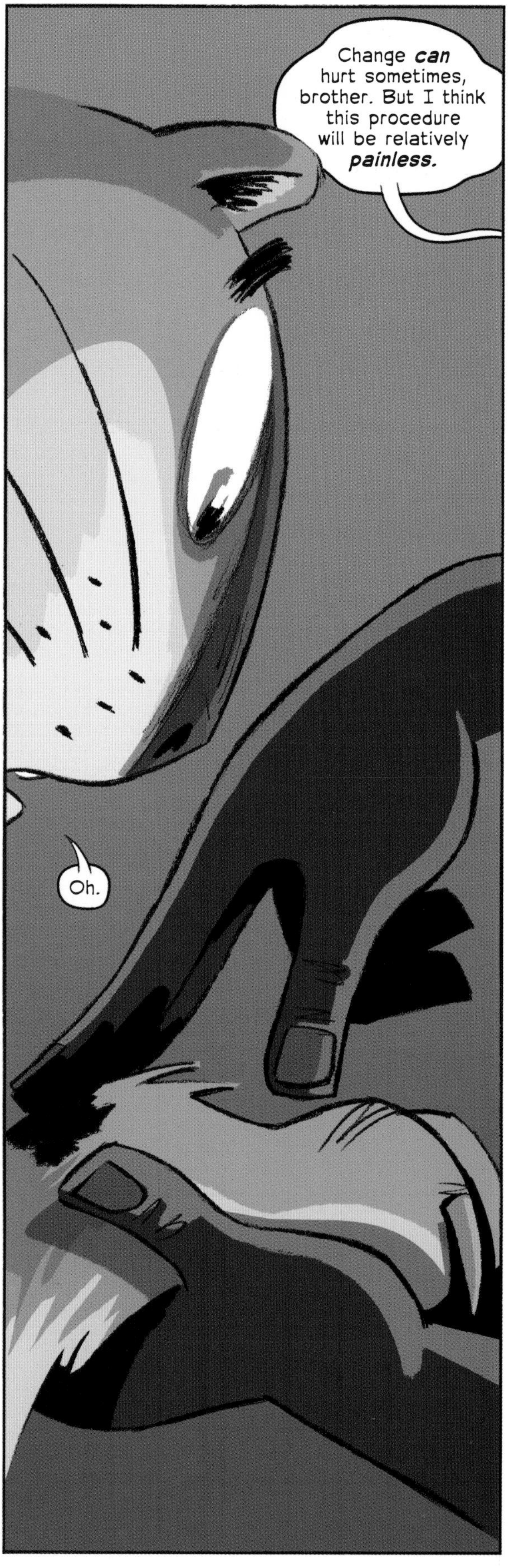
Change *can* hurt sometimes, brother. But I think this procedure will be relatively *painless.*
Oh.

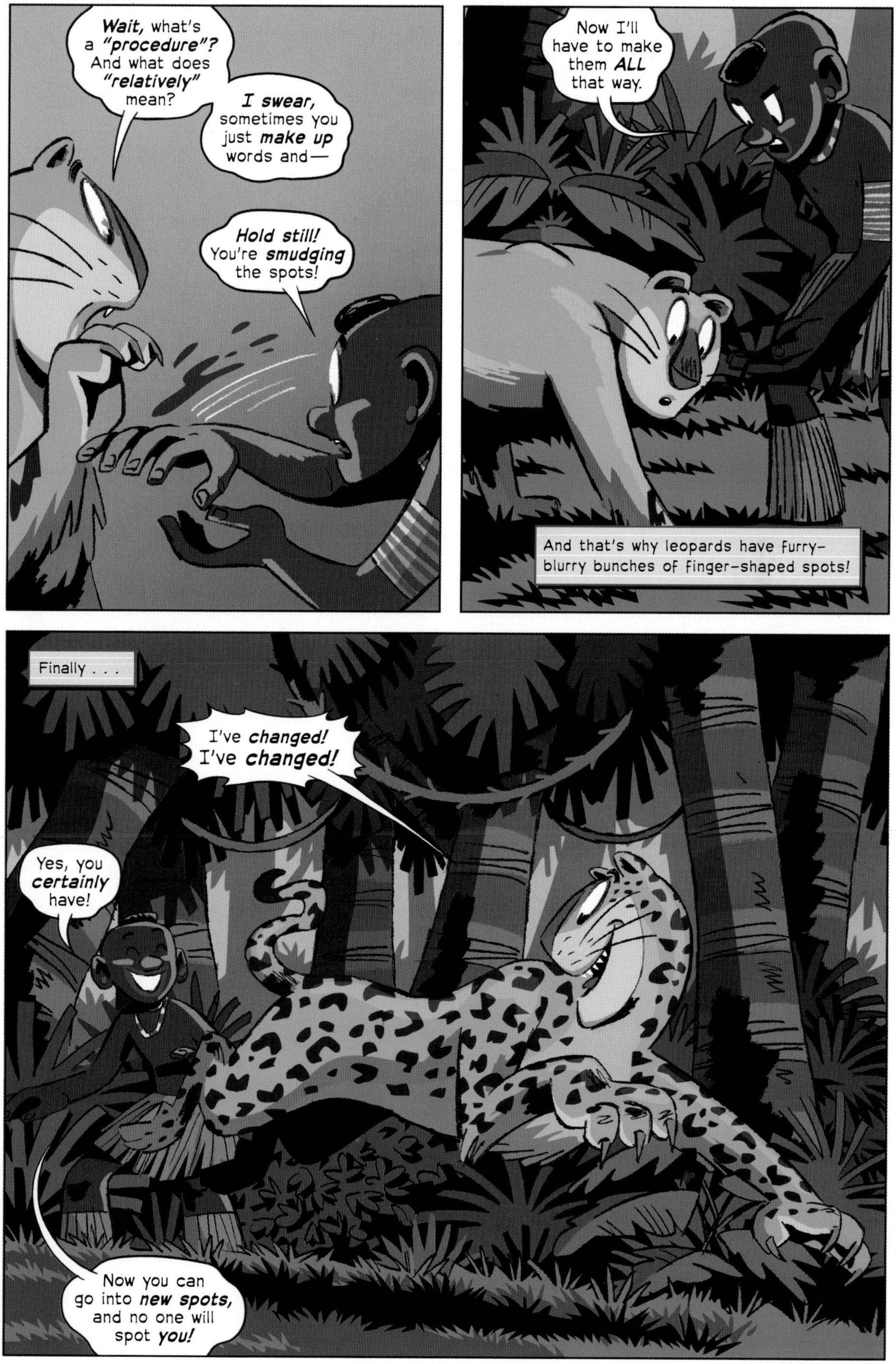
Wait, what's a "procedure"? And what does "relatively" mean?
I swear, sometimes you just make up words and—
Hold still! You're smudging the spots!
Now I'll have to make them ALL that way.
And that's why leopards have furry-blurry bunches of finger-shaped spots!
Finally . . .
I've changed! I've changed!
Yes, you certainly have!
Now you can go into new spots, and no one will spot you!

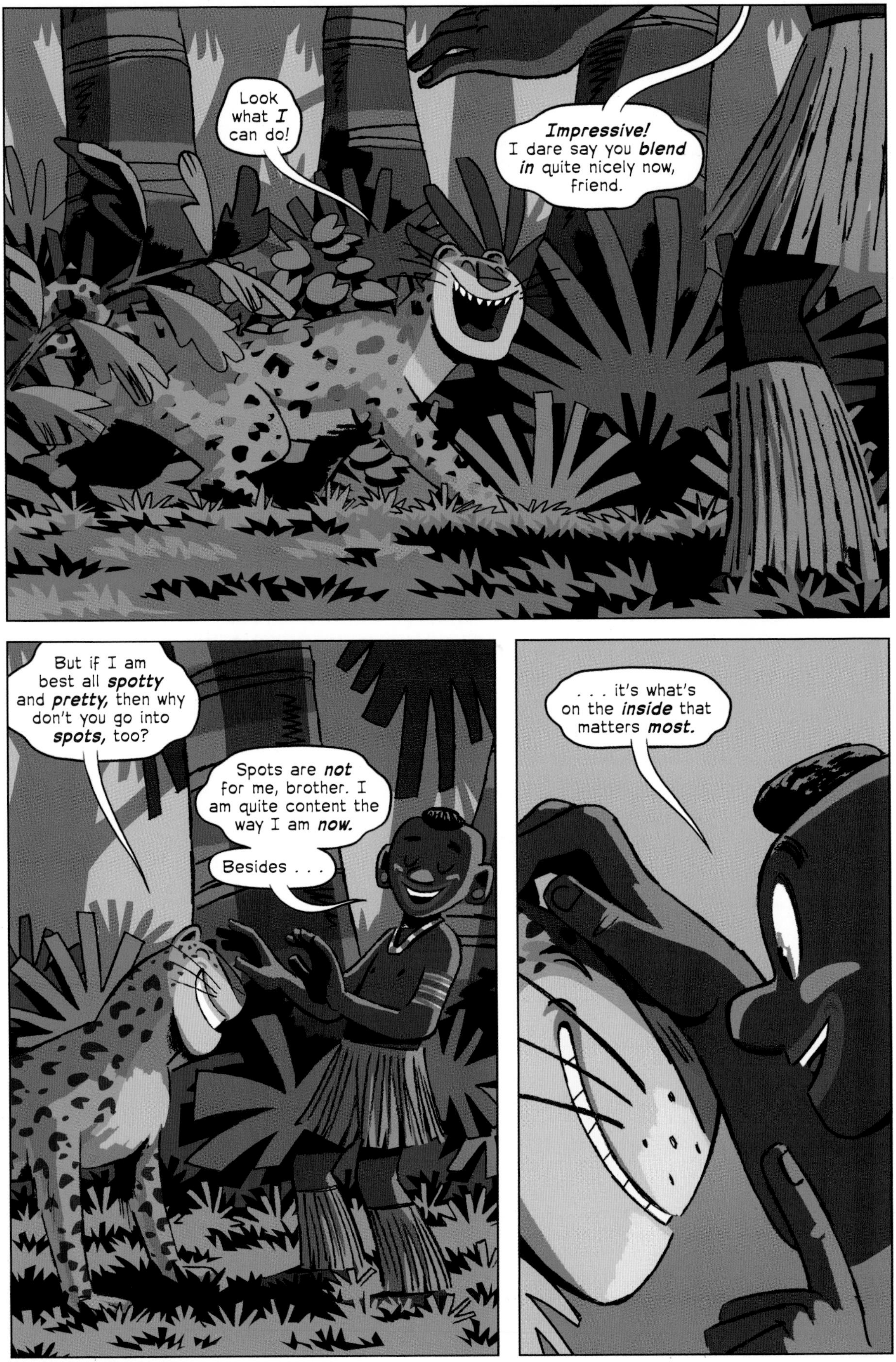
Look what *I* can do!
***Impressive!*** I dare say you ***blend in*** quite nicely now, friend.
But if I am best all ***spotty*** and ***pretty,*** then why don't you go into ***spots,*** too?
Spots are ***not*** for me, brother. I am quite content the way I am ***now.***
Besides . . .
. . . it's what's on the ***inside*** that matters ***most.***

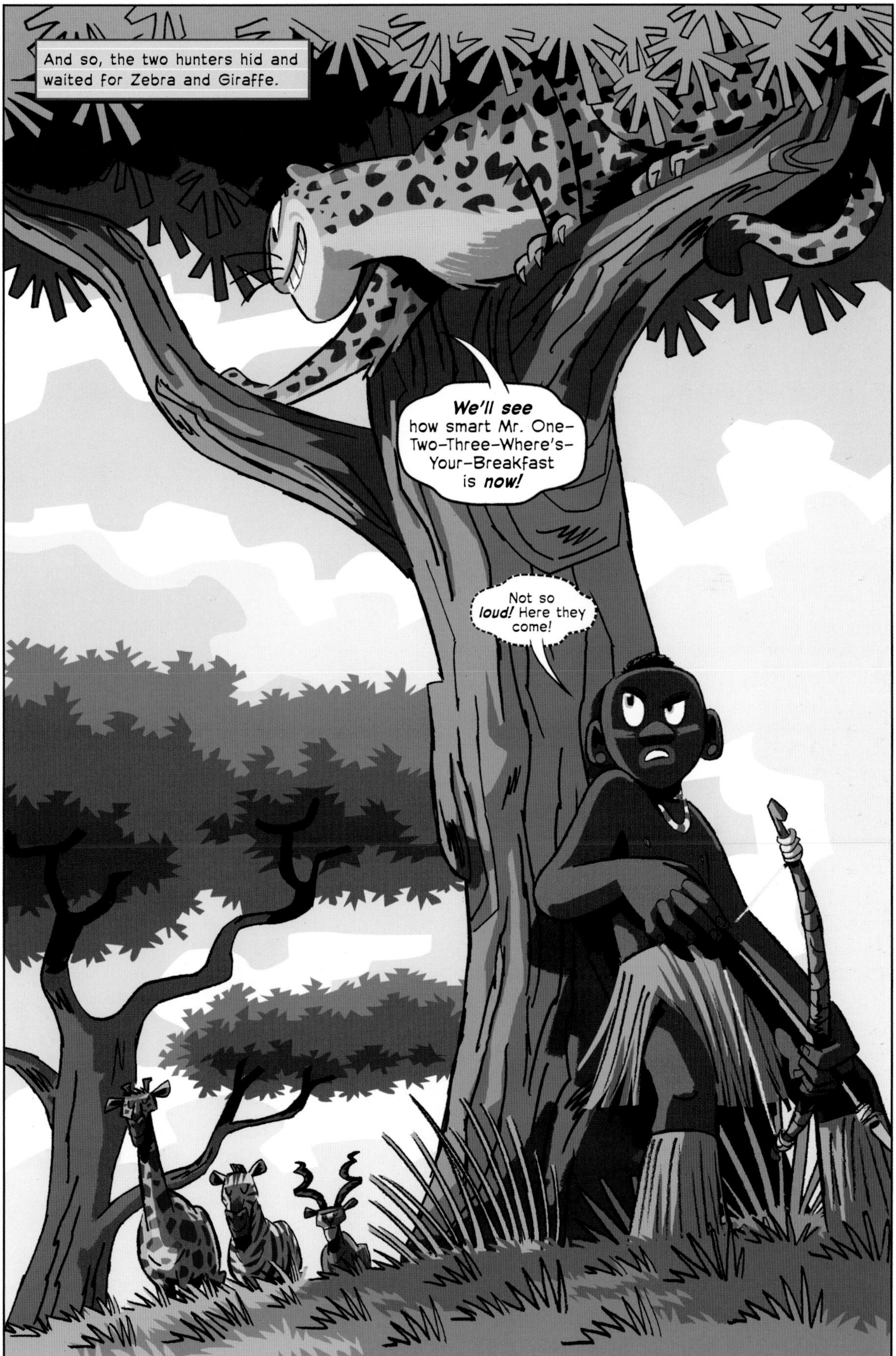

And so, the two hunters hid and waited for Zebra and Giraffe.
We'll see how smart Mr. One-Two-Three-Where's-Your-Breakfast is now!
Not so loud! Here they come!

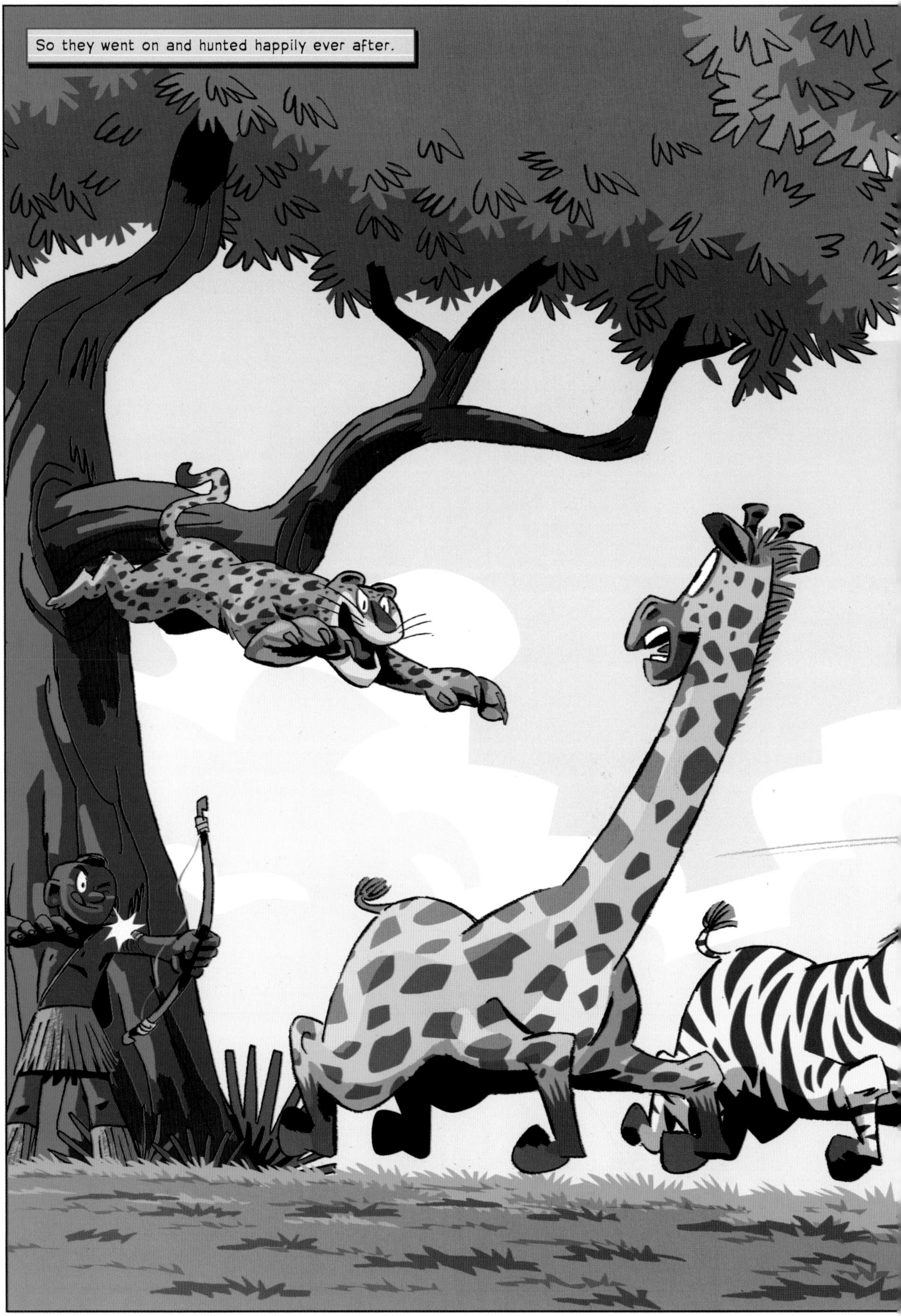
So they went on and hunted happily ever after.

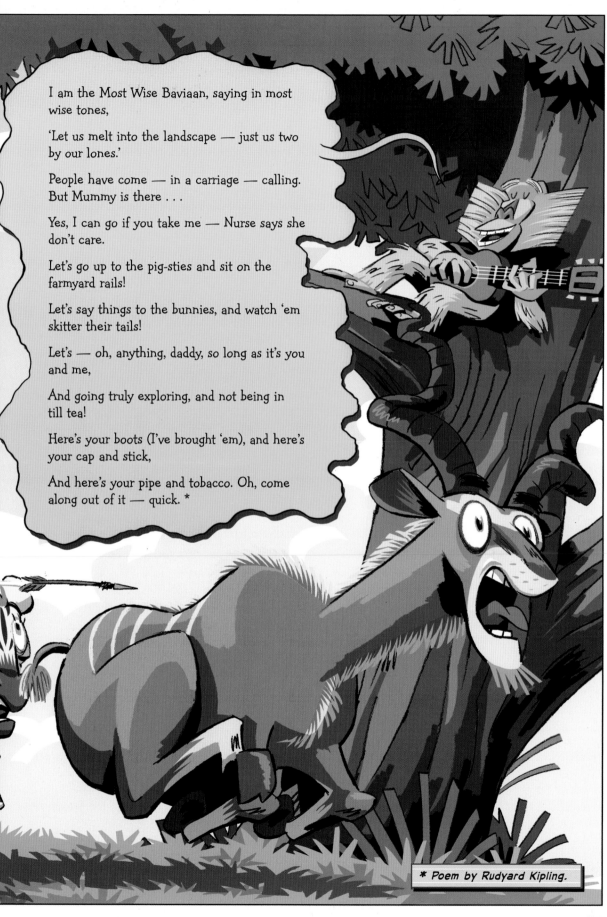

I am the Most Wise Baviaan, saying in most wise tones,

'Let us melt into the landscape — just us two by our lones.'

People have come — in a carriage — calling. But Mummy is there . . .

Yes, I can go if you take me — Nurse says she don't care.

Let's go up to the pig-sties and sit on the farmyard rails!

Let's say things to the bunnies, and watch 'em skitter their tails!

Let's — oh, anything, daddy, so long as it's you and me,

And going truly exploring, and not being in till tea!

Here's your boots (I've brought 'em), and here's your cap and stick,

And here's your pipe and tobacco. Oh, come along out of it — quick. *

* *Poem by Rudyard Kipling.*

RUDYARD KIPLING

3

# CONCLUSION

NEW SPECIMENS:
SUPERBLY-SPOTTED LEOPARD (Fig. A)

THE ETHIOPIAN (Fig. B)
STRIPED ZEBRA (Fig. C)
BANDED KUDU (Fig. D)
SPOTTED GIRAFFE (Fig. E)

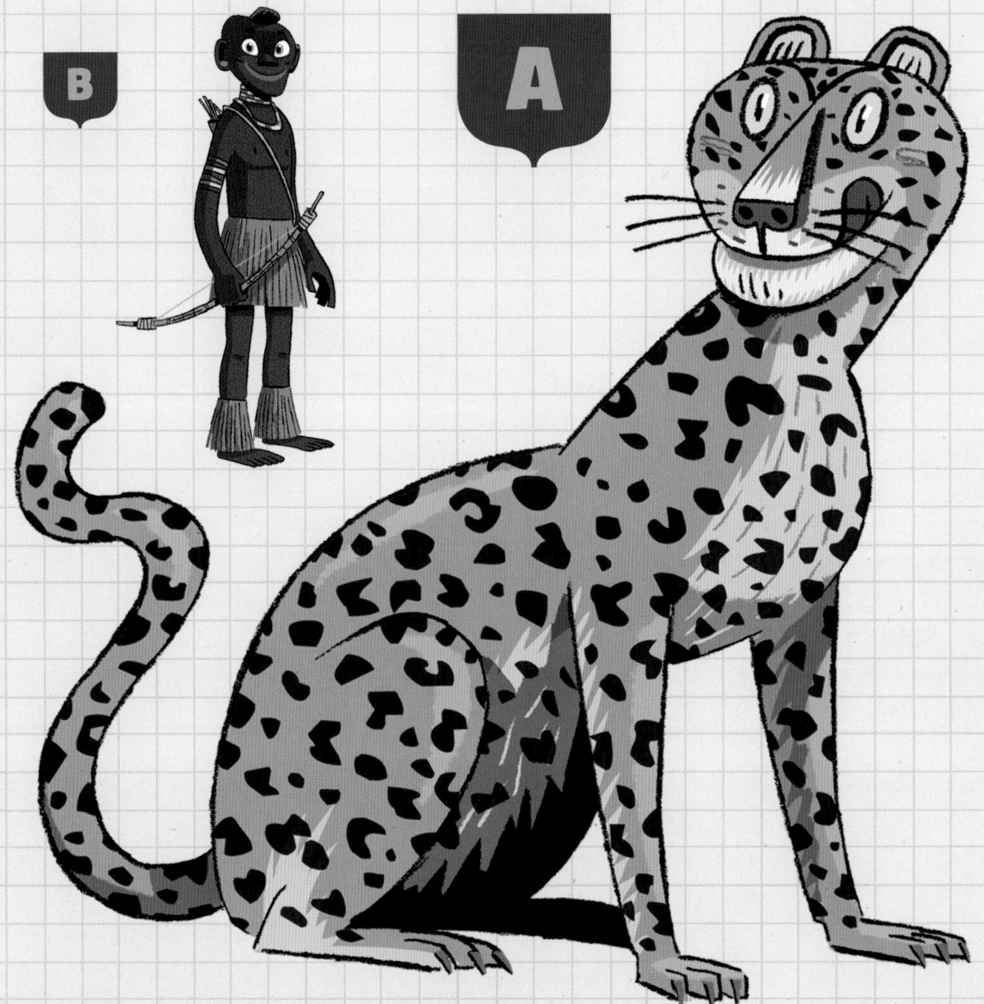
B
A

# NOTES:

The leopard is the smallest of the four big cats. Not sure if he suffers from low self-esteem when tiger, lion, or jaguar is around.

Leopards hunt about ninety species of animals, including antelope, rodents, birds, reptiles, and even insects. Not at risk for being labeled "picky eaters."

Leopards can hear five times more sounds than humans. Be thankful that your parents are not leopards.

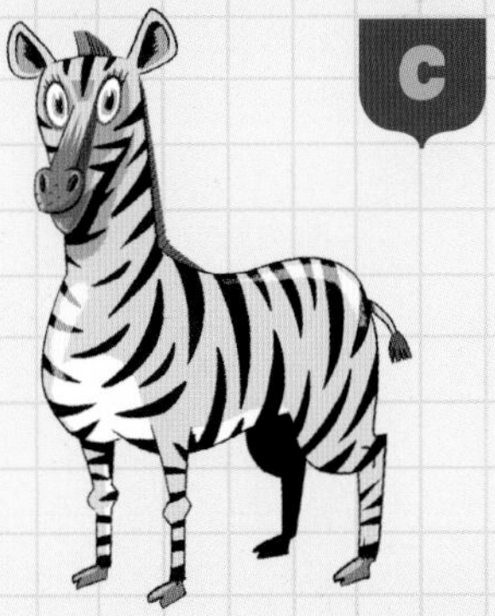
C

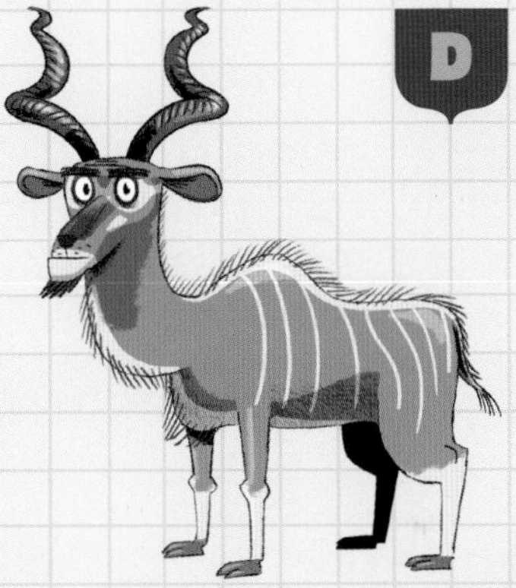
D

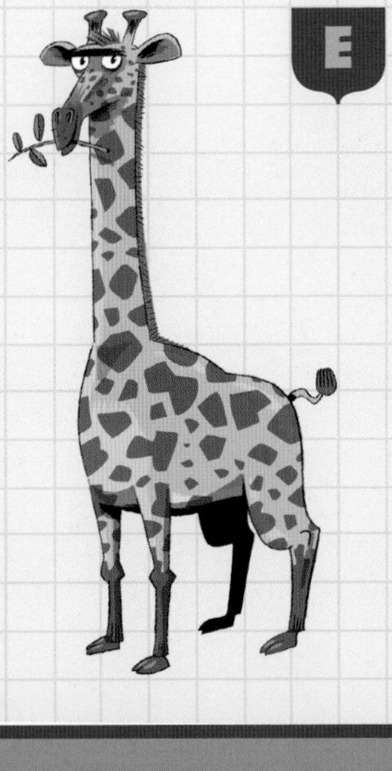
E

1

2

3

**RUDYARD KIPLING**

EST.
1865

# HOW THE ELEPHANT GOT HIS TRUNK

as retold by

## BLAKE A. HOENA
### TEAM WRITER

RUDYARD KIPLING

1

# RESEARCH

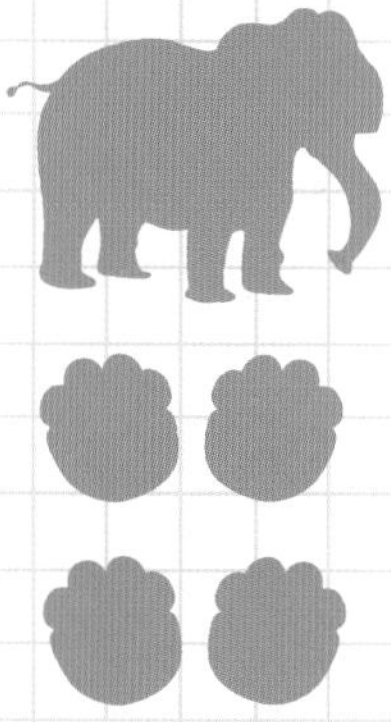

**SPECIMEN:**

## BOOT-NOSED ELEPHANT

(Fig. A)

HABITAT: **South Africa, near the Limpopo River (Fig. C)**
SOCIAL BEHAVIOR: **Insatiably curious**
PARENTAL UNIT: **Mother elephant (Fig. B)**
ADVISOR: **Mr. Snake (Fig. D)**
ELDERS: **Hippopotomus (Fig. E), Giraffe (Fig. F), Baboon (Fig. G), Aunty Ozzy (Fig. H)**
PREDATOR: **Crocodile (Fig. I)**

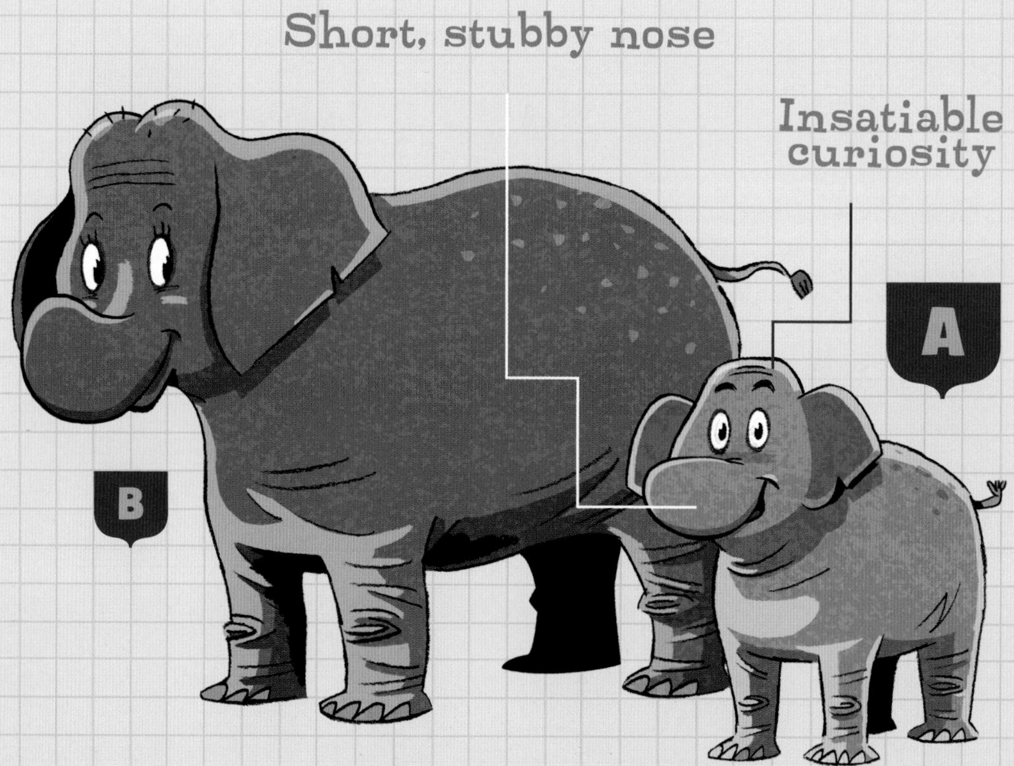
Short, stubby nose
Insatiable curiosity
A
B

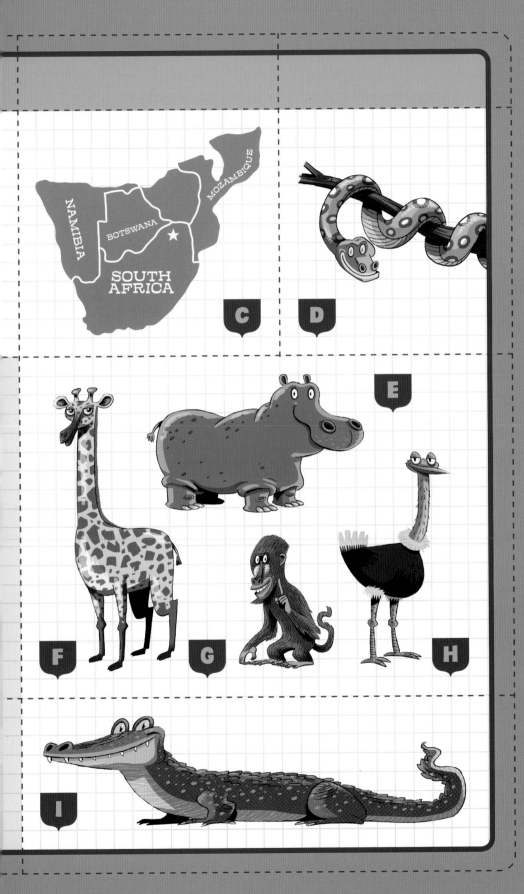

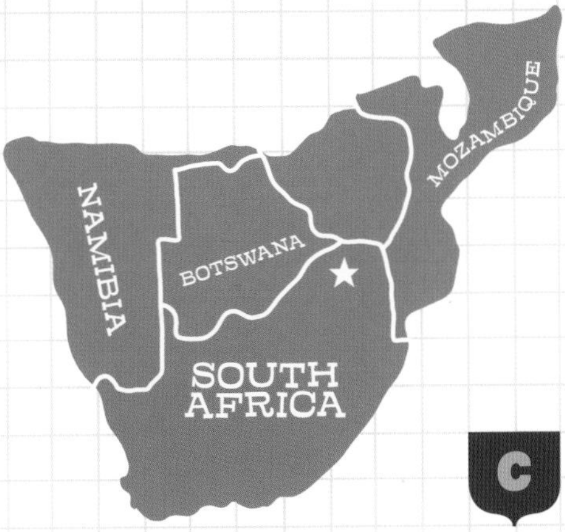
MOZAMBIQUE
NAMIBIA
BOTSWANA
SOUTH AFRICA

C

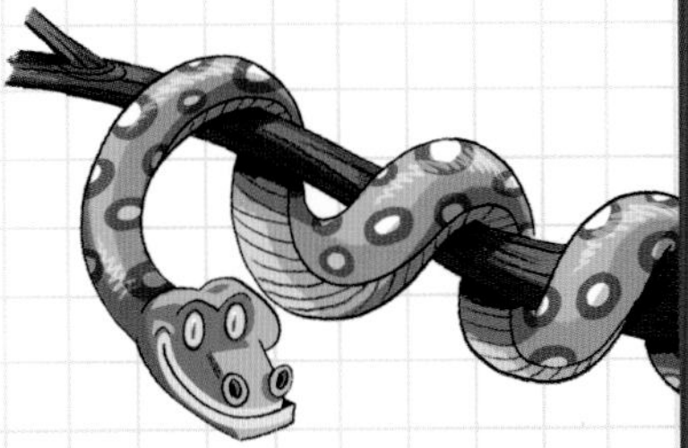

D

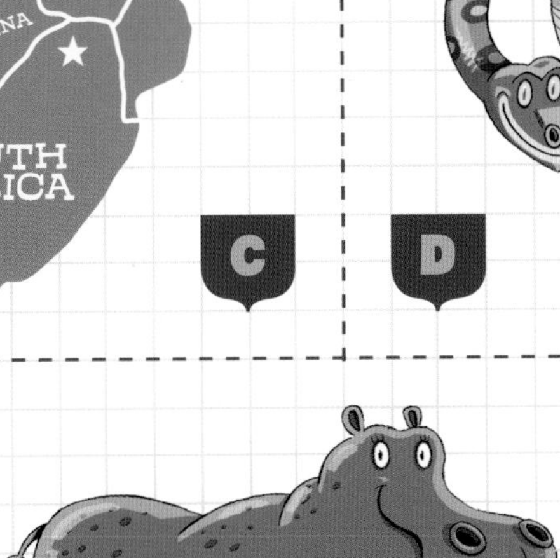

E

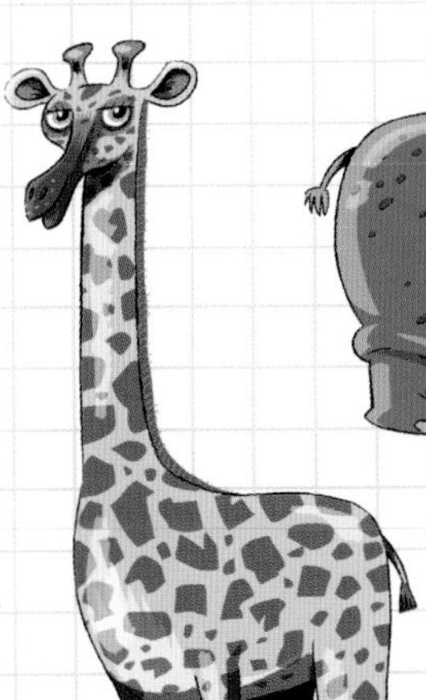

F

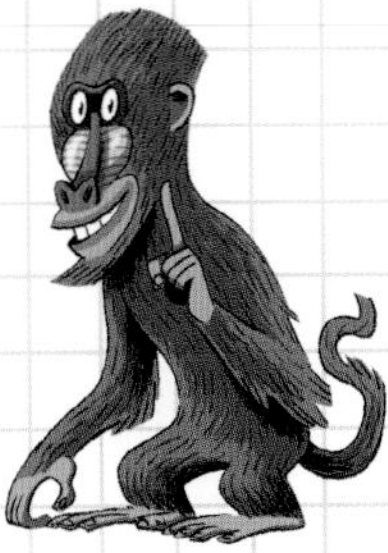

G

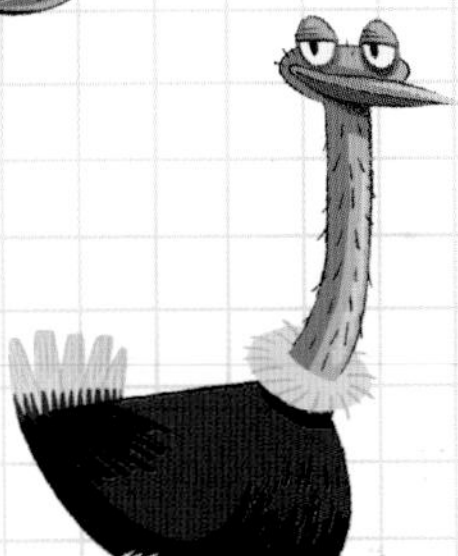

H

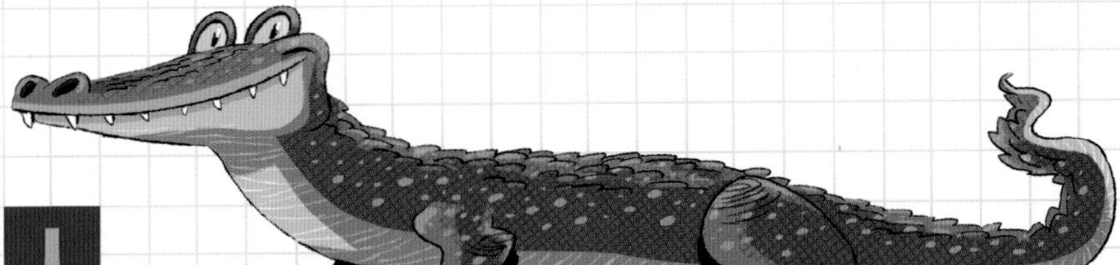

I

# KIPLING'S OBSERVATION

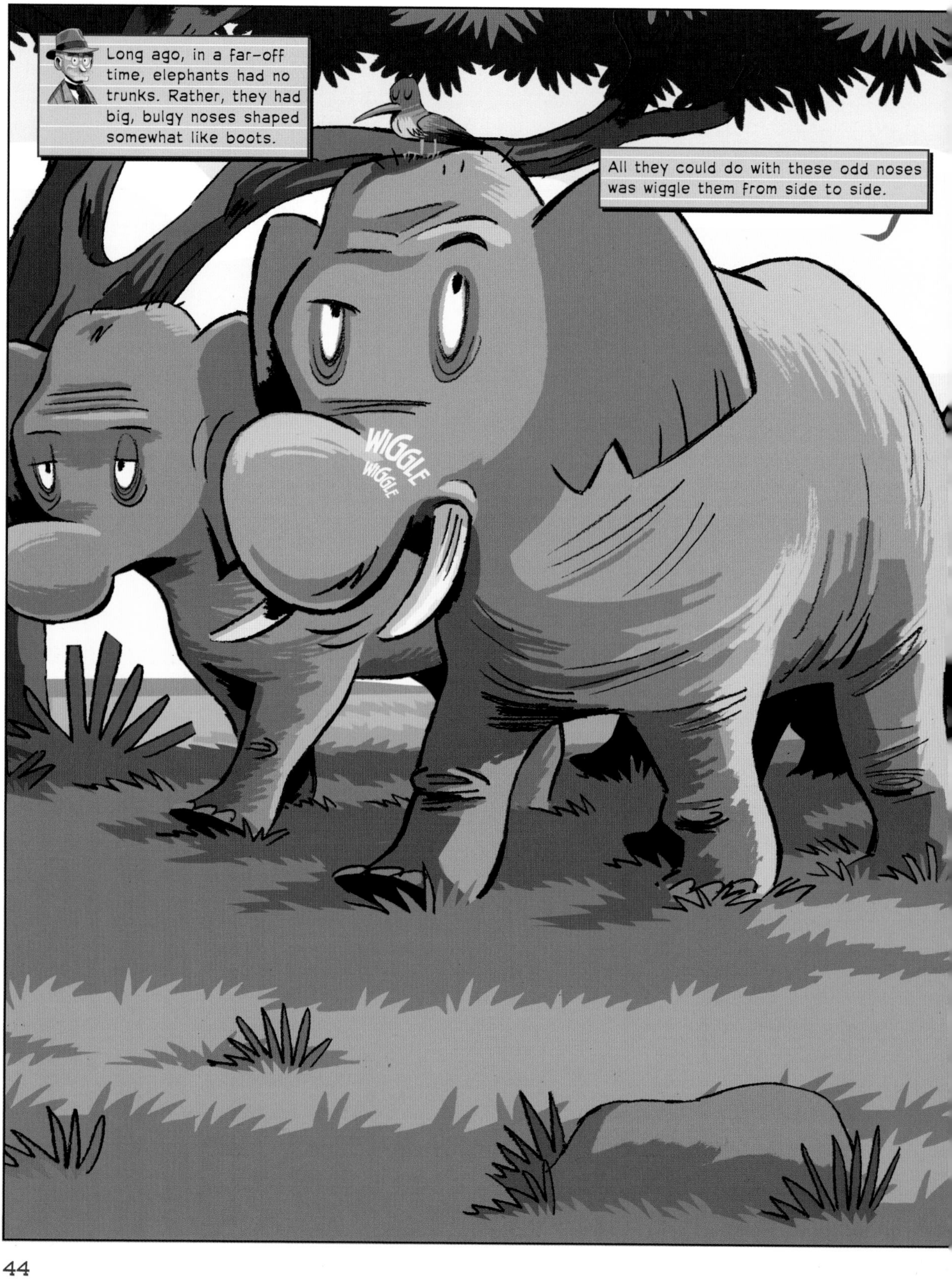
Long ago, in a far-off time, elephants had no trunks. Rather, they had big, bulgy noses shaped somewhat like boots.
All they could do with these odd noses was wiggle them from side to side.
WIGGLE
WIGGLE
WIGGLE

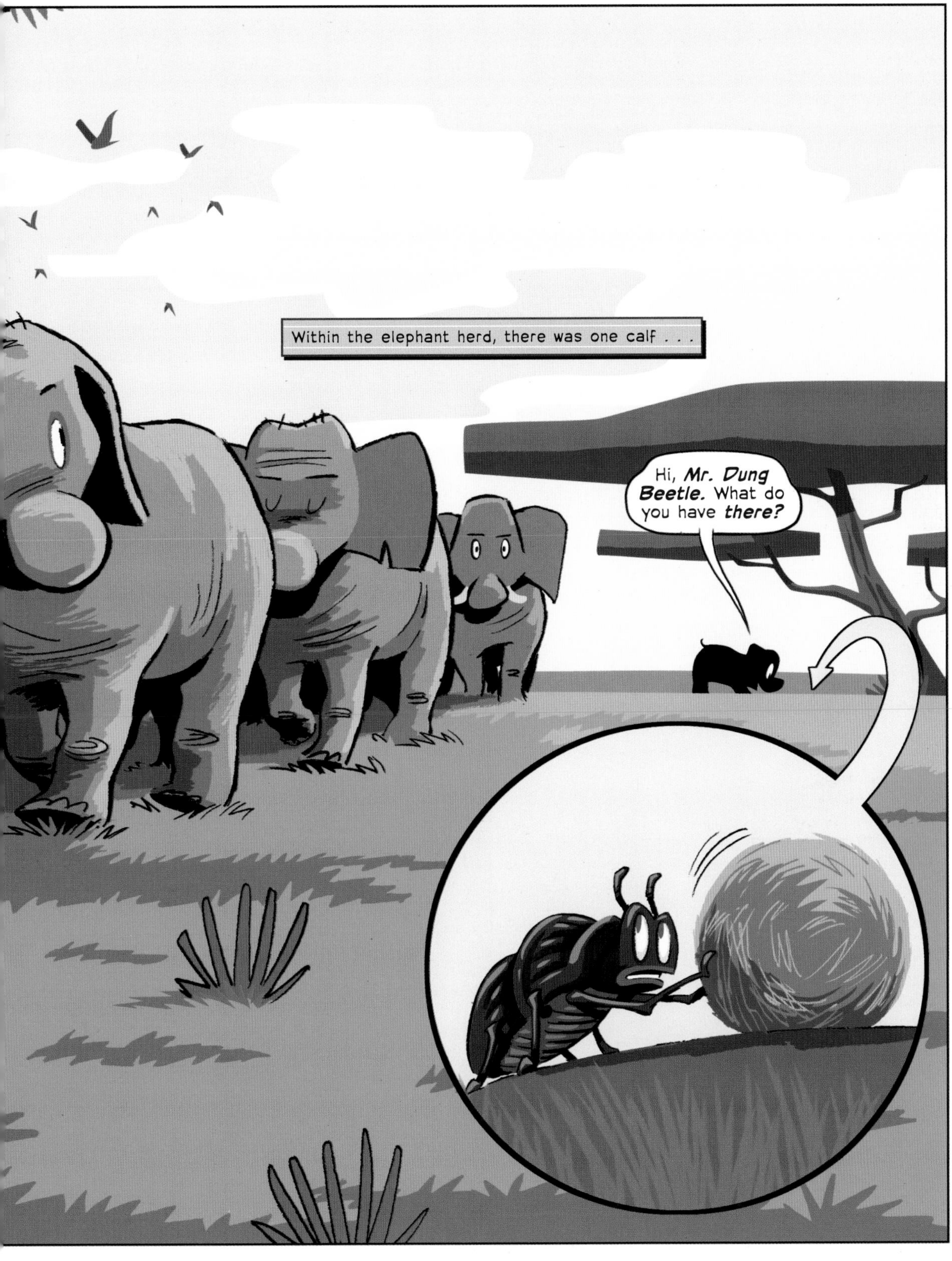
Within the elephant herd, there was one calf . . .
Hi, *Mr. Dung Beetle.* What do you have *there?*

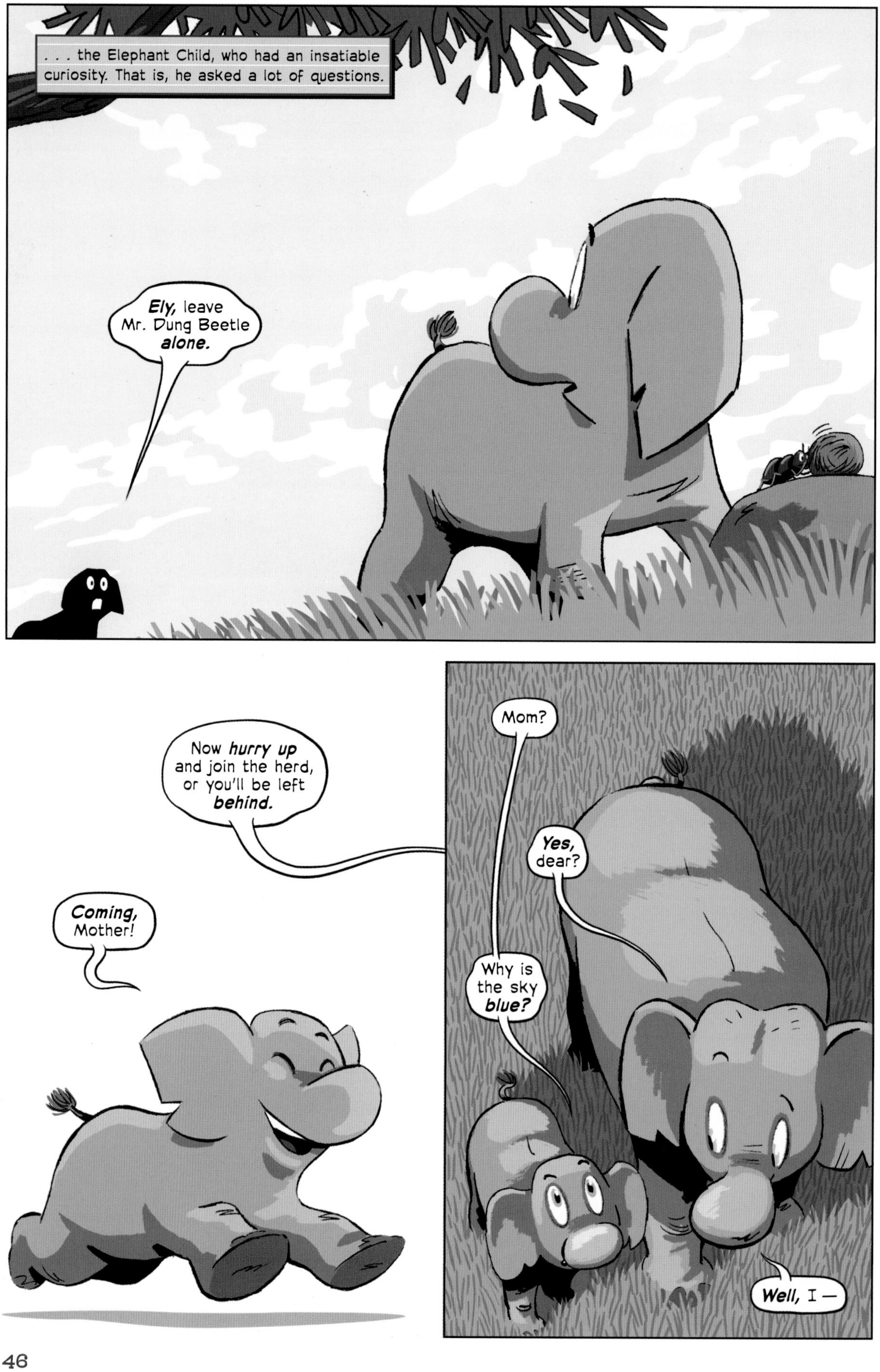

. . . the Elephant Child, who had an insatiable curiosity. That is, he asked a lot of questions.
Ely, leave Mr. Dung Beetle alone.
Now hurry up and join the herd, or you'll be left behind.
Coming, Mother!
Mom?
Yes, dear?
Why is the sky blue?
Well, I —

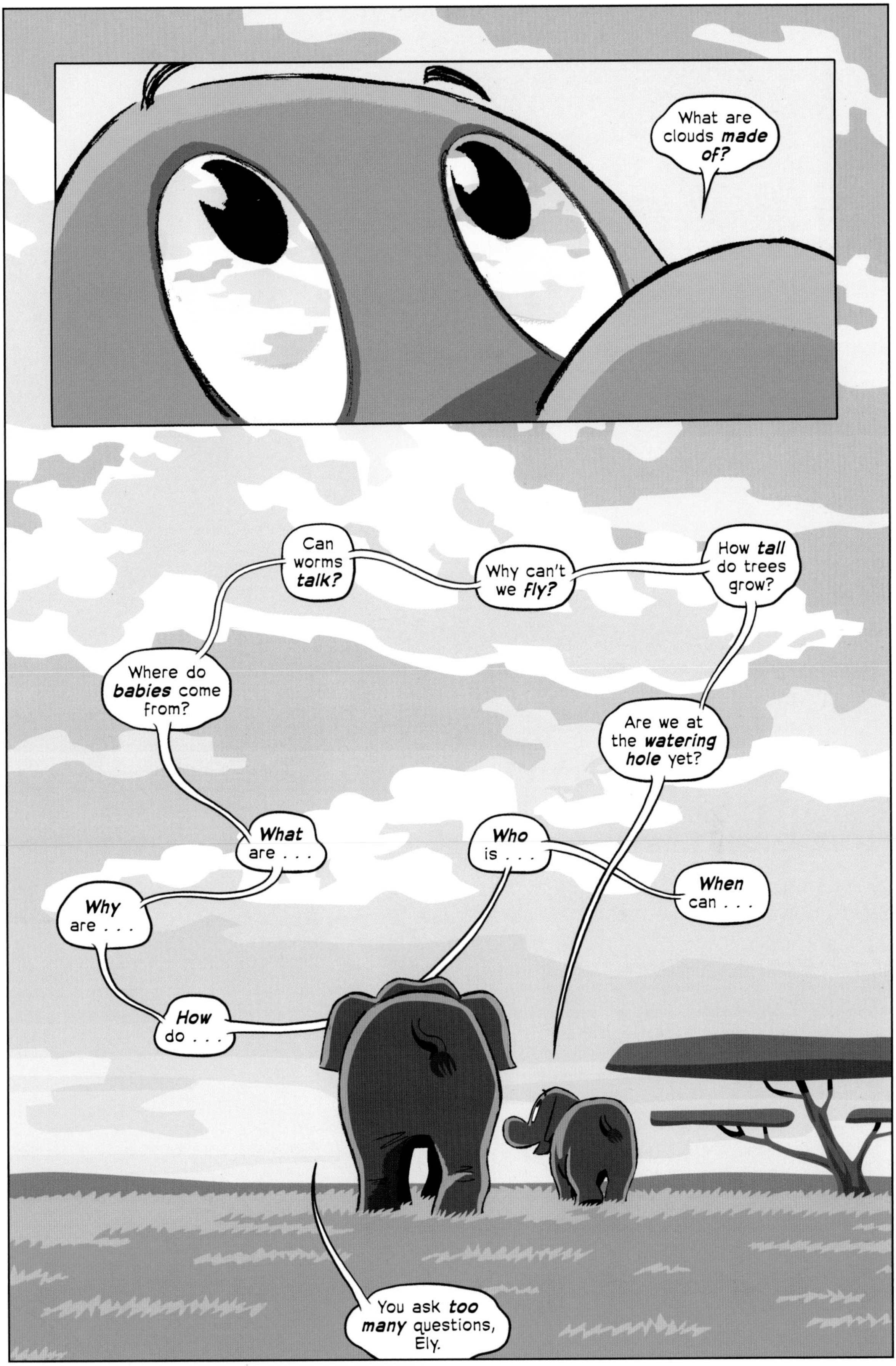

What are clouds made of?
Where do babies come from?
Can worms talk?
Why can't we fly?
How tall do trees grow?
Are we at the watering hole yet?
What are . . .
Why are . . .
How do . . .
Who is . . .
When can . . .
You ask too many questions, Ely.

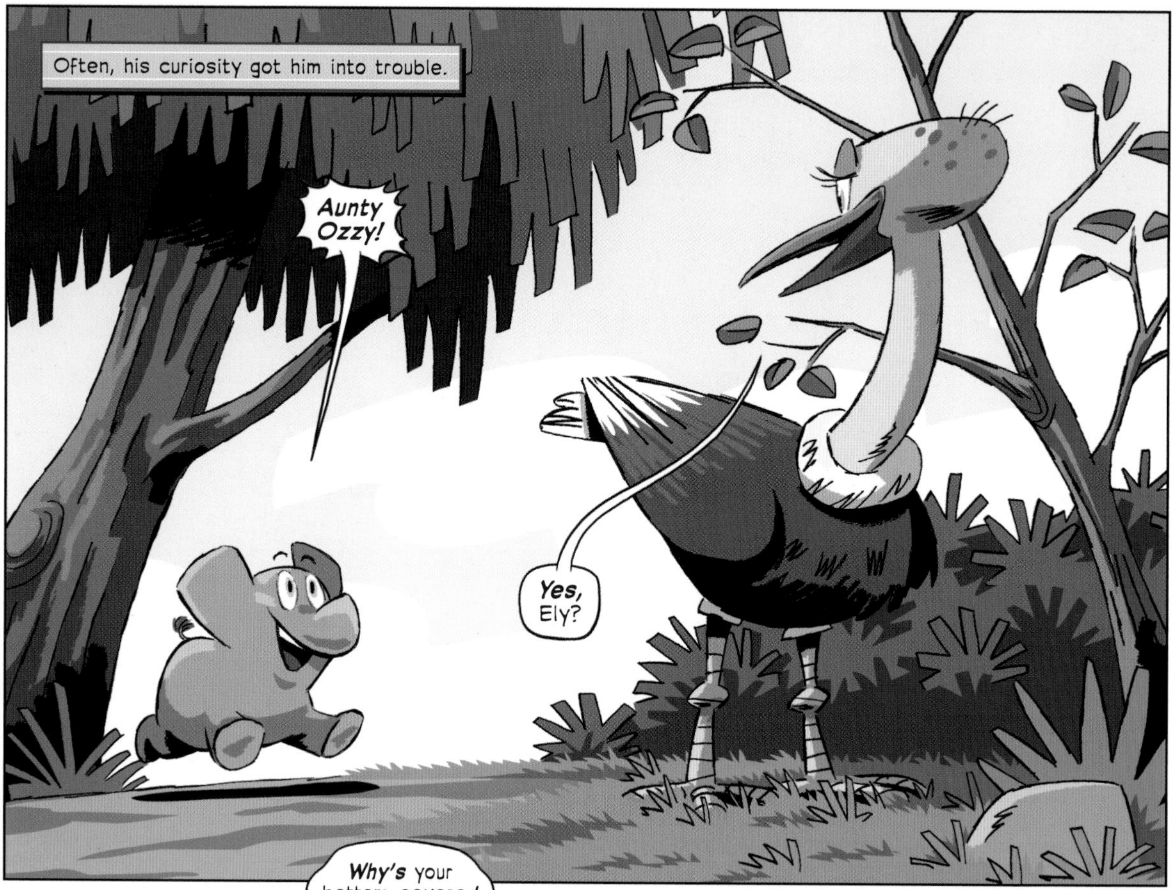
Often, his curiosity got him into trouble.
Aunty Ozzy!
Yes, Ely?

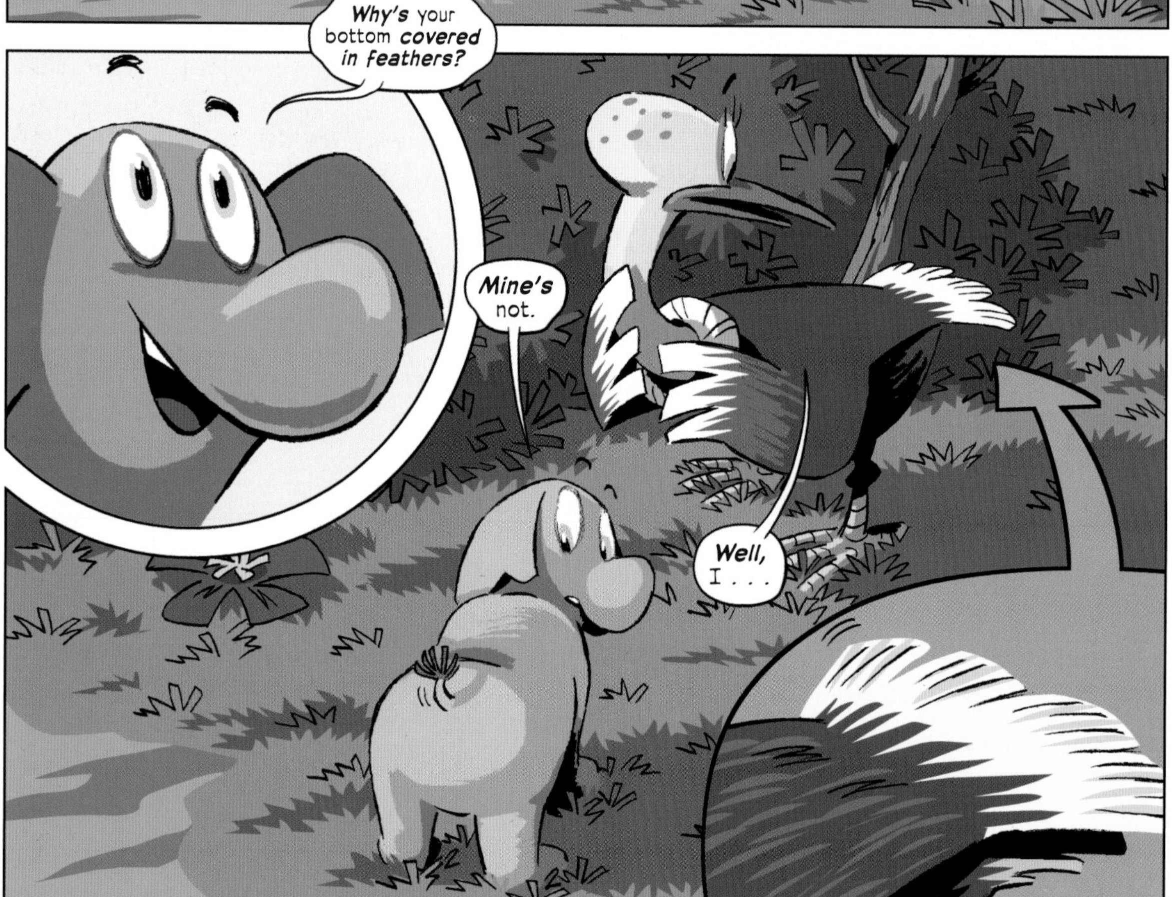
Why's your bottom covered in feathers?
Mine's not.
Well, I . . .

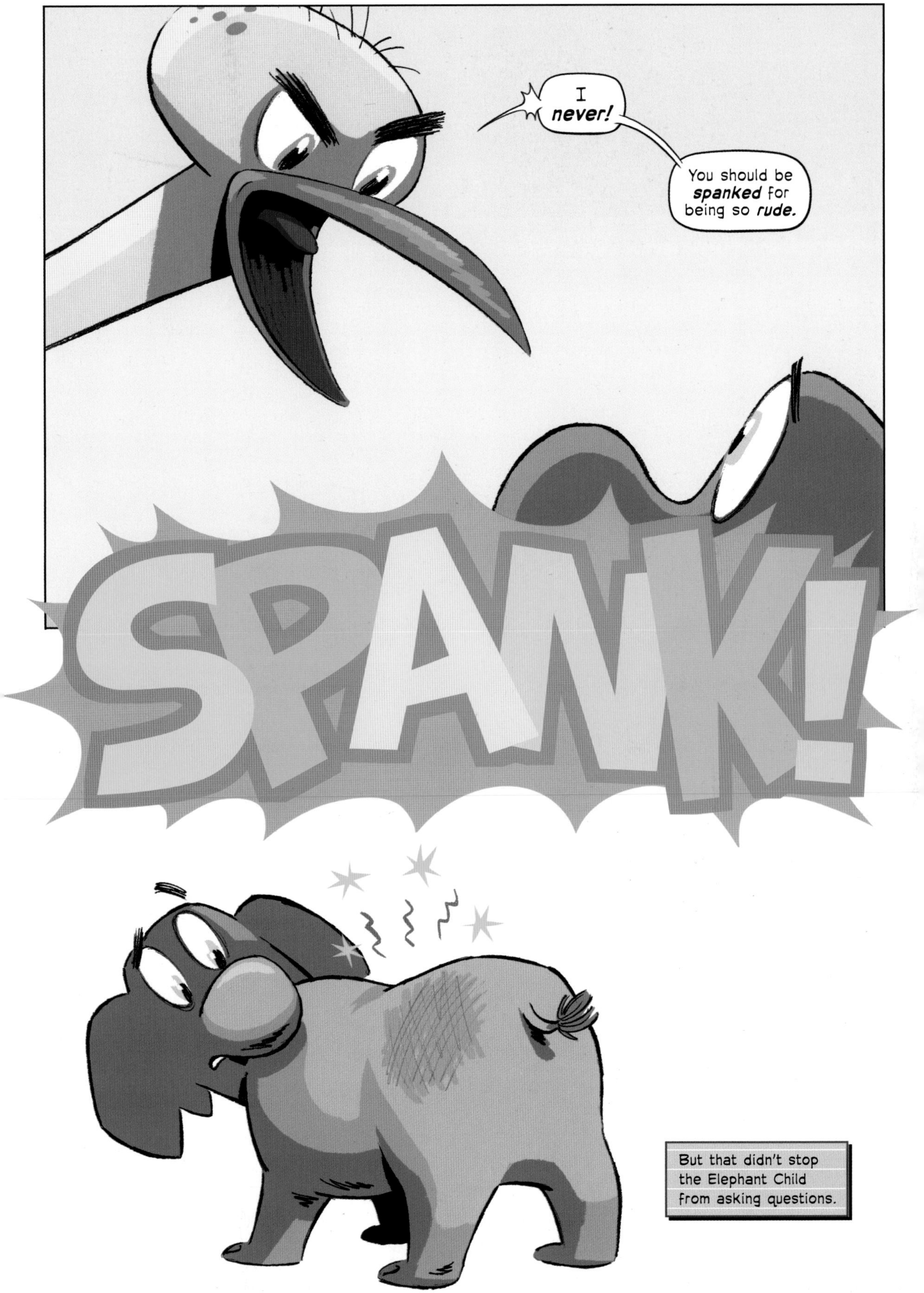
I never!
You should be spanked for being so rude.
SPANK!
But that didn't stop the Elephant Child from asking questions.

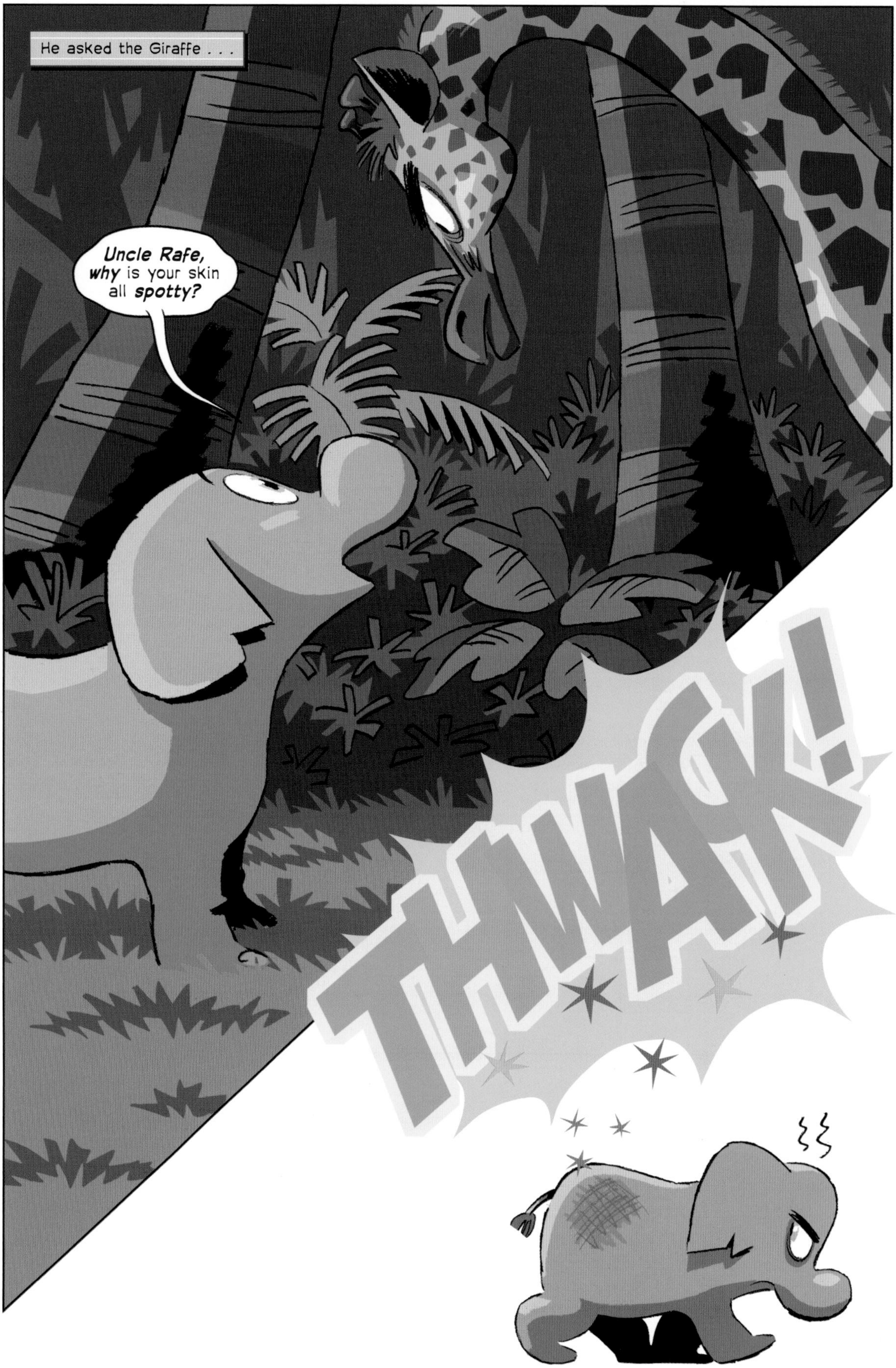
He asked the Giraffe . . .
*Uncle Rafe,* ***why*** is your skin all ***spotty?***
THWAK!

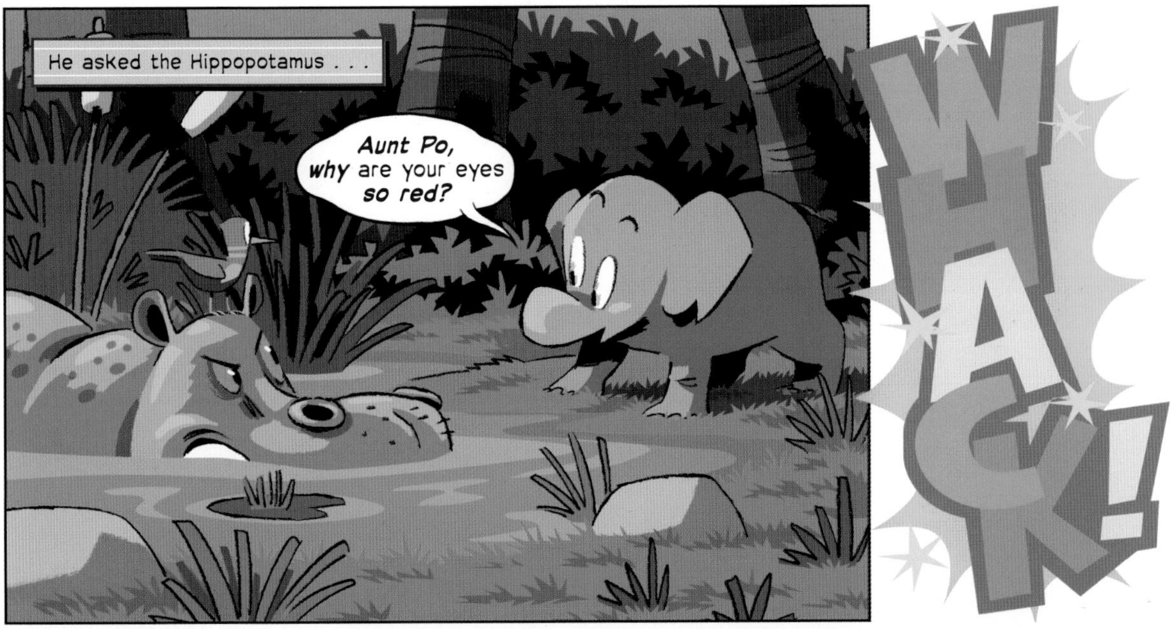
He asked the Hippopotamus . . .
Aunt Po, why are your eyes so red?
WHACK!

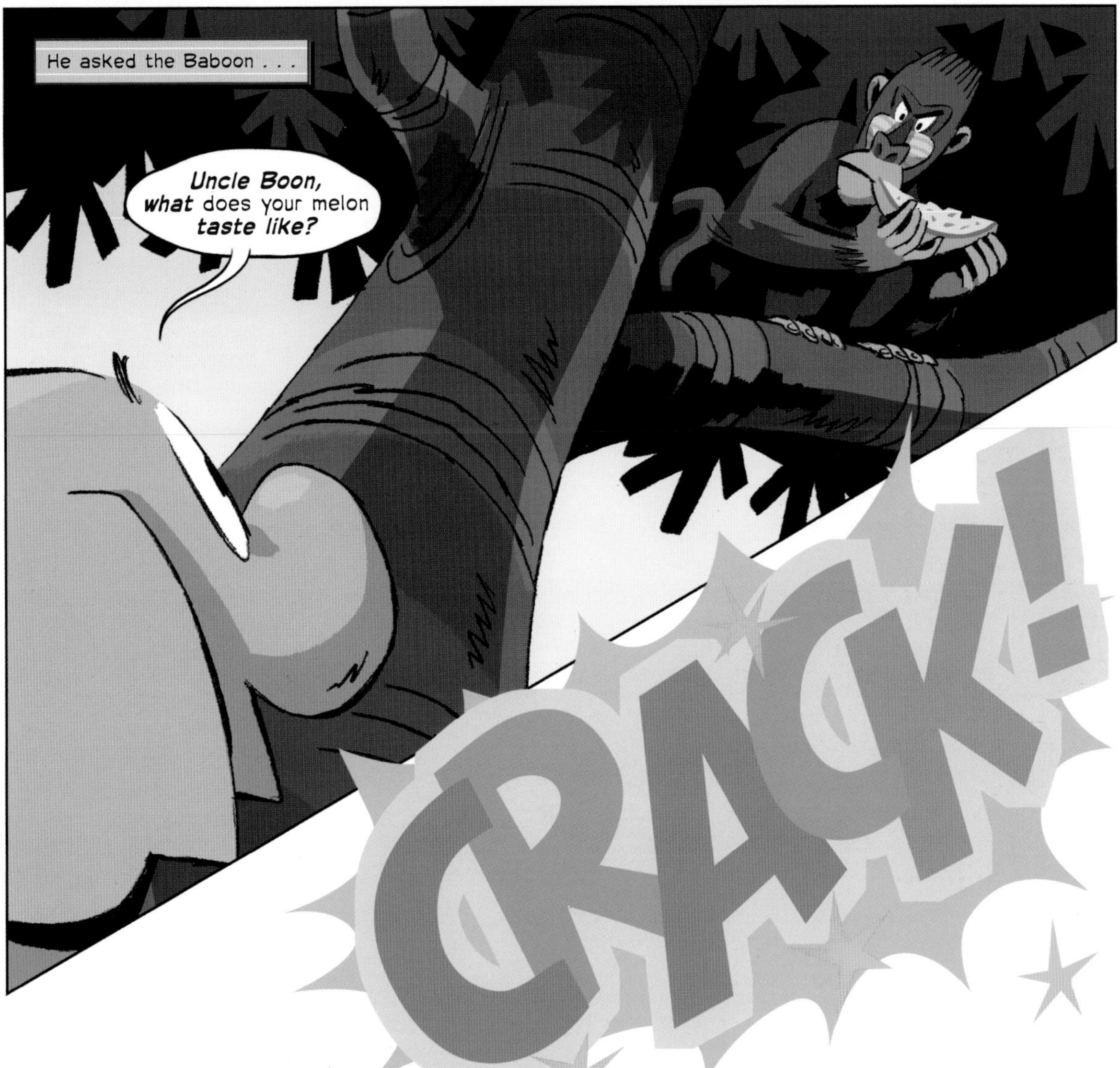
He asked the Baboon . . .
Uncle Boon, what does your melon taste like?
CRACK!

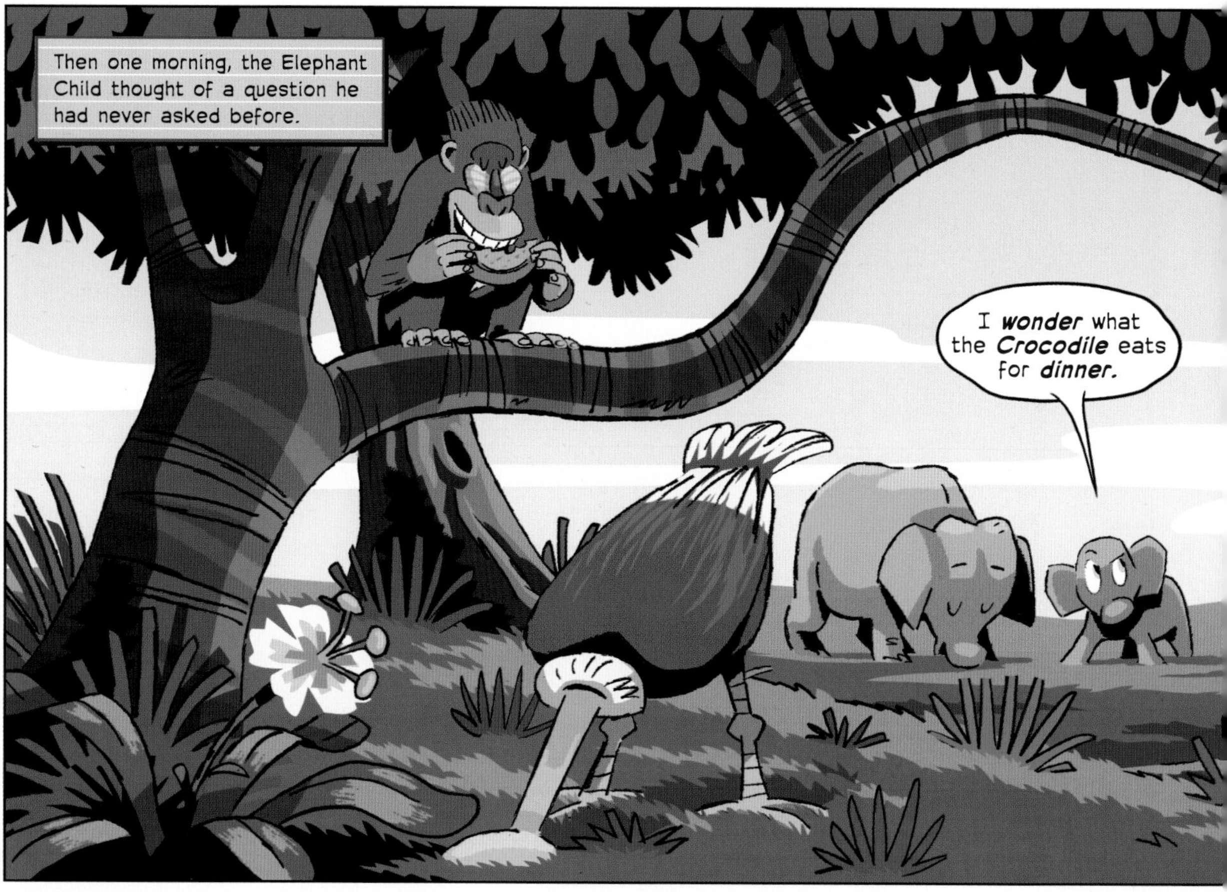
Then one morning, the Elephant Child thought of a question he had never asked before.
I *wonder* what the *Crocodile* eats for *dinner.*

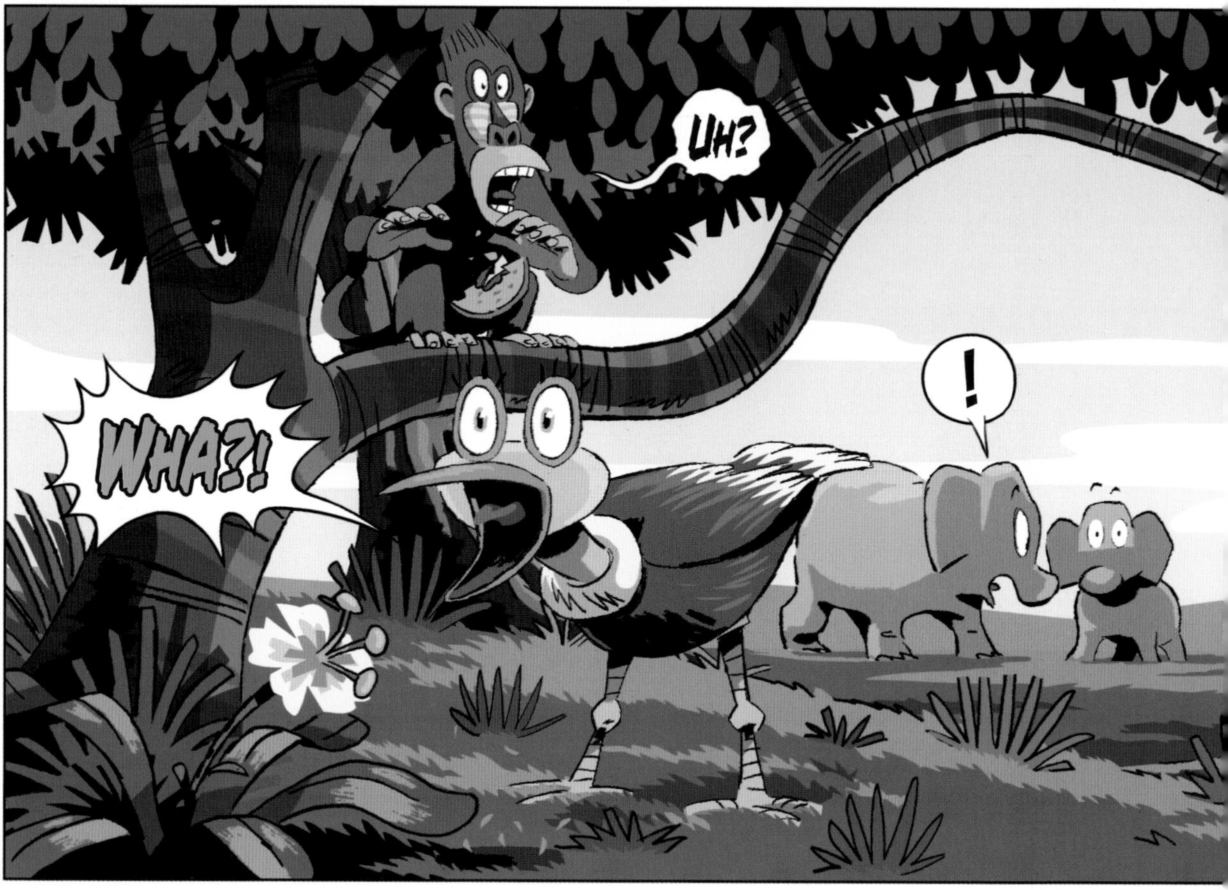
UH?
!
WHA?!

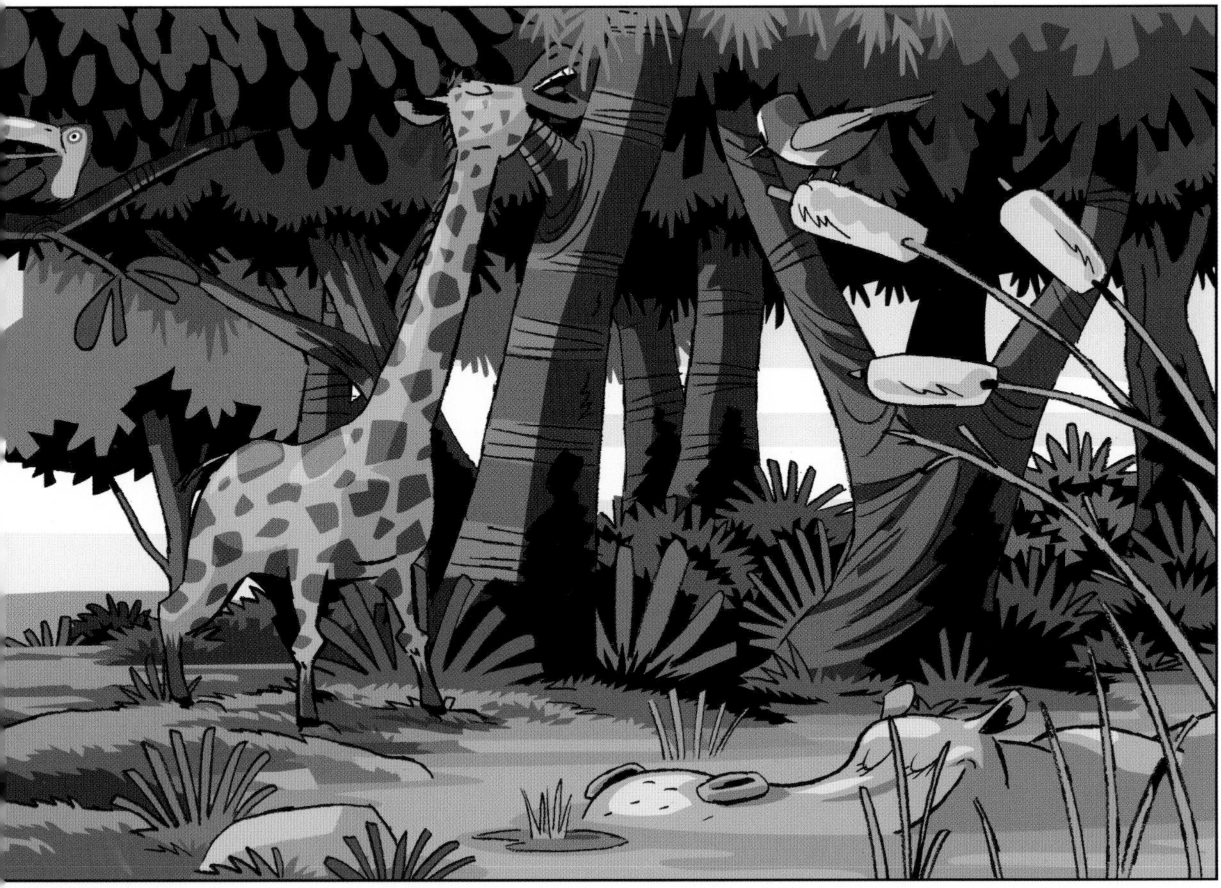

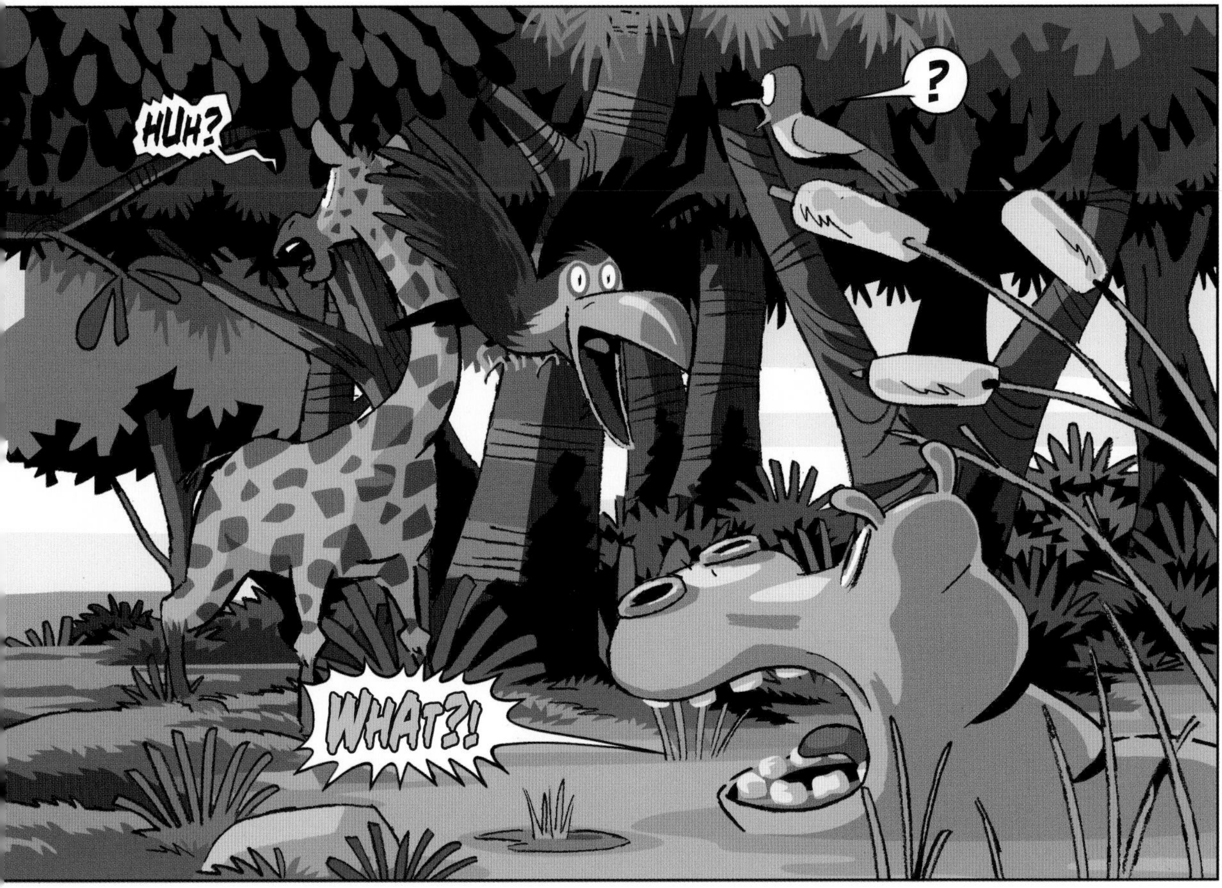
HUH?
?
WHAT?!

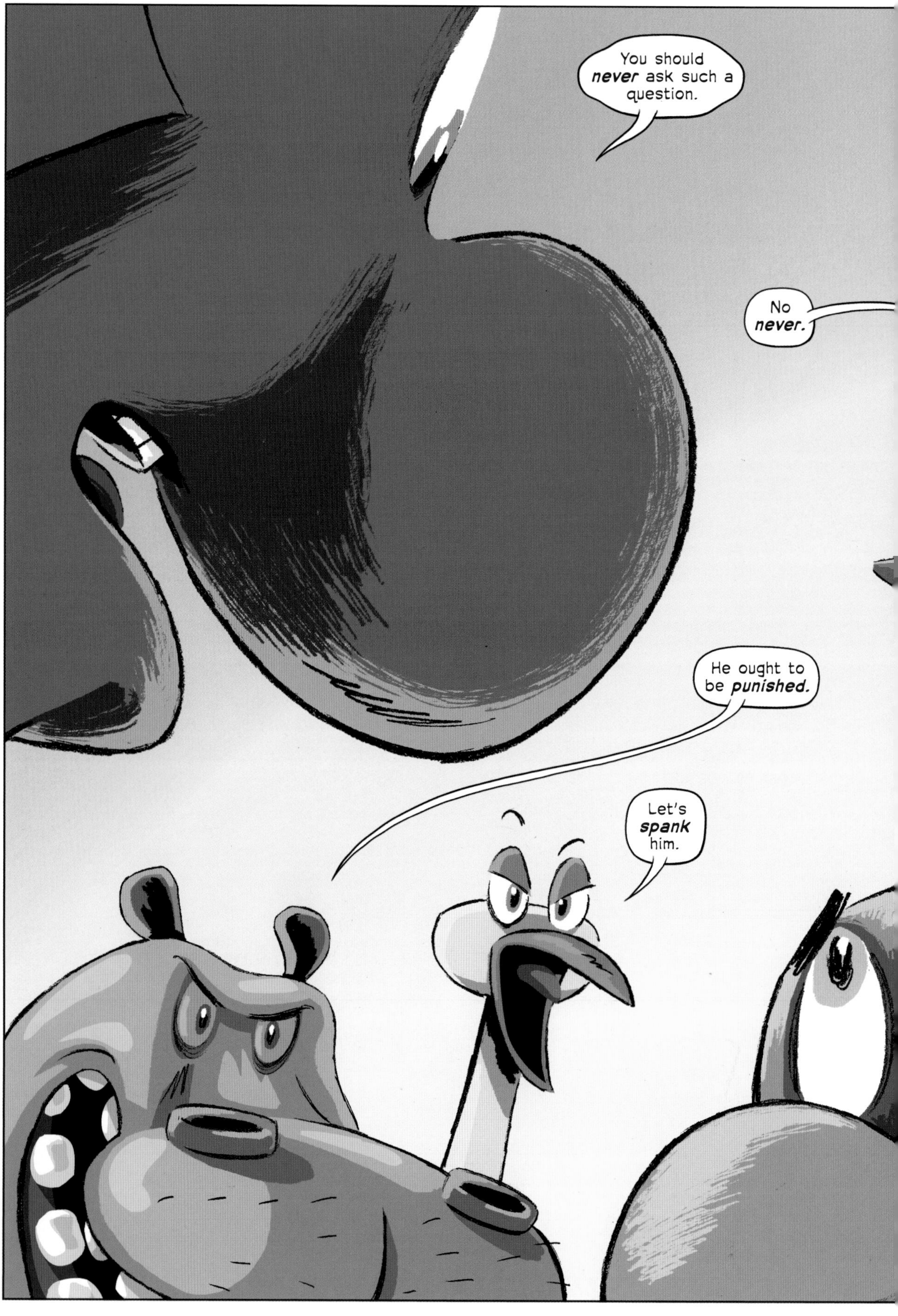

You should *never* ask such a question.
No *never.*
He ought to be *punished.*
Let's *spank* him.

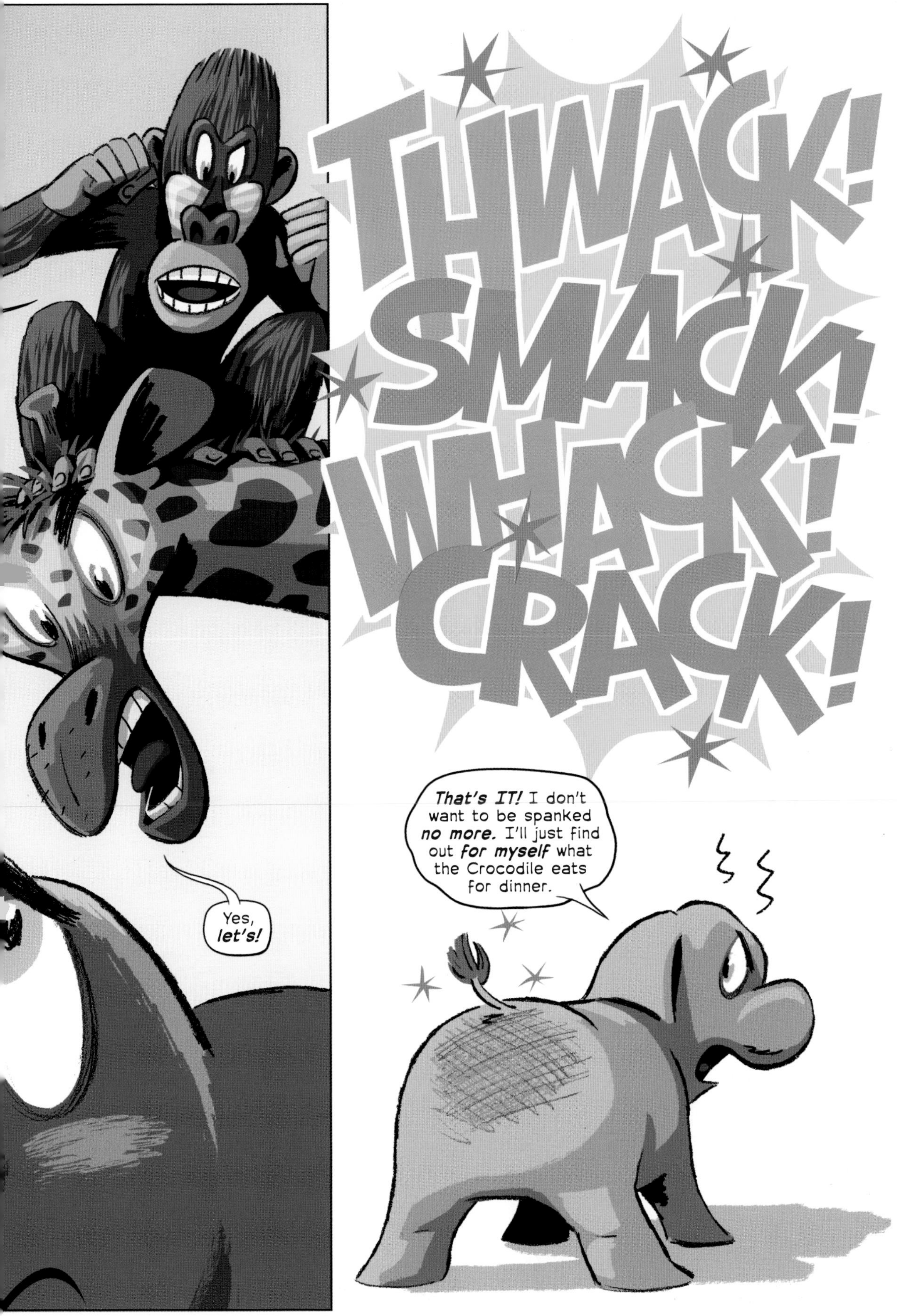
THWACK!
SMACK!
WHACK!
CRACK!
Yes, *let's!*
*That's IT!* I don't want to be spanked *no more.* I'll just find out *for myself* what the Crocodile eats for dinner.

As he walked away, the Elephant Child came across the Kolokolo Bird.

*Why* so *glum*, Ely, my chum?

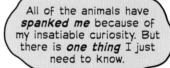

*This* is why!

*Oh my*, your rump is as *red* as Baboon's *butt!*

All of the animals have *spanked me* because of my insatiable curiosity. But there is *one thing* I just need to know.

What is *that*, my *curious* elephant?

56

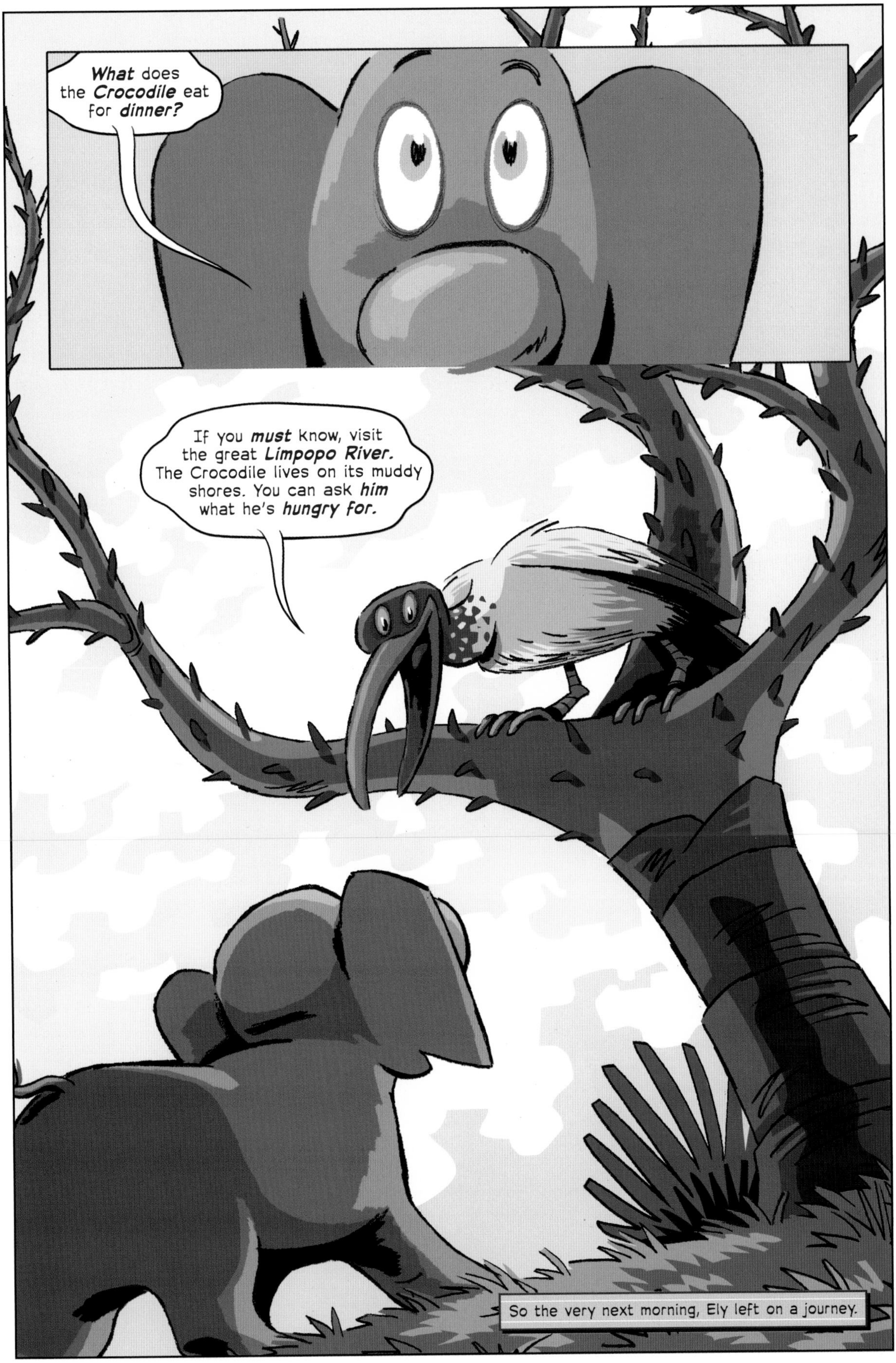
What does the Crocodile eat for dinner?
If you must know, visit the great Limpopo River. The Crocodile lives on its muddy shores. You can ask him what he's hungry for.
So the very next morning, Ely left on a journey.

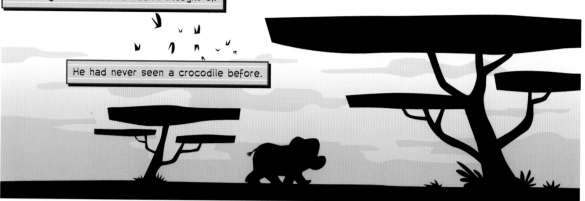

As the Elephant Child traveled, there was one thing he realized he hadn't thought of.

He had never seen a crocodile before.

Excuse me, *Mr. Snake.* But have you ever *seen* a *crocodile?*

Why yes, *I have.*

Then do you *know* where I can *find* one?

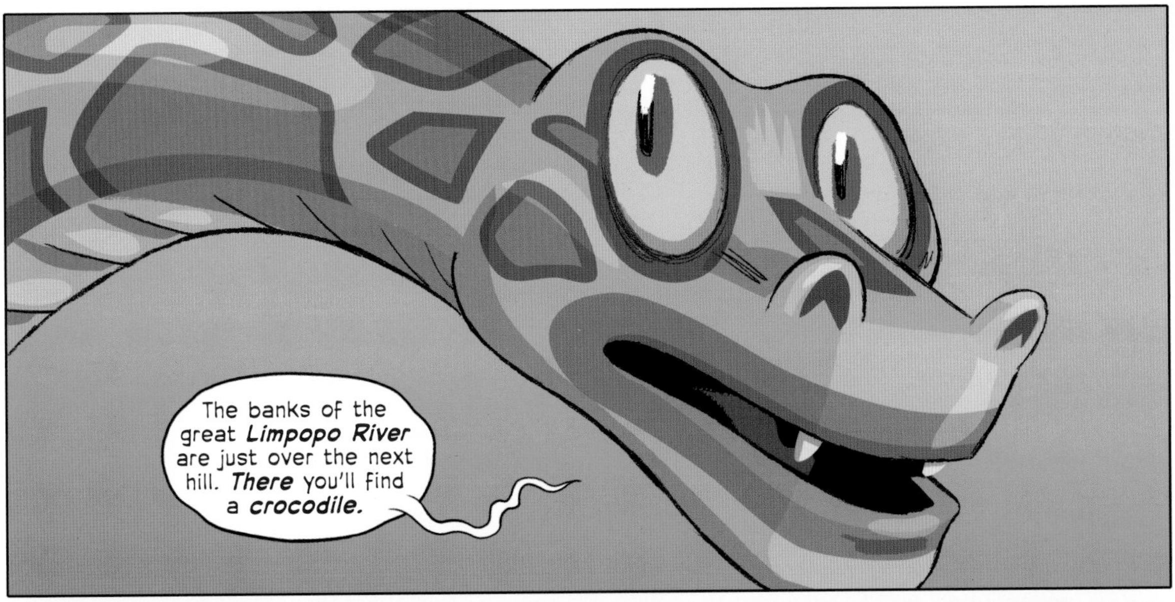
The banks of the great *Limpopo River* are just over the next hill. *There* you'll find a *crocodile.*

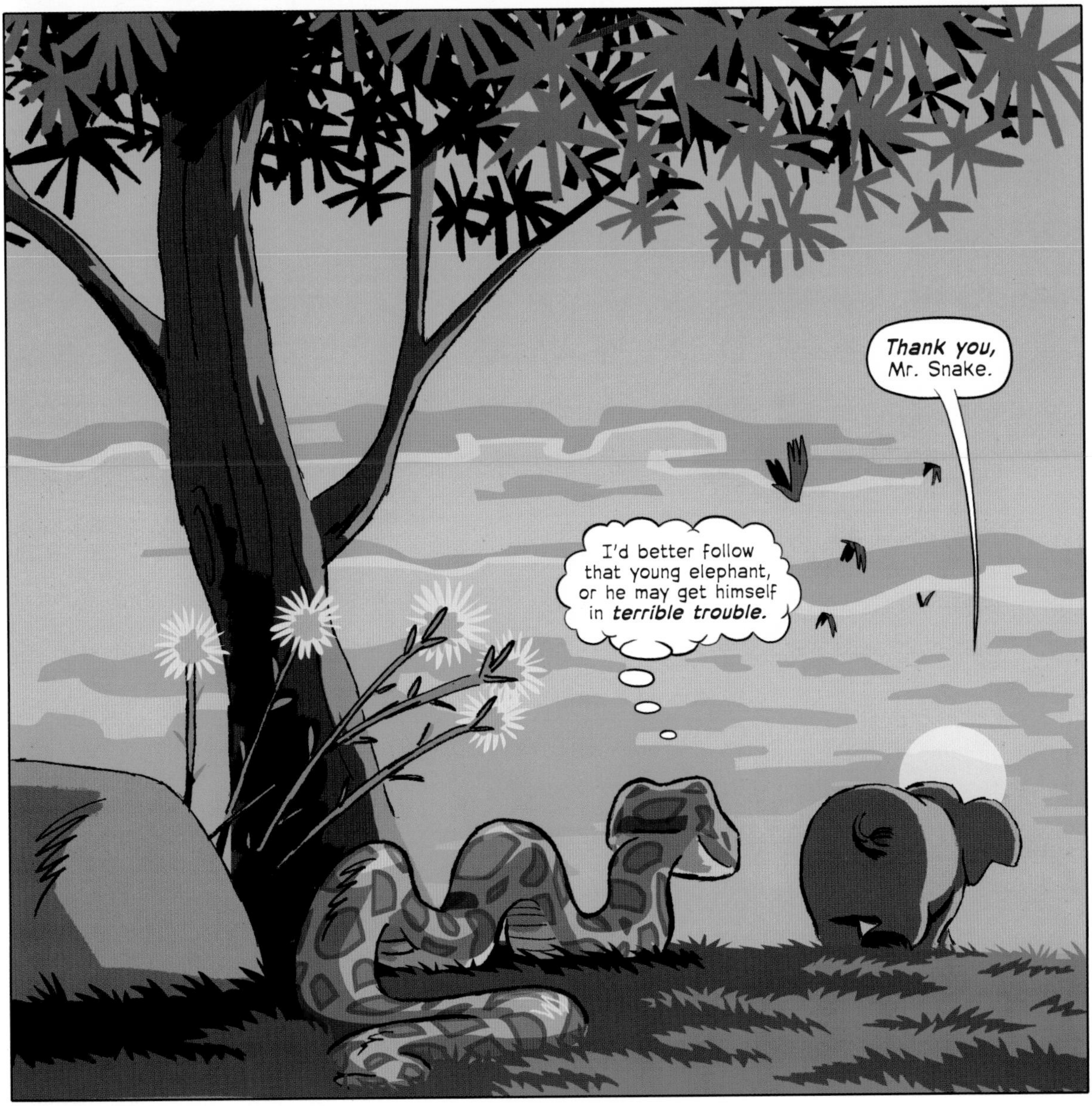
*Thank you,* Mr. Snake.
I'd better follow that young elephant, or he may get himself in *terrible trouble.*

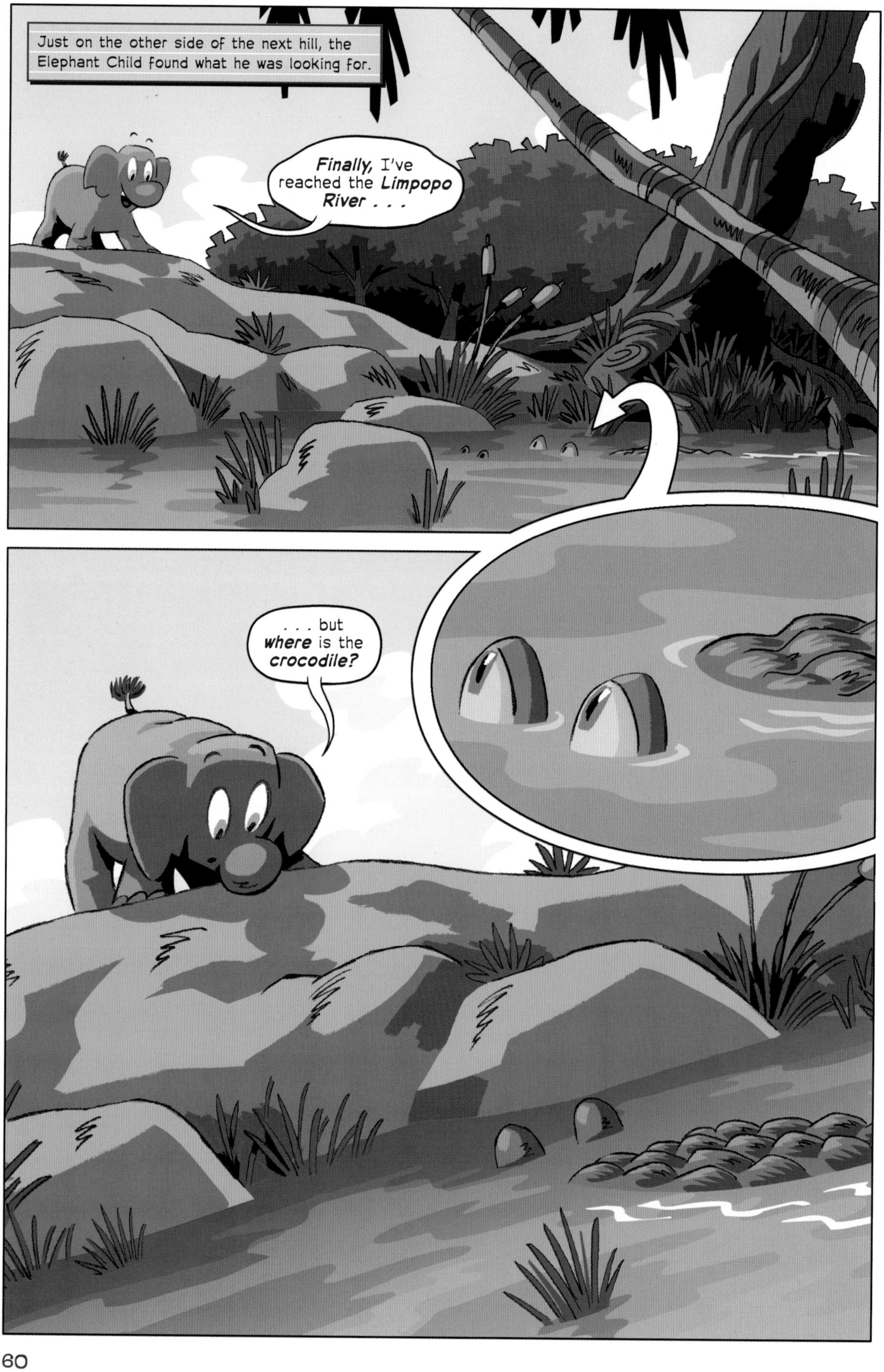
Just on the other side of the next hill, the Elephant Child found what he was looking for.
Finally, I've reached the Limpopo River . . .
. . . but where is the crocodile?

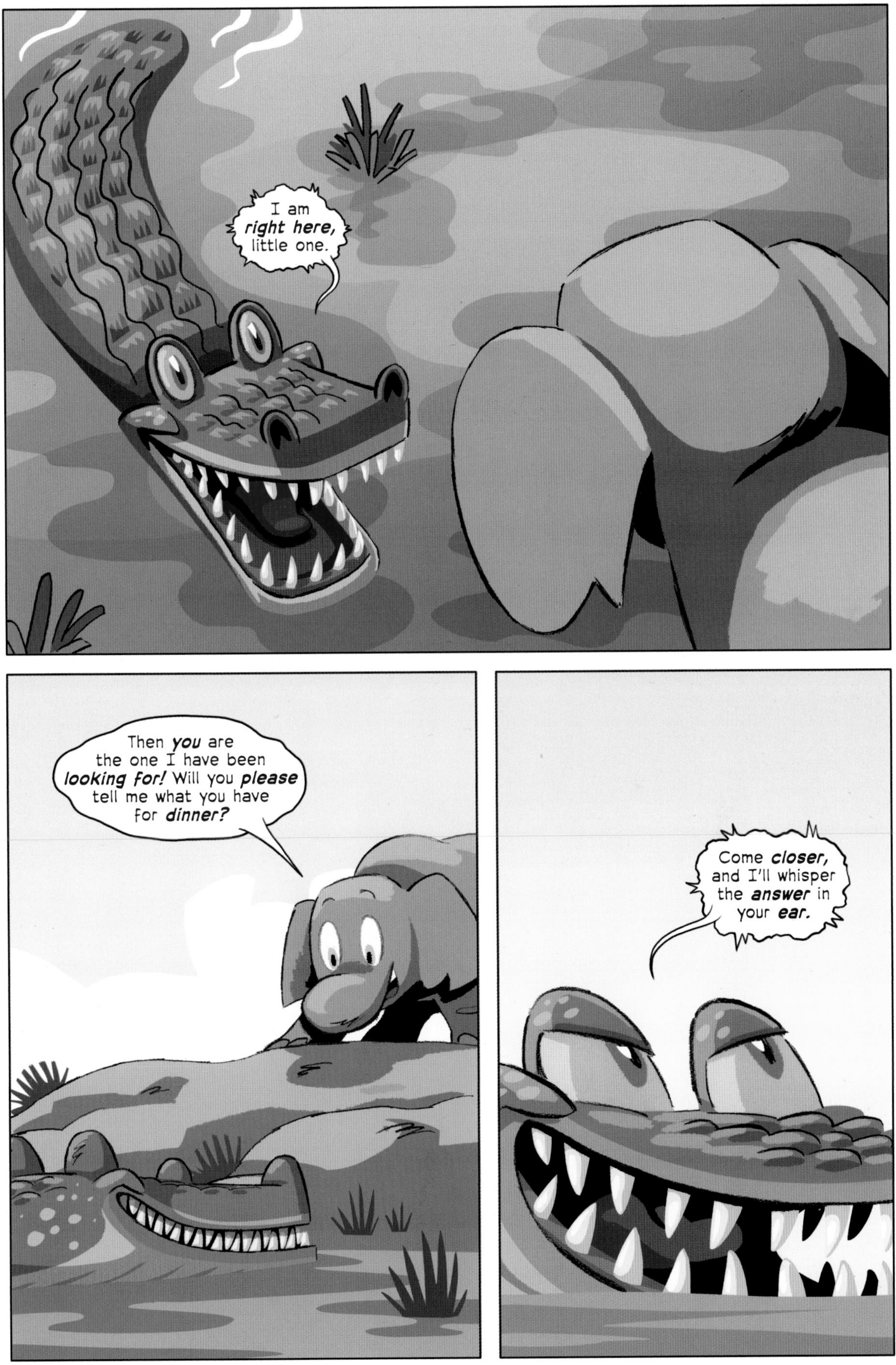
I am right here, little one.
Then you are the one I have been looking for! Will you please tell me what you have for dinner?
Come closer, and I'll whisper the answer in your ear.

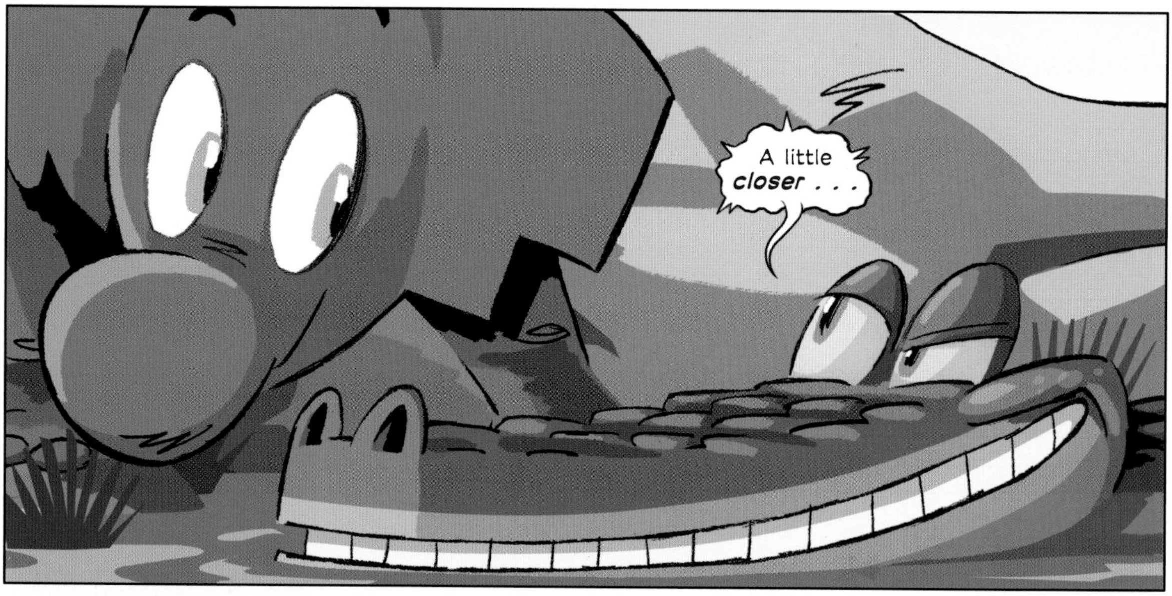
A little *closer* . . .

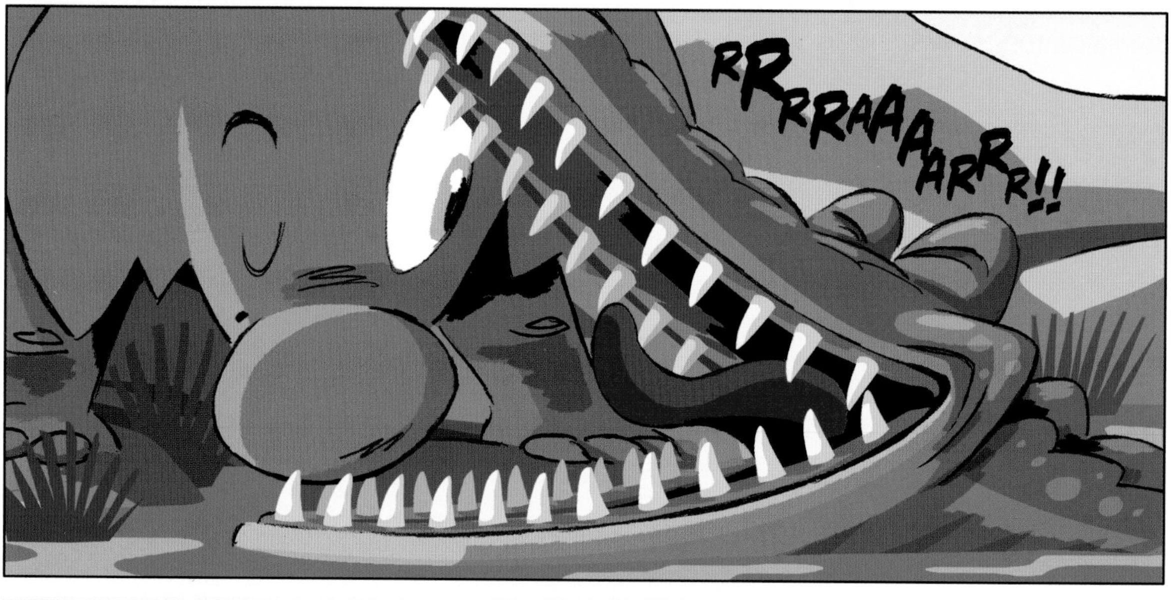
RRRRAAAAARRR!!

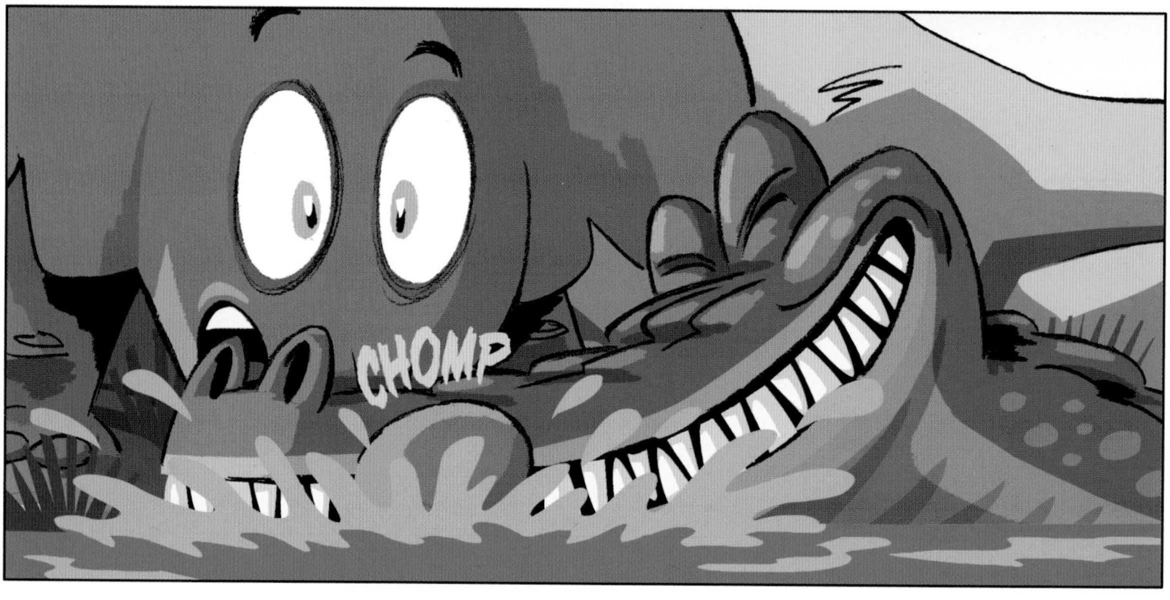
CHOMP

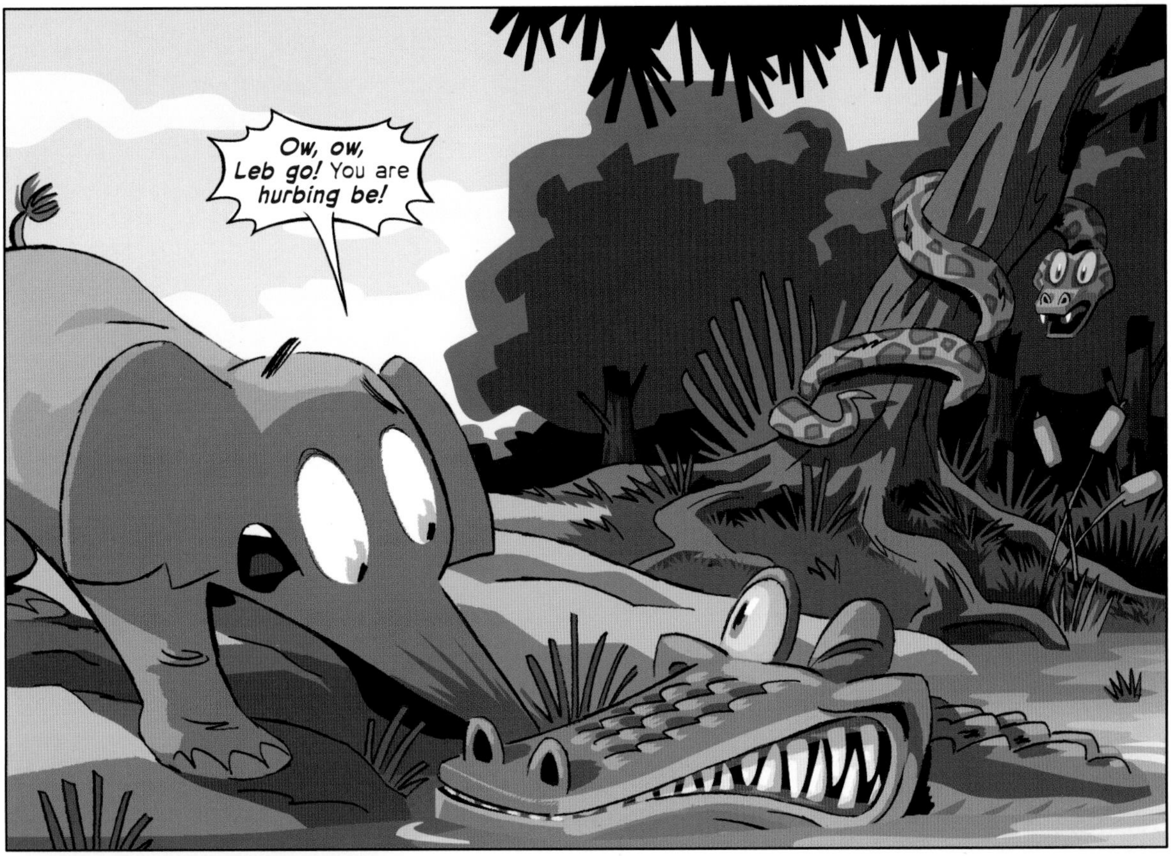
Ow, ow, Leb go! You are hurbing be!

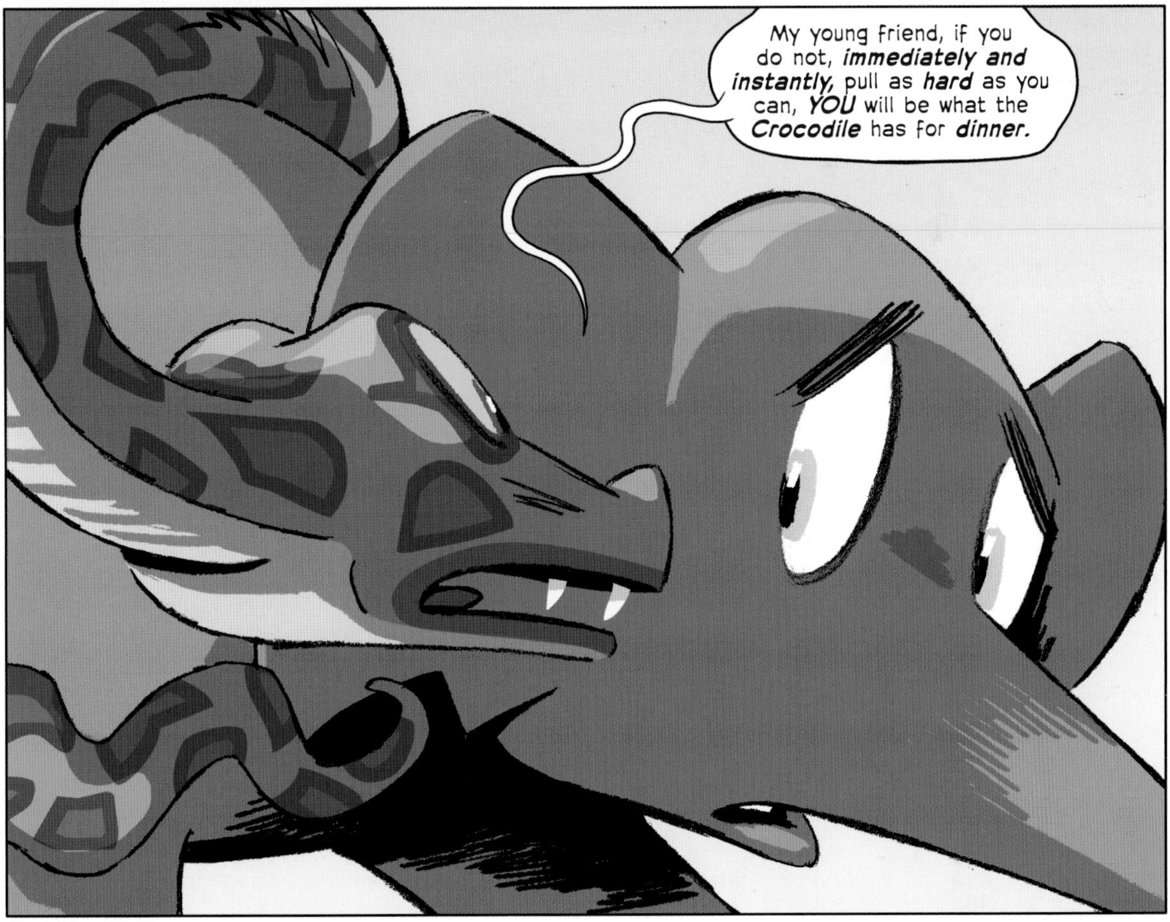
My young friend, if you do not, immediately and instantly, pull as hard as you can, YOU will be what the Crocodile has for dinner.

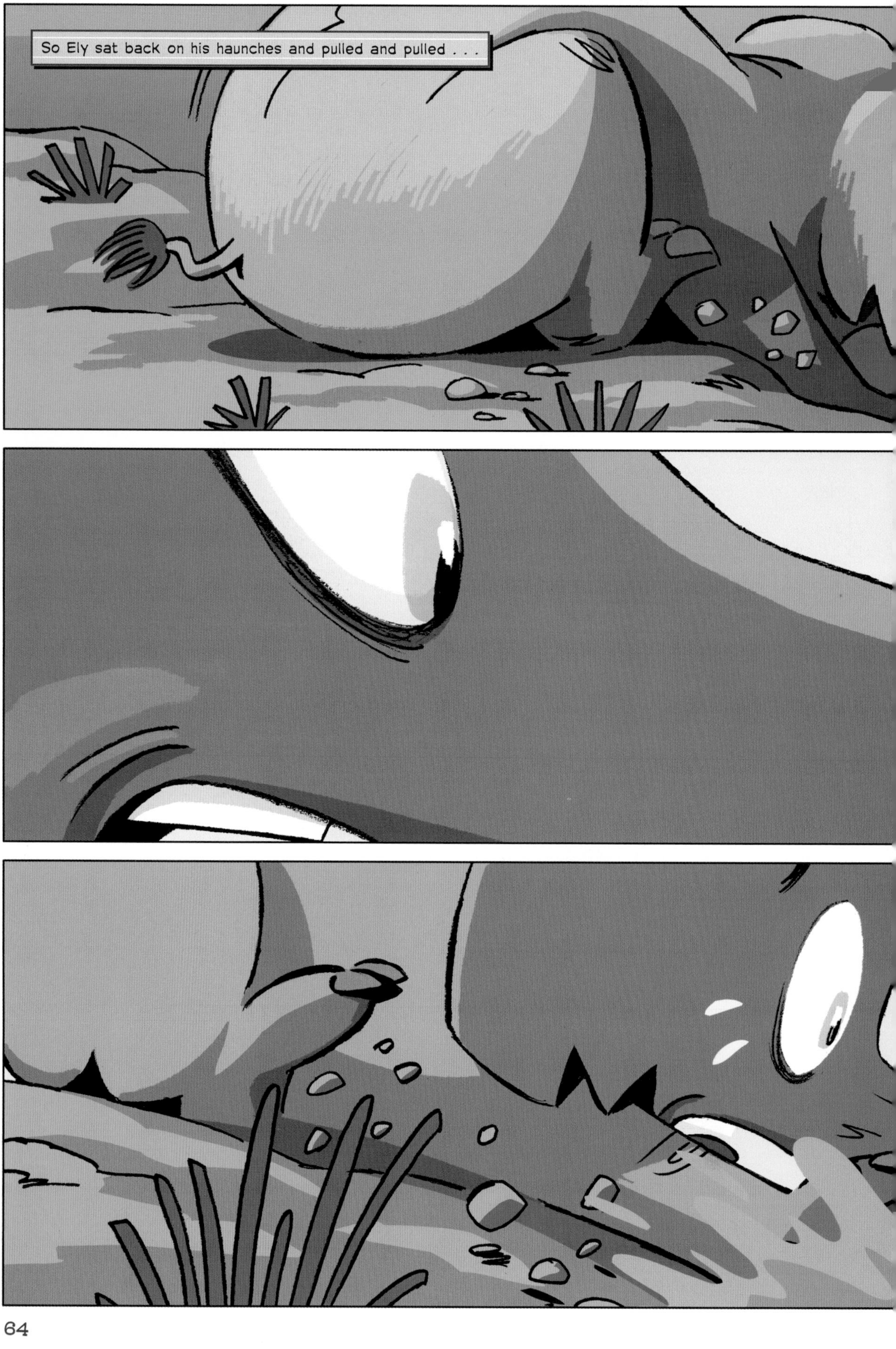
So Ely sat back on his haunches and pulled and pulled . . .

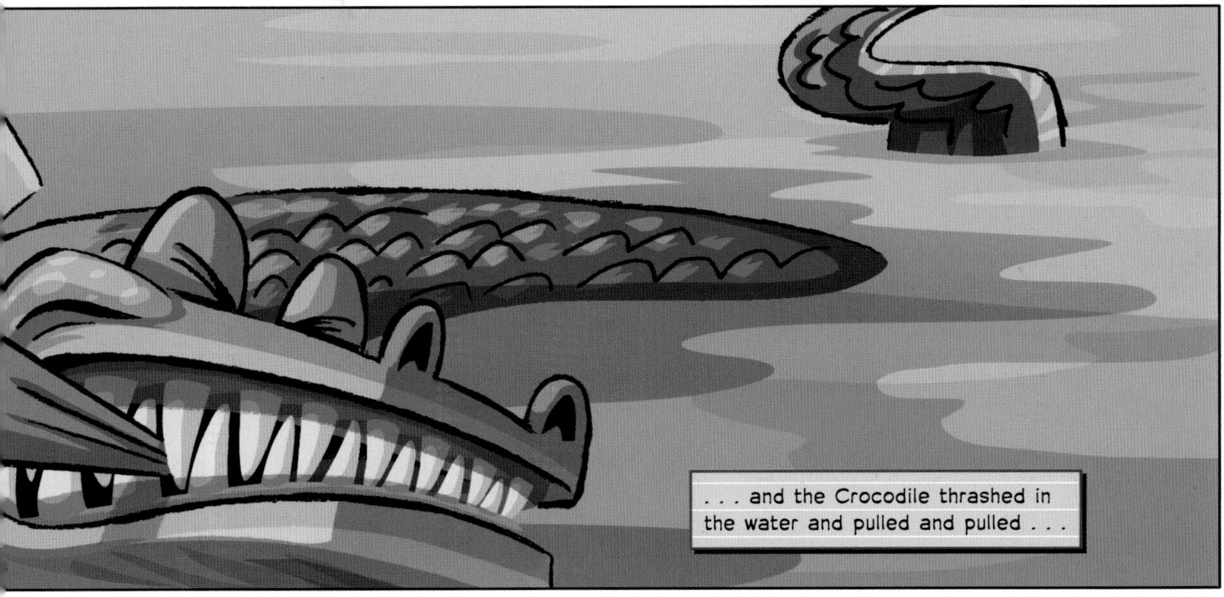
. . . and the Crocodile thrashed in the water and pulled and pulled . . .

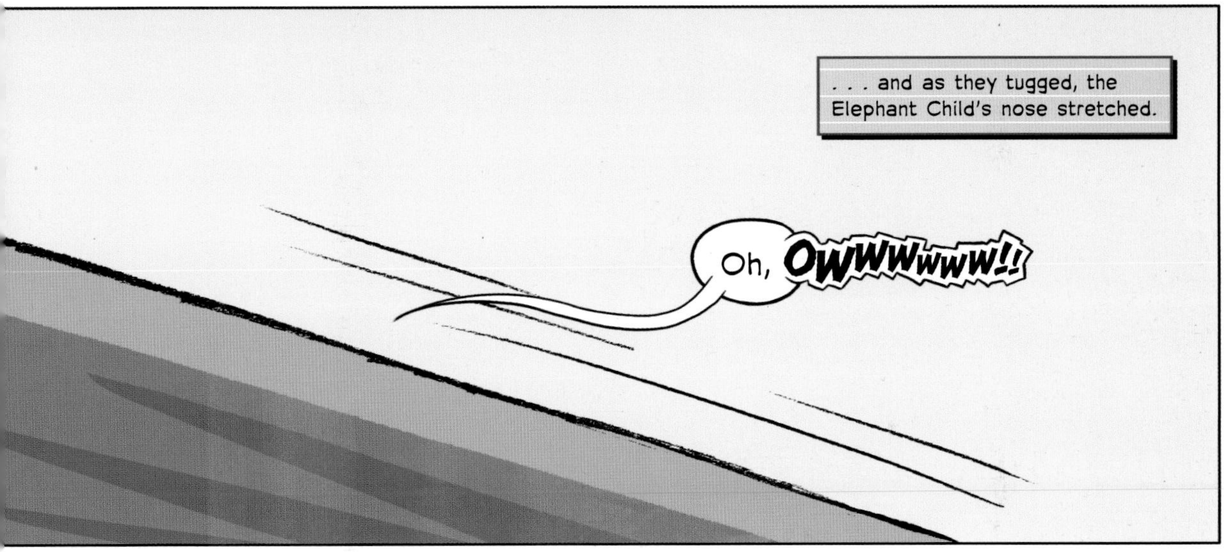
. . . and as they tugged, the Elephant Child's nose stretched.
Oh, OWWWWWW!!

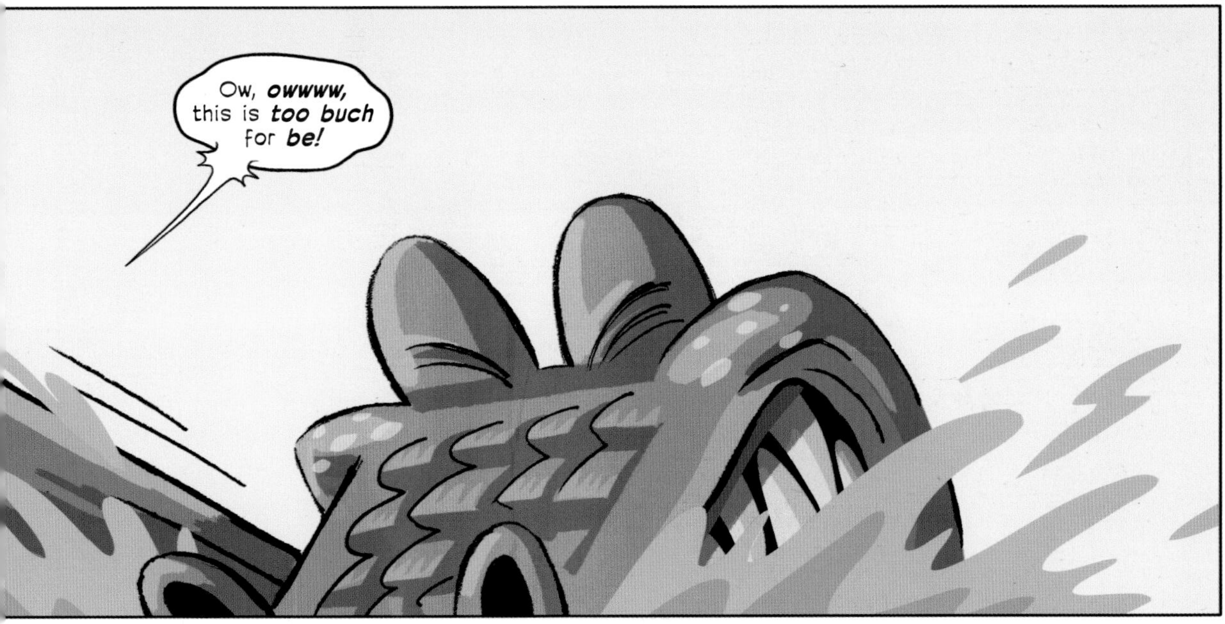
Ow, owwww, this is too buch for be!

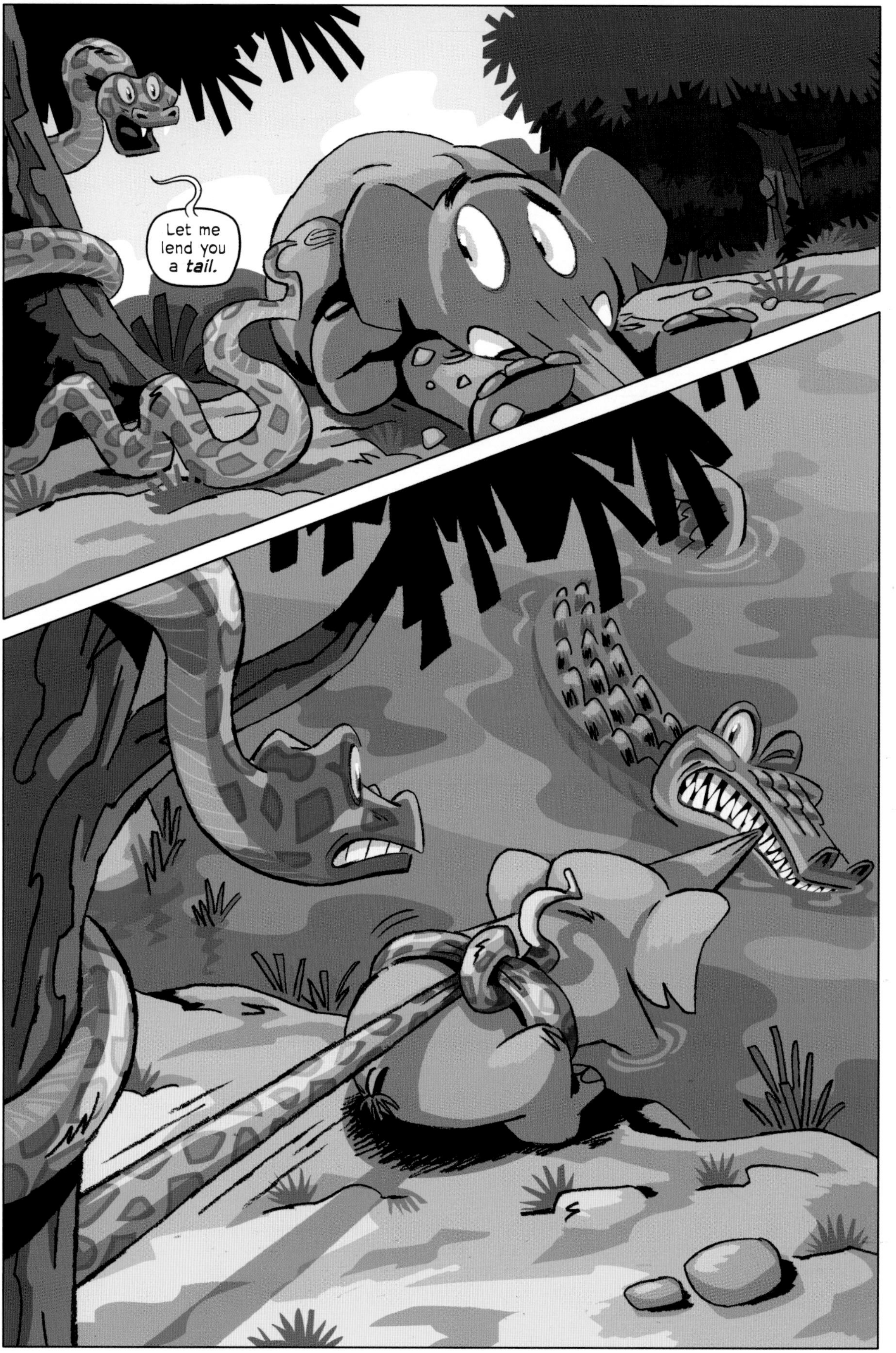
Let me lend you a *tail.*

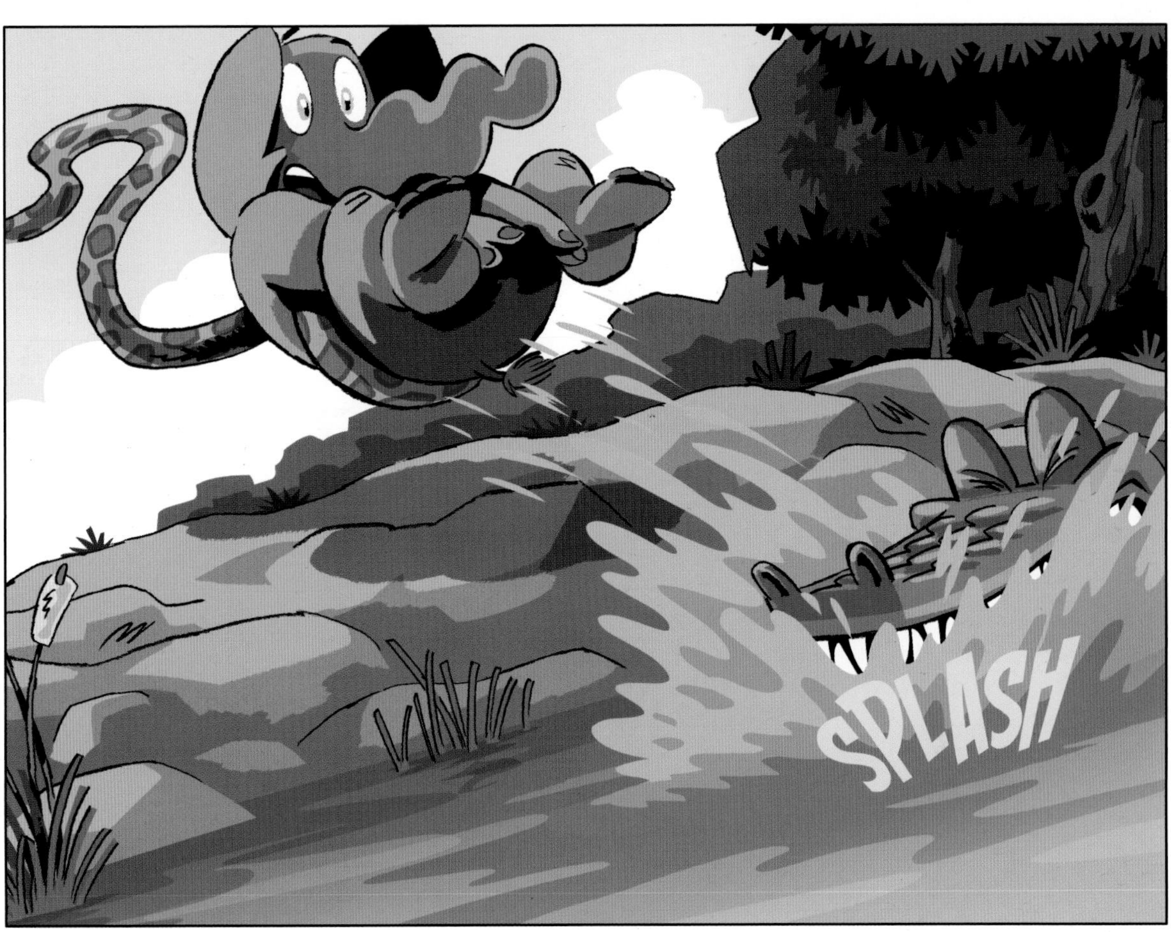
SPLASH

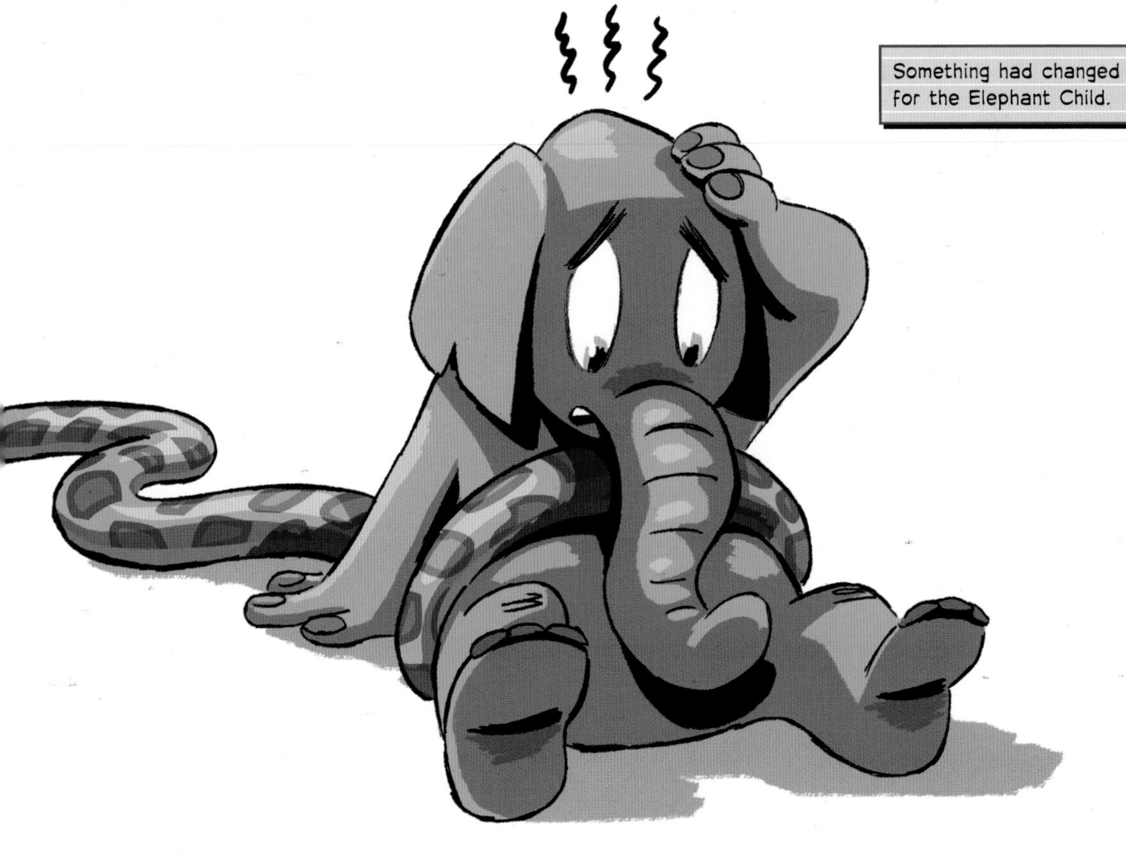
Something had changed
for the Elephant Child.

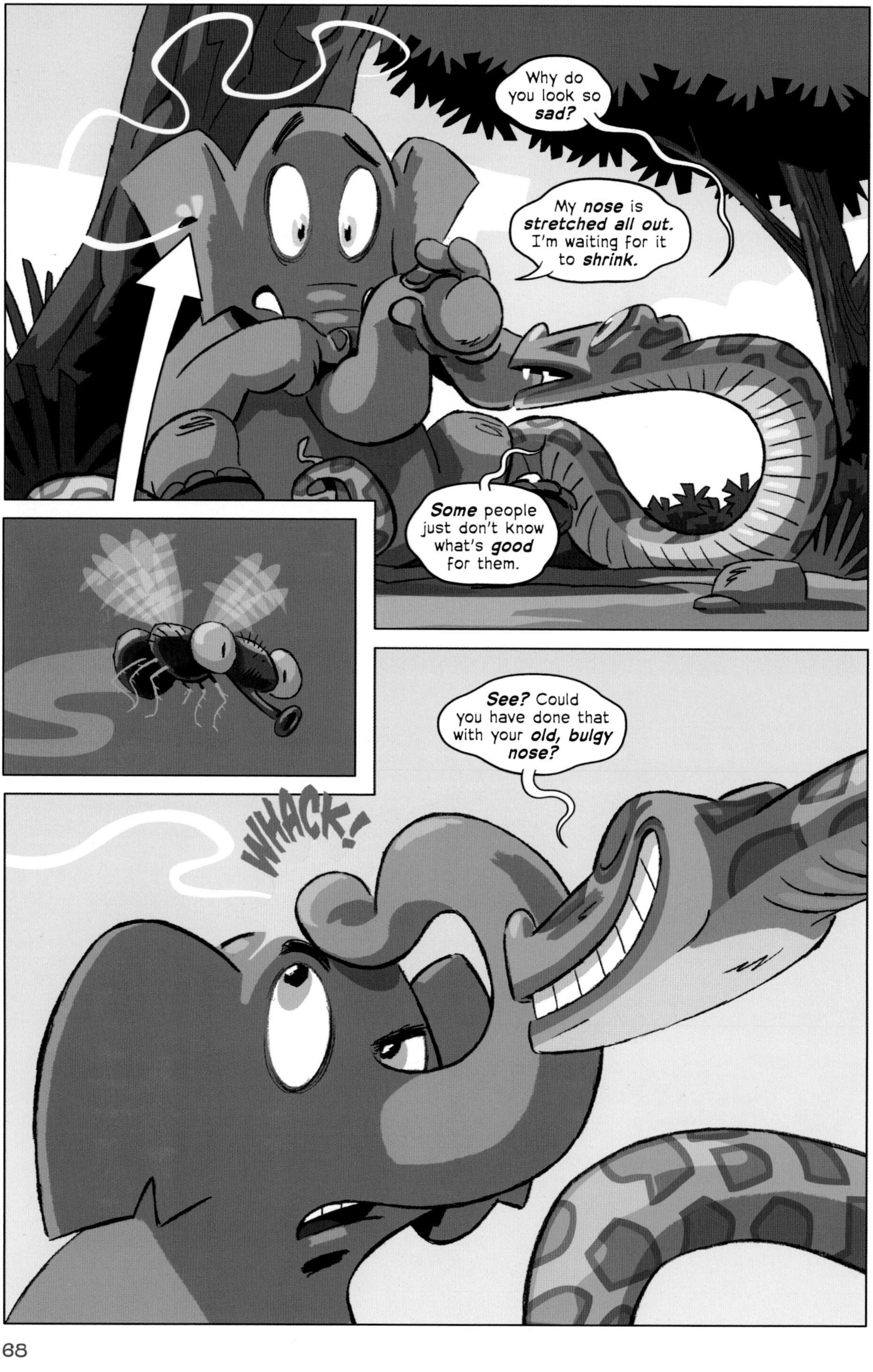
Why do you look so sad?
My nose is stretched all out. I'm waiting for it to shrink.
Some people just don't know what's good for them.
See? Could you have done that with your old, bulgy nose?
WHACK!

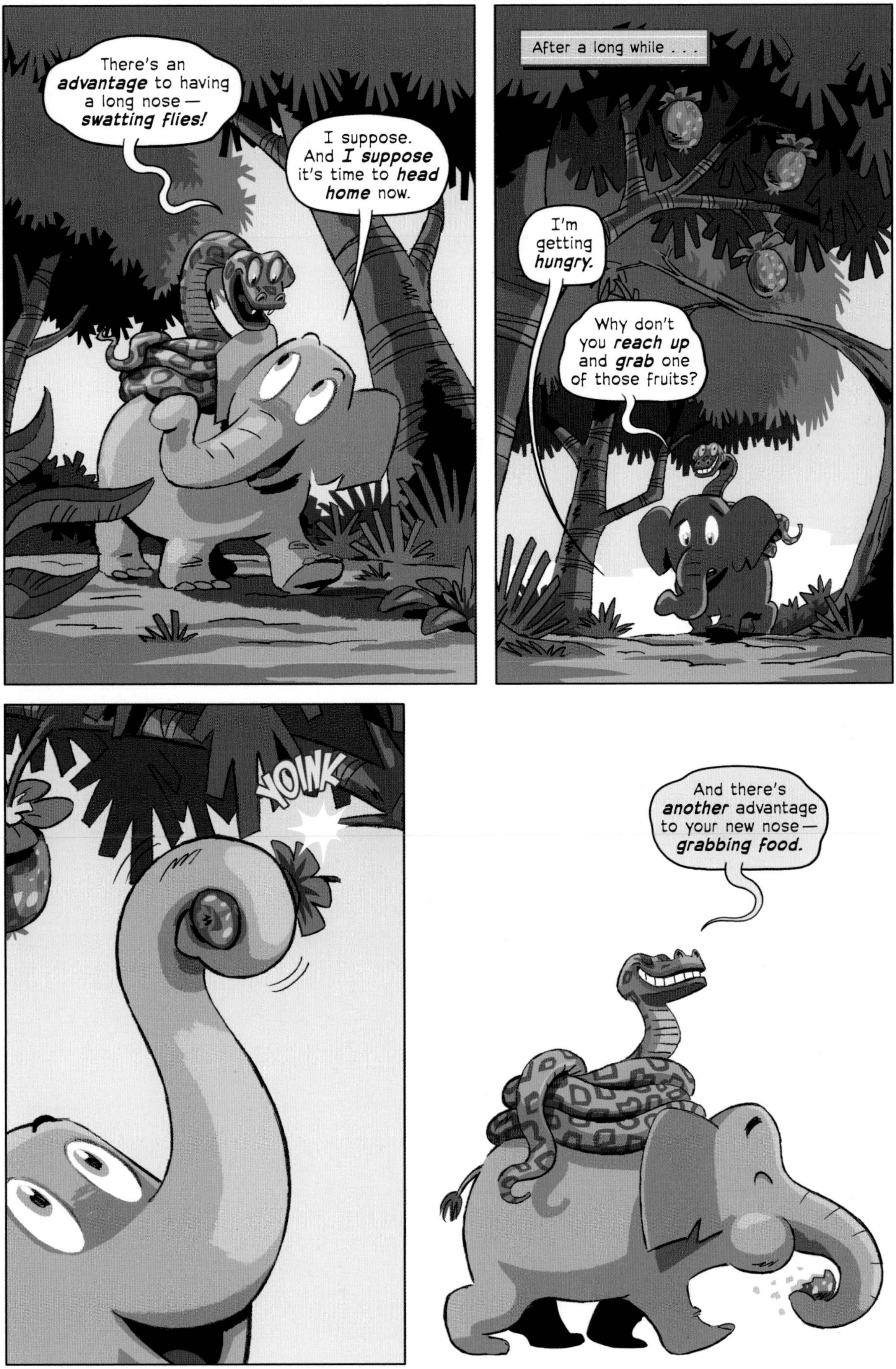
There's an advantage to having a long nose — swatting flies!
I suppose. And I suppose it's time to head home now.
After a long while . . .
I'm getting hungry.
Why don't you reach up and grab one of those fruits?
YOINK
And there's another advantage to your new nose — grabbing food.

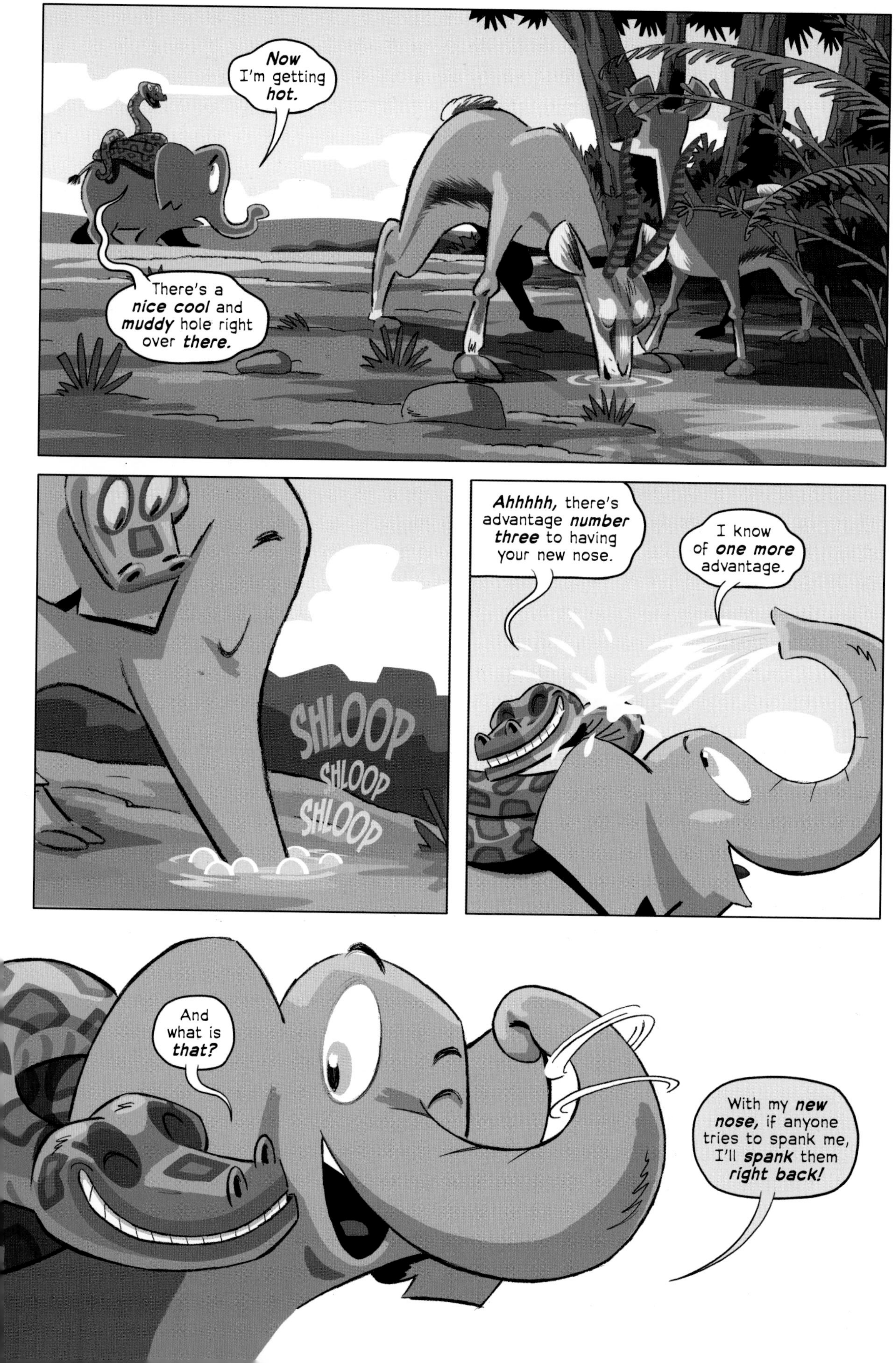
Now I'm getting hot.
There's a nice cool and muddy hole right over there.
SHLOOP
SHLOOP
SHLOOP
Ahhhhh, there's advantage number three to having your new nose.
I know of one more advantage.
And what is that?
With my new nose, if anyone tries to spank me, I'll spank them right back!

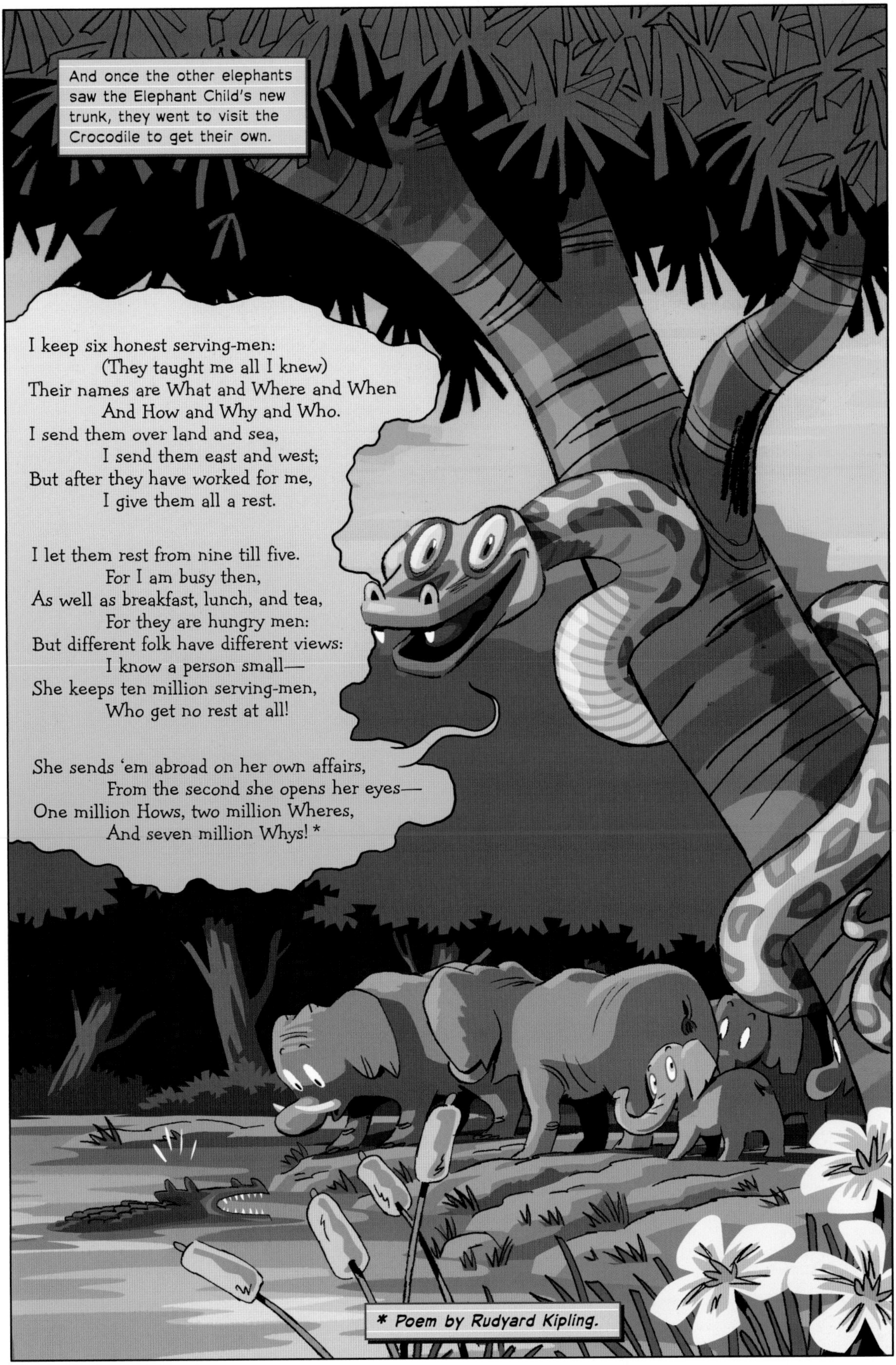
And once the other elephants saw the Elephant Child's new trunk, they went to visit the Crocodile to get their own.
I keep six honest serving-men:
(They taught me all I knew)
Their names are What and Where and When
And How and Why and Who.
I send them over land and sea,
I send them east and west;
But after they have worked for me,
I give them all a rest.

I let them rest from nine till five.
For I am busy then,
As well as breakfast, lunch, and tea,
For they are hungry men:
But different folk have different views:
I know a person small—
She keeps ten million serving-men,
Who get no rest at all!

She sends 'em abroad on her own affairs,
From the second she opens her eyes—
One million Hows, two million Wheres,
And seven million Whys! *
* Poem by Rudyard Kipling.

RUDYARD KIPLING

3

# CONCLUSION

## NEW SPECIMEN:
## LONG-TRUNKED ELEPHANT

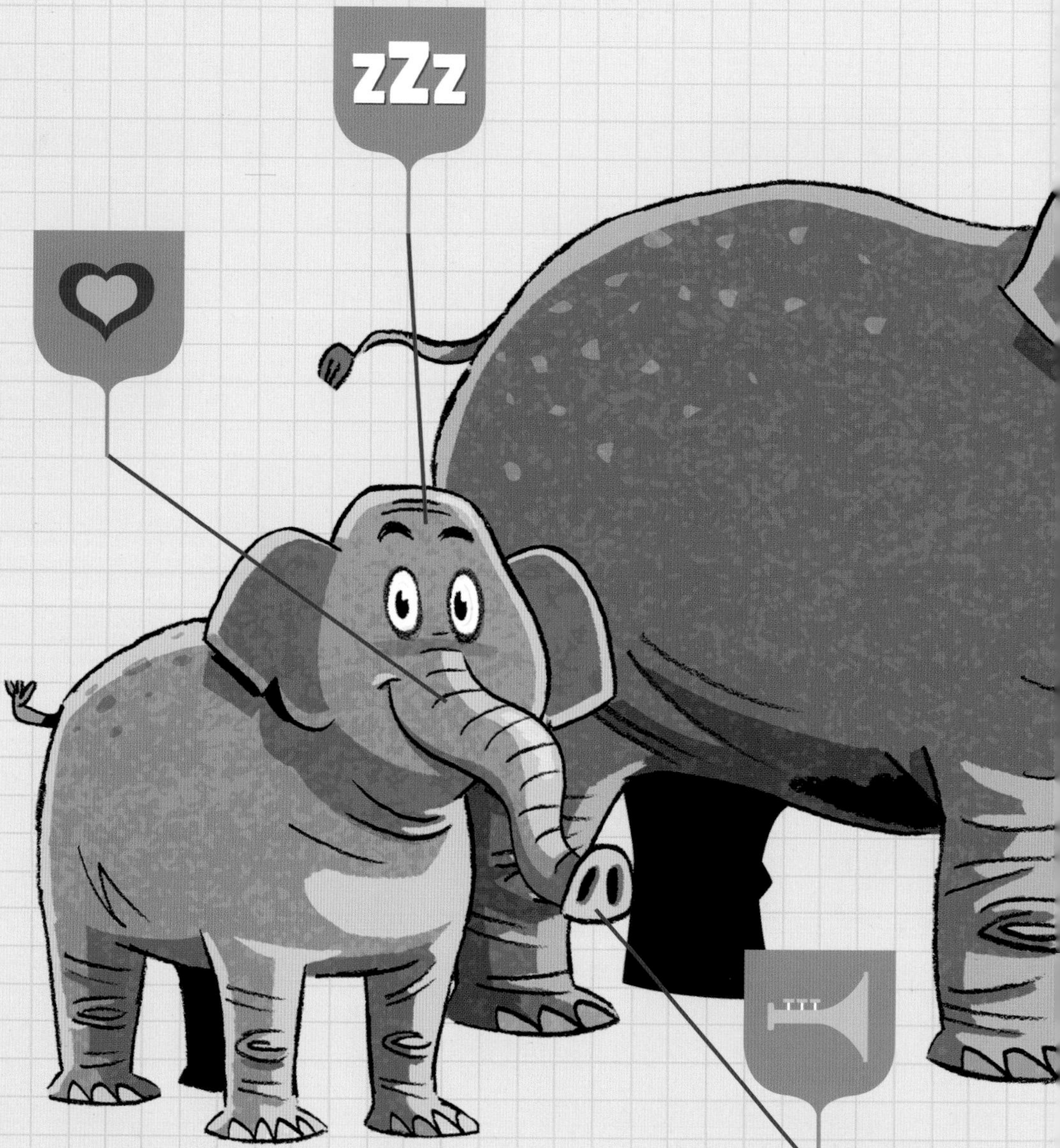
zZz

An adult African elephant's trunk is about seven feet long. Even though noses are very long, nose jobs are unheard of in elephant social circles.

If threatened, an elephant uses its trunk to make loud trumpeting noises. Would love to hear a jazz combo built around this incredible sound.

Elephants sometimes hug each other with their trunks. Must be a hugger to run with this group.

An elephant sleeps an average of just two hours during a 24-hour period. No wonder the young elephant's mother was so cranky.

84

84

1

2

3

RUDYARD KIPLING
EST.
1865

# HOW THE RHINOCEROS GOT HIS SKIN

as retold by

## MARTIN POWELL
### TEAM WRITER

**RUDYARD KIPLING**

**1**

# RESEARCH

SPECIMEN:

SMOOTH-SKINNED RHINOCEROS
(Fig. A)

HABITAT: An island in the Red Sea (Fig. B)
FOOD SOURCE: Cake (Fig. C)
RIVAL: The Parsee (Fig. D)
SOCIAL BEHAVIOR: Rude and selfish

**A**

Large horn

Mischievous grin

Smooth skin

B

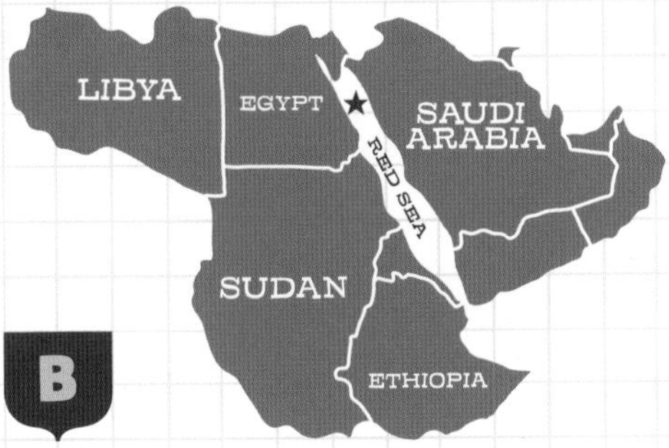
LIBYA
EGYPT
SAUDI ARABIA
RED SEA
SUDAN
ETHIOPIA

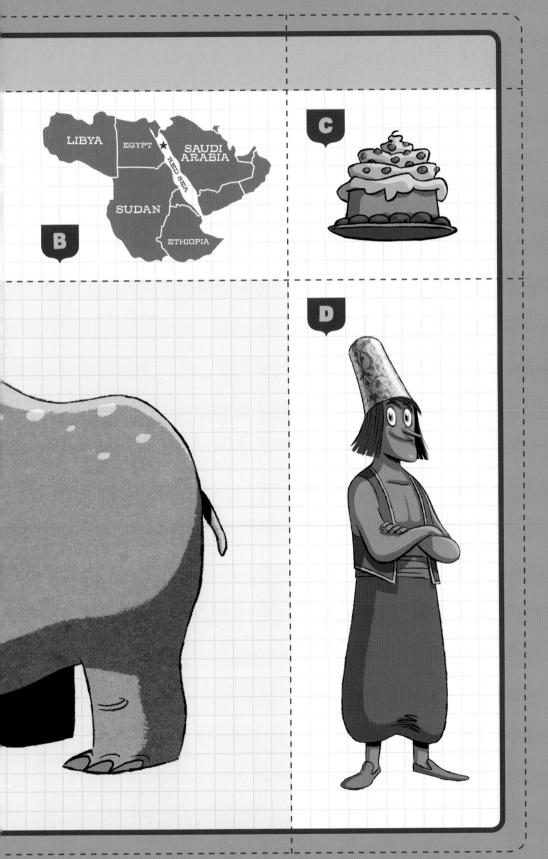

C

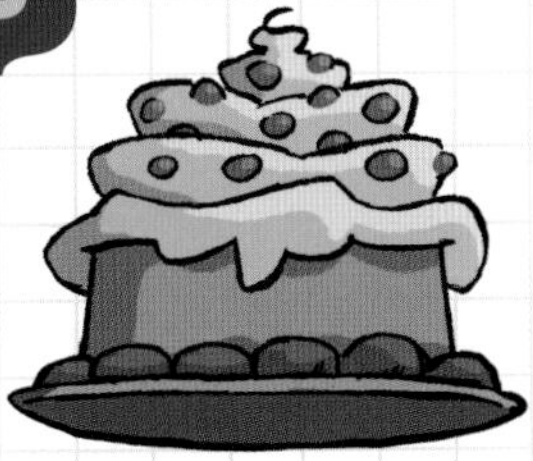

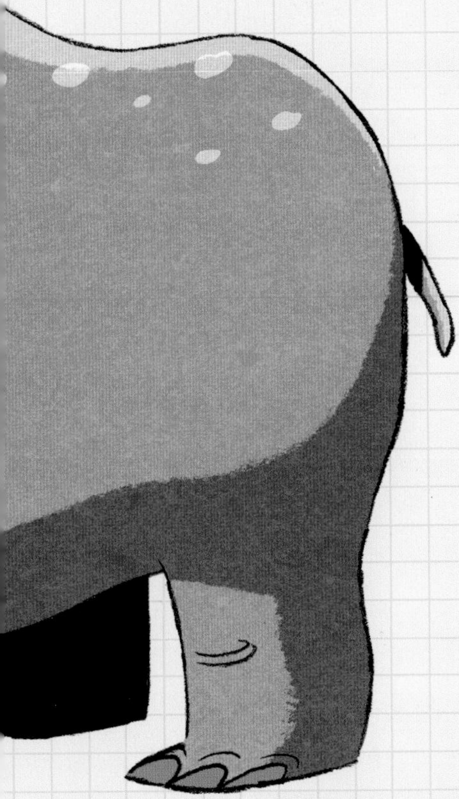

D

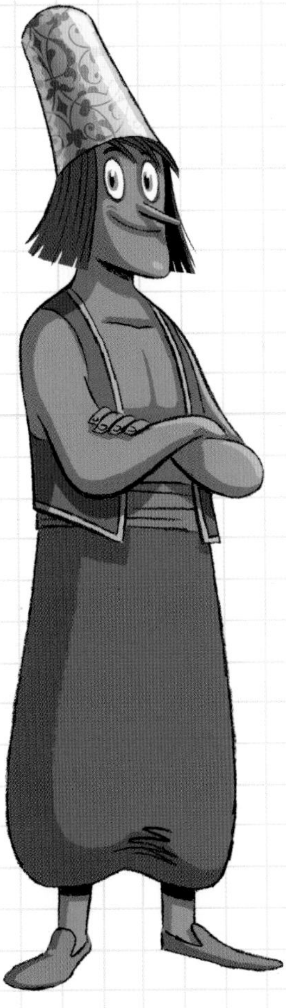

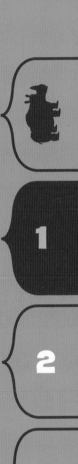

1

2

3

RUDYARD KIPLING 2

# KIPLING'S OBSERVATION

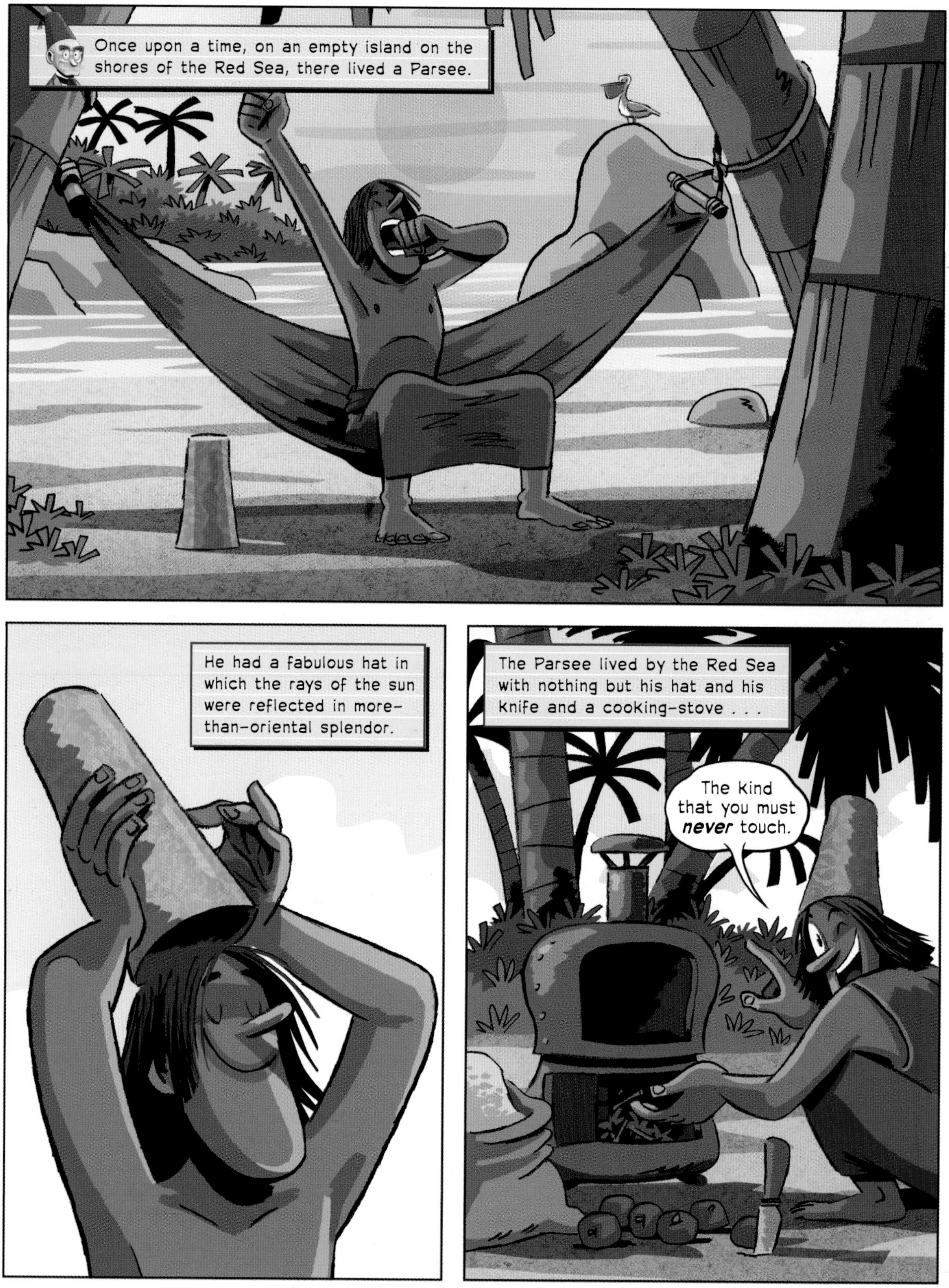
Once upon a time, on an empty island on the shores of the Red Sea, there lived a Parsee.
He had a fabulous hat in which the rays of the sun were reflected in more-than-oriental splendor.
The Parsee lived by the Red Sea with nothing but his hat and his knife and a cooking-stove . . .
The kind that you must ***never*** touch.

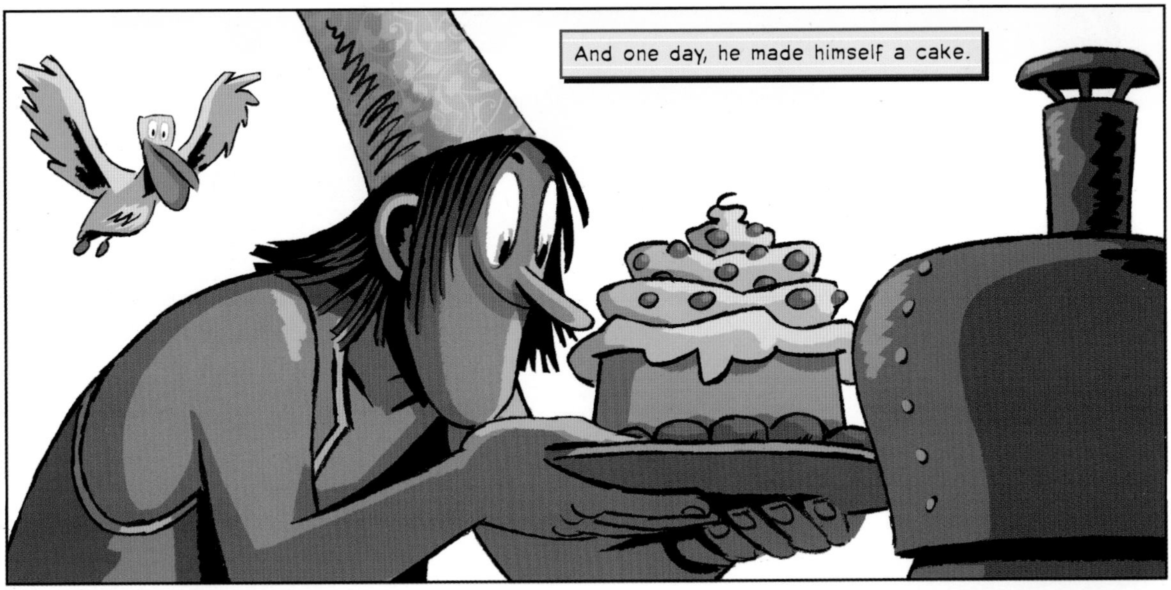
And one day, he made himself a cake.

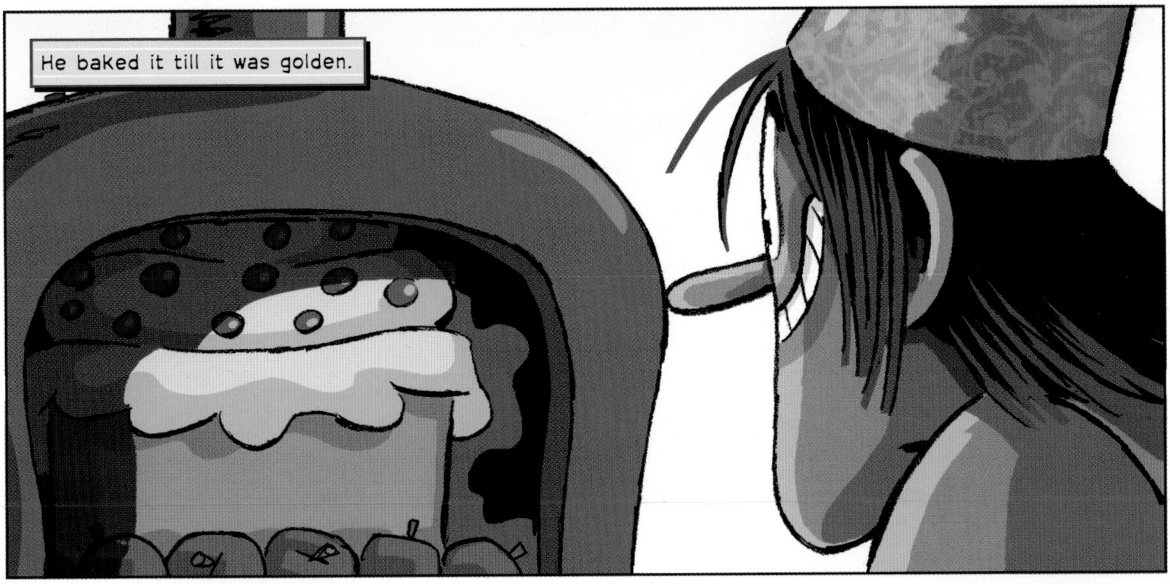
He baked it till it was golden.

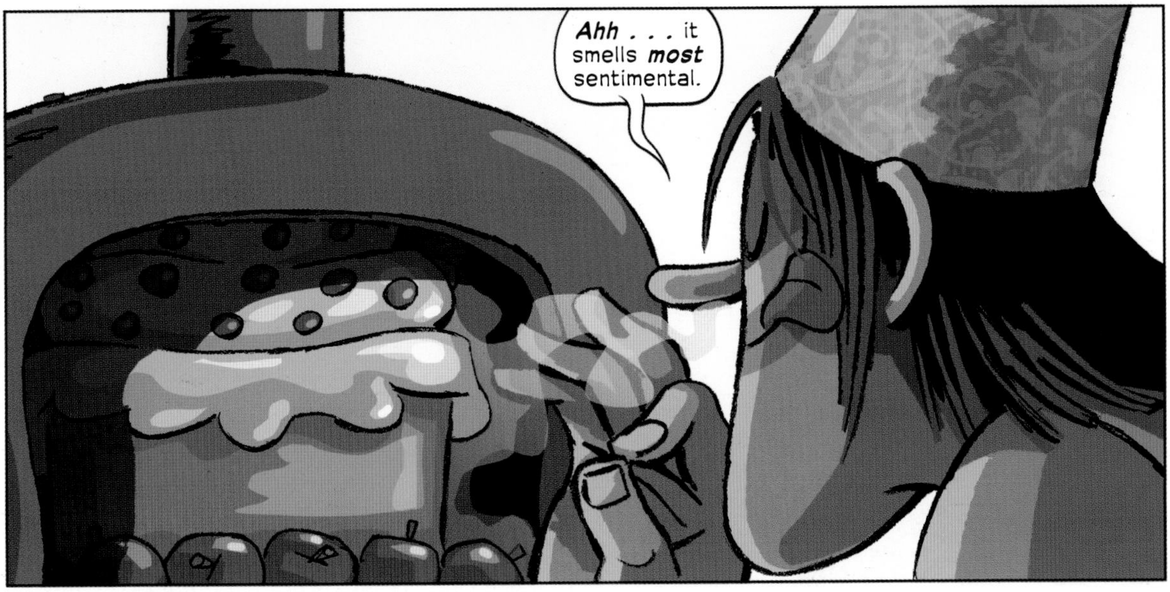
***Ahh . . .*** it smells ***most*** sentimental.

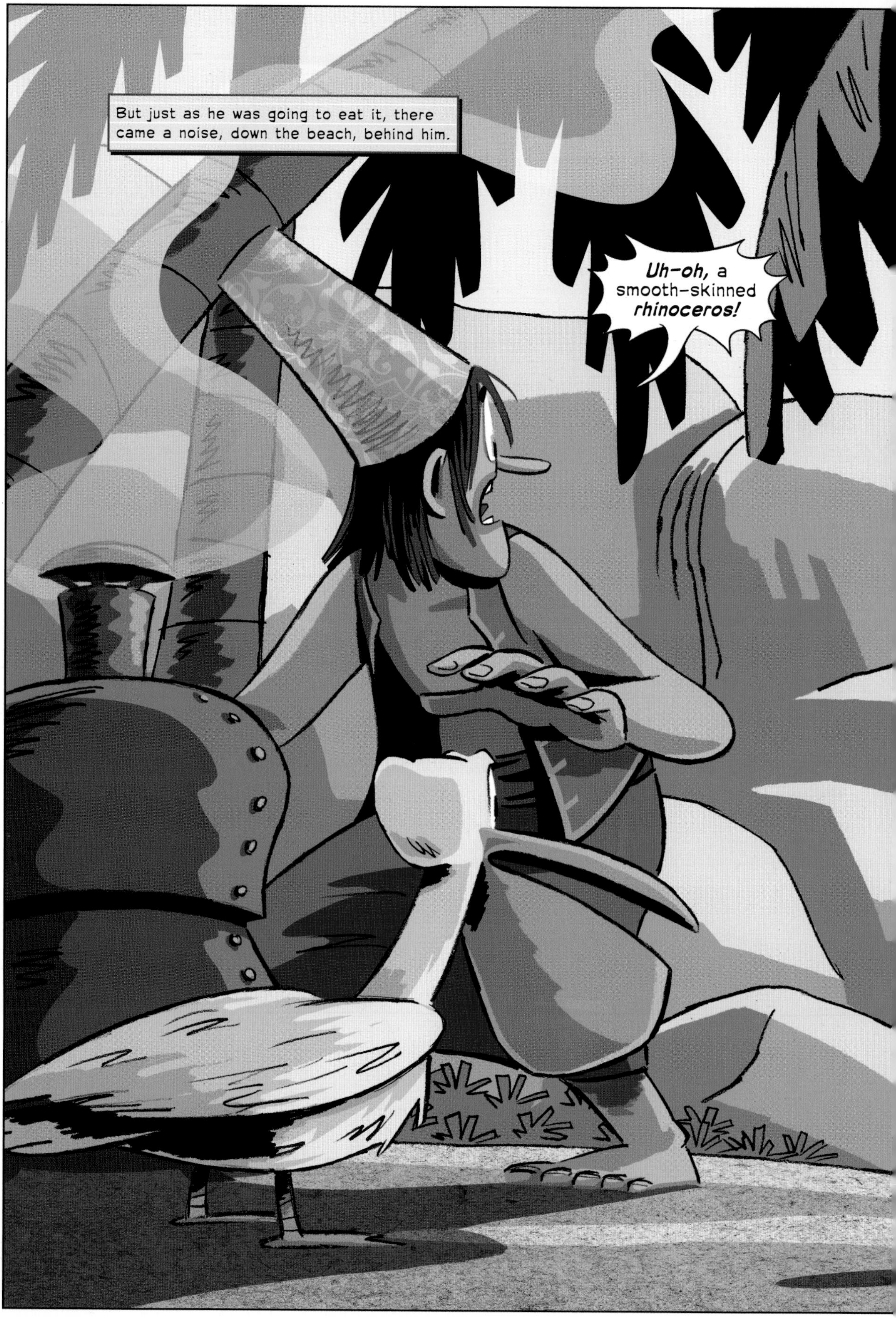
But just as he was going to eat it, there came a noise, down the beach, behind him.
*Uh-oh,* a smooth-skinned ***rhinoceros!***

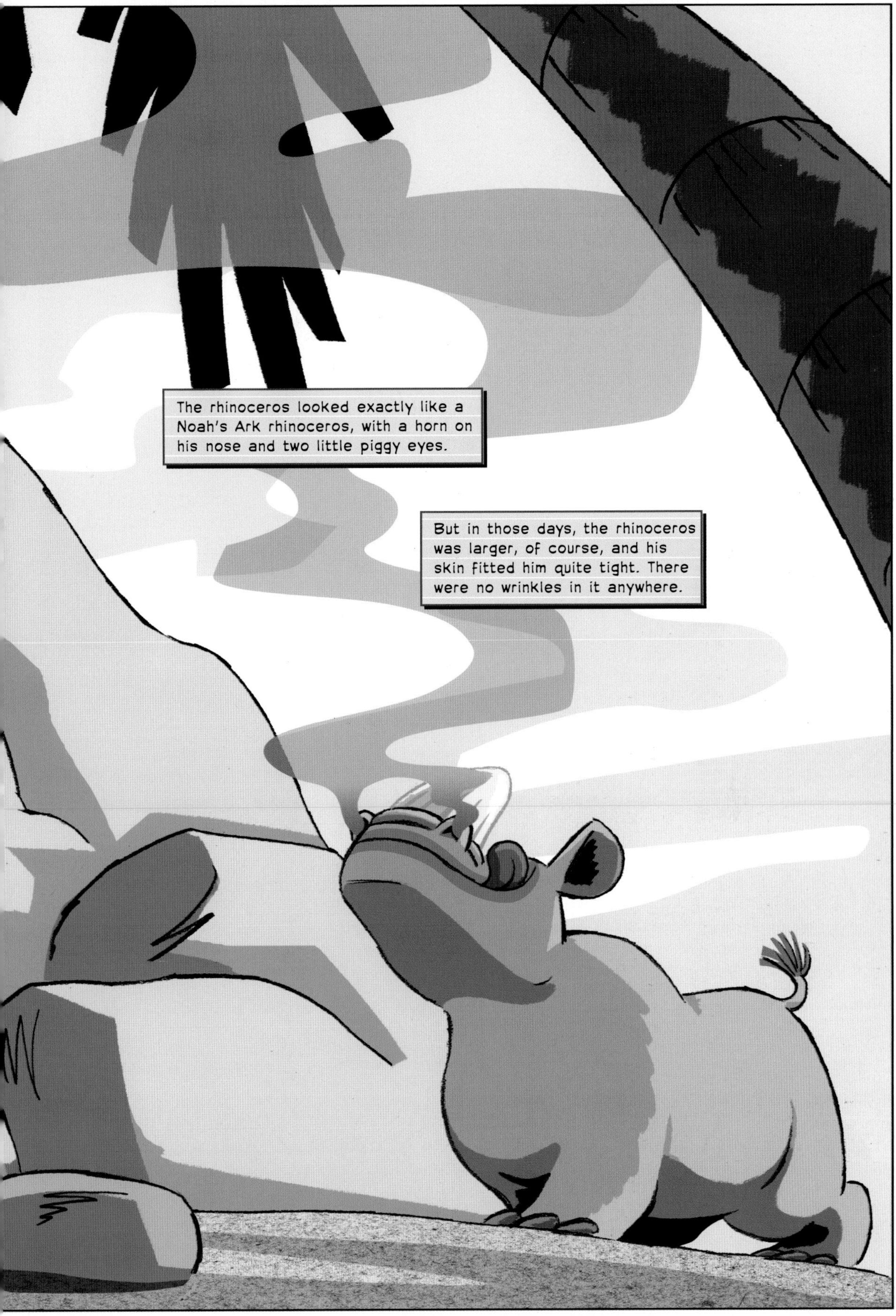
The rhinoceros looked exactly like a Noah's Ark rhinoceros, with a horn on his nose and two little piggy eyes.
But in those days, the rhinoceros was larger, of course, and his skin fitted him quite tight. There were no wrinkles in it anywhere.

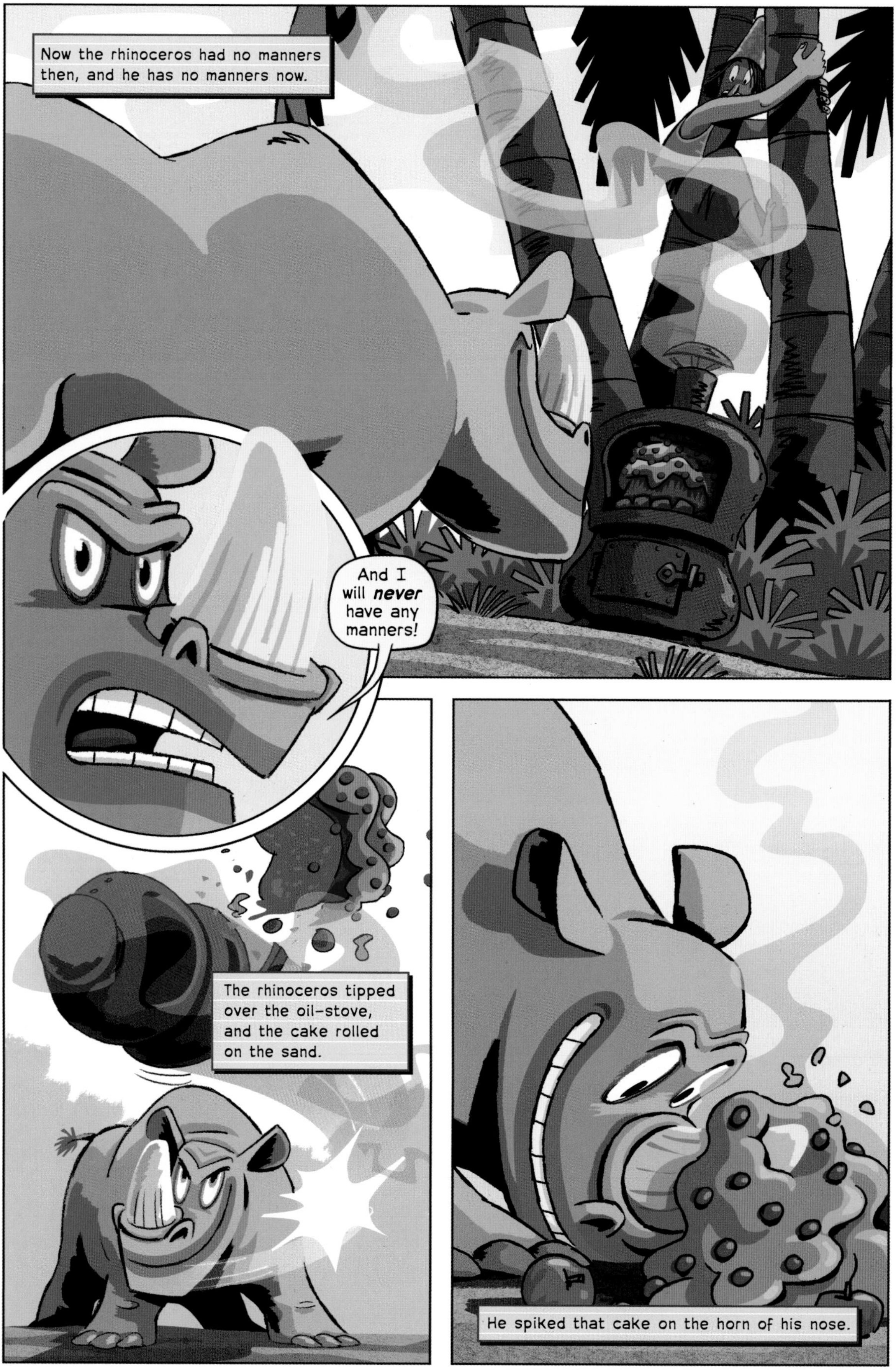
Now the rhinoceros had no manners then, and he has no manners now.
And I will ***never*** have any manners!
The rhinoceros tipped over the oil-stove, and the cake rolled on the sand.
He spiked that cake on the horn of his nose.

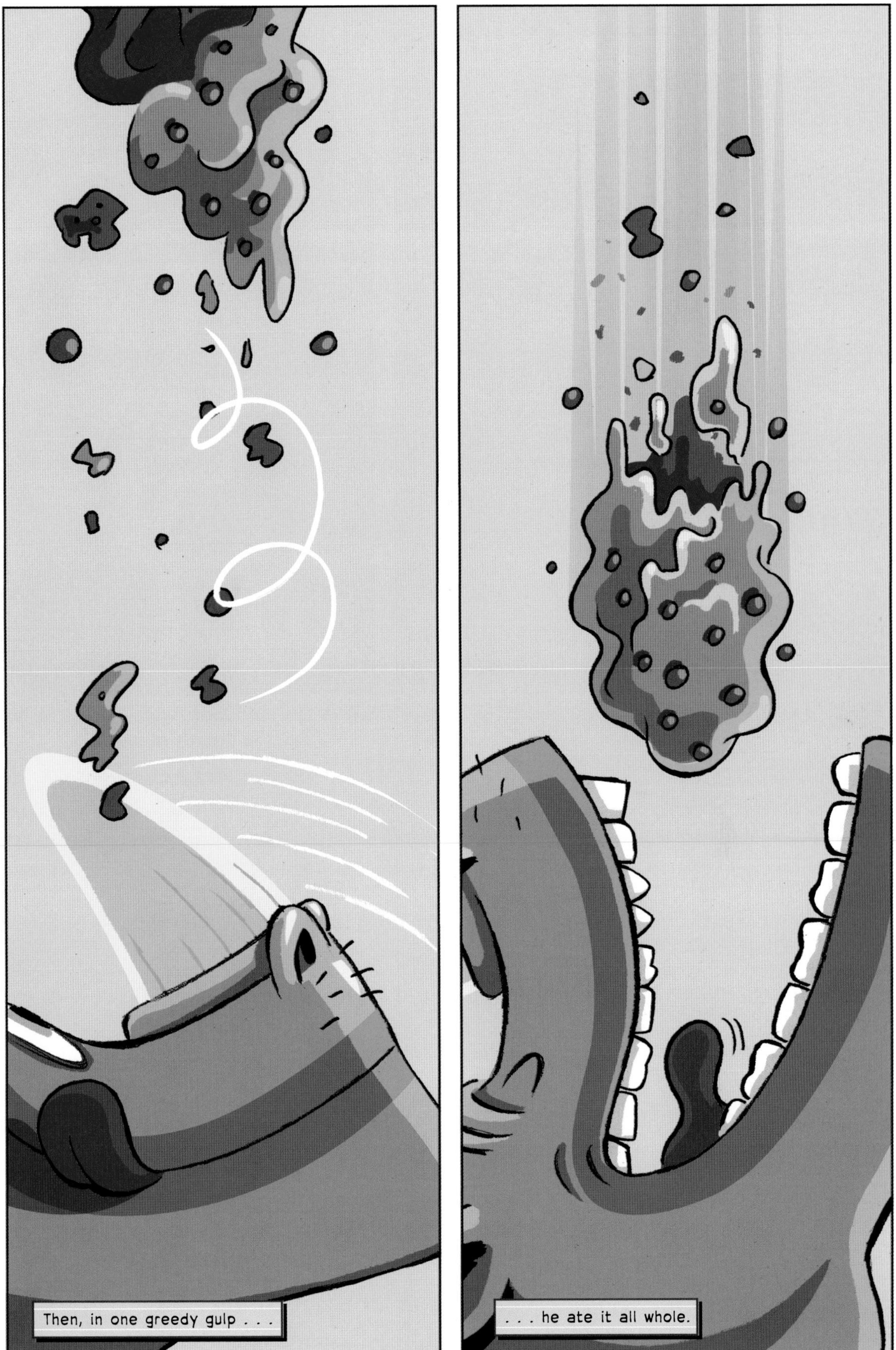
Then, in one greedy gulp . . .
. . . he ate it all whole.

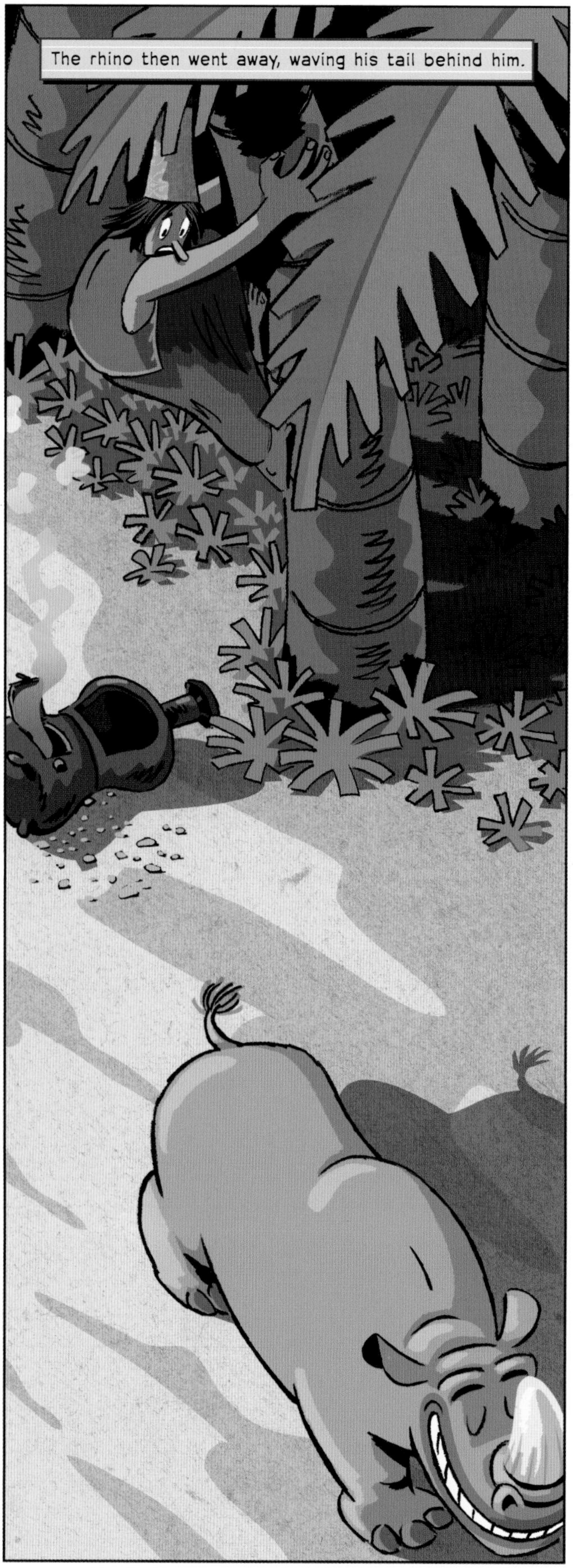
The rhino then went away, waving his tail behind him.

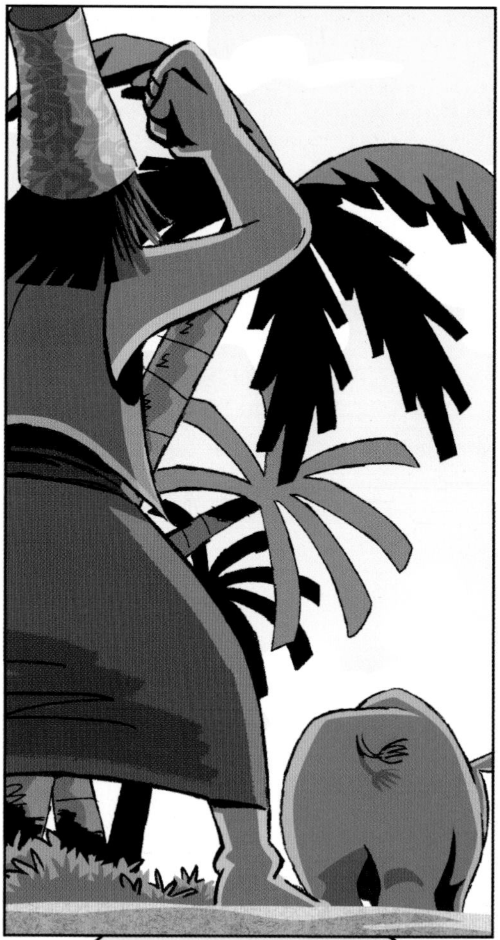

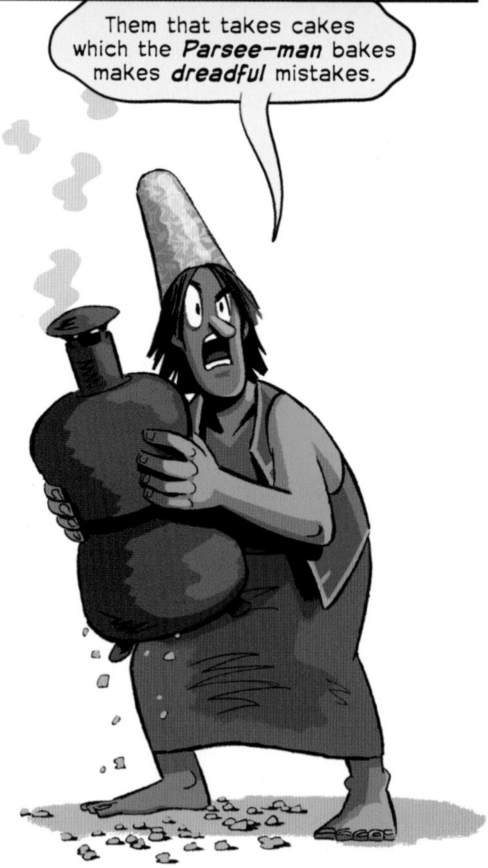
Them that takes cakes which the *Parsee-man* bakes makes *dreadful* mistakes.

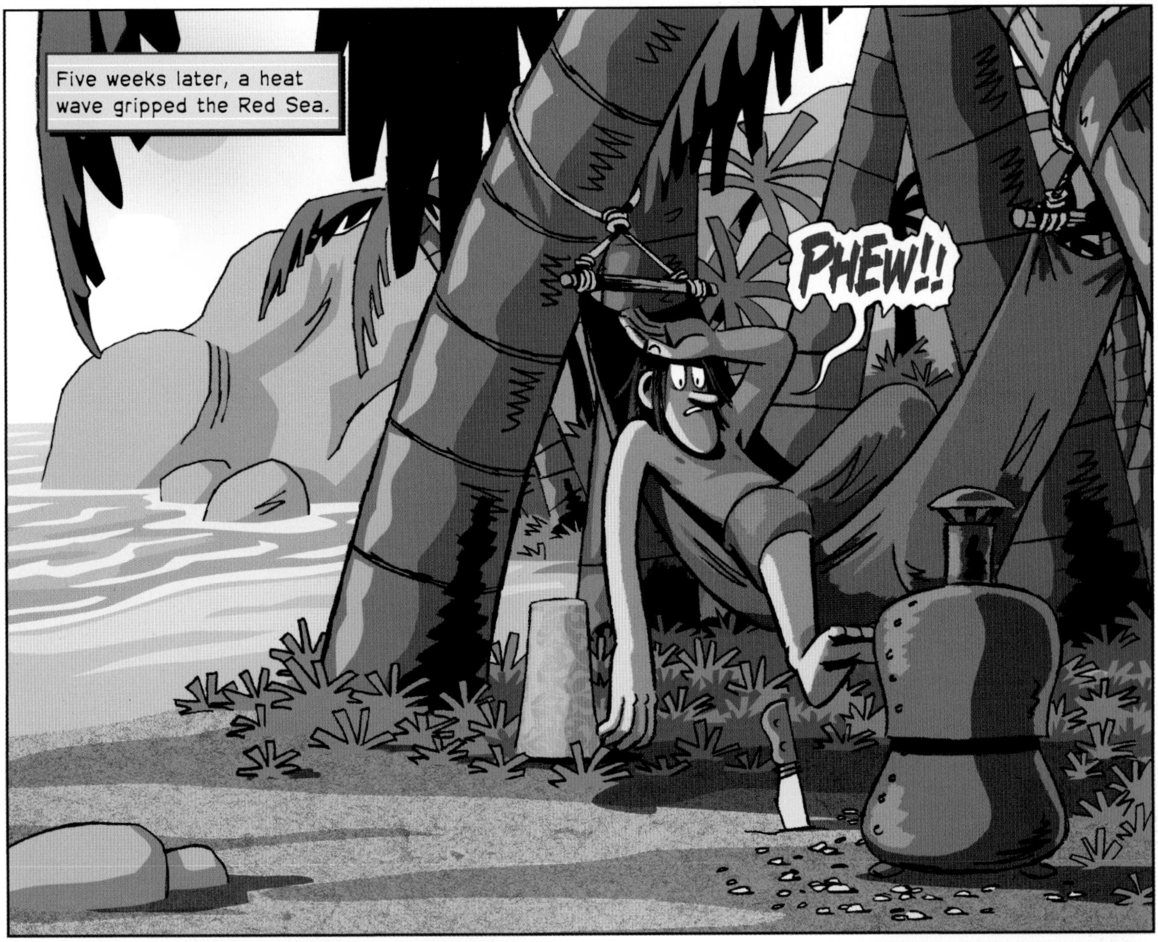
Five weeks later, a heat wave gripped the Red Sea.
PHEW!!

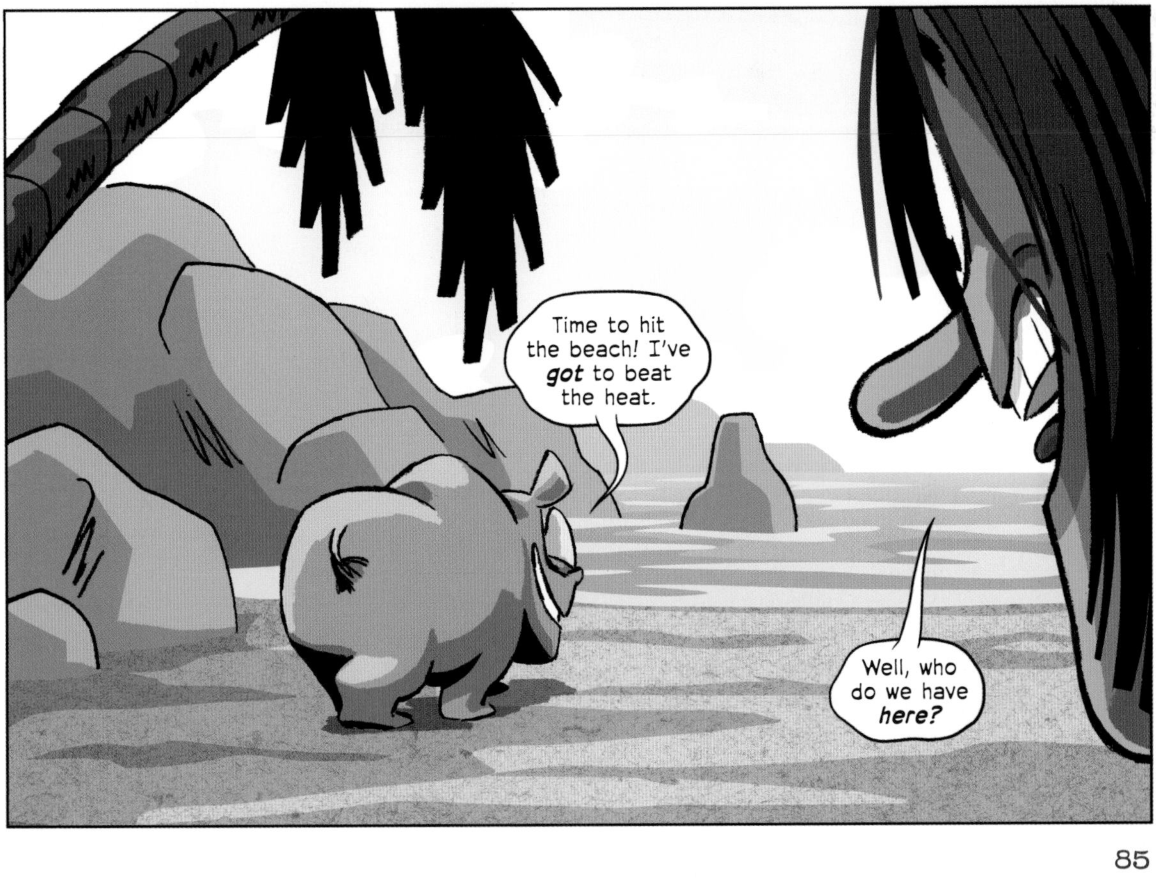
Time to hit the beach! I've **got** to beat the heat.
Well, who do we have ***here?***

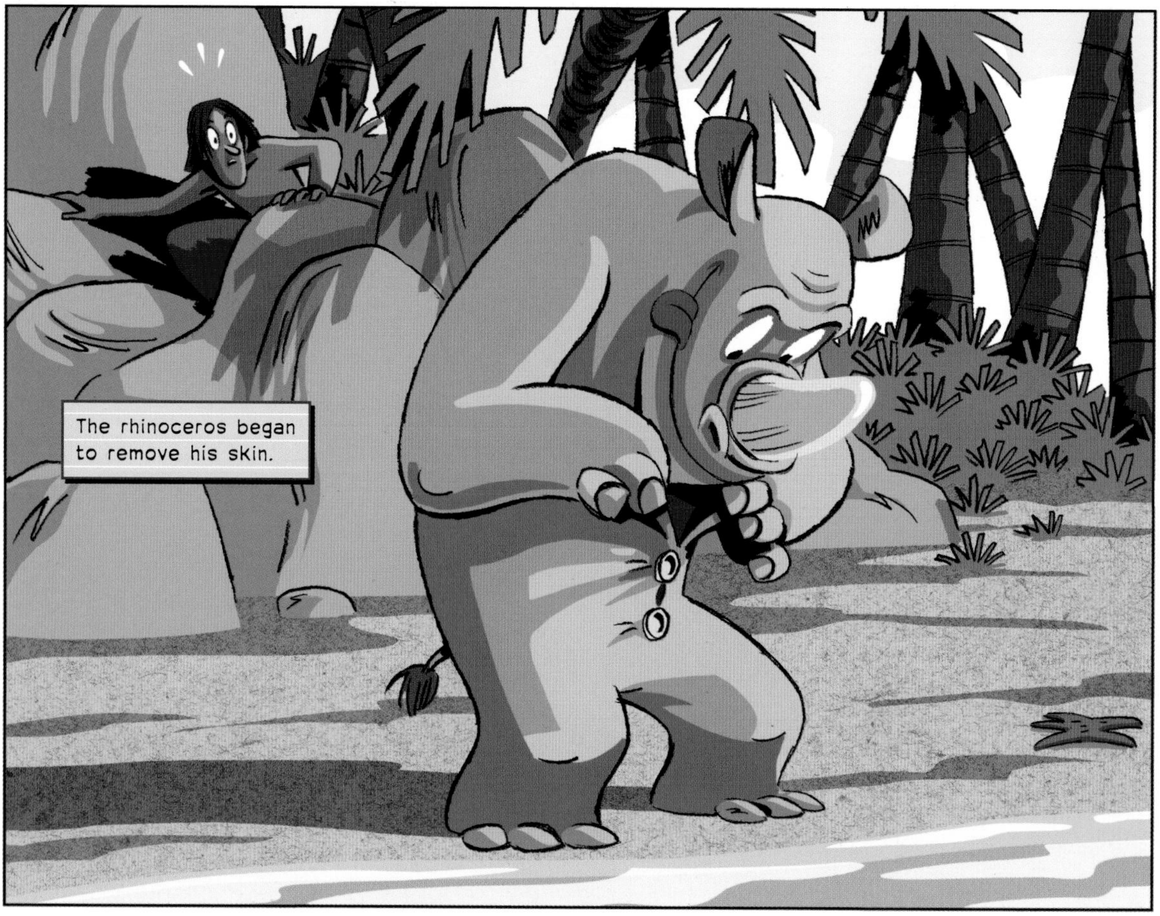
The rhinoceros began to remove his skin.

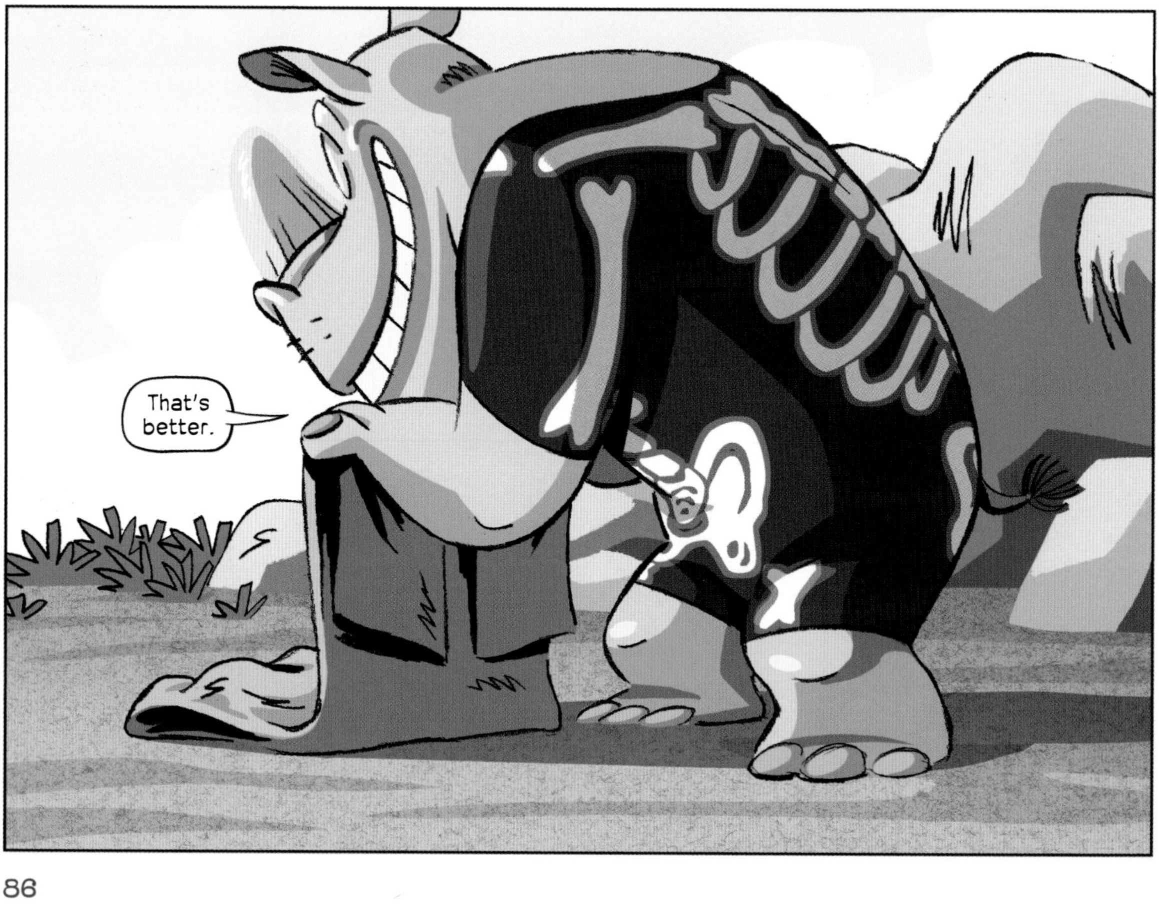
That's better.

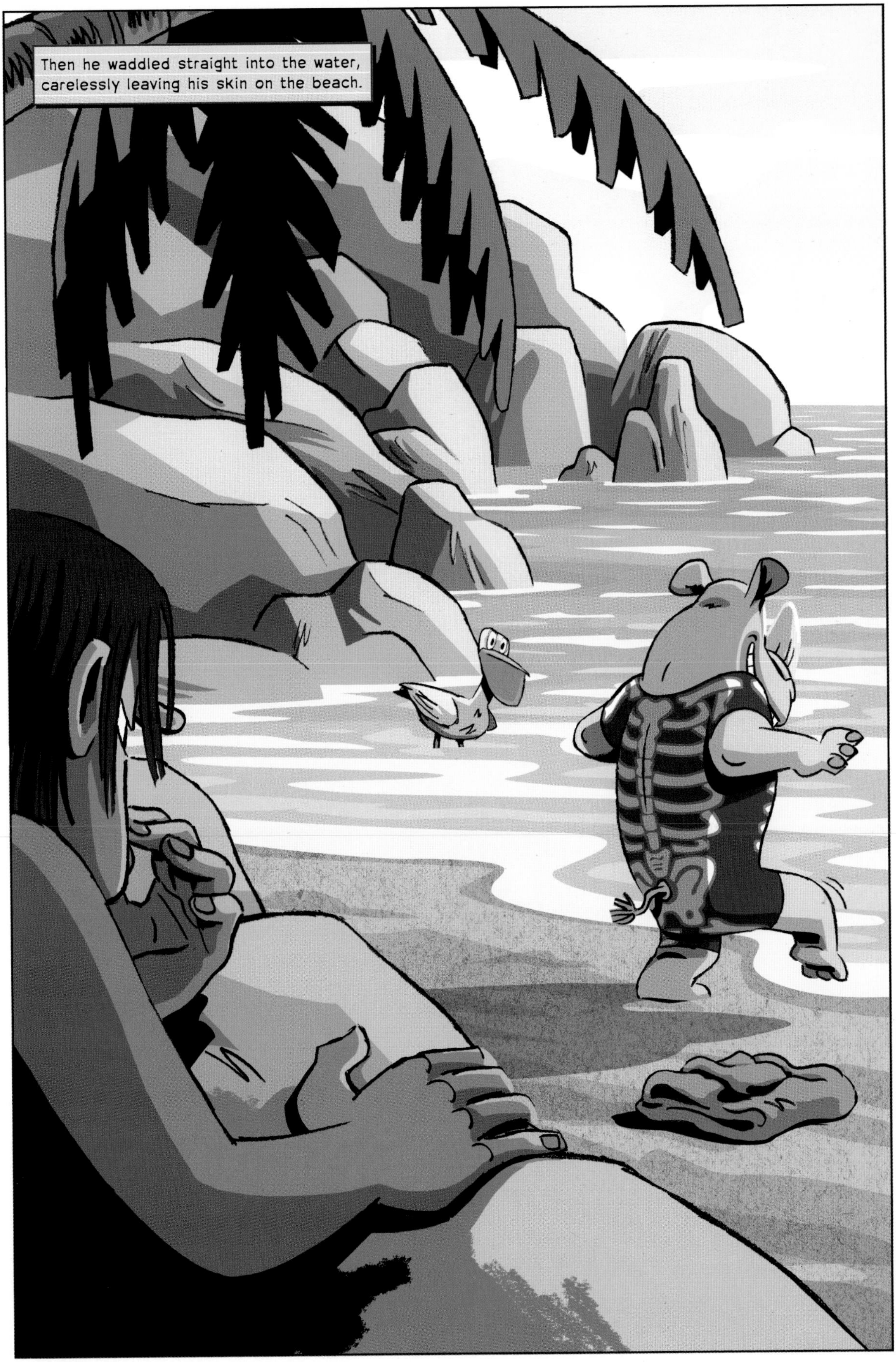
Then he waddled straight into the water,
carelessly leaving his skin on the beach.

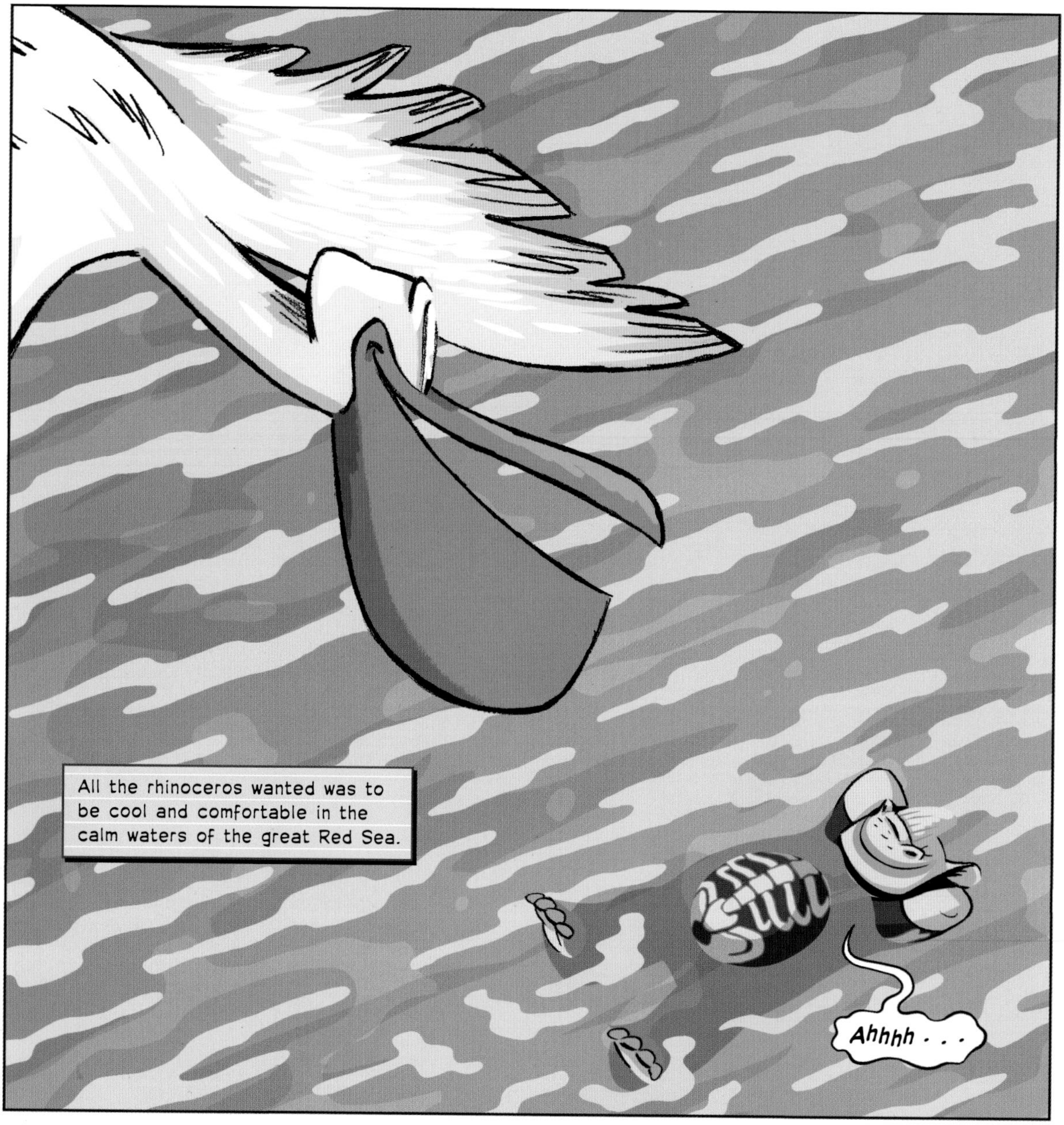
All the rhinoceros wanted was to be cool and comfortable in the calm waters of the great Red Sea.
Ahhhh . . .

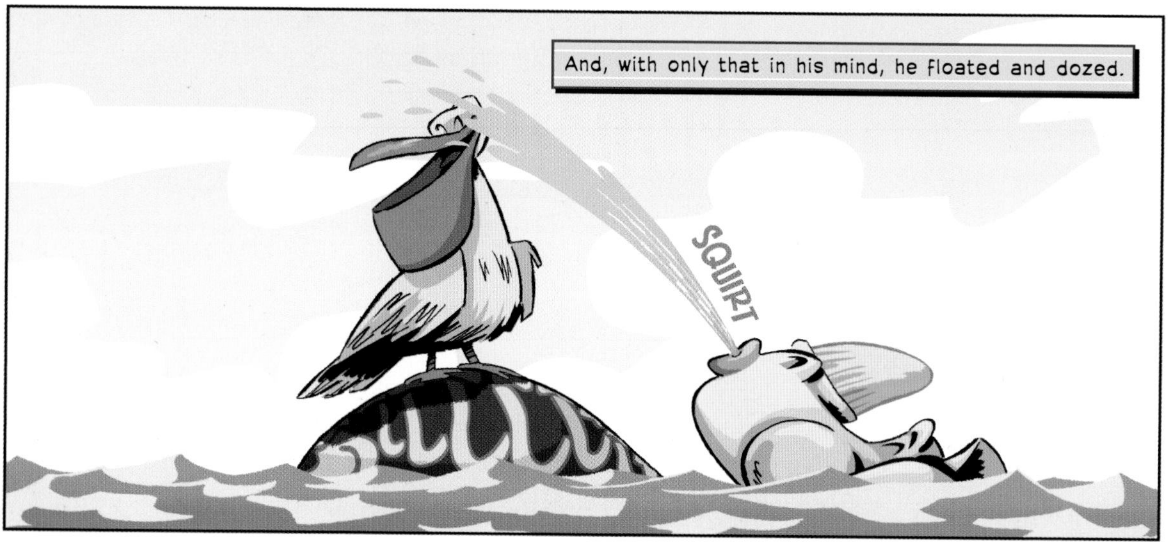
And, with only that in his mind, he floated and dozed.
SQUIRT

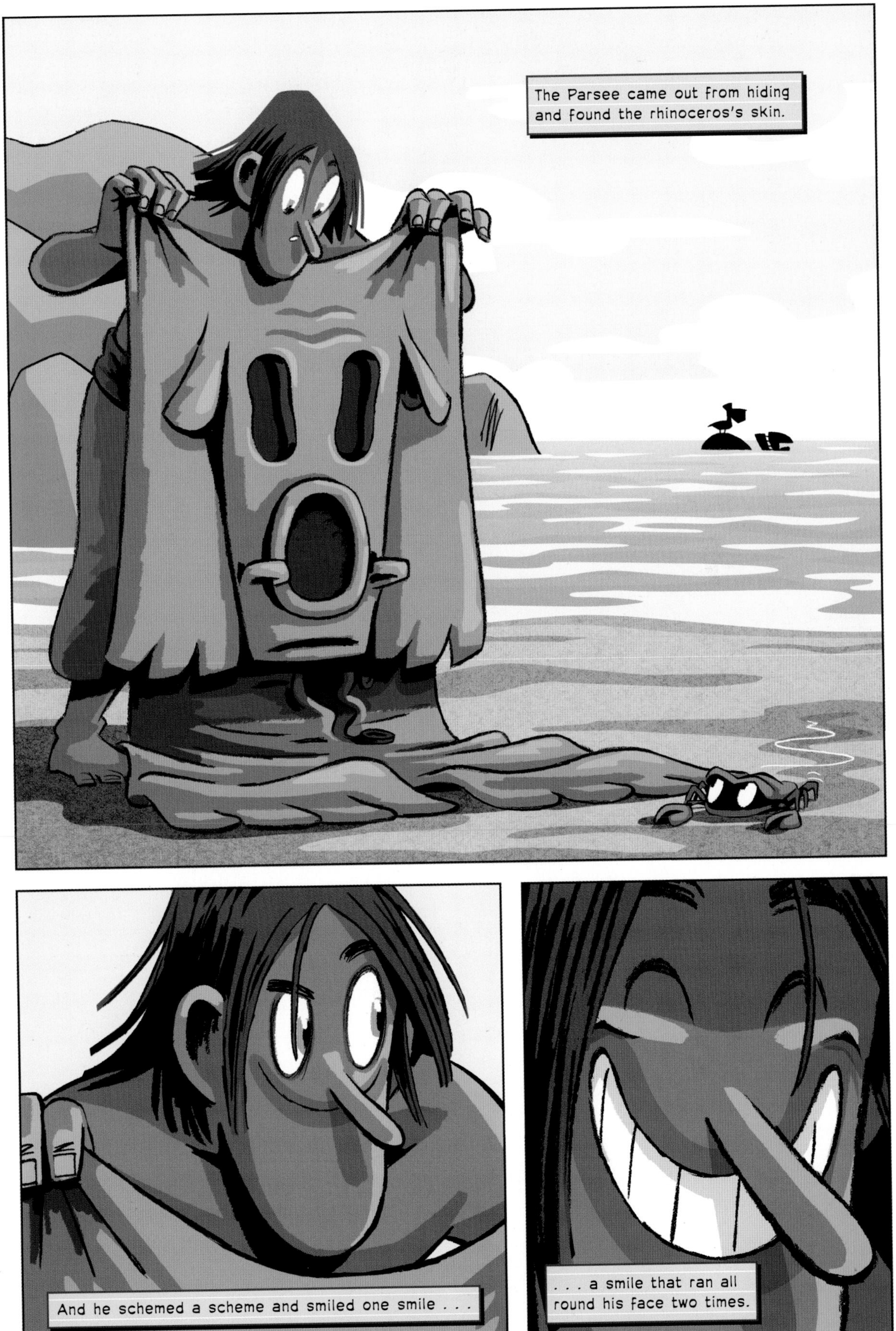
The Parsee came out from hiding and found the rhinoceros's skin.
And he schemed a scheme and smiled one smile . . .
. . . a smile that ran all round his face two times.

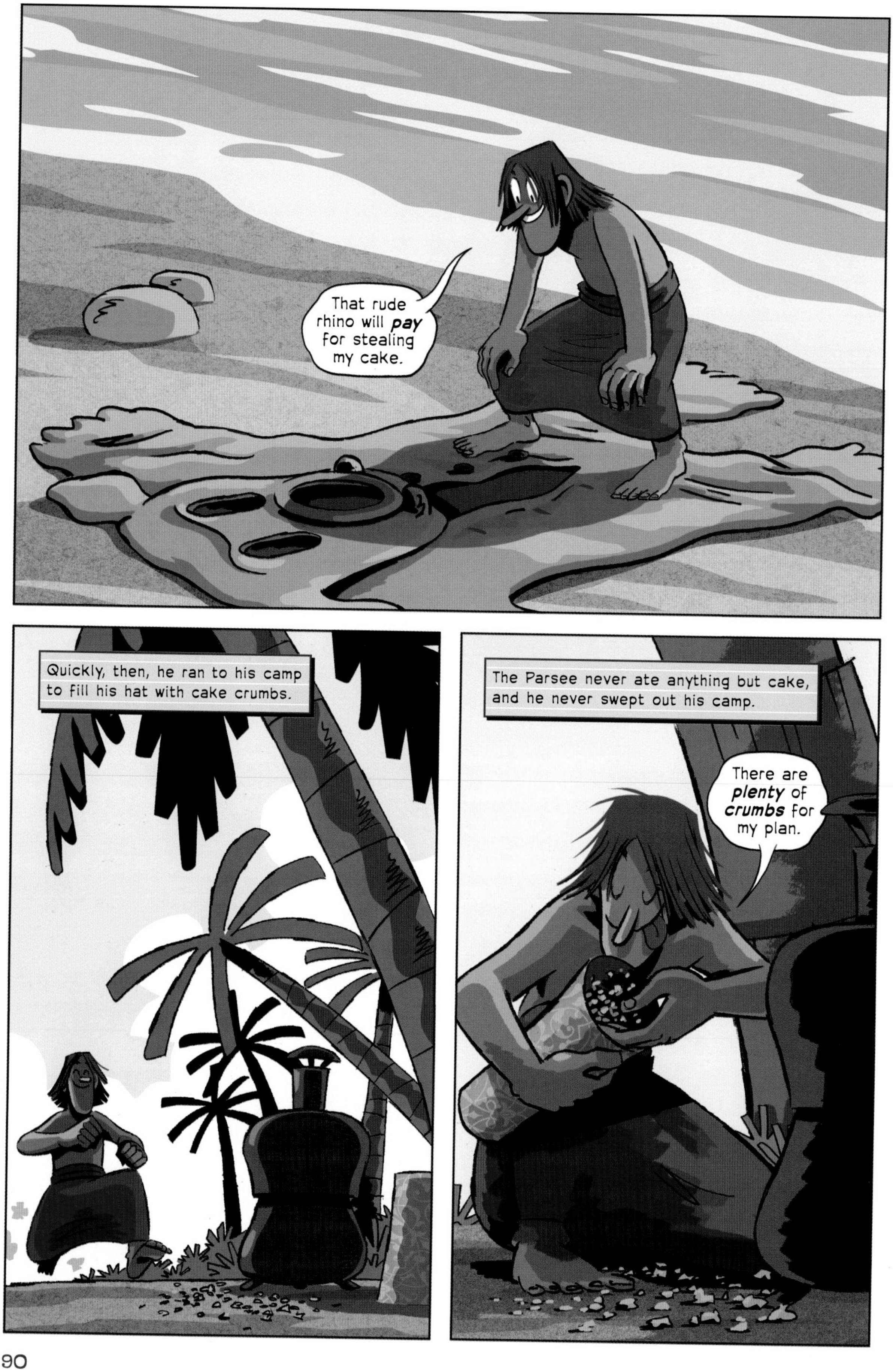
That rude rhino will *pay* for stealing my cake.
Quickly, then, he ran to his camp to fill his hat with cake crumbs.
The Parsee never ate anything but cake, and he never swept out his camp.
There are *plenty* of *crumbs* for my plan.

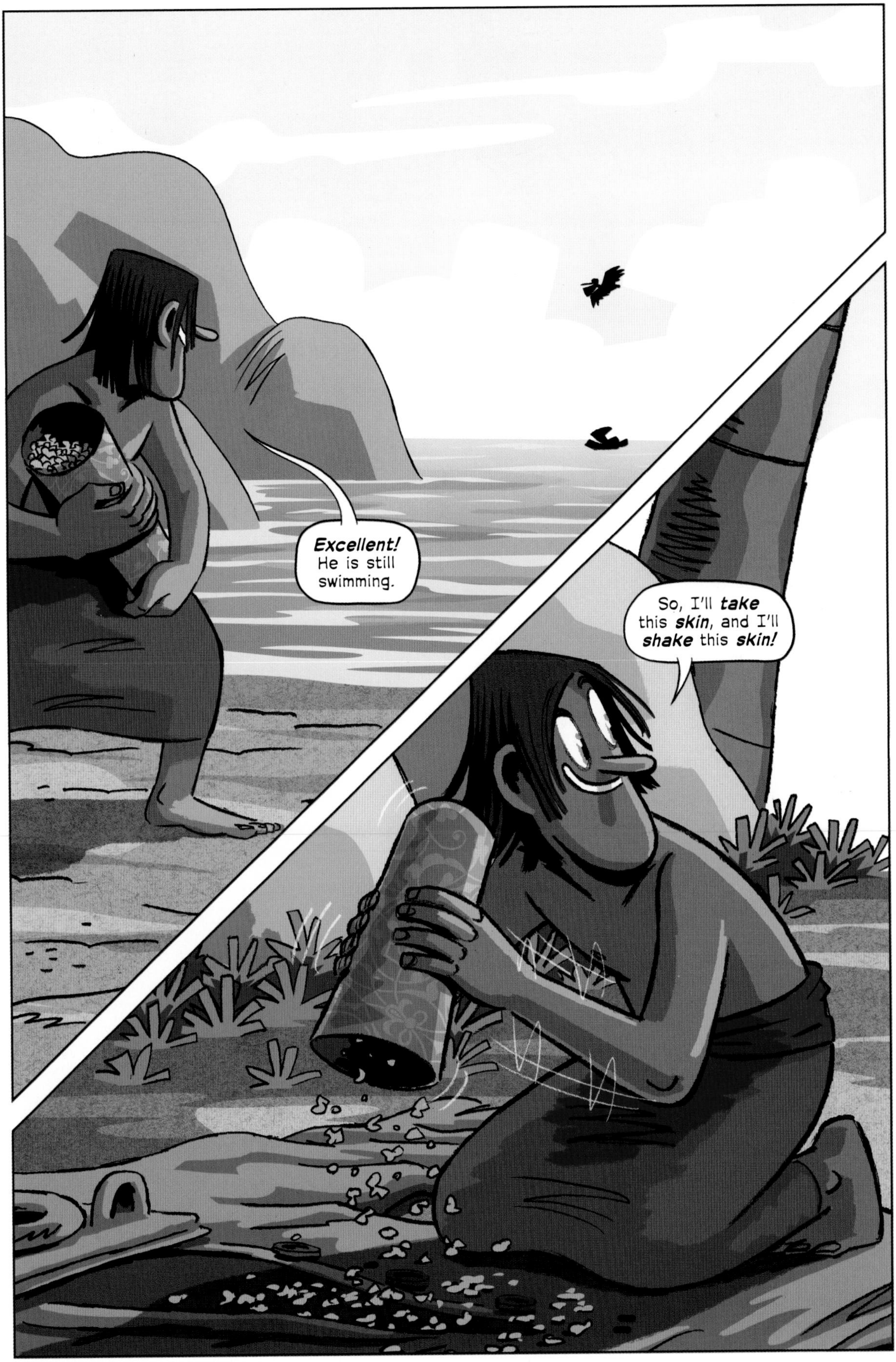

*Excellent!* He is still swimming.
So, I'll ***take*** this ***skin***, and I'll ***shake*** this ***skin!***

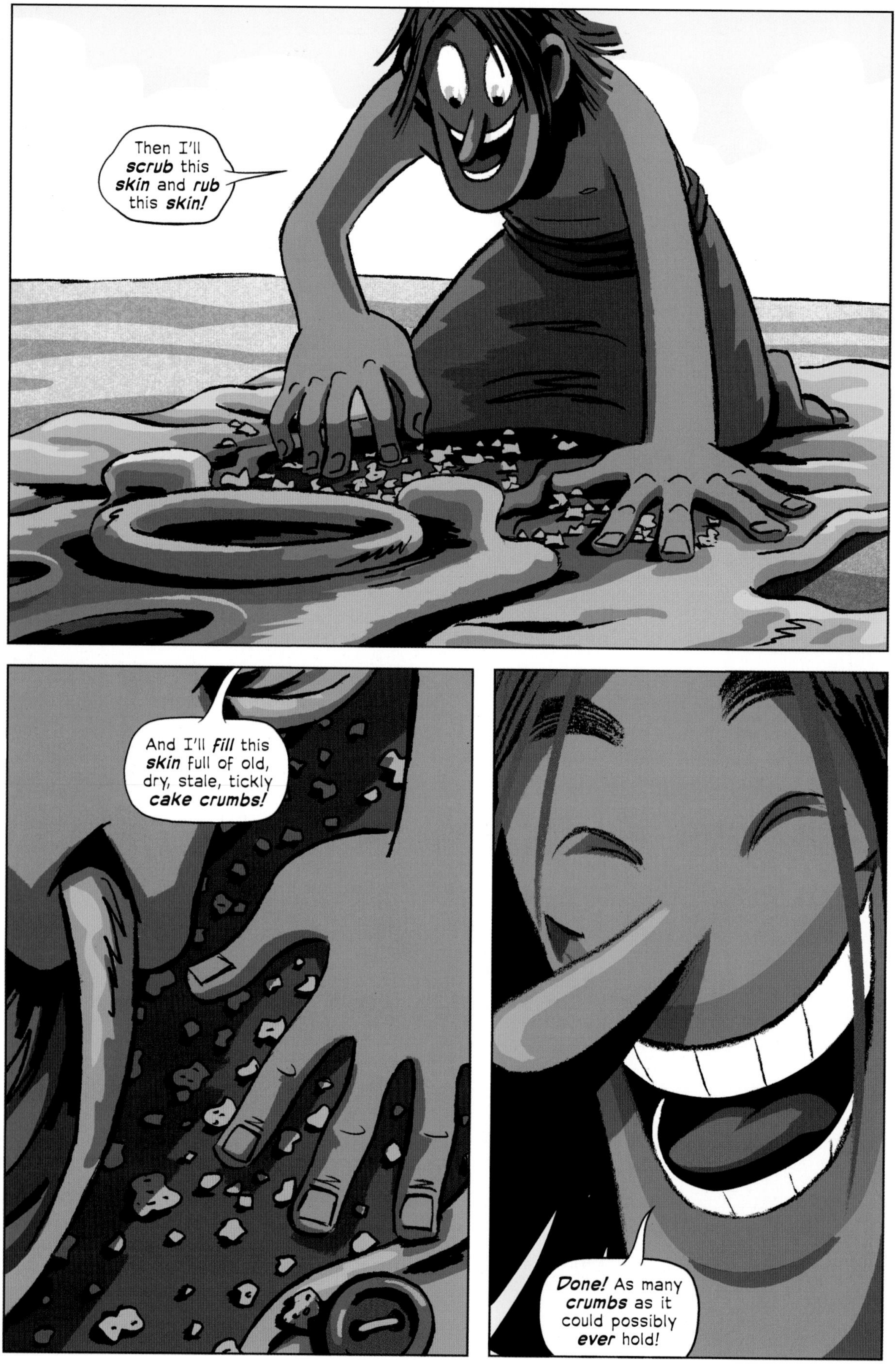
Then I'll *scrub* this *skin* and *rub* this *skin!*
And I'll *fill* this *skin* full of old, dry, stale, tickly *cake crumbs!*
*Done!* As many *crumbs* as it could possibly *ever* hold!

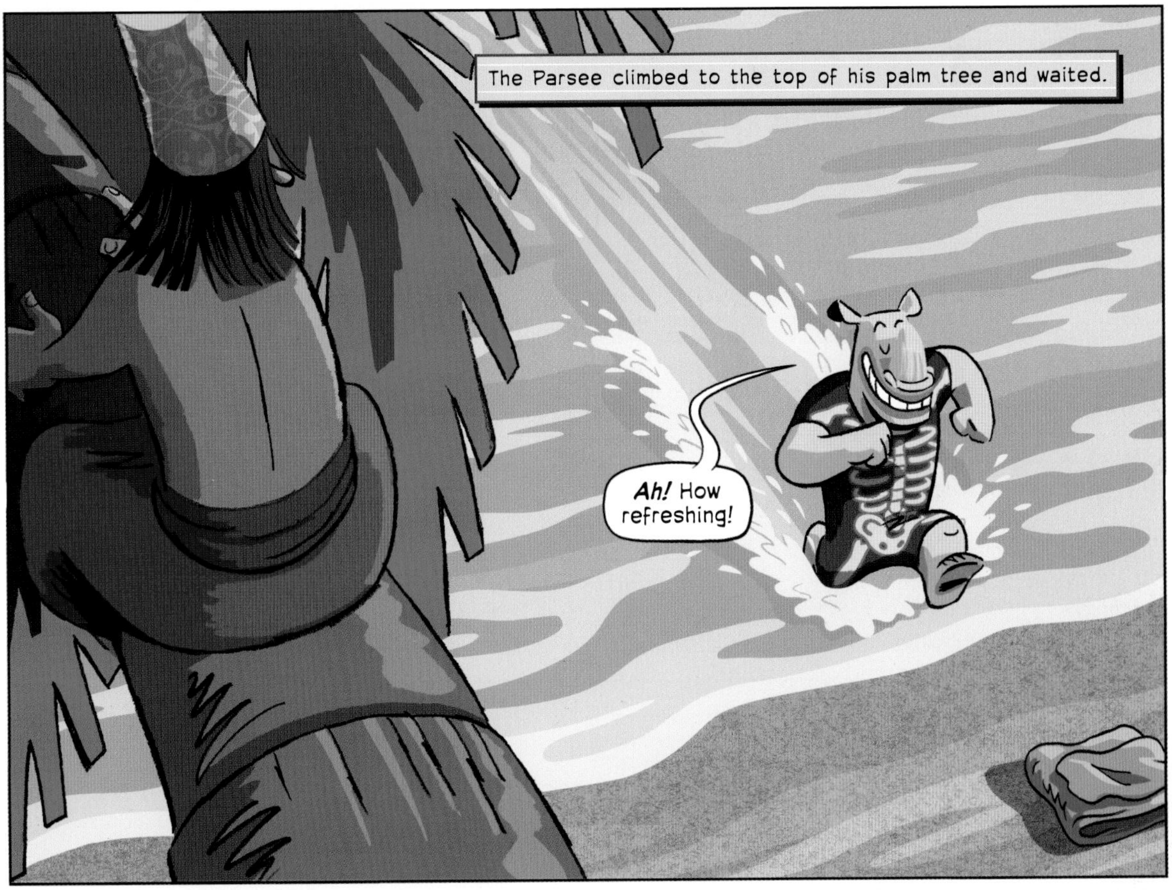
The Parsee climbed to the top of his palm tree and waited.
Ah! How refreshing!

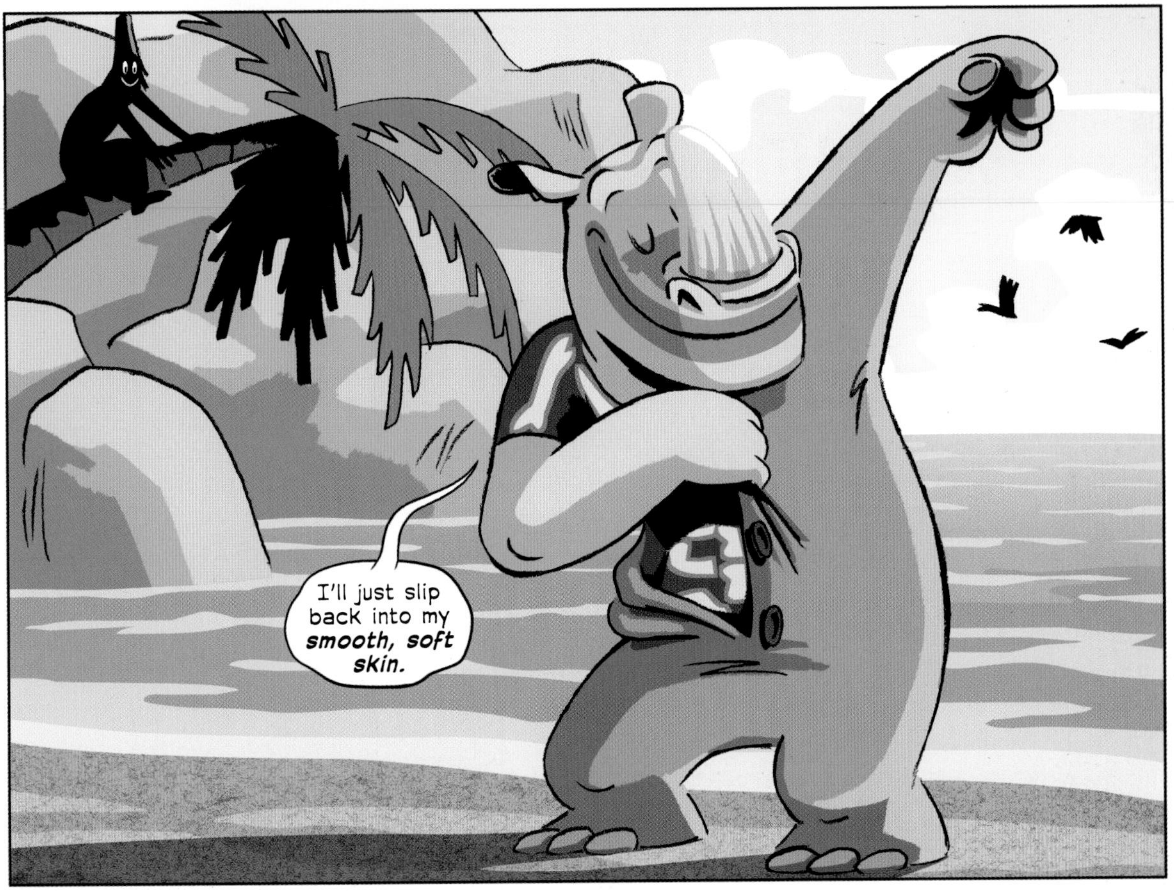
I'll just slip back into my smooth, soft skin.

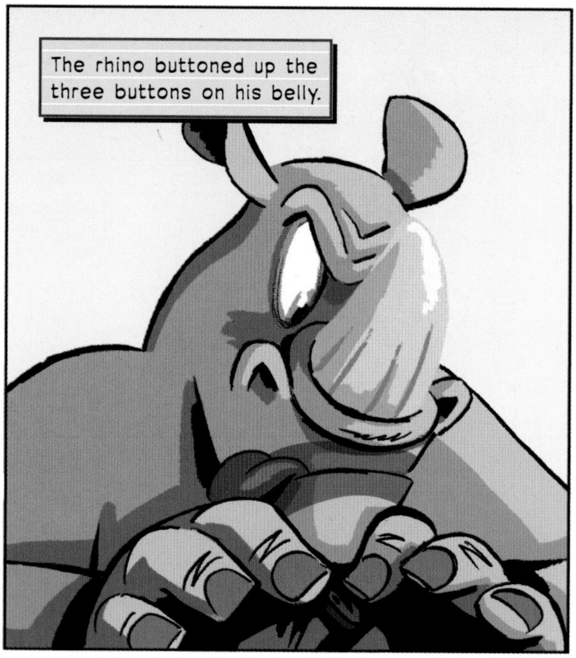
The rhino buttoned up the three buttons on his belly.

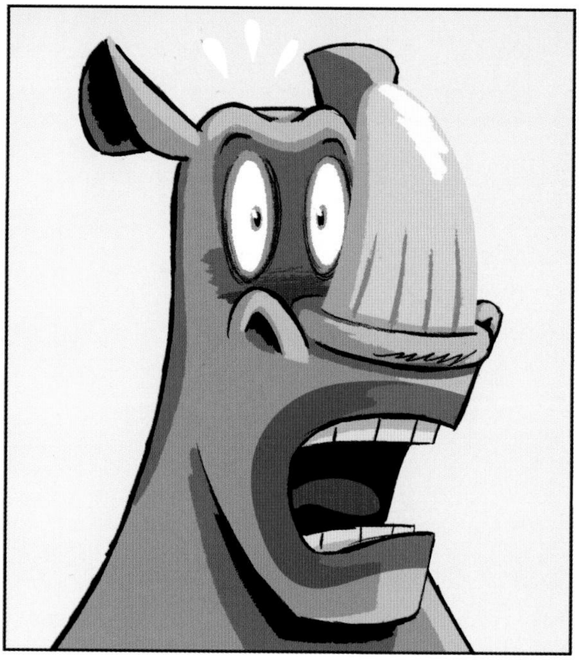

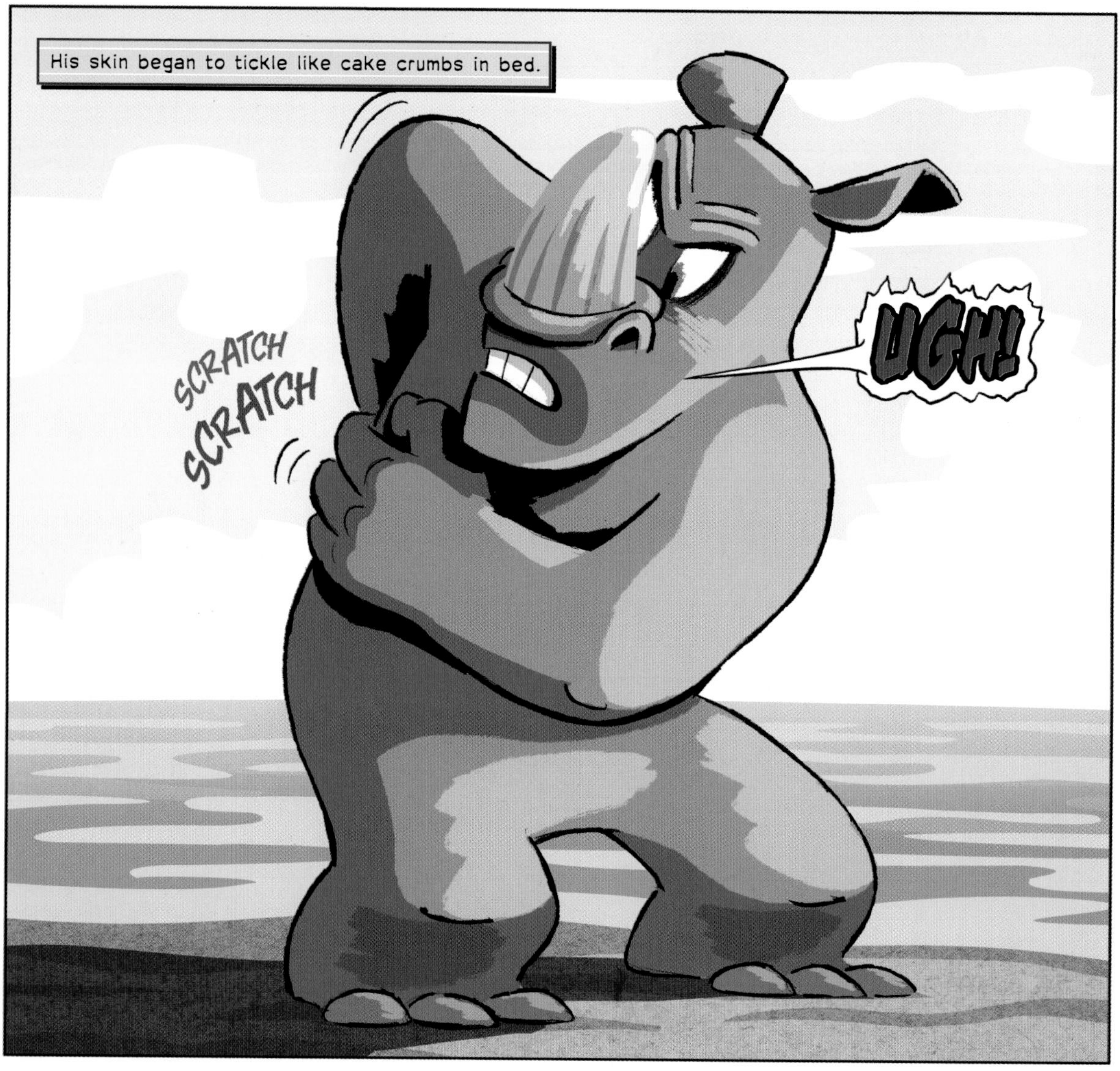
His skin began to tickle like cake crumbs in bed.
SCRATCH SCRATCH
UGH!

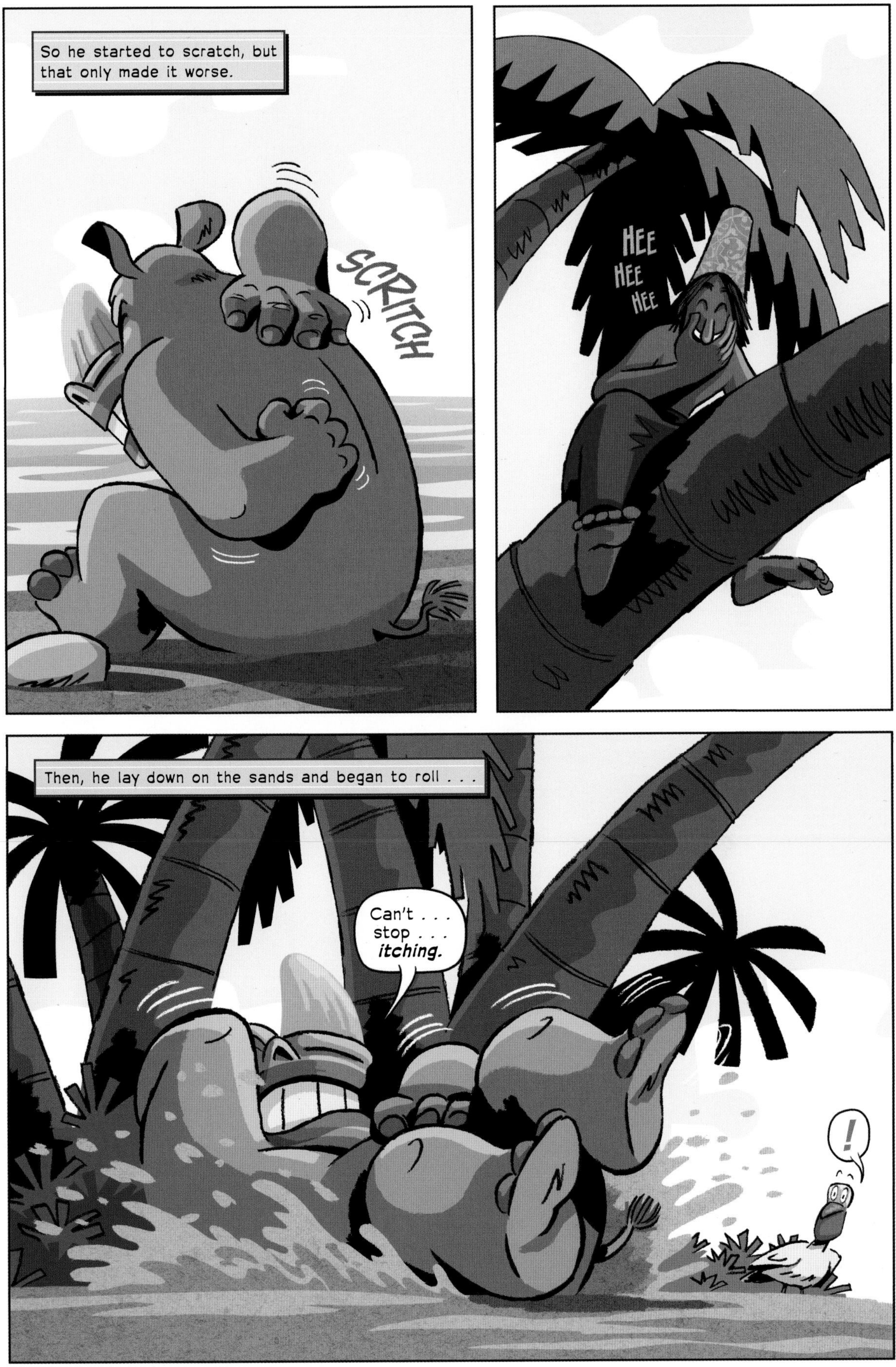
So he started to scratch, but that only made it worse.
SCRITCH
HEE HEE HEE
Then, he lay down on the sands and began to roll . . .
Can't . . . stop . . . *itching.*
!

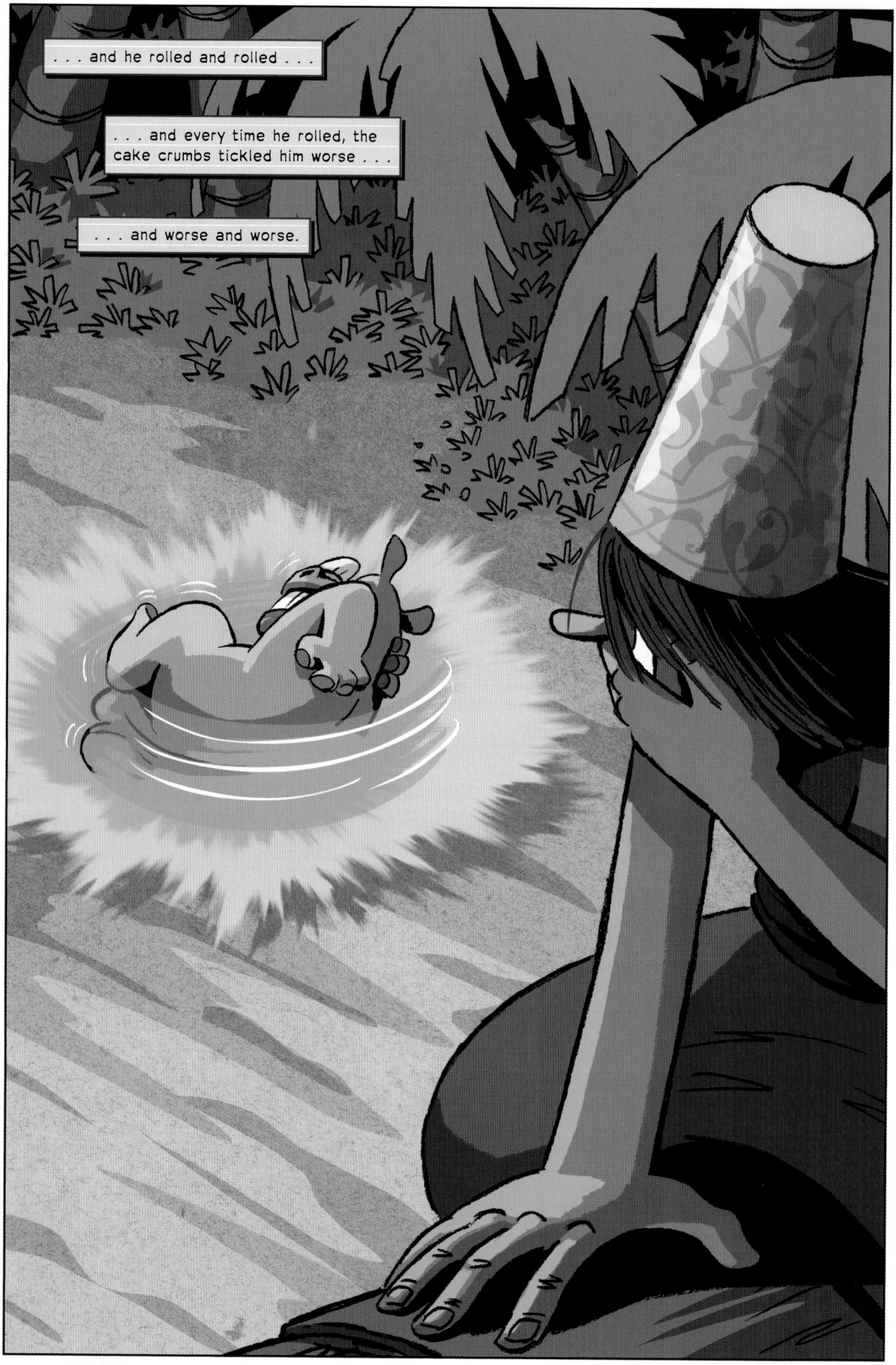
. . . and he rolled and rolled . . .
. . . and every time he rolled, the cake crumbs tickled him worse . . .
. . . and worse and worse.

And even *worse!*

Finally, the rhino noticed the rough bark of the palm tree.

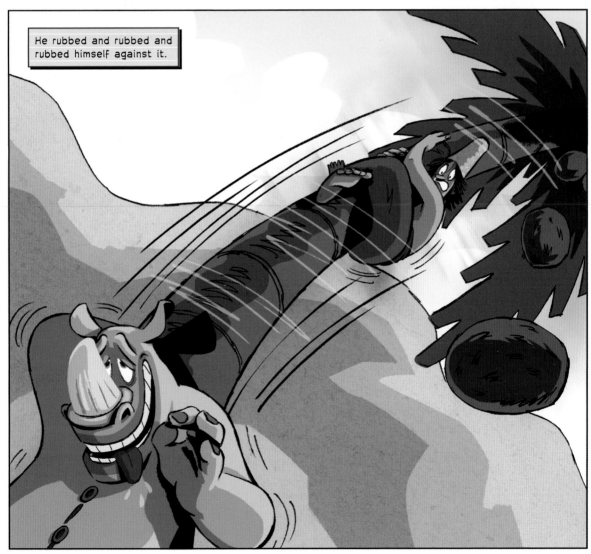

He rubbed and rubbed and rubbed himself against it.

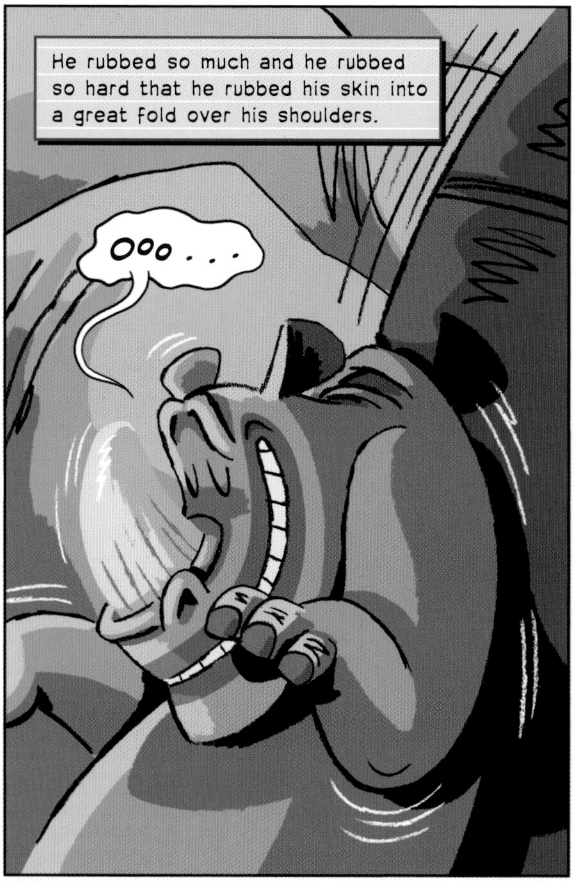
He rubbed so much and he rubbed so hard that he rubbed his skin into a great fold over his shoulders.
Ooo . . .

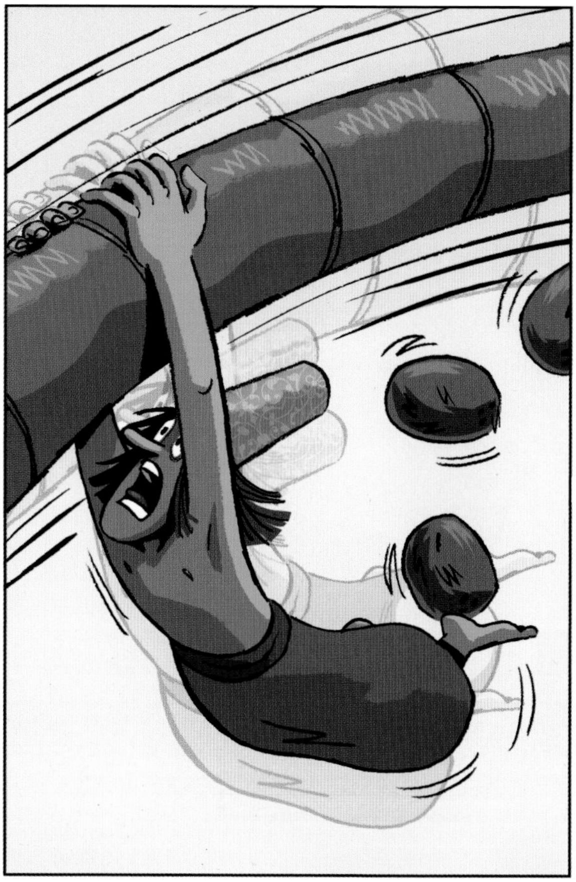

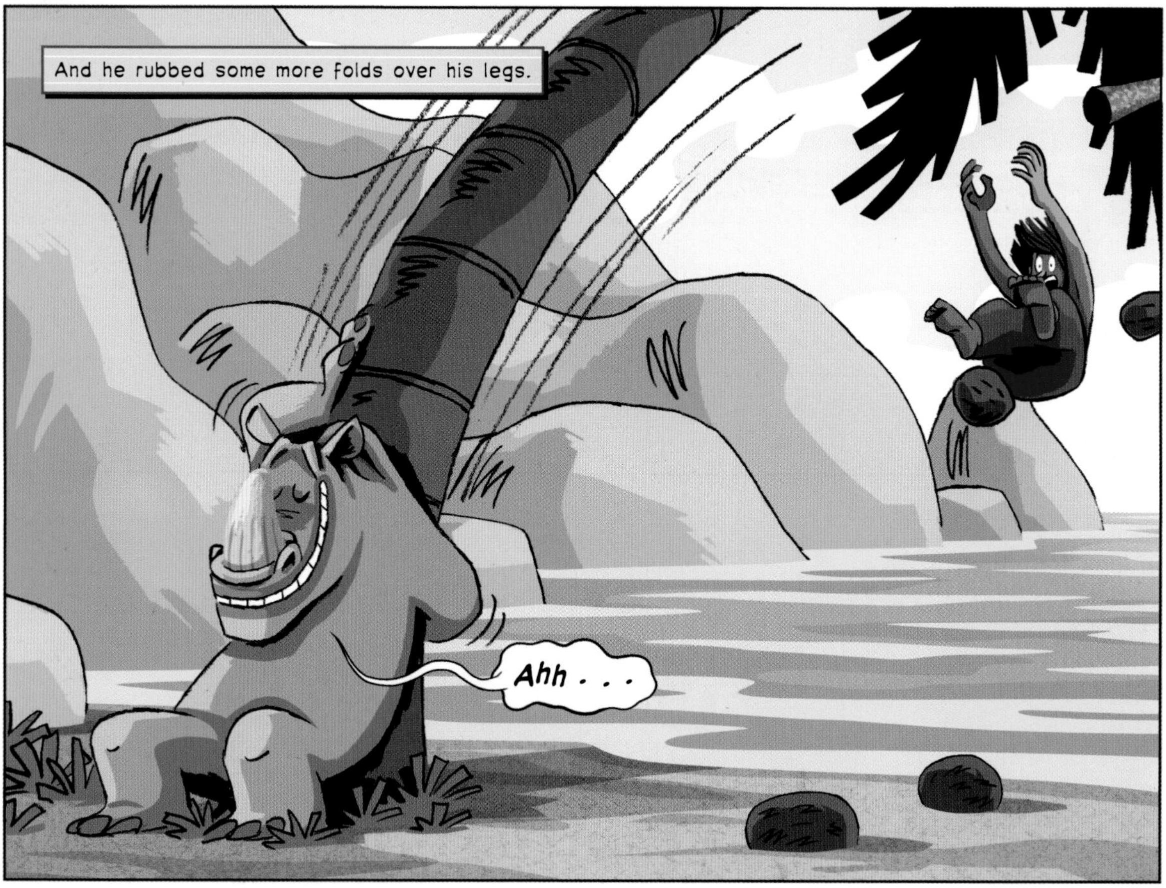
And he rubbed some more folds over his legs.
Ahh . . .

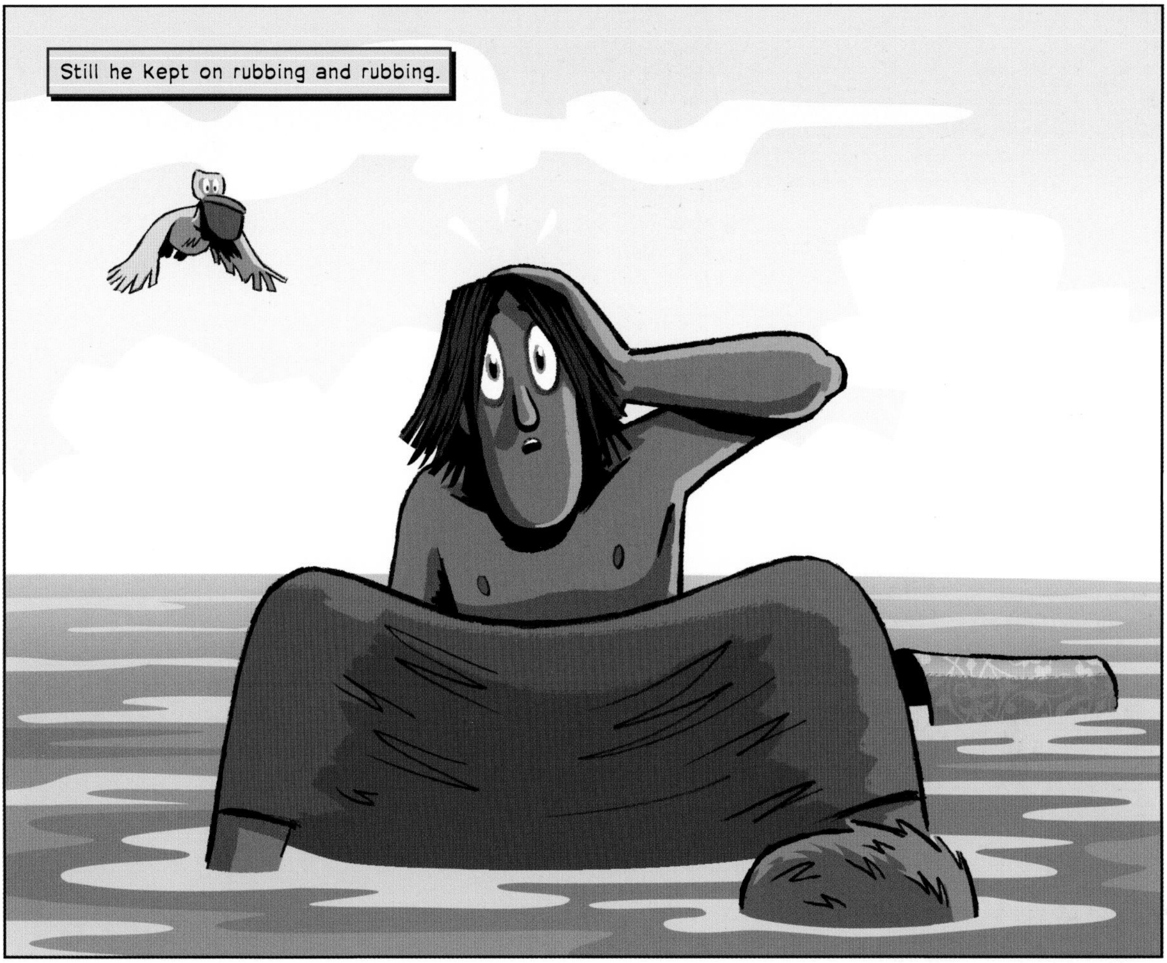
Still he kept on rubbing and rubbing.

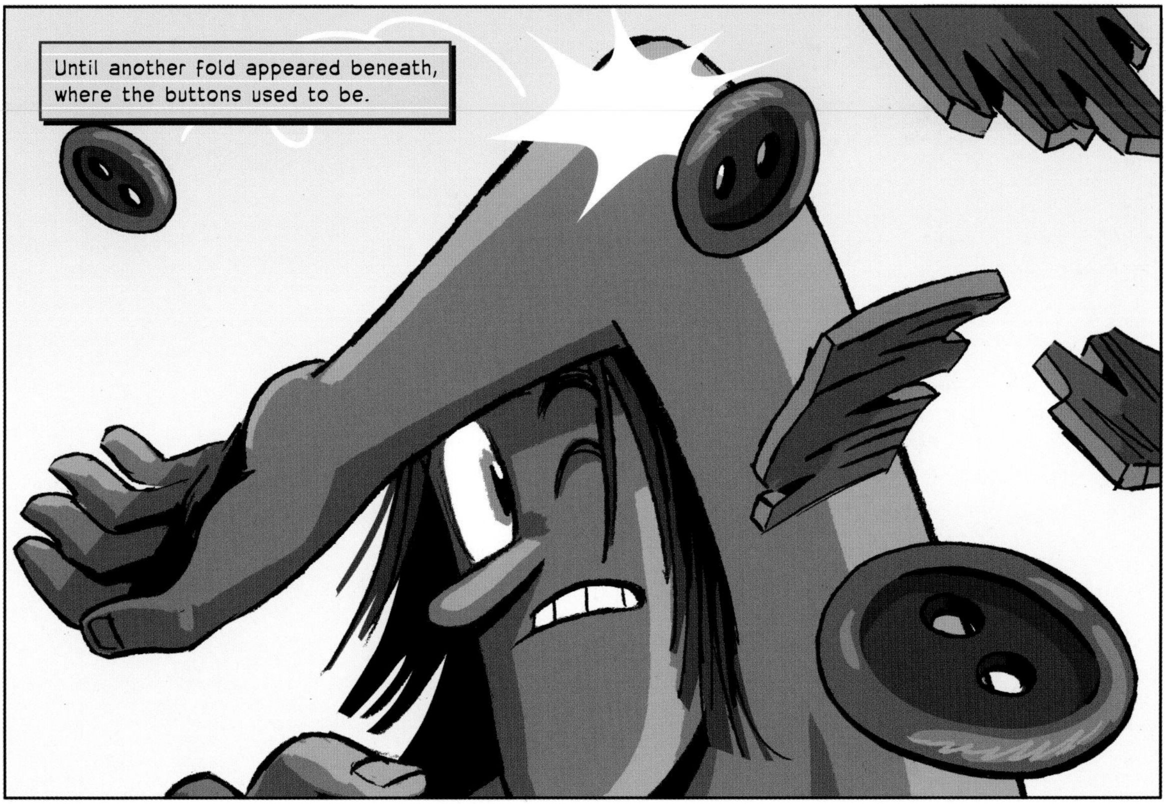
Until another fold appeared beneath,
where the buttons used to be.

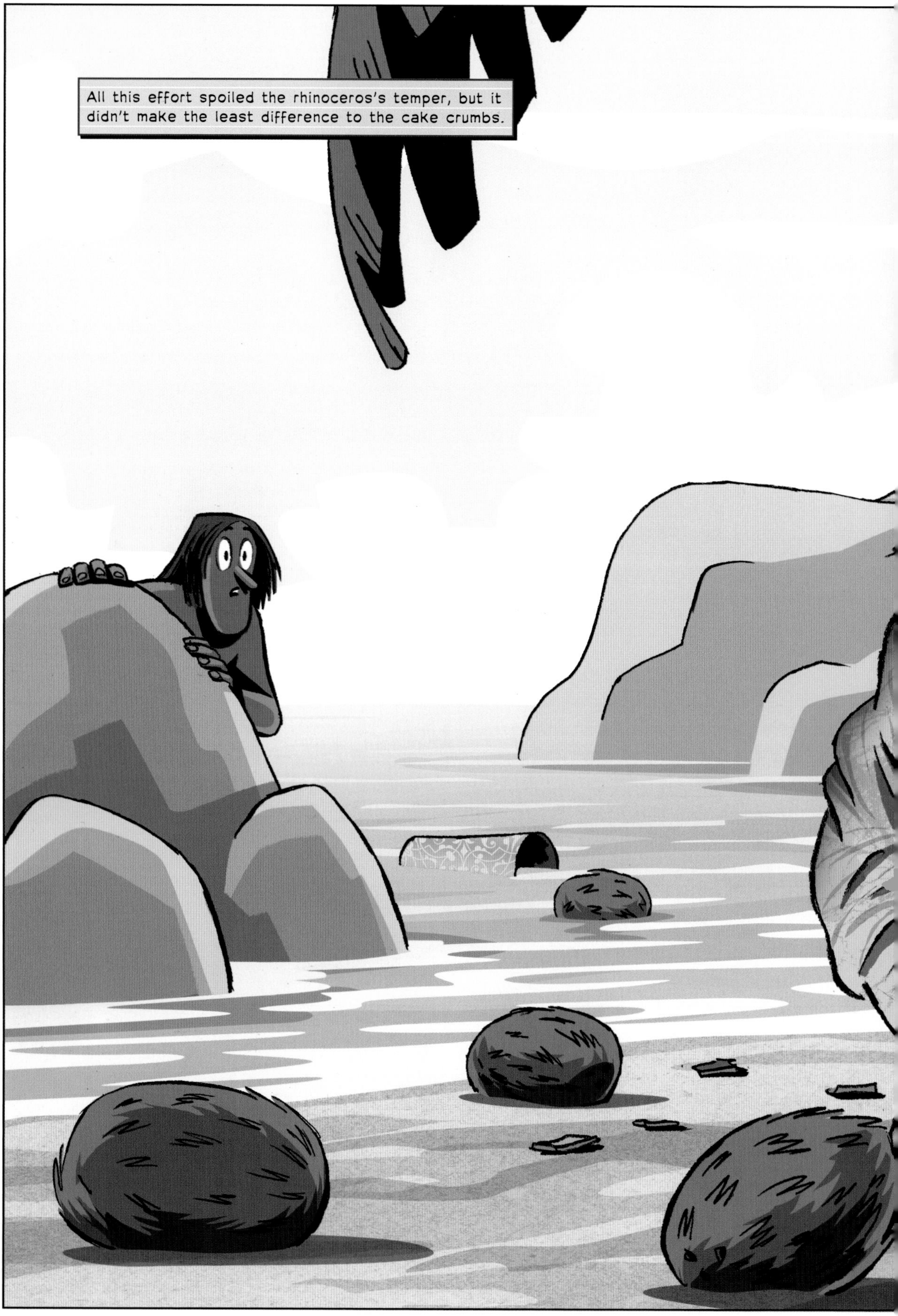
All this effort spoiled the rhinoceros's temper, but it didn't make the least difference to the cake crumbs.

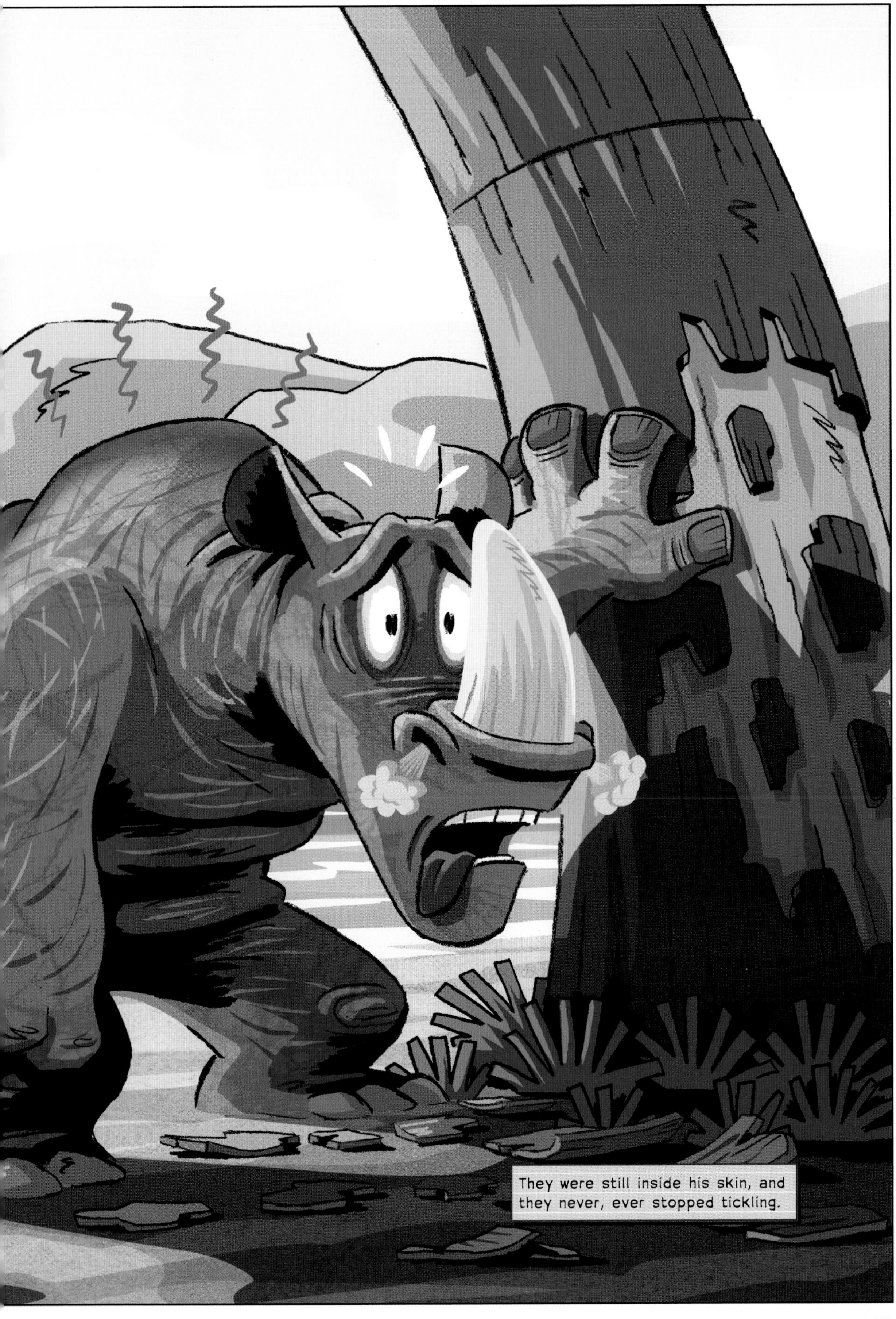
They were still inside his skin, and they never, ever stopped tickling.

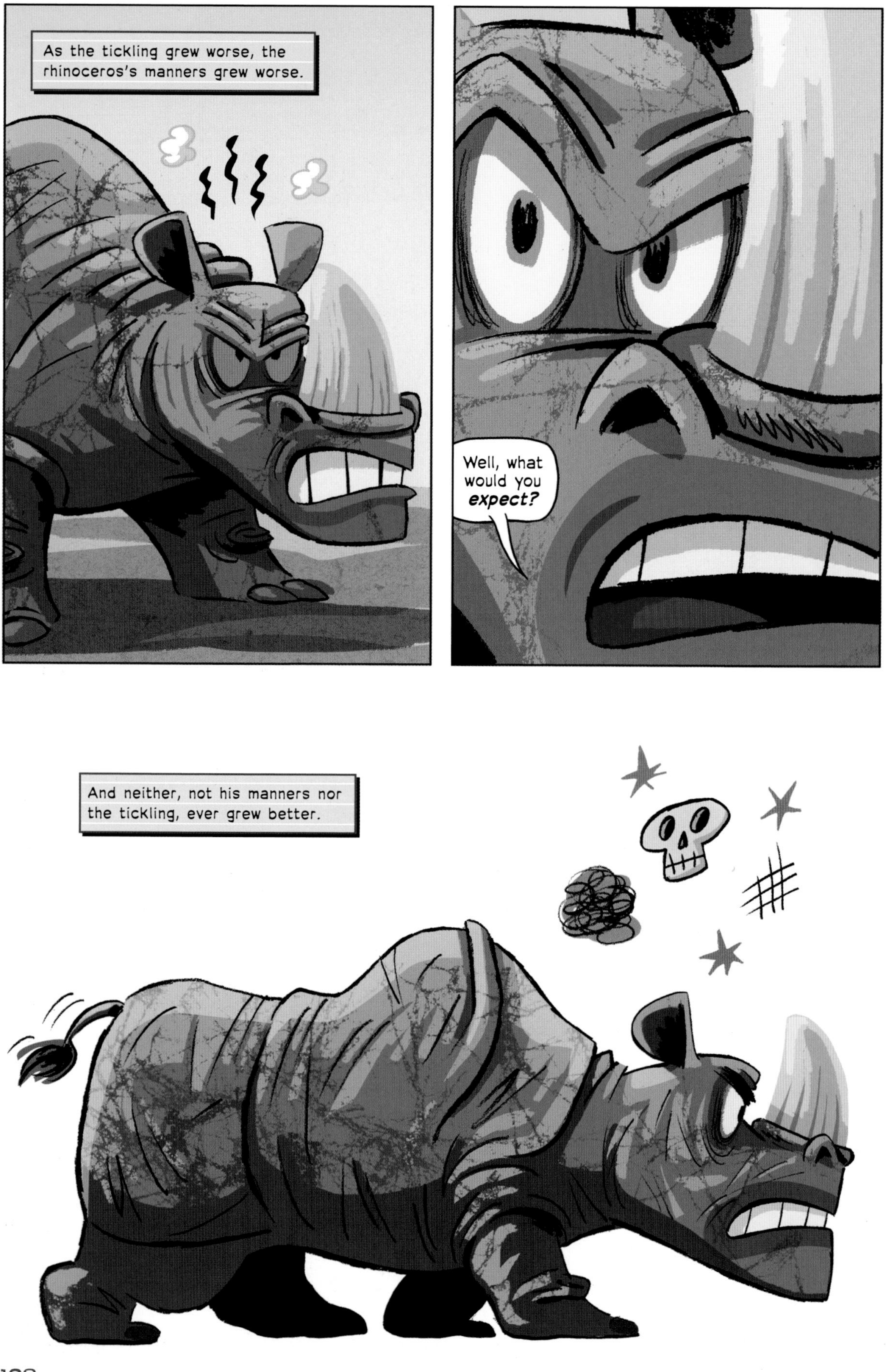
As the tickling grew worse, the rhinoceros's manners grew worse.
Well, what would you *expect?*
And neither, not his manners nor the tickling, ever grew better.

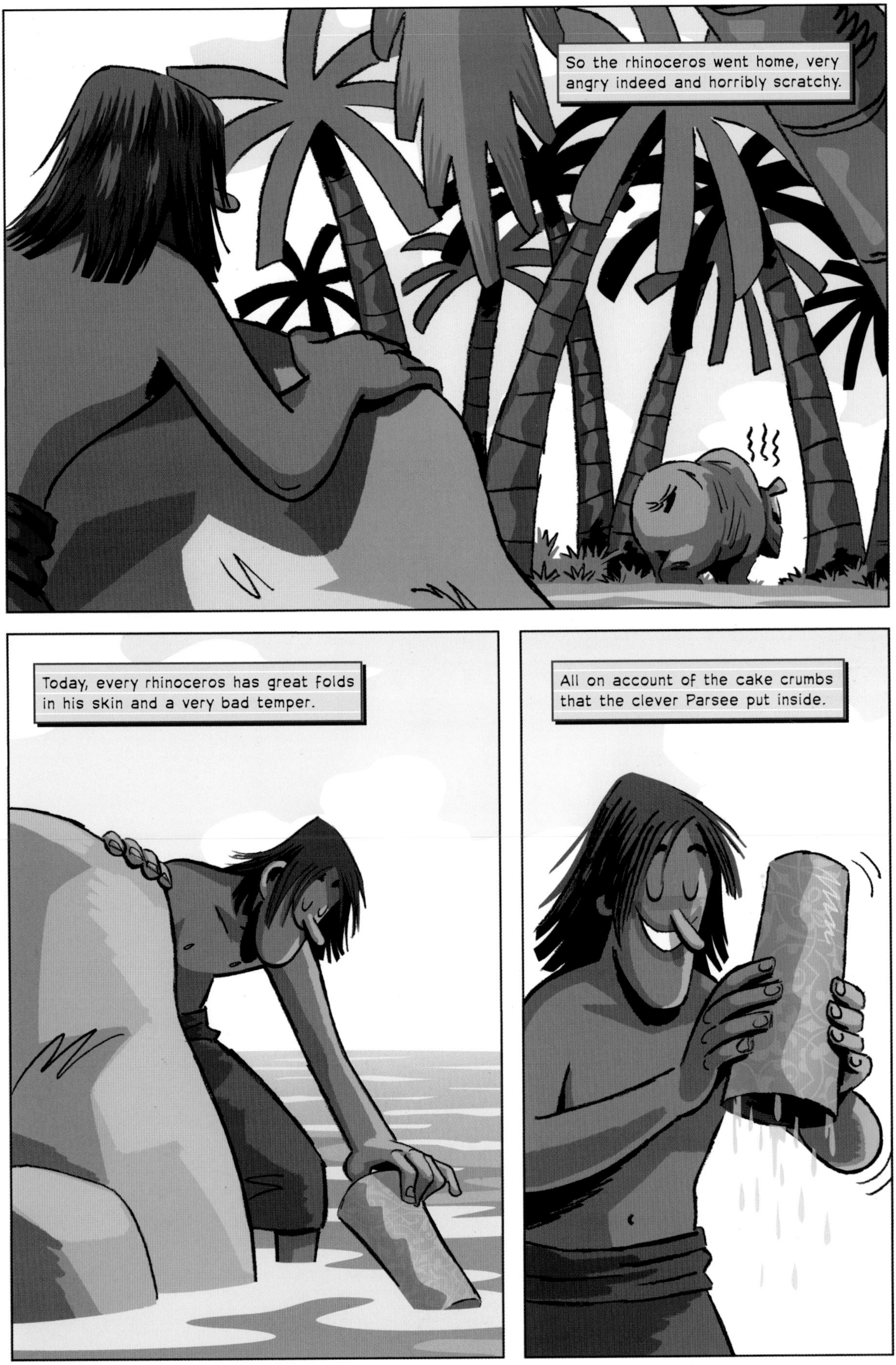
So the rhinoceros went home, very angry indeed and horribly scratchy.
Today, every rhinoceros has great folds in his skin and a very bad temper.
All on account of the cake crumbs that the clever Parsee put inside.

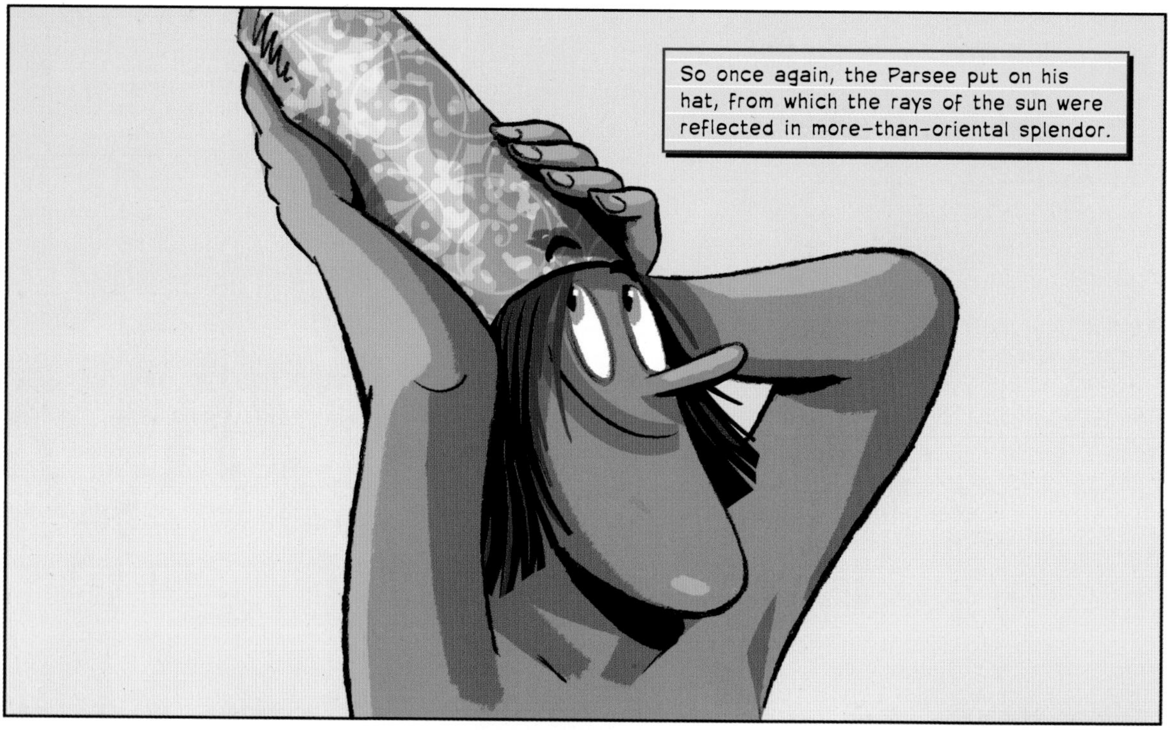
So once again, the Parsee put on his hat, from which the rays of the sun were reflected in more-than-oriental splendor.

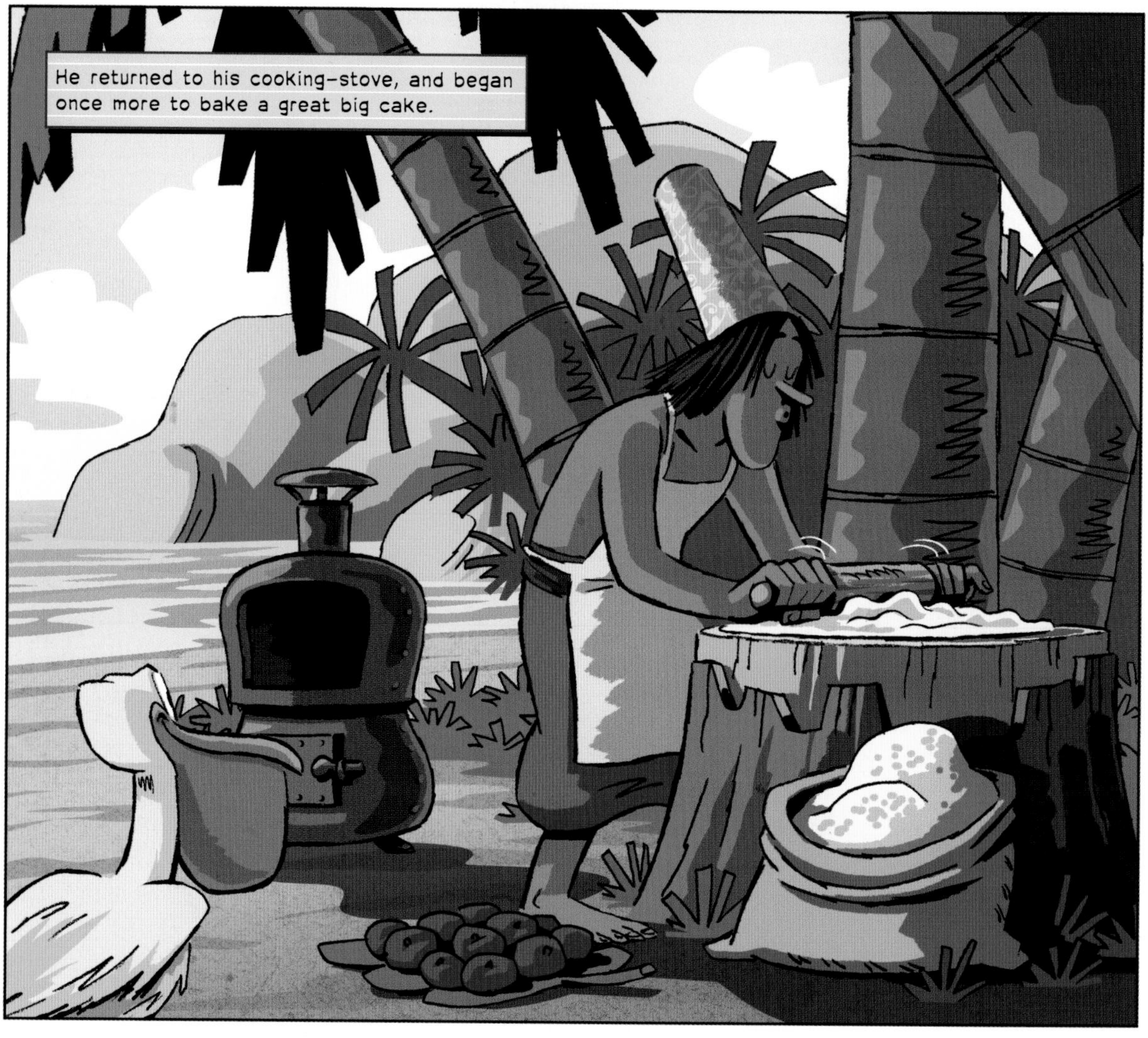
He returned to his cooking-stove, and began once more to bake a great big cake.

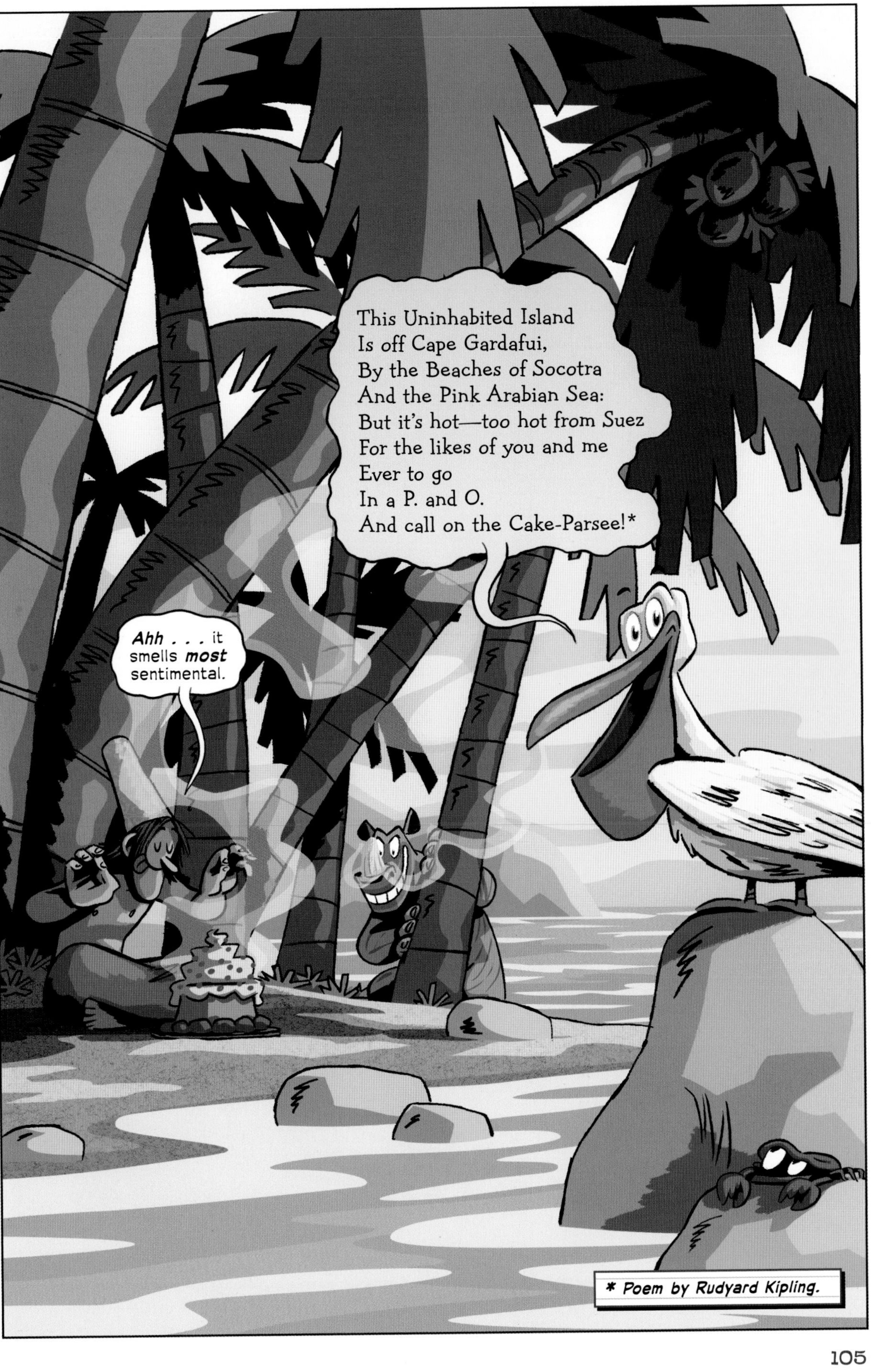
This Uninhabited Island
Is off Cape Gardafui,
By the Beaches of Socotra
And the Pink Arabian Sea:
But it's hot—too hot from Suez
For the likes of you and me
Ever to go
In a P. and O.
And call on the Cake-Parsee!*
Ahh . . . it smells most sentimental.
* Poem by Rudyard Kipling.

RUDYARD KIPLING
3

# CONCLUSION

## NEW SPECIMEN:
## ROUGH & PLATED RHINOCEROS

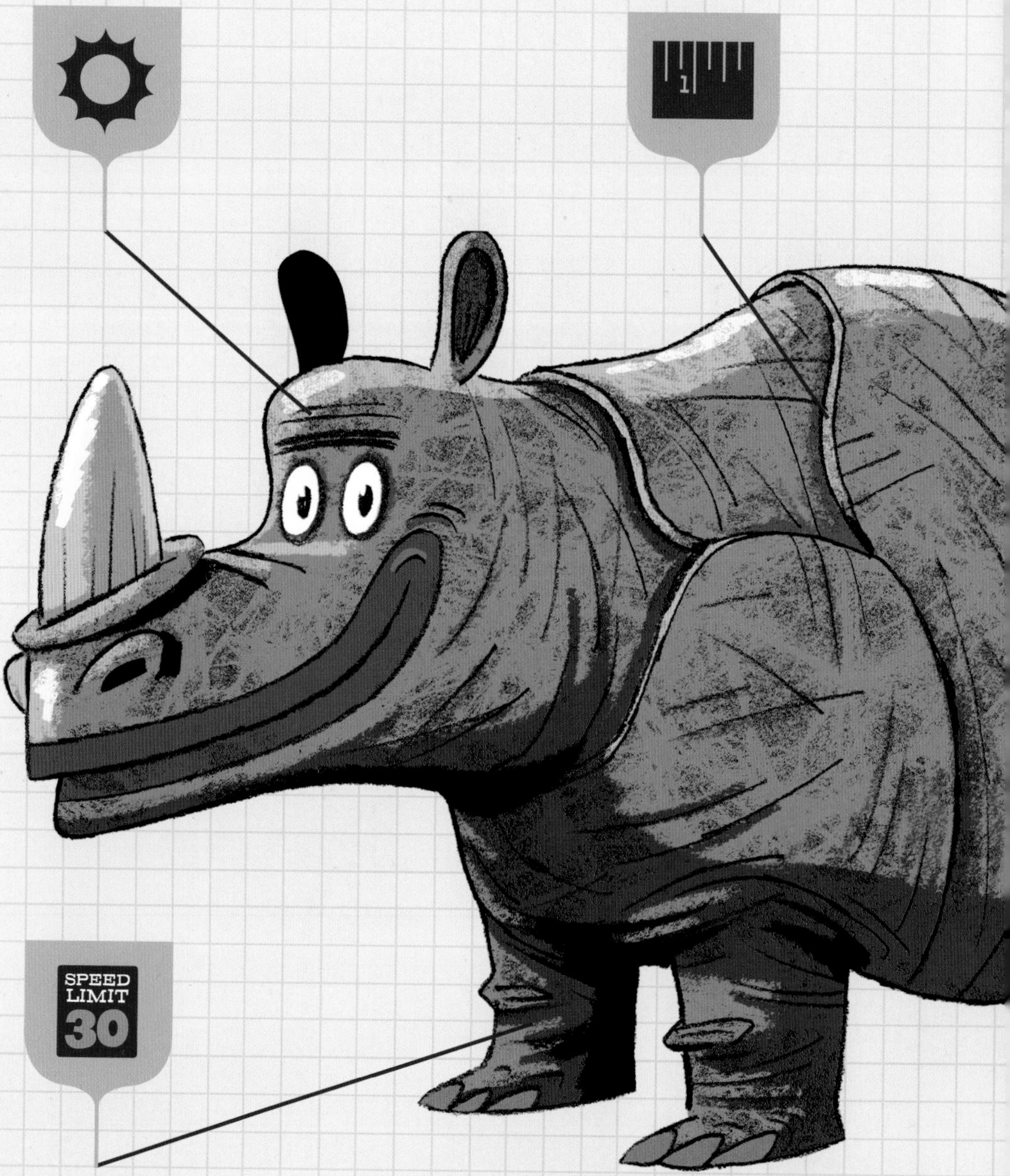
SPEED
LIMIT
30

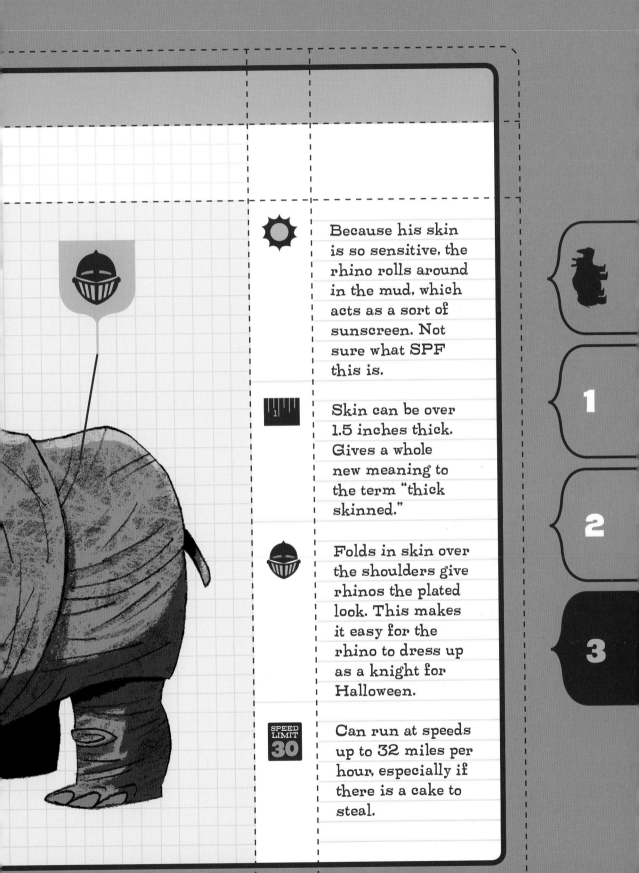

Because his skin is so sensitive, the rhino rolls around in the mud, which acts as a sort of sunscreen. Not sure what SPF this is.

Skin can be over 1.5 inches thick. Gives a whole new meaning to the term "thick skinned."

Folds in skin over the shoulders give rhinos the plated look. This makes it easy for the rhino to dress up as a knight for Halloween.

Can run at speeds up to 32 miles per hour, especially if there is a cake to steal.

1

2

3

RUDYARD
KIPLING
EST.
1865

# HOW THE CAMEL GOT HIS HUMP

as retold by

## LOUISE SIMONSON
TEAM WRITER

RUDYARD KIPLING

1

# RESEARCH

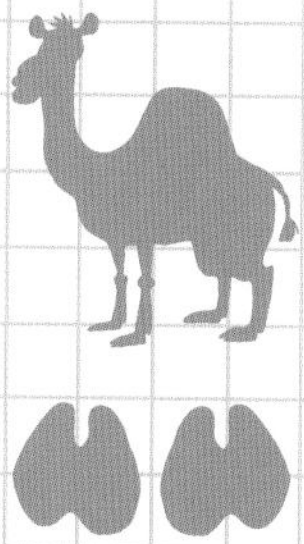

**SPECIMEN:**
FLAT-BACKED CAMEL (Fig. A)

SOCIAL BEHAVIOR: 'Scruciatingly idle
DIET: Milkweed, tamarisks, and prickles (Fig. B)
HABITAT: Howling Desert (Fig. C)
FELLOW DESERT DWELLER: Djinn (Fig. D)
NEARBY ANIMALS: Dog (Fig. E); Oxen (Fig. F); and Horse (Fig. G)

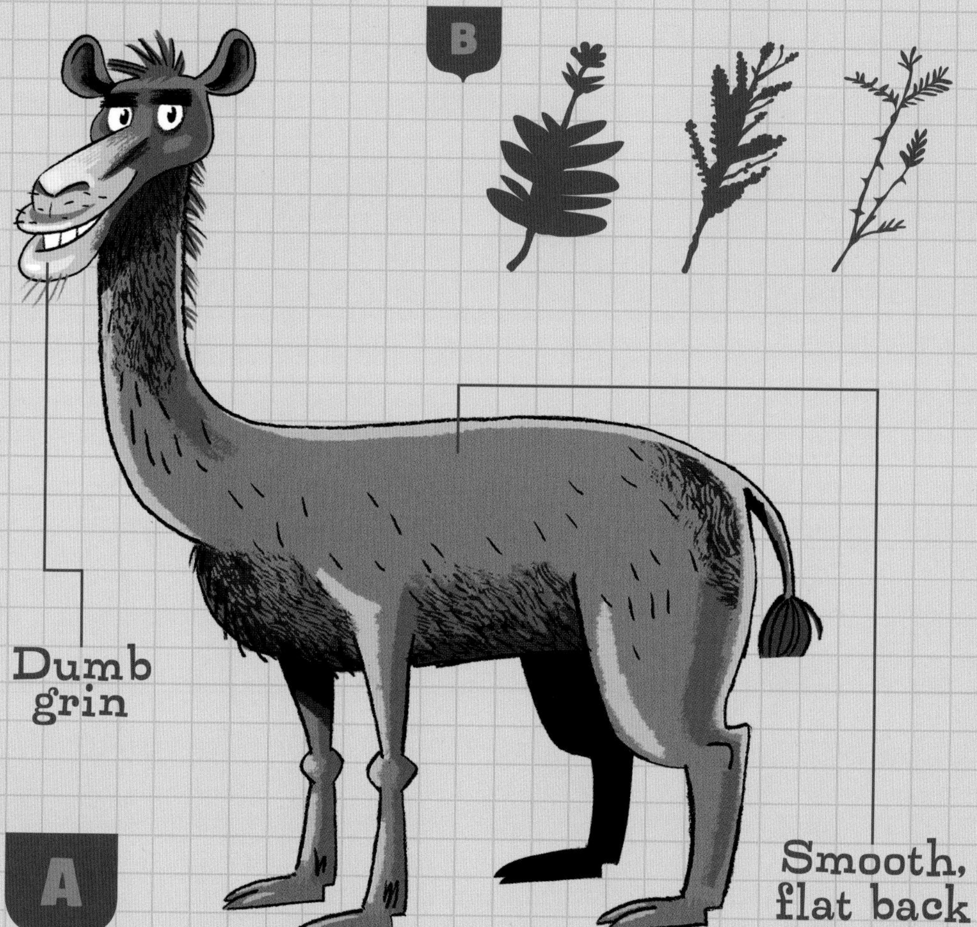
B
Dumb grin
A
Smooth, flat back

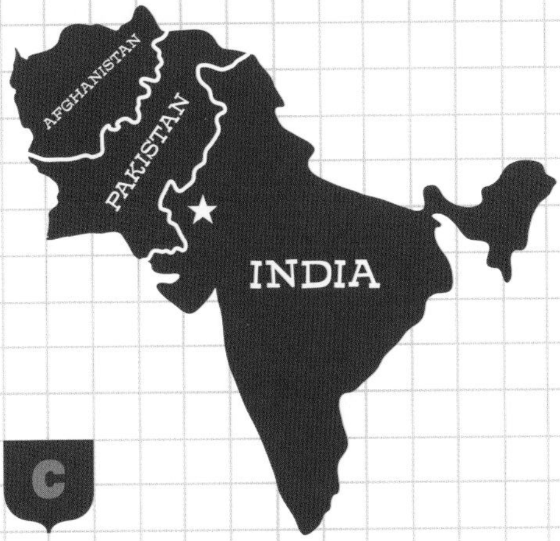
AFGHANISTAN
PAKISTAN
INDIA

C

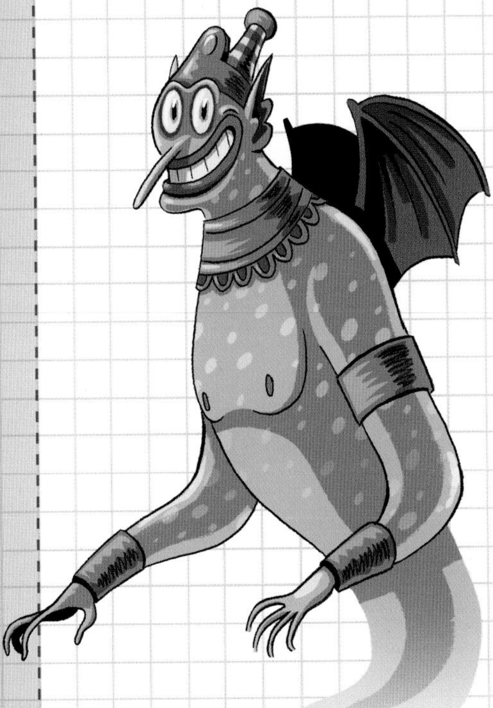

D

E

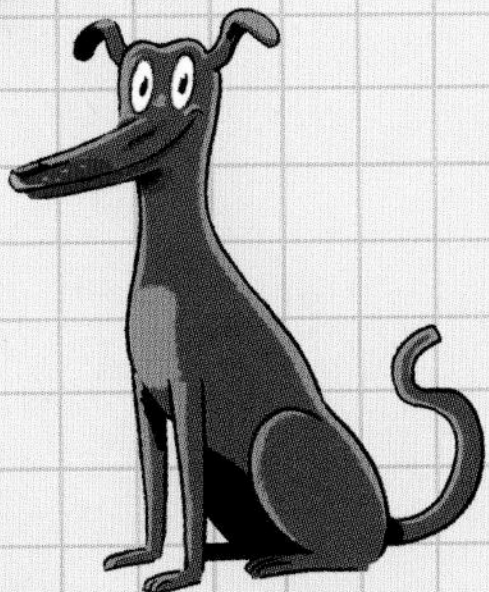

F

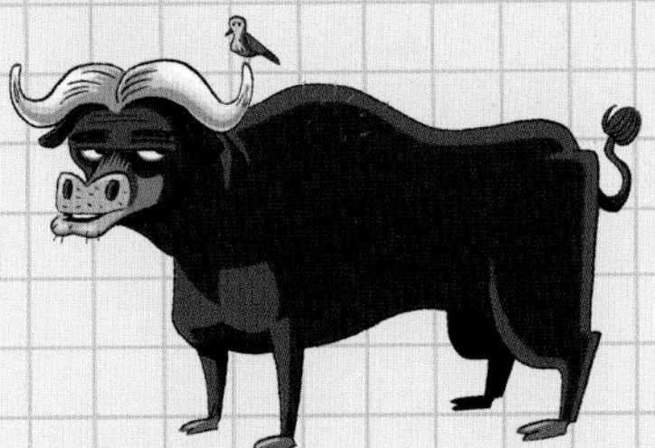

G

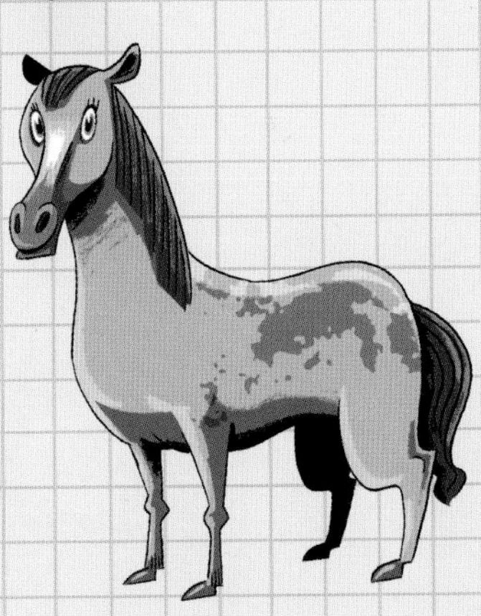

1

2

3

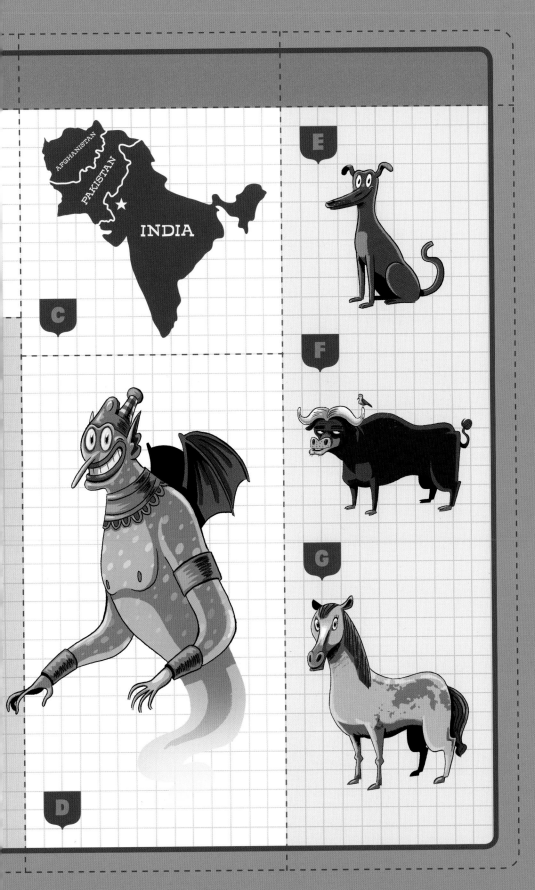

RUDYARD KIPLING

2

# KIPLING'S OBSERVATION

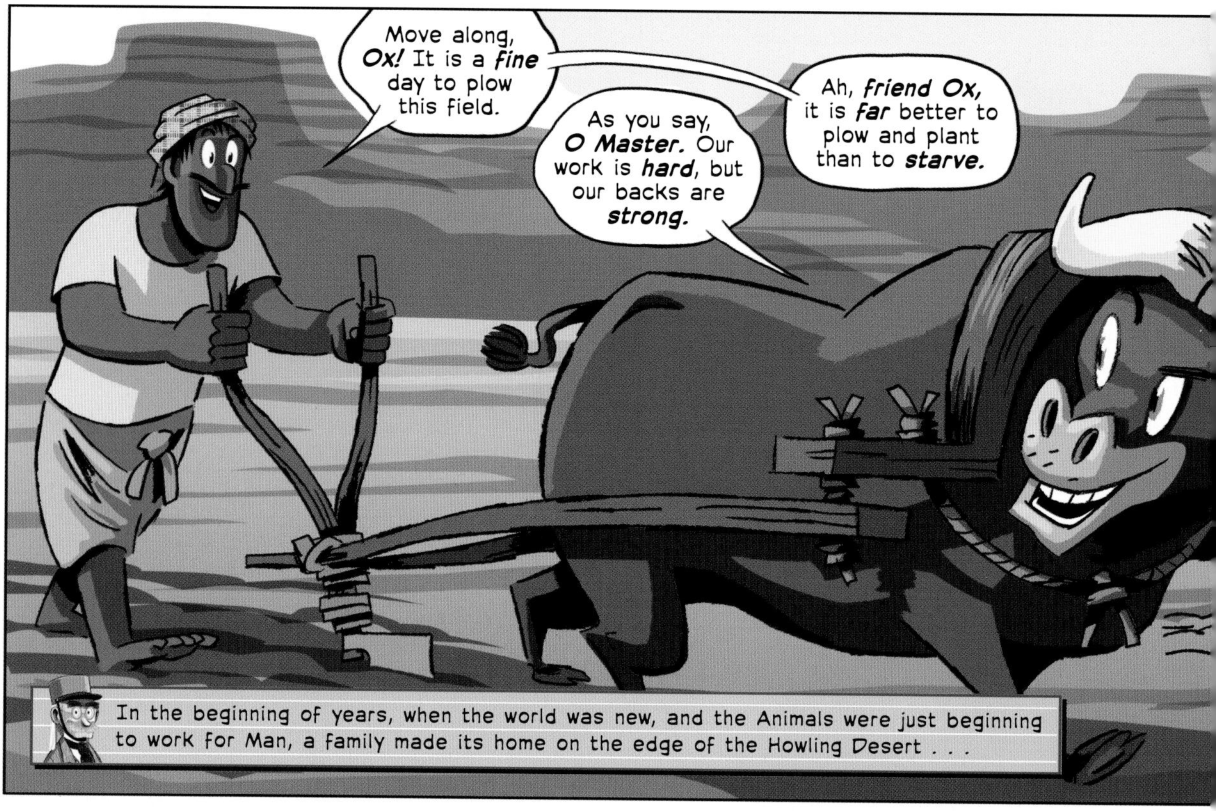
Move along, *Ox!* It is a *fine* day to plow this field.
As you say, ***O Master.*** Our work is ***hard***, but our backs are ***strong.***
Ah, ***friend Ox,*** it is ***far*** better to plow and plant than to ***starve.***
In the beginning of years, when the world was new, and the Animals were just beginning to work for Man, a family made its home on the edge of the Howling Desert . . .

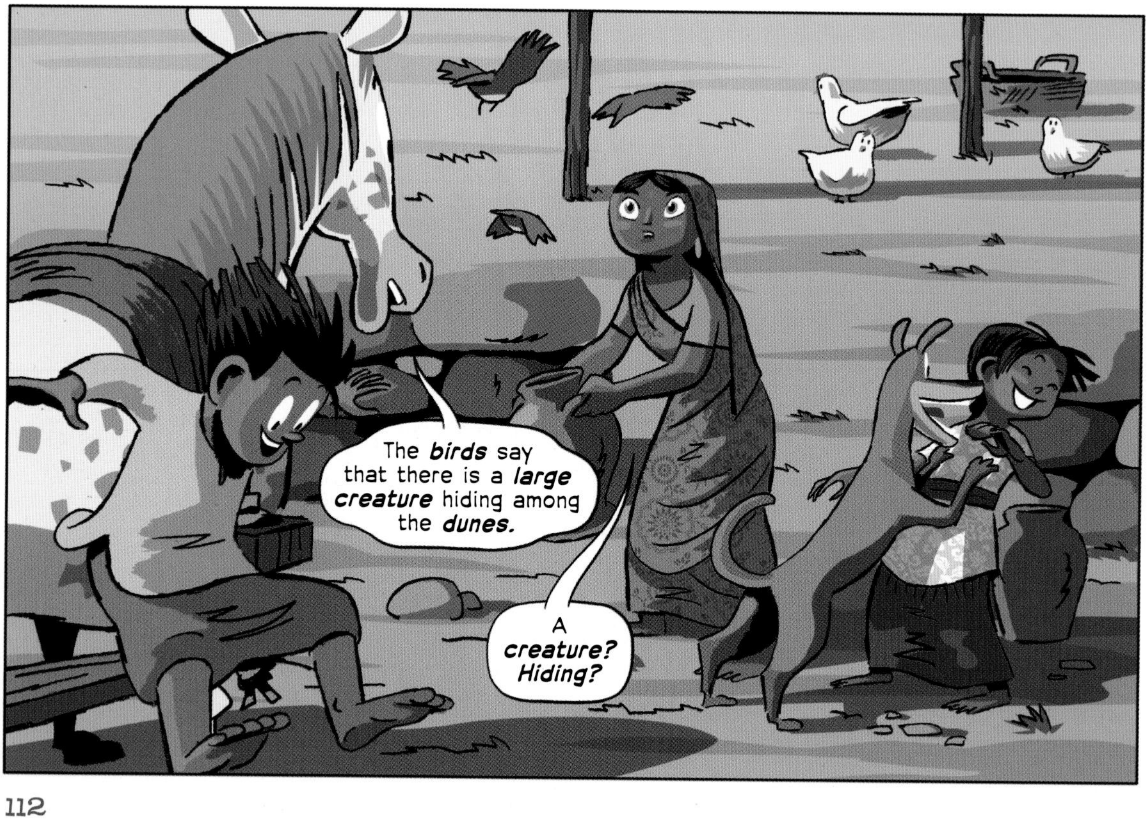
The ***birds*** say that there is a ***large creature*** hiding among the ***dunes.***
A ***creature? Hiding?***

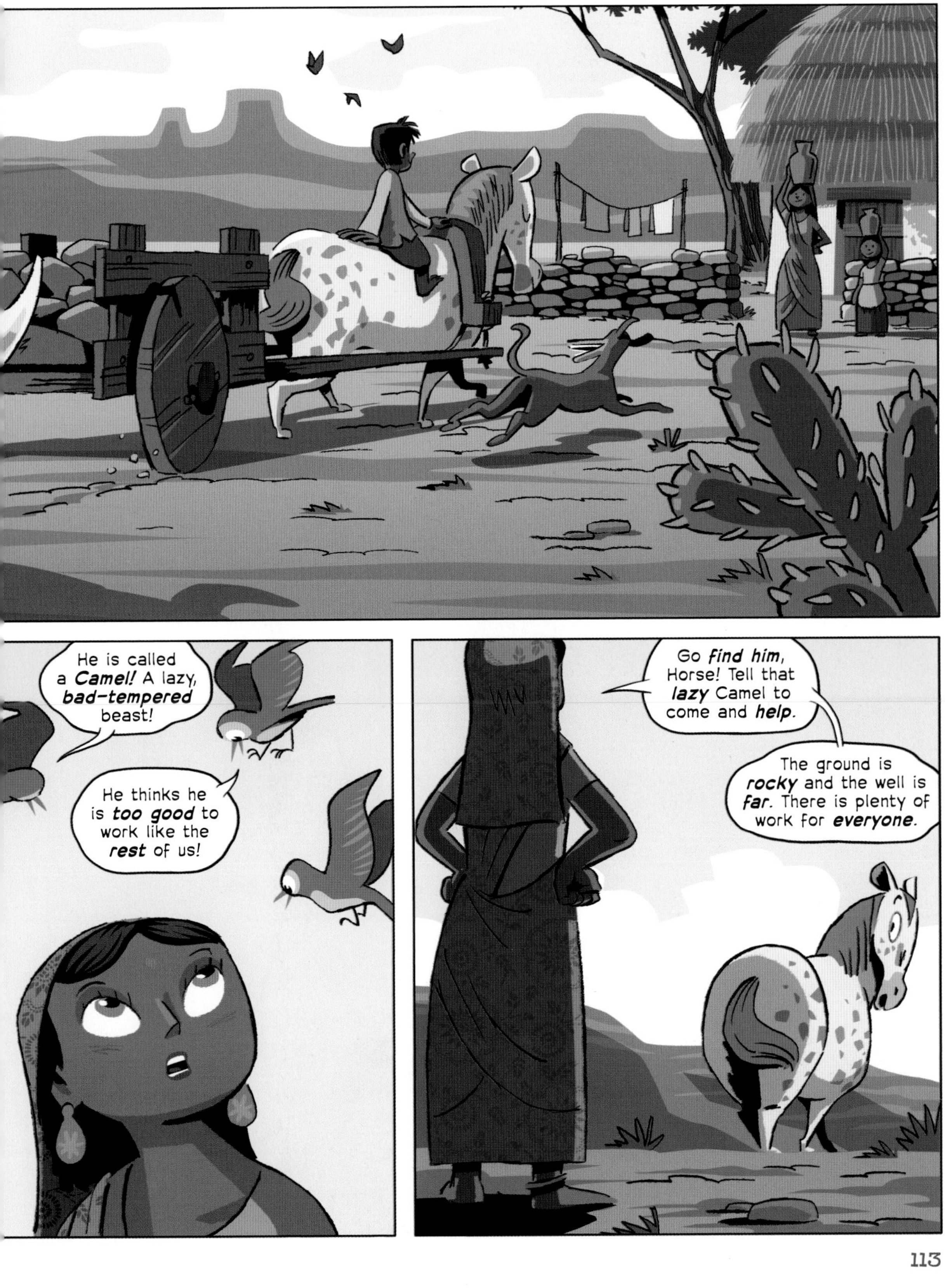
He is called a Camel! A lazy, bad-tempered beast!
He thinks he is too good to work like the rest of us!
Go find him, Horse! Tell that lazy Camel to come and help.
The ground is rocky and the well is far. There is plenty of work for everyone.

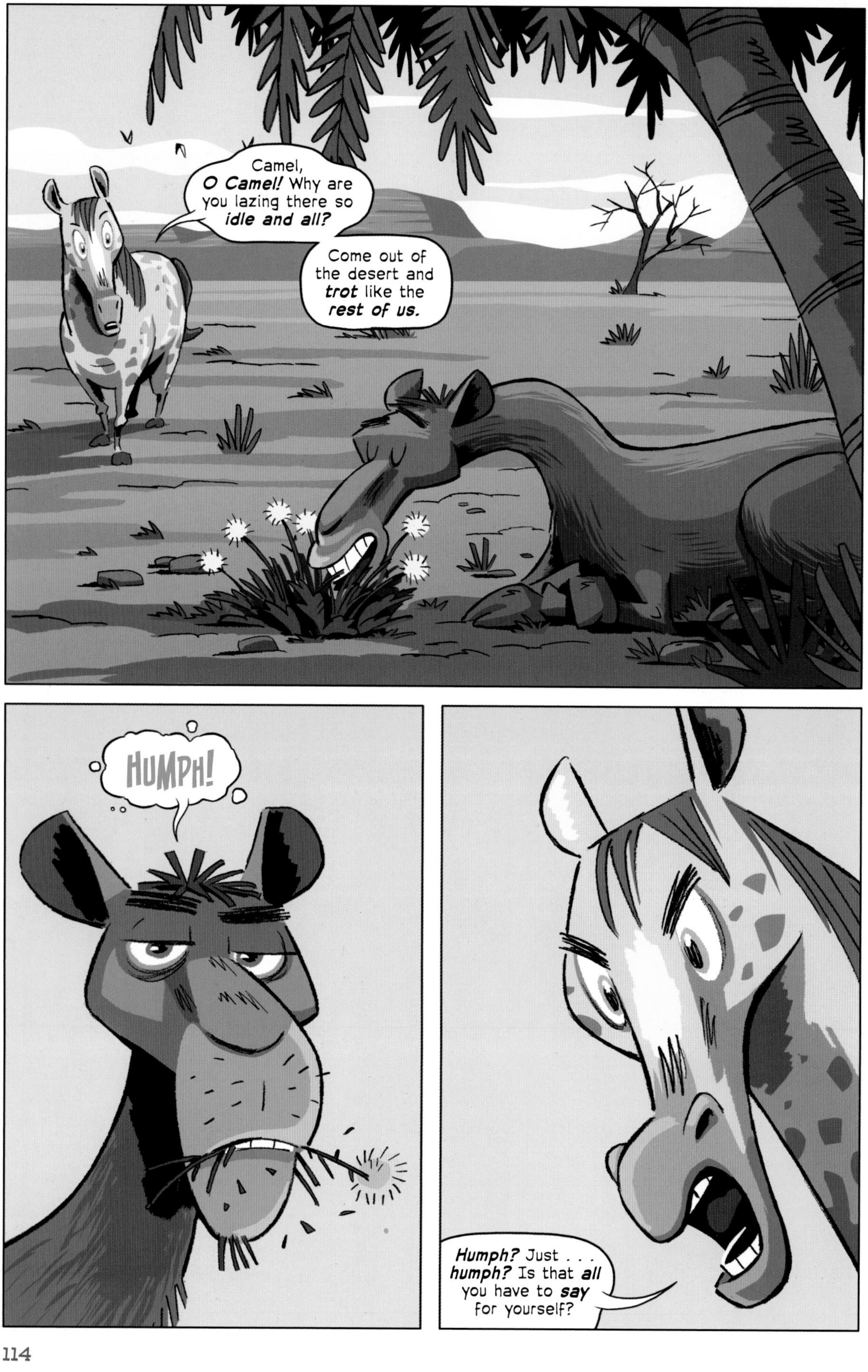
Camel, *O Camel!* Why are you lazing there so *idle and all?*
Come out of the desert and *trot* like the *rest of us.*
HUMPH!
*Humph?* Just . . . *humph?* Is that *all* you have to *say* for yourself?

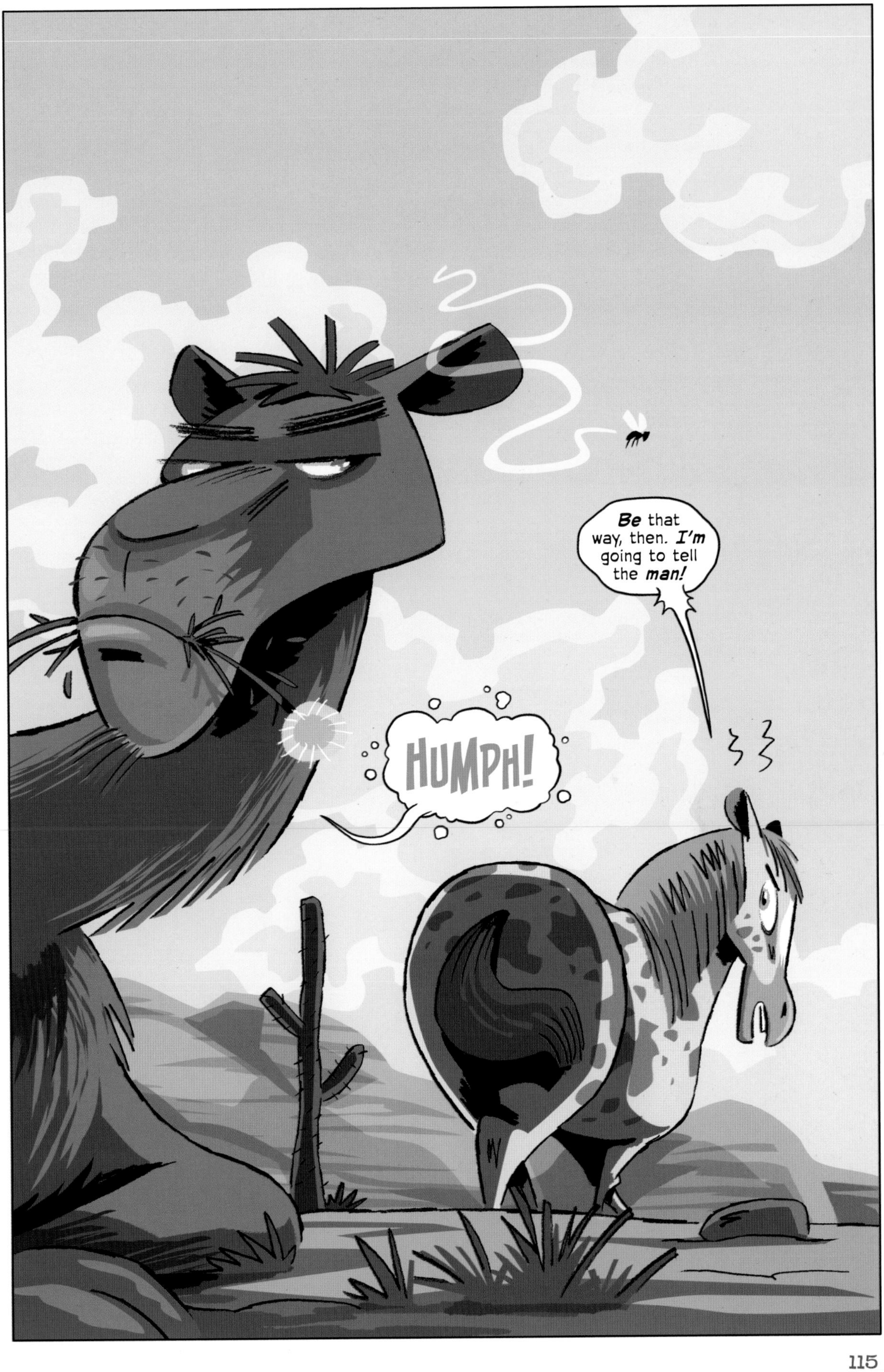
HUMPH!
Be that way, then. I'm going to tell the man!

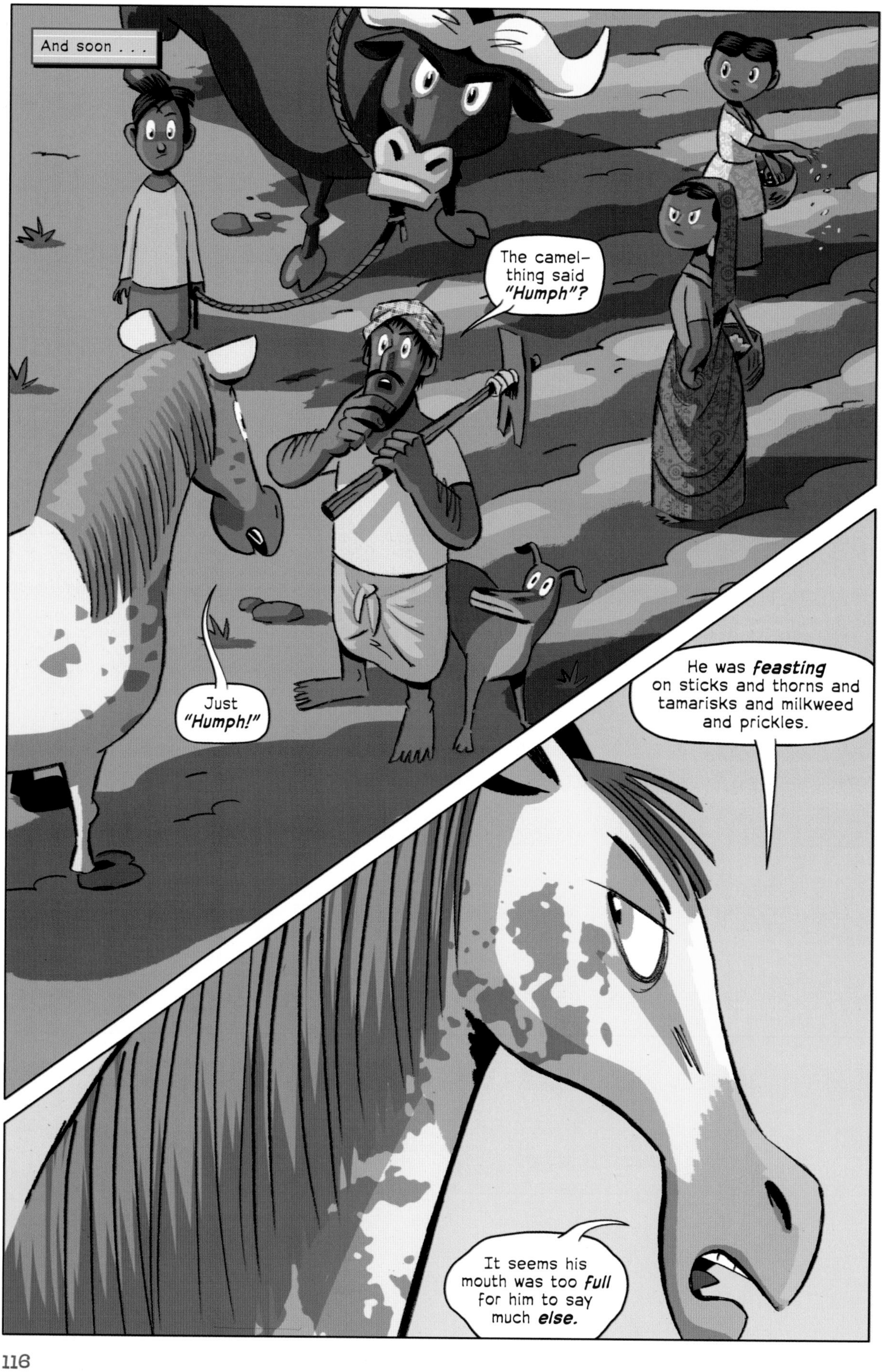
And soon . . .
The camel-thing said *"Humph"*?
Just *"Humph!"*
He was ***feasting*** on sticks and thorns and tamarisks and milkweed and prickles.
It seems his mouth was too *full* for him to say much ***else.***

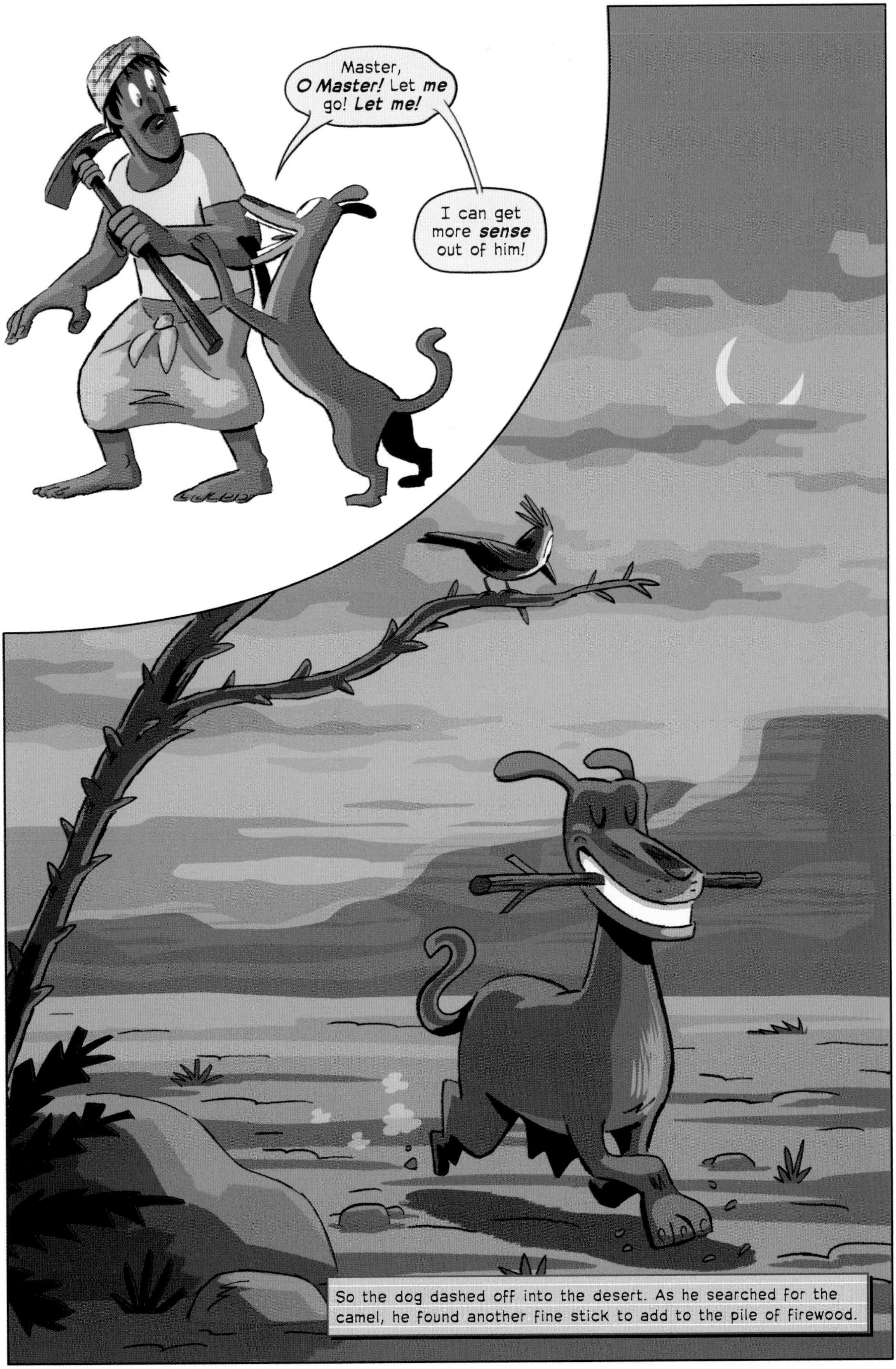

Master, O Master! Let me go! Let me!
I can get more sense out of him!
So the dog dashed off into the desert. As he searched for the camel, he found another fine stick to add to the pile of firewood.

Finally, he found the camel beside a small oasis.

Wake up, O Camel!

DOINK

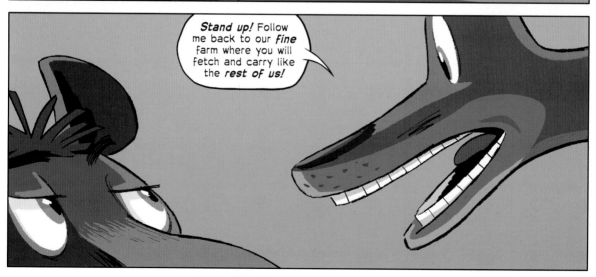

*Stand up!* Follow me back to our *fine* farm where you will fetch and carry like the *rest of us!*

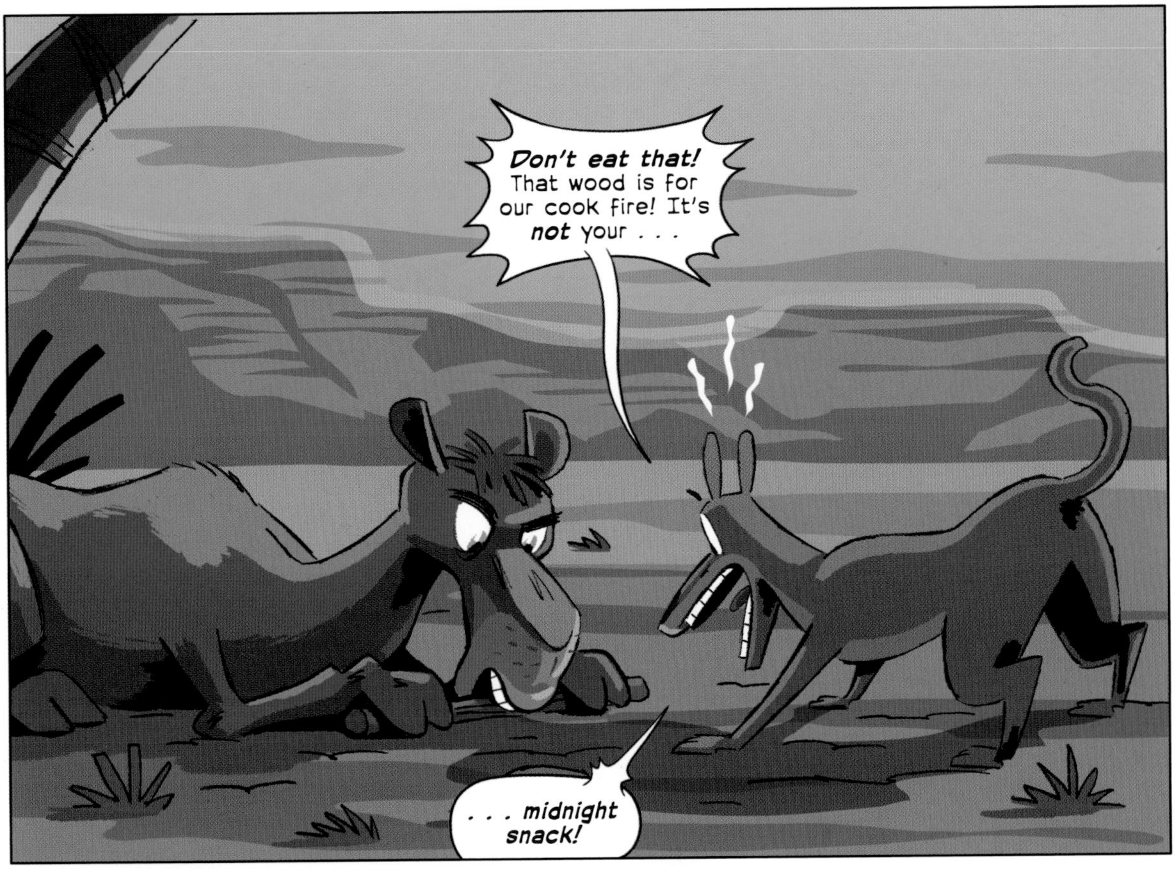
Don't eat that! That wood is for our cook fire! It's not your . . .
. . . midnight snack!

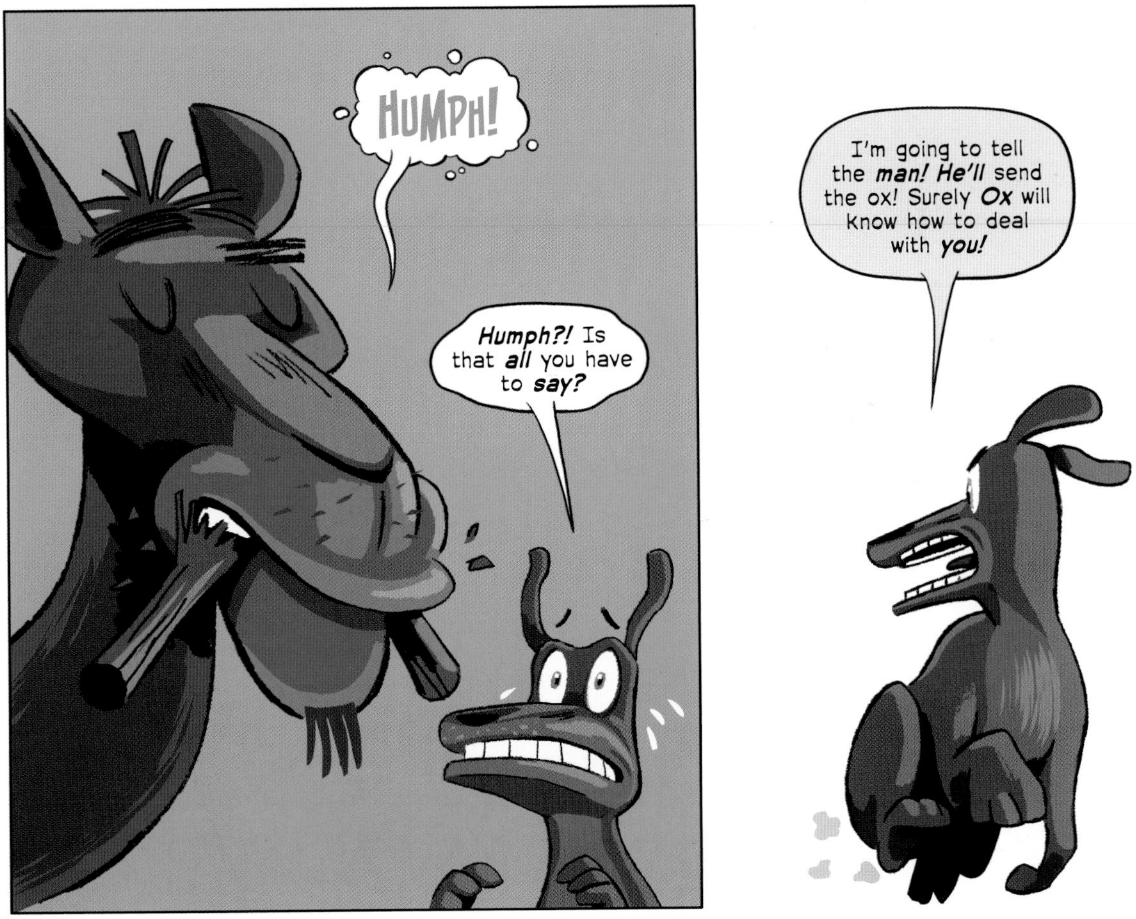
HUMPH!
Humph?! Is that all you have to say?
I'm going to tell the man! He'll send the ox! Surely Ox will know how to deal with you!

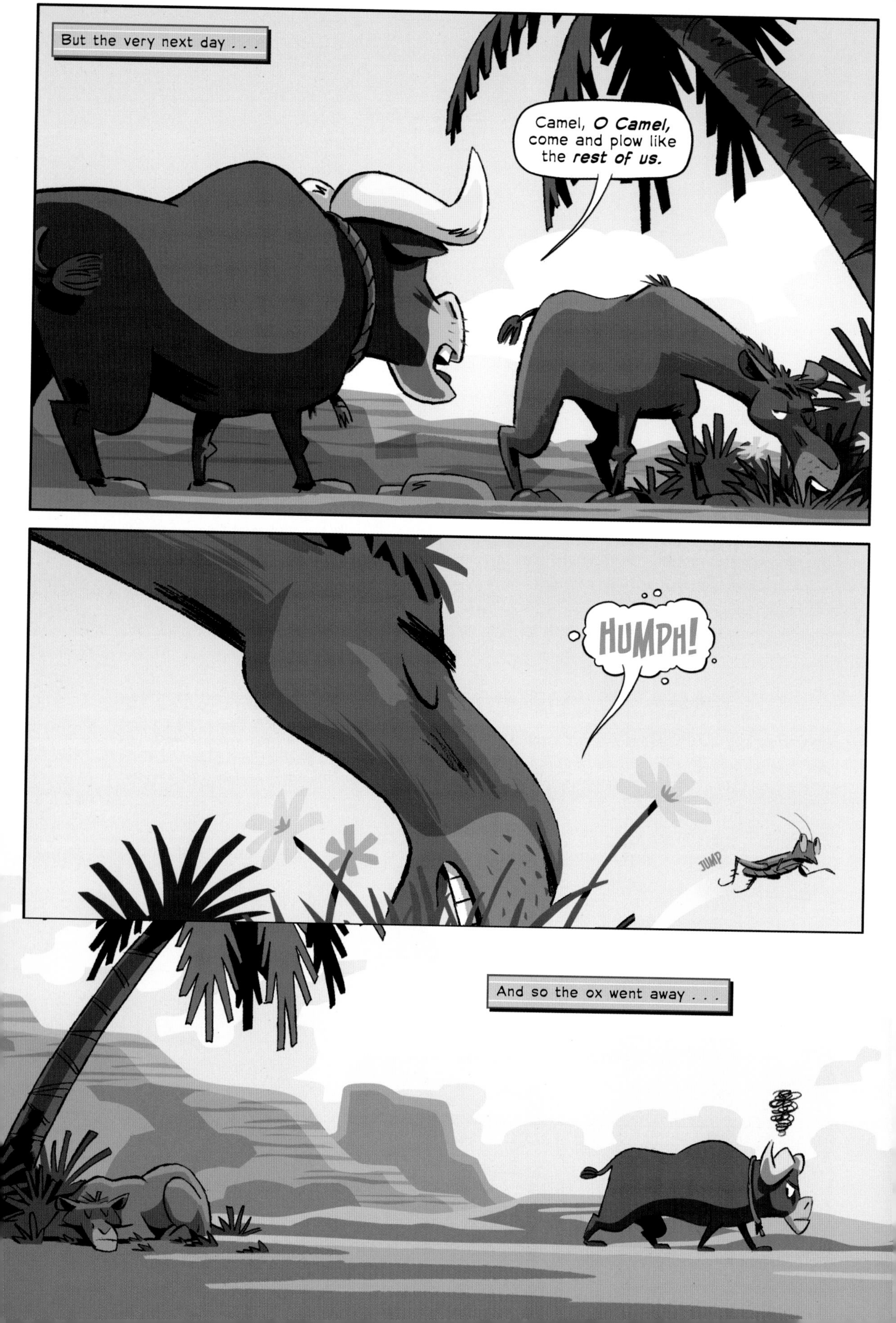

But the very next day . . .
Camel, O Camel, come and plow like the rest of us.
HUMPH!
JUMP
And so the ox went away . . .

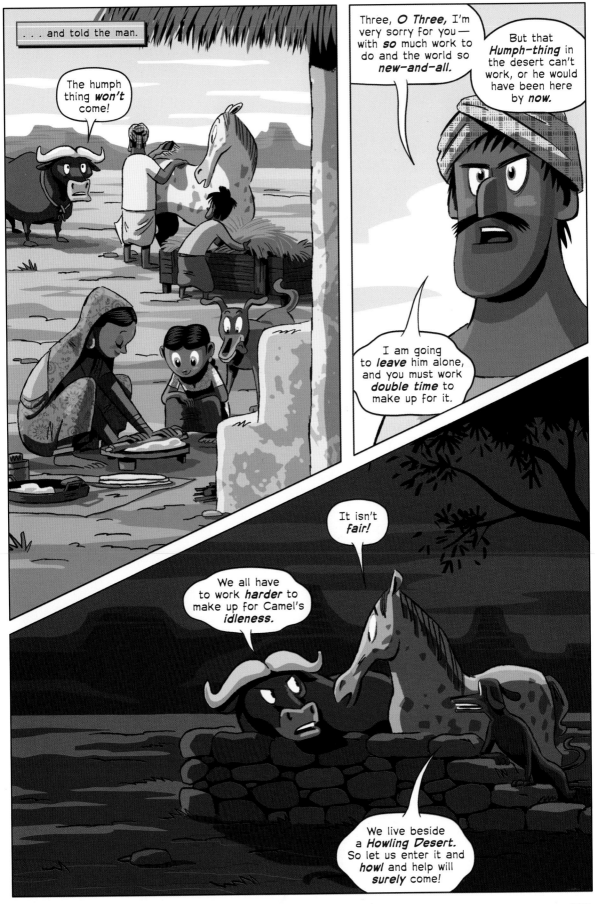

... and told the man.

The humph thing *won't* come!

Three, *O Three,* I'm very sorry for you—with *so* much work to do and the world so *new-and-all.*

But that *Humph-thing* in the desert can't work, or he would have been here by *now.*

I am going to *leave* him alone, and you must work *double time* to make up for it.

It isn't *fair!*

We all have to work *harder* to make up for Camel's *idleness.*

We live beside a *Howling Desert.* So let us enter it and *howl* and help will *surely* come!

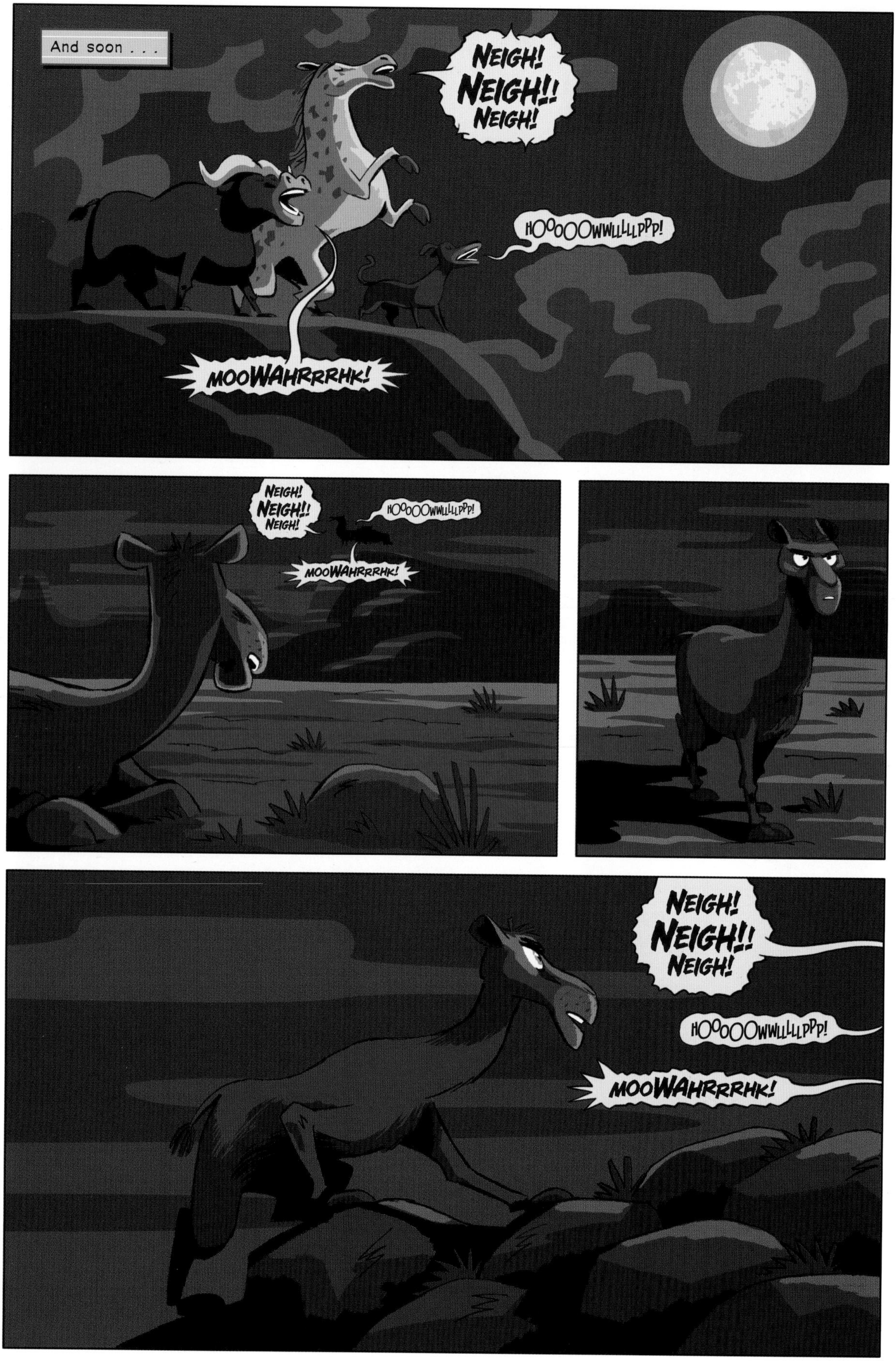

And soon . . .
NEIGH! NEIGH!! NEIGH!
HOOOOOWWLLLLPPP!
MOOWAHRRRHK!
NEIGH! NEIGH!! NEIGH!
HOOOOOWWLLLLPPP!
MOOWAHRRRHK!
NEIGH! NEIGH!! NEIGH!
HOOOOOWWLLLLPPP!
MOOWAHRRRHK!

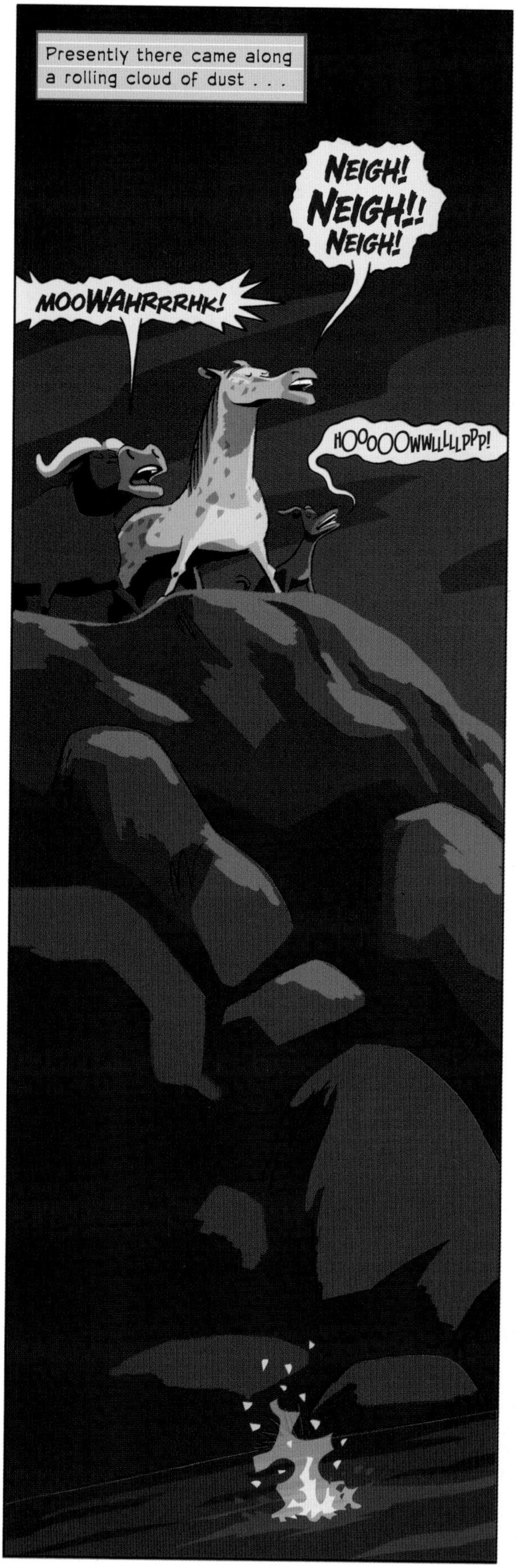
Presently there came along a rolling cloud of dust . . .
NEIGH! NEIGH!! NEIGH!
MOOWAHRRRHK!
HOOOOOWWLLLLPPP!

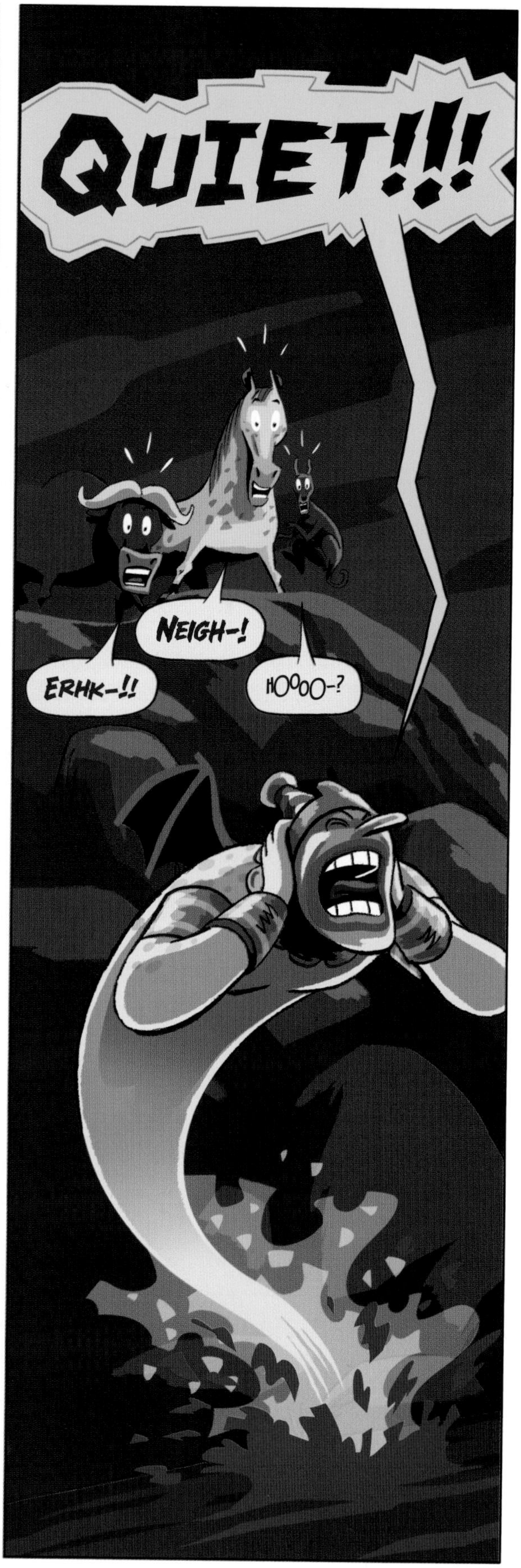
QUIET!!!
NEIGH-!
ERHK-!!
HOOOO-?

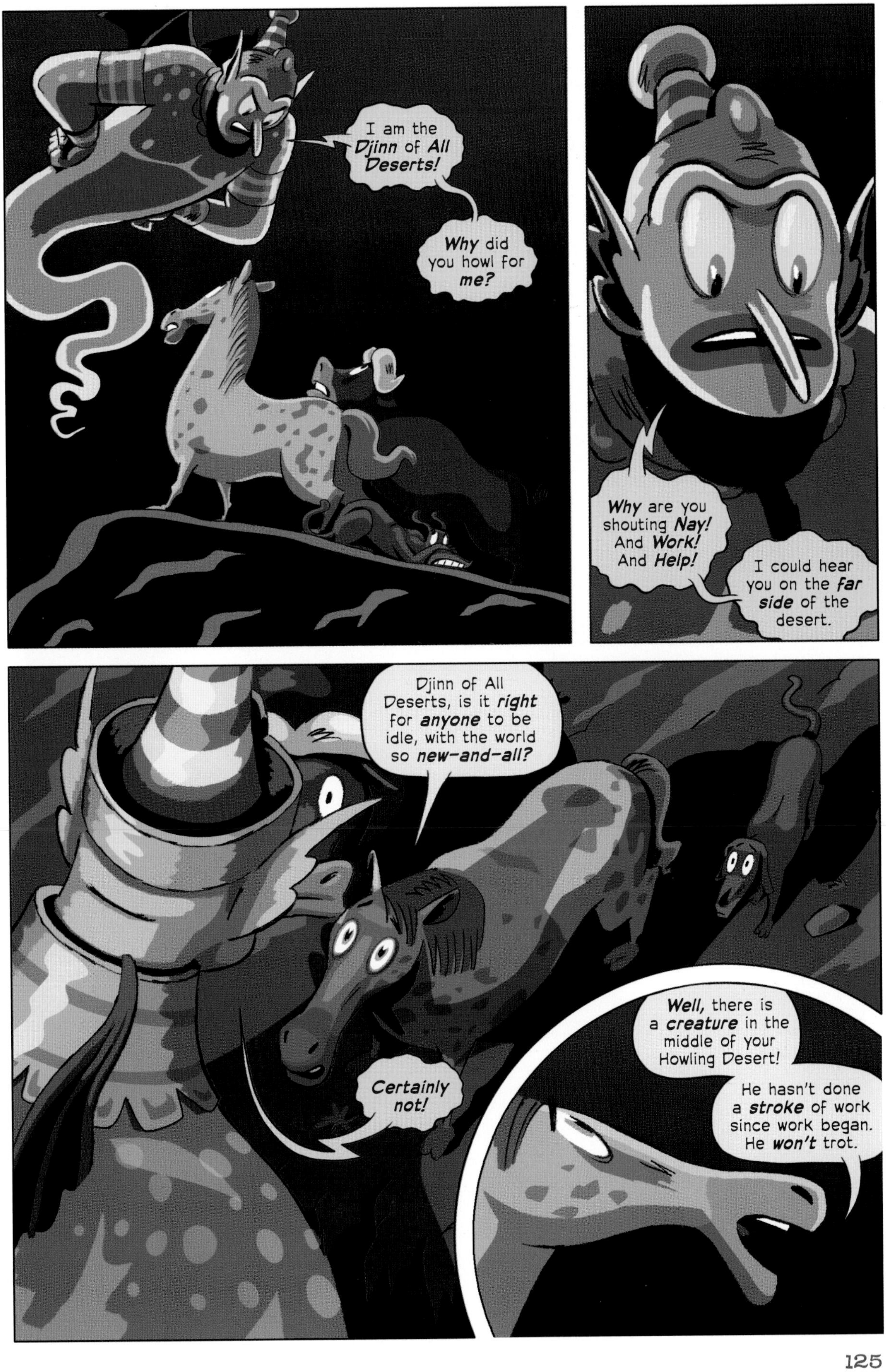

I am the *Djinn* of *All Deserts!*
*Why* did you howl for *me?*
*Why* are you shouting *Nay!* And *Work!* And *Help!*
I could hear you on the *far side* of the desert.
Djinn of All Deserts, is it *right* for *anyone* to be idle, with the world so *new-and-all?*
*Certainly not!*
*Well,* there is a *creature* in the middle of your Howling Desert!
He hasn't done a *stroke* of work since work began. He *won't* trot.

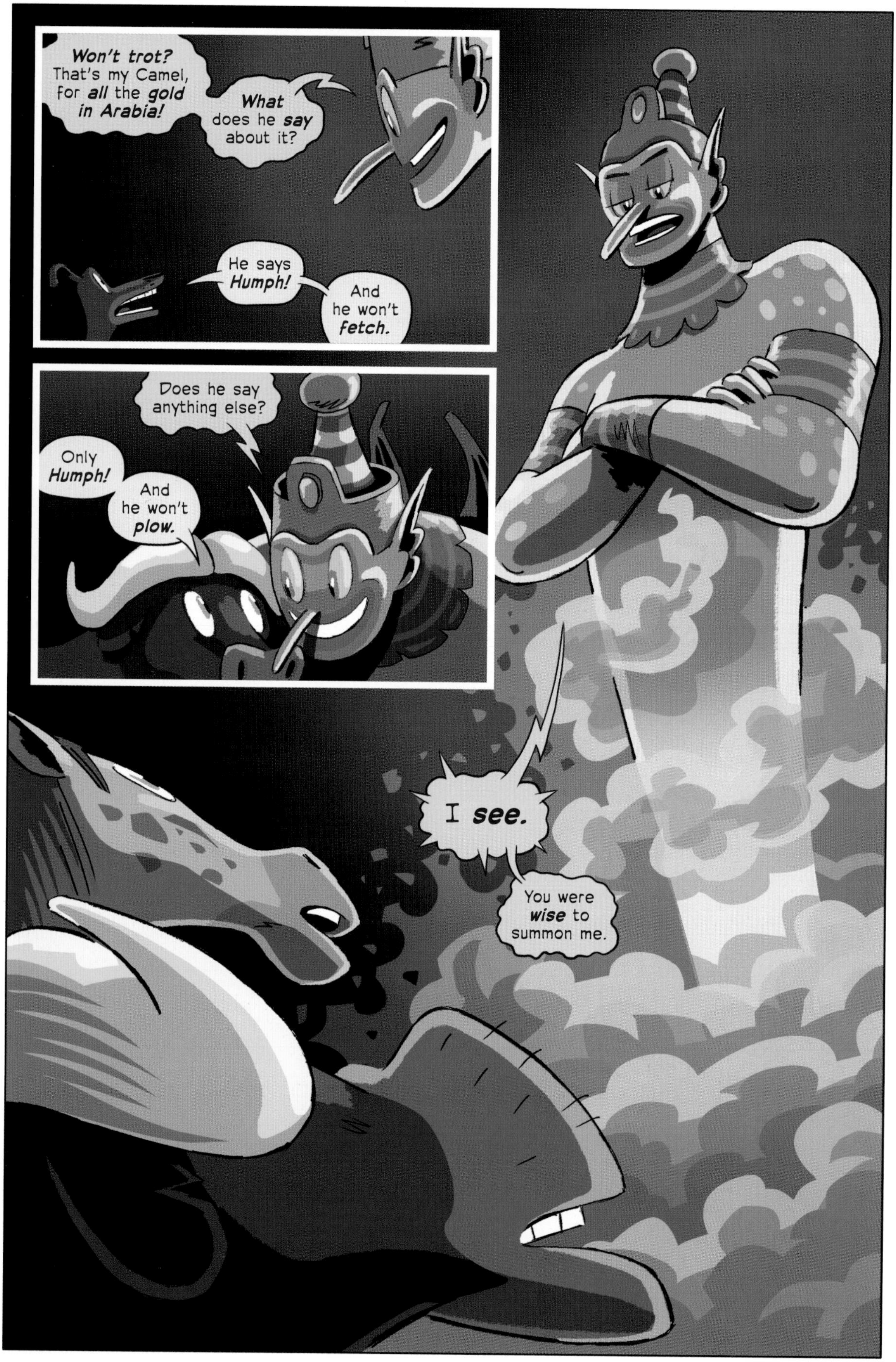

Won't trot? That's my Camel, for all the gold in Arabia!
What does he say about it?
He says Humph!
And he won't fetch.
Does he say anything else?
Only Humph!
And he won't plow.
I see.
You were wise to summon me.

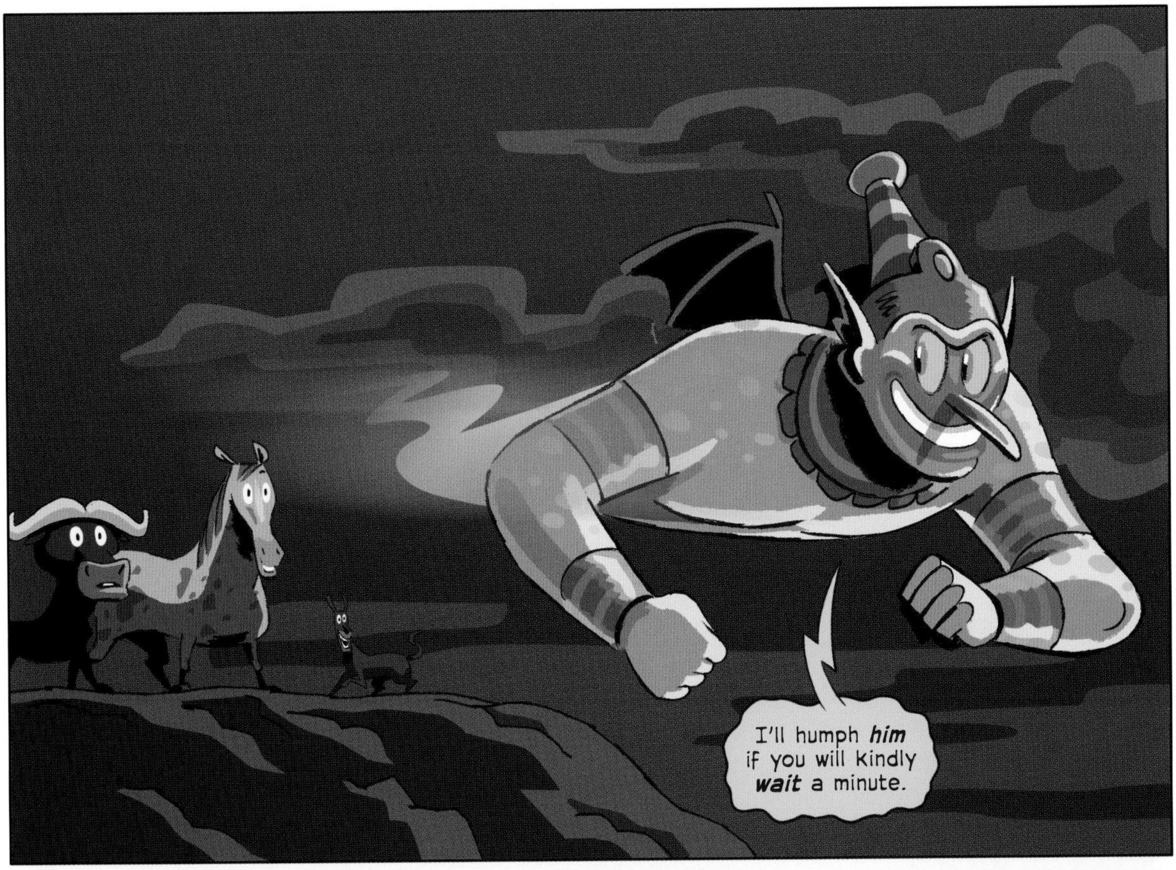
I'll humph *him* if you will kindly *wait* a minute.

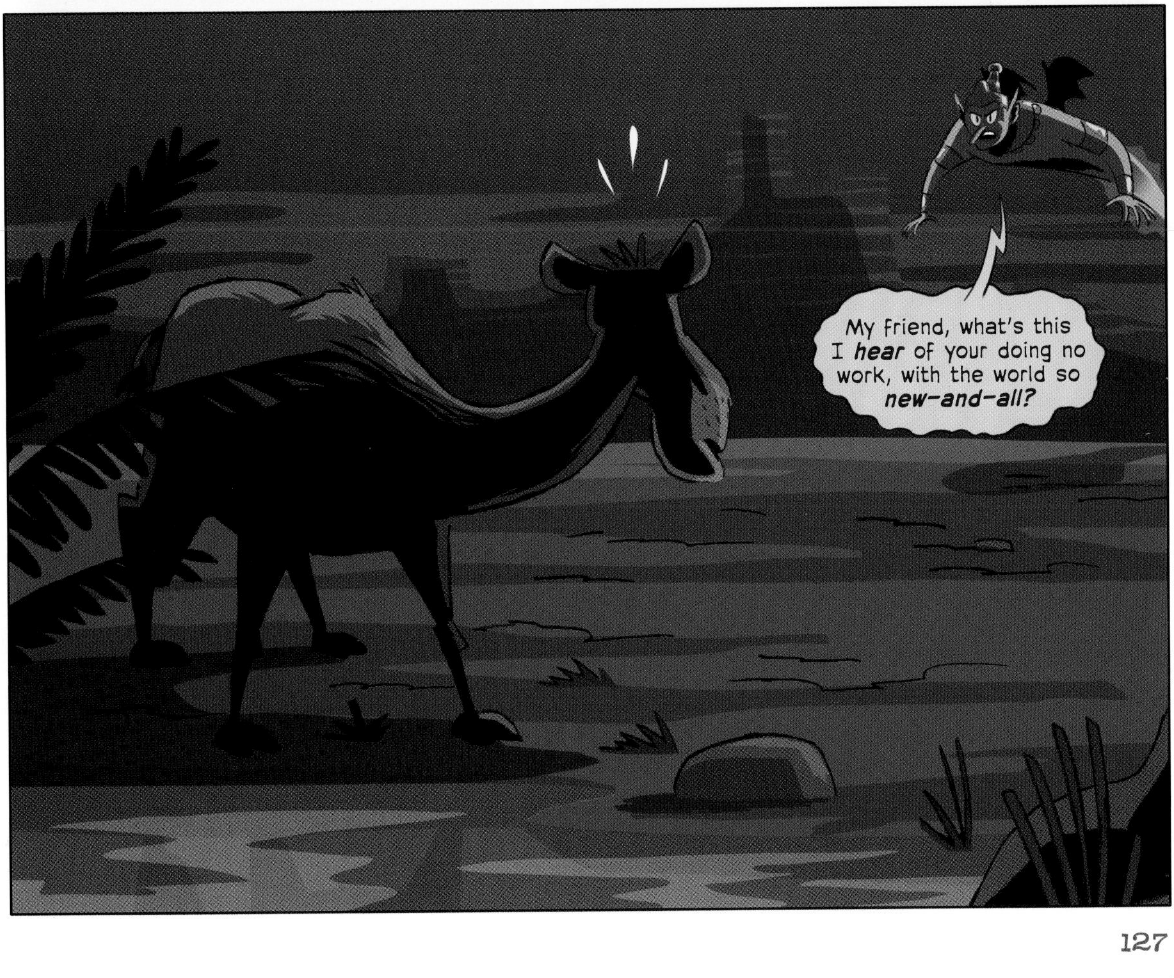
My friend, what's this I *hear* of your doing no work, with the world so *new-and-all?*

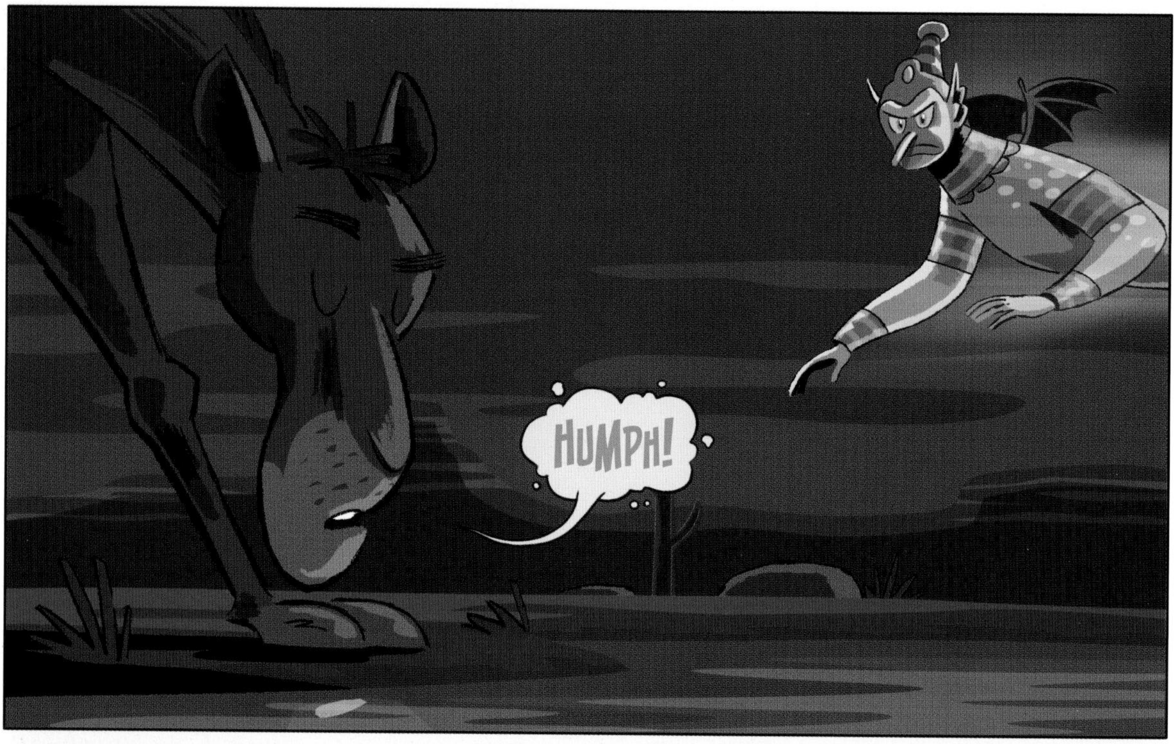
HUMPH!

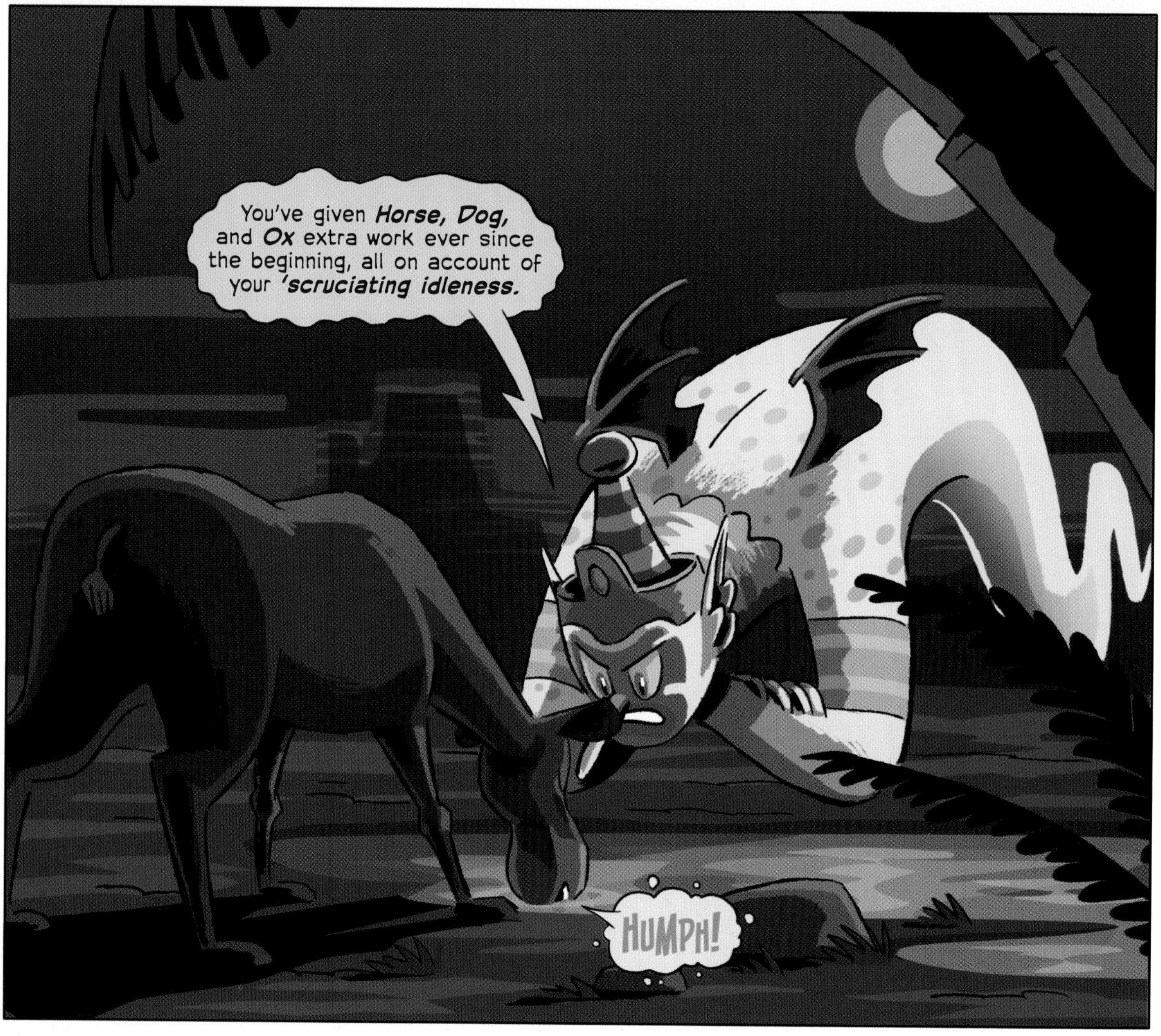
You've given Horse, Dog, and Ox extra work ever since the beginning, all on account of your 'scruciating idleness.
HUMPH!

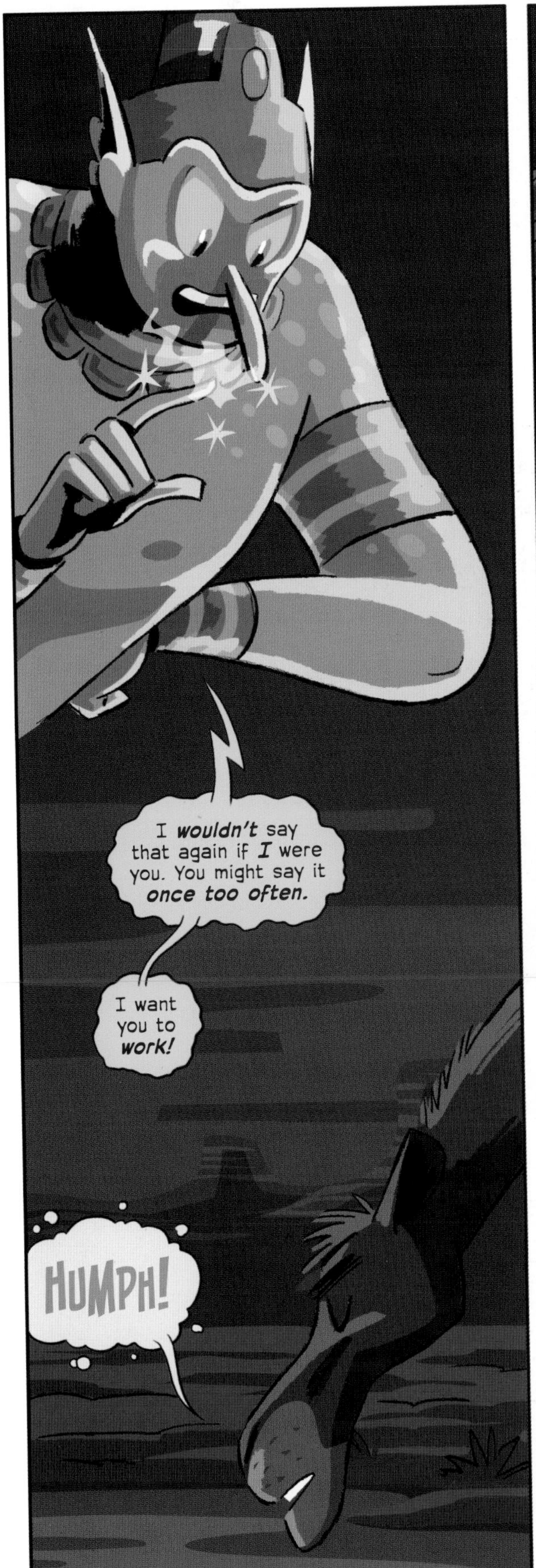
I *wouldn't* say that again if *I* were you. You might say it *once too often.*
I want you to *work!*
HUMPH!
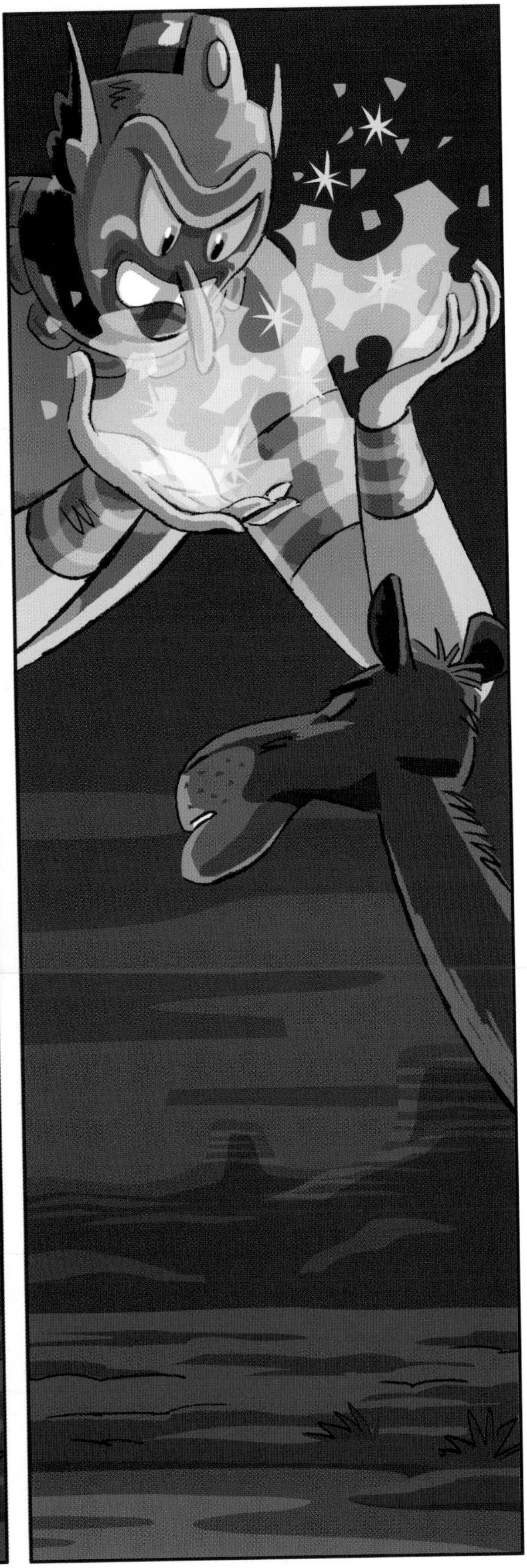

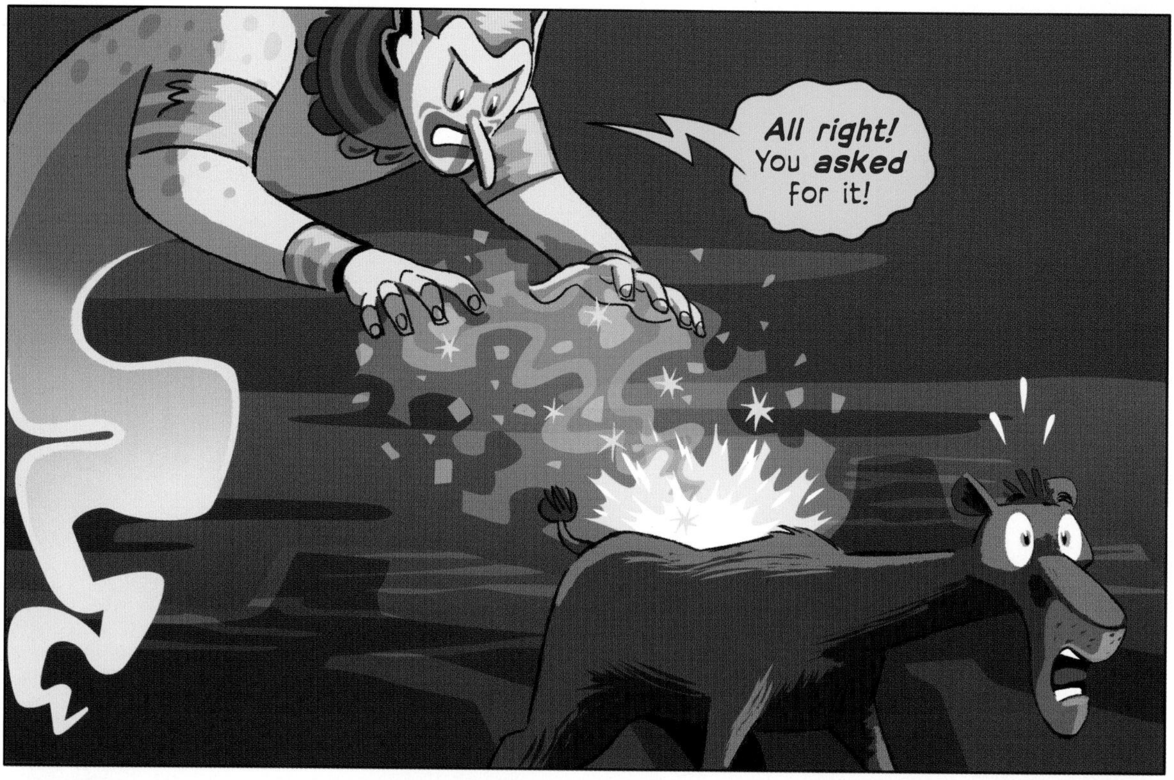
All right! You asked for it!

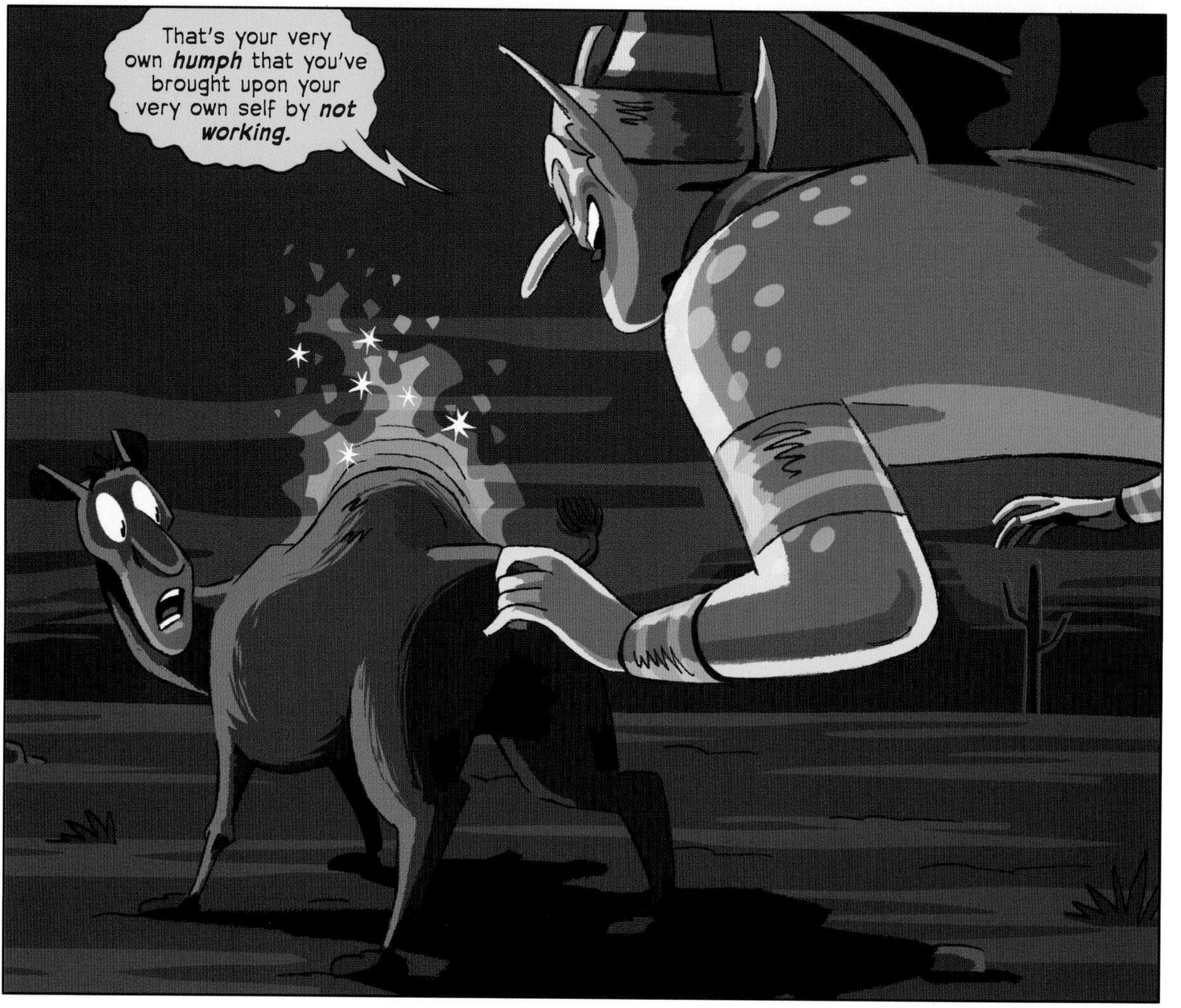
That's your very own humph that you've brought upon your very own self by not working.

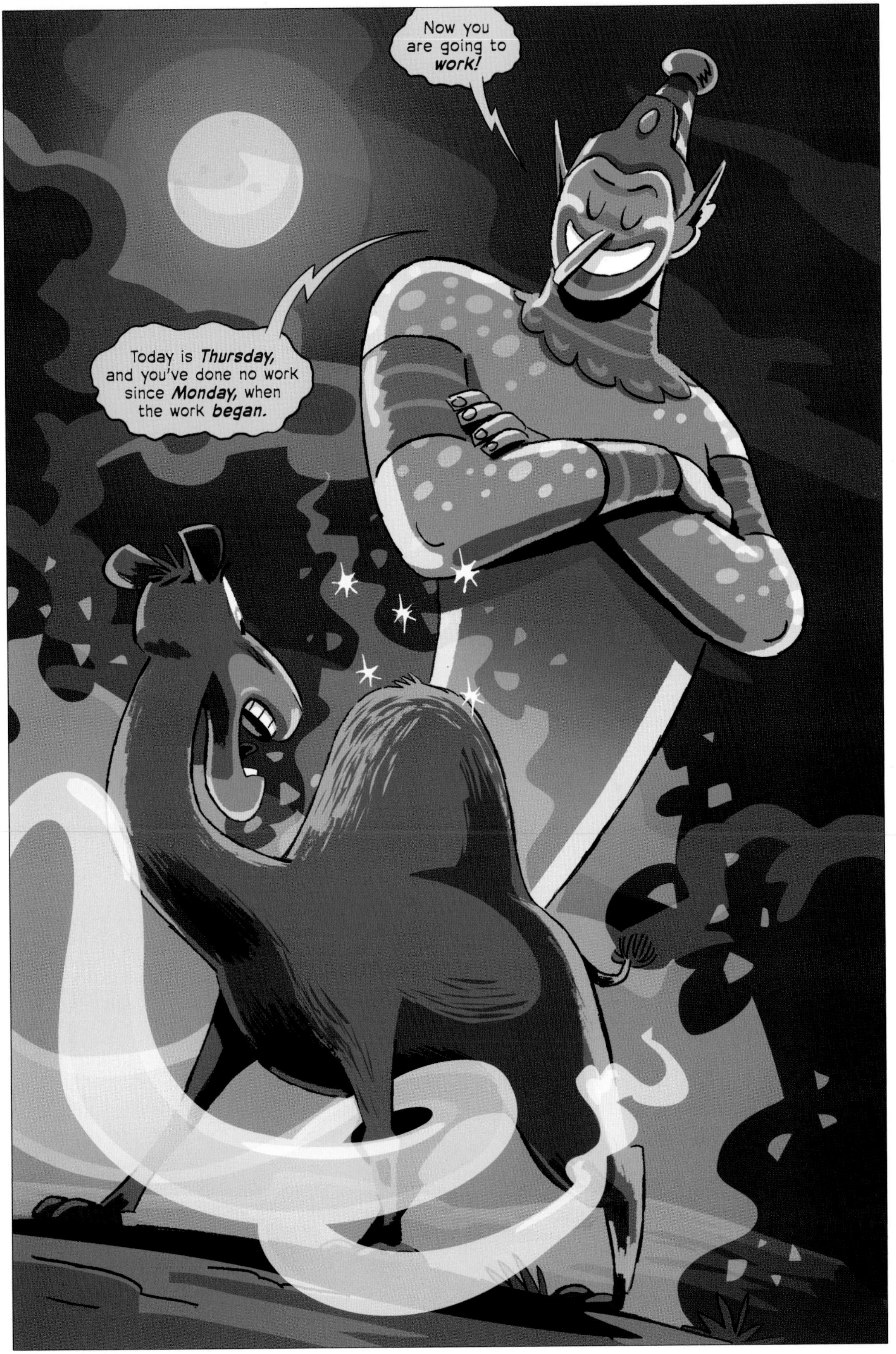
Now you are going to work!
Today is Thursday, and you've done no work since Monday, when the work began.

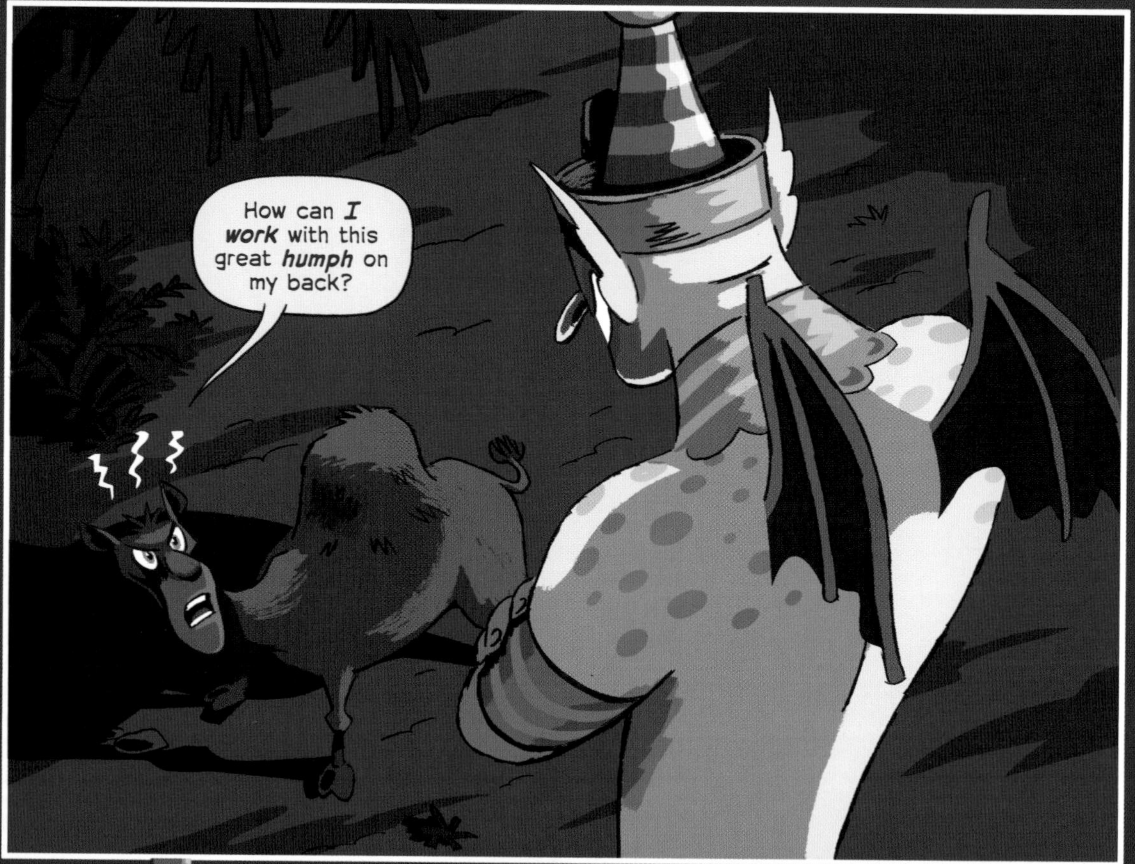
How can *I* *work* with this great *humph* on my back?

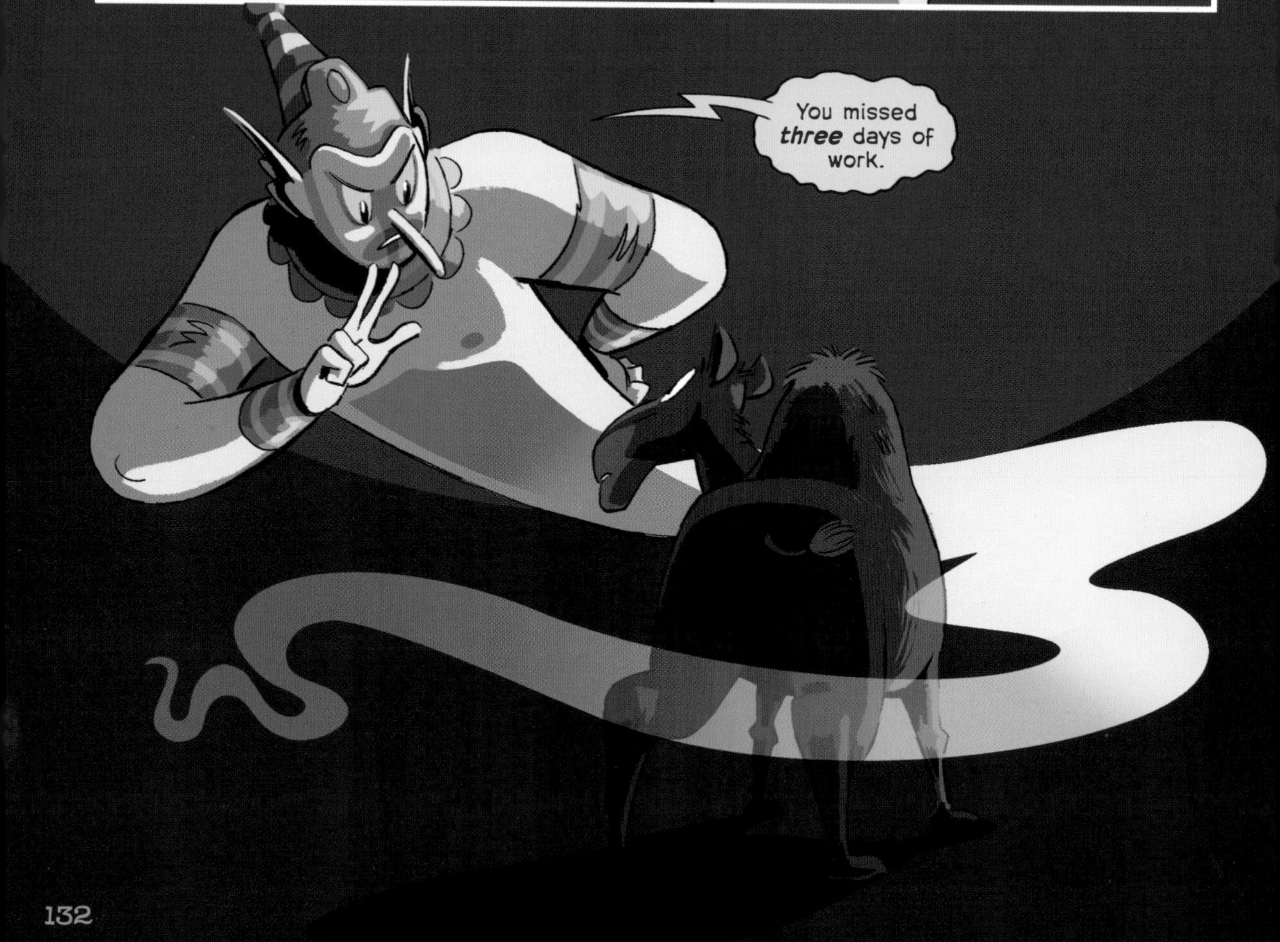
You missed *three* days of work.

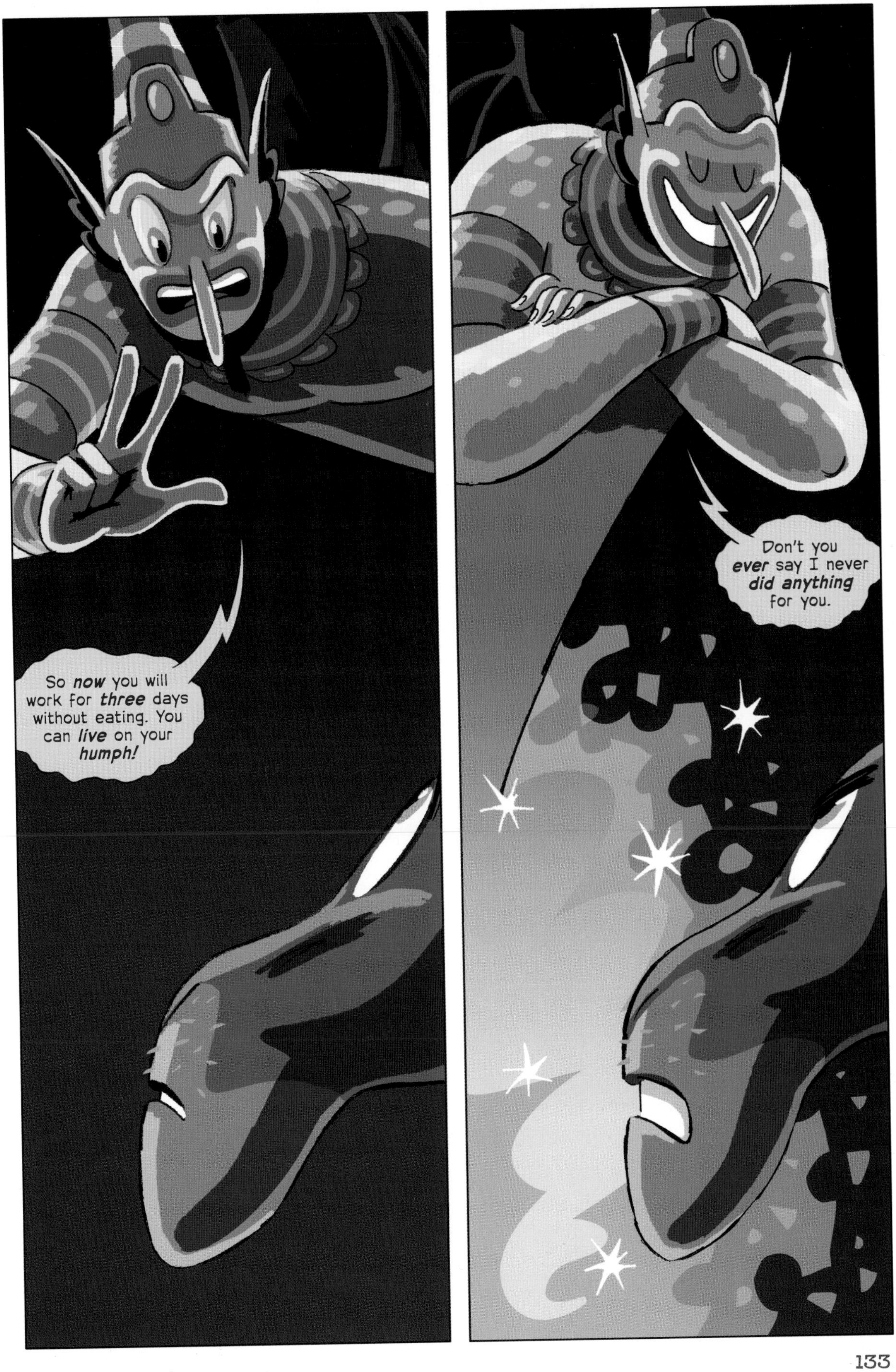
So *now* you will work for *three* days without eating. You can *live* on your *humph!*
Don't you *ever* say I never *did anything* for you.

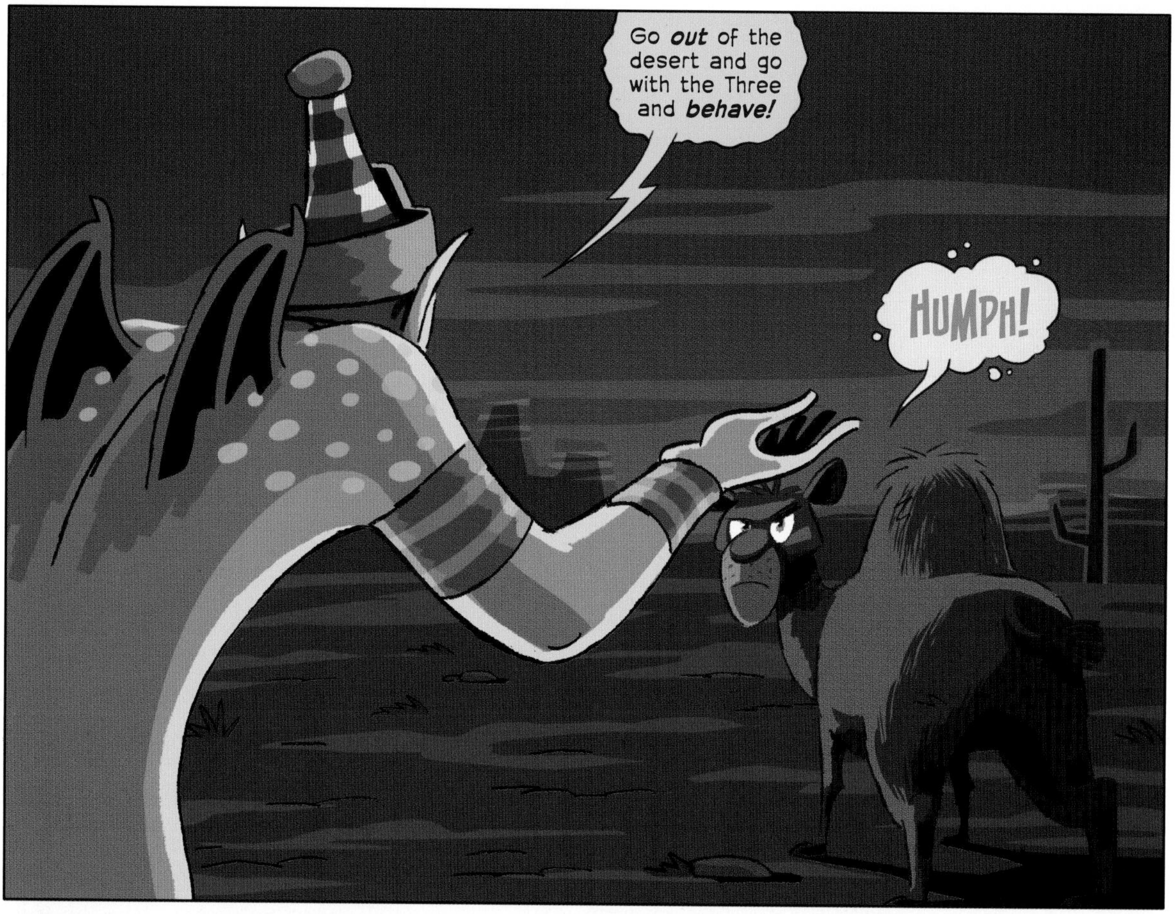
Go *out* of the desert and go with the Three and *behave!*
HUMPH!

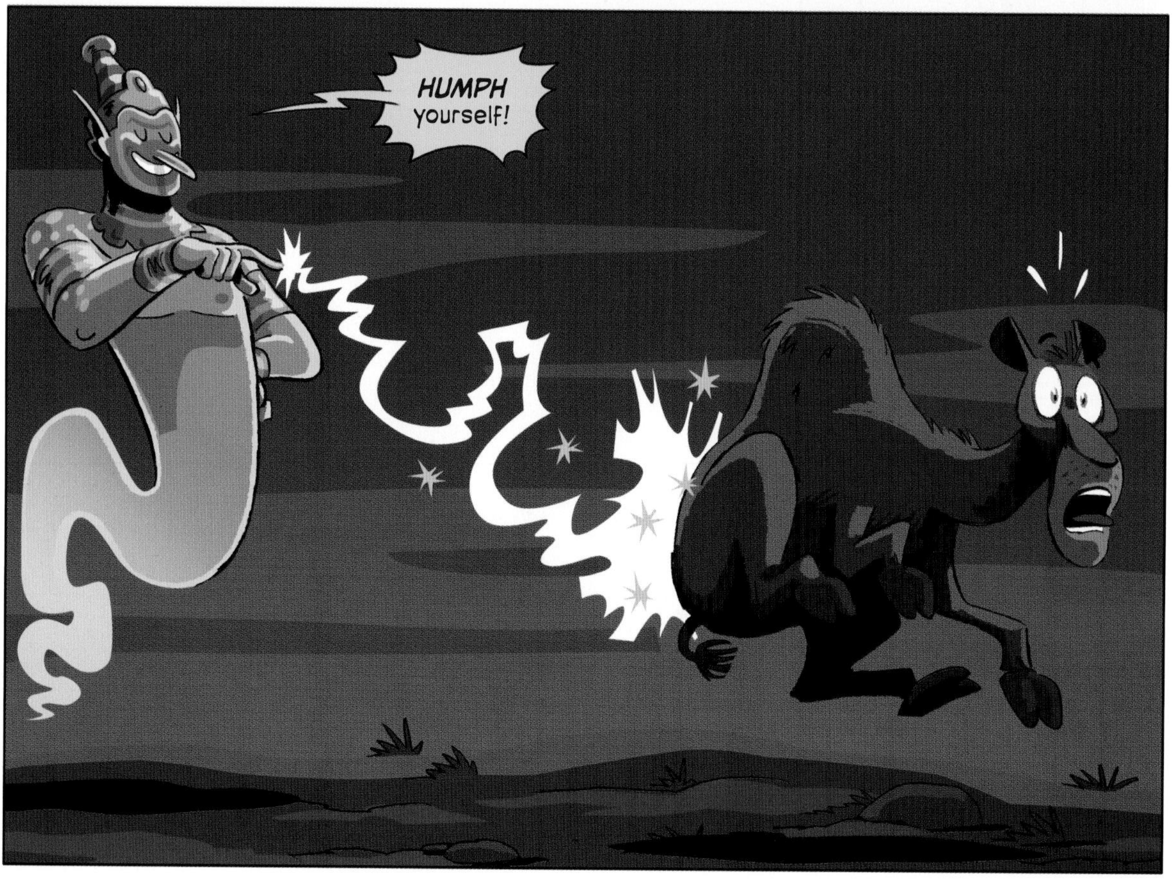
*HUMPH* yourself!

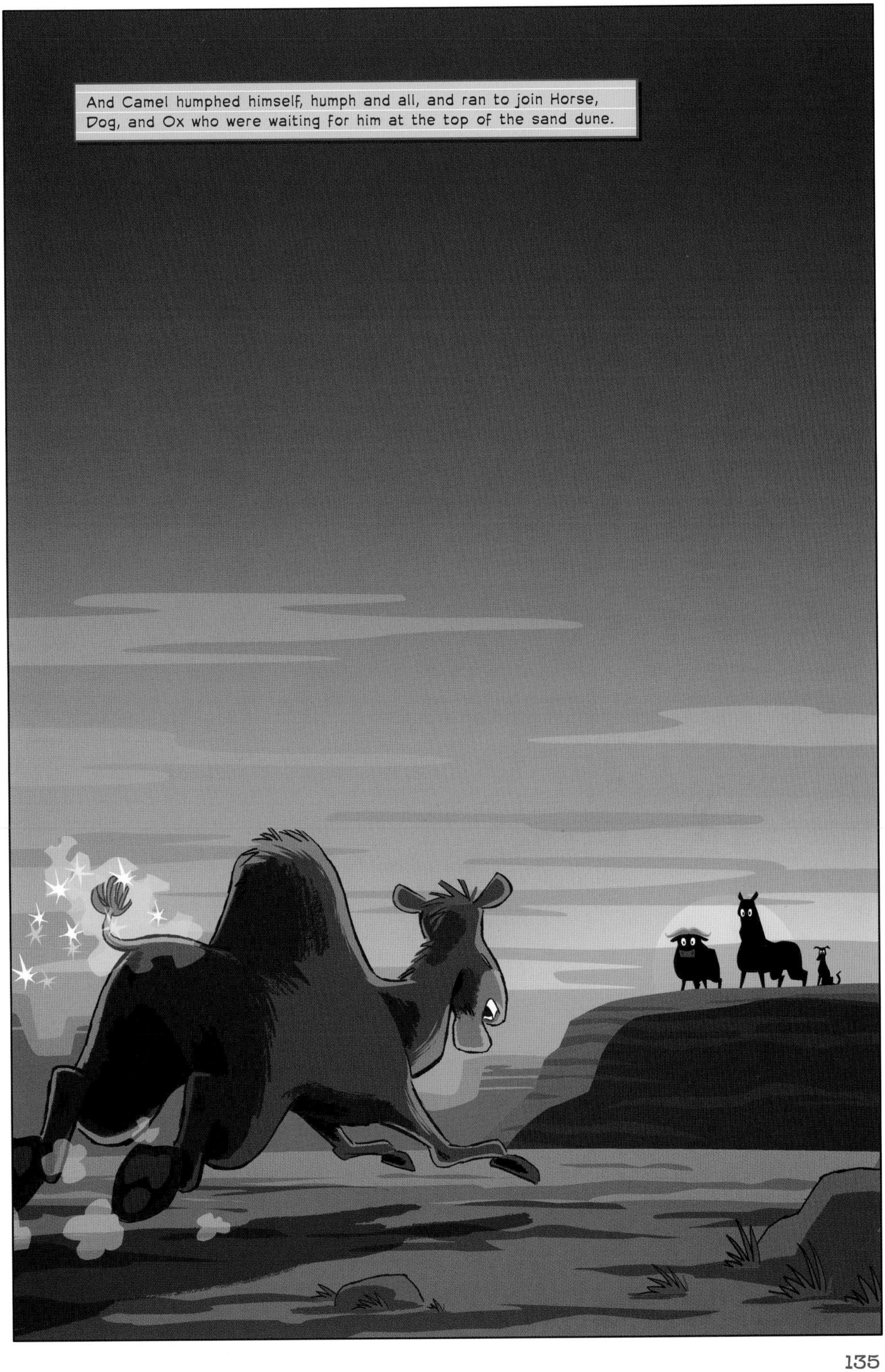
And Camel humphed himself, humph and all, and ran to join Horse, Dog, and Ox who were waiting for him at the top of the sand dune.

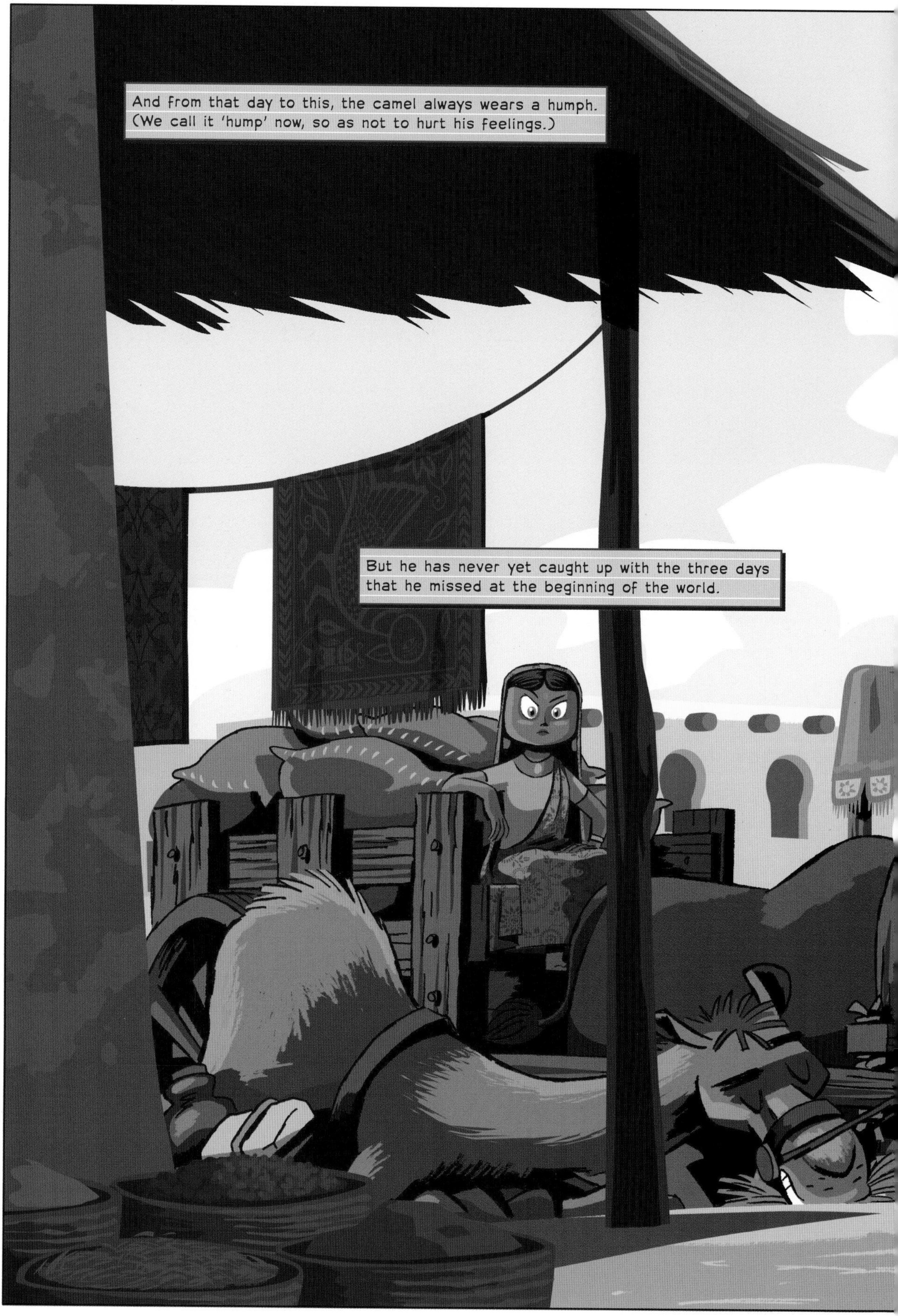
And from that day to this, the camel always wears a humph. (We call it 'hump' now, so as not to hurt his feelings.)
But he has never yet caught up with the three days that he missed at the beginning of the world.

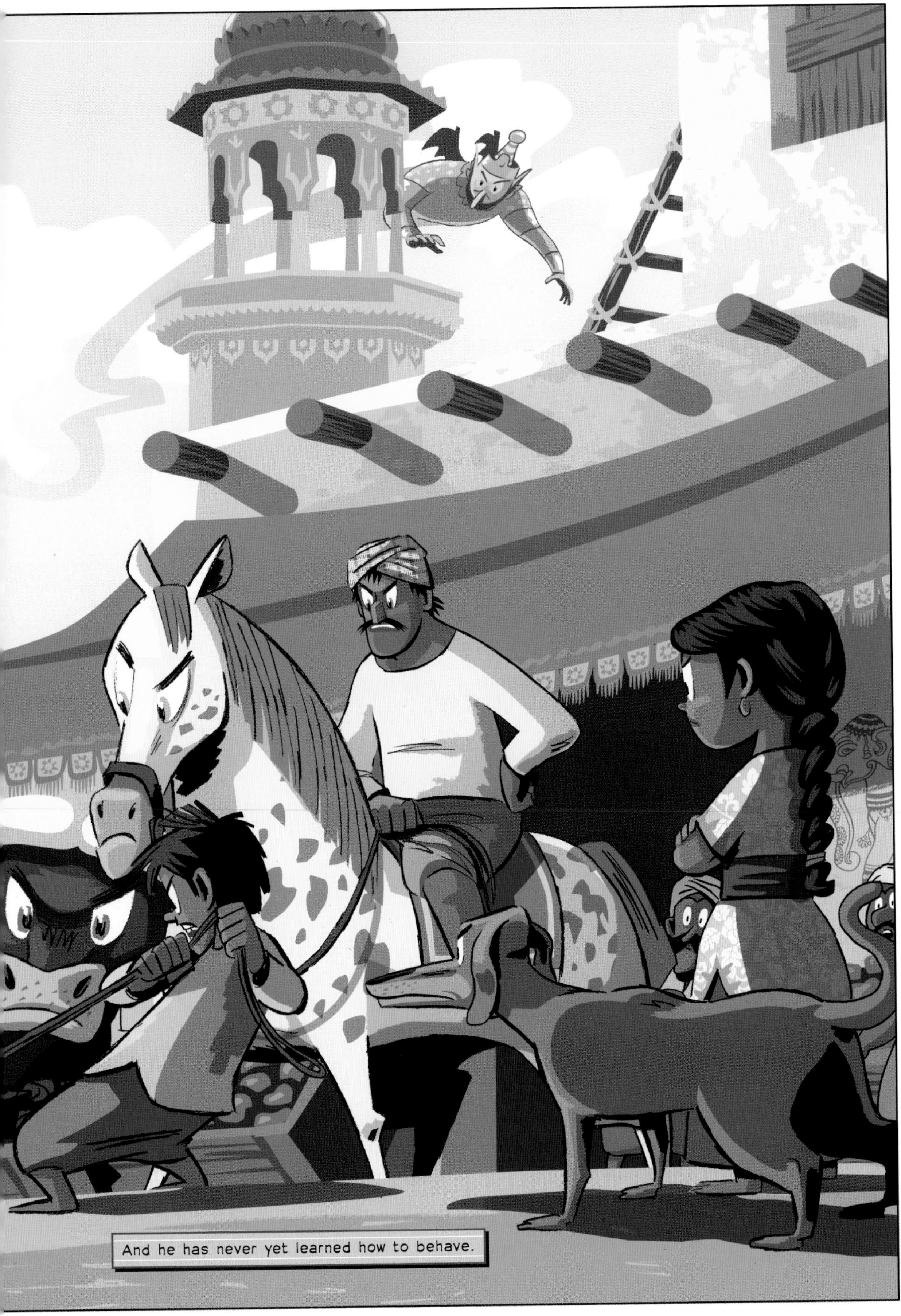
And he has never yet learned how to behave.

THE Camel's hump is an ugly lump
    Which well you may see at the Zoo;
But uglier yet is the hump we get
    From having too little to do.

Kiddies and grown-ups too-oo-oo,
If we haven't enough to do-oo-oo,
    We get the hump—
    Cameelious hump—
The hump that is black and blue!

We climb out of bed with a frouzly head
    And a snarly-yarly voice.
We shiver and scowl and we grunt and we growl
    At our bath and our boots and our toys;

And there ought to be a corner for me
(And I know there is one for you)
    When we get the hump—
    Cameelious hump—
The hump that is black and blue!

The cure for this ill is not to sit still,
    Or frowst with a book by the fire;
But to take a large hoe and a shovel also,
    And dig till you gently perspire;

And then you will find that the sun and the wind.
And the Djinn of the Garden too,
    Have lifted the hump—
    The horrible hump—
The hump that is black and blue!

I get it as well as you-oo-oo—
If I haven't enough to do-oo-oo—
    We all get hump—
    Cameelious hump—
Kiddies and grown-ups too! *

* Poem by Rudyard Kipling.

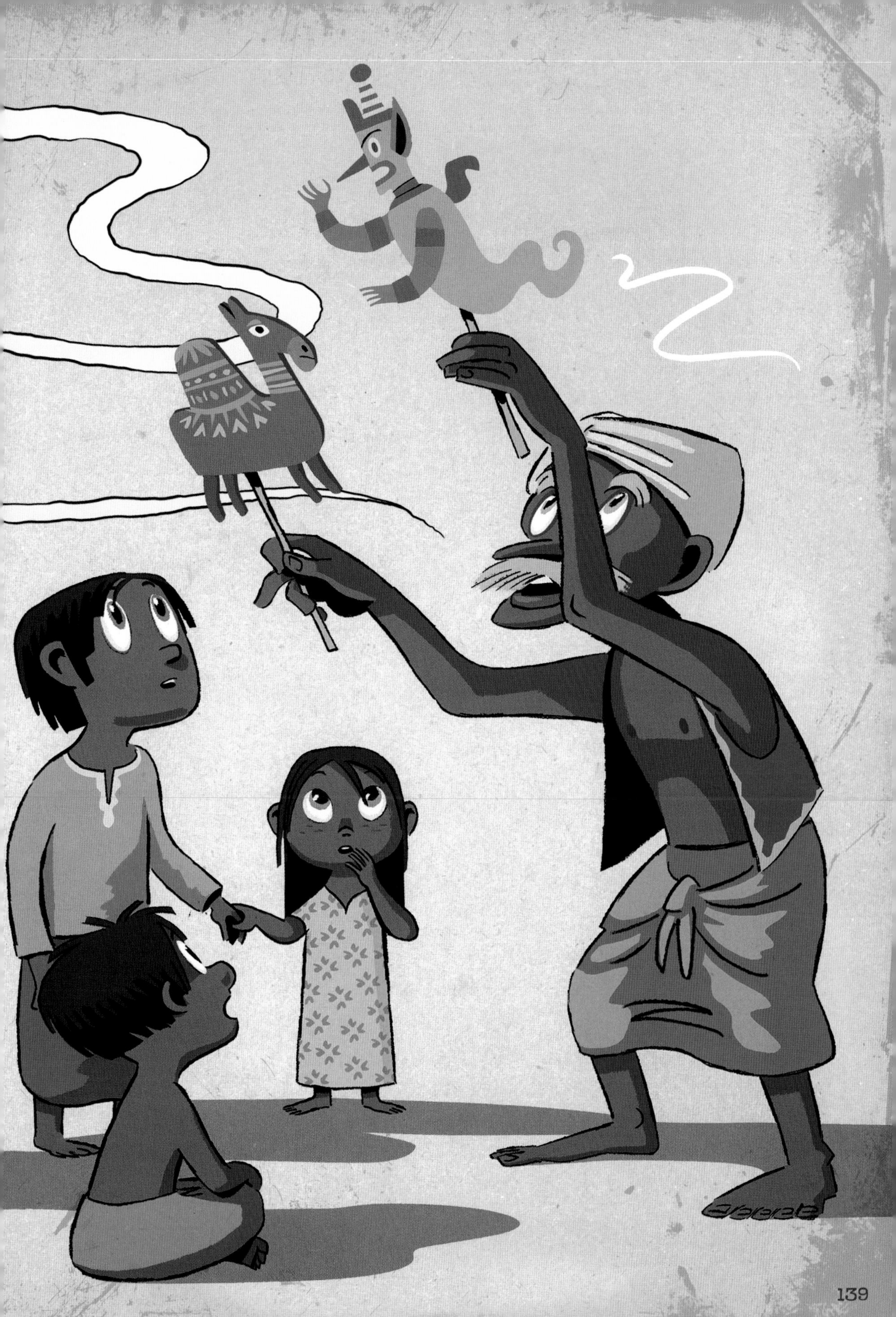

RUDYARD KIPLING 3

# CONCLUSION

## NEW SPECIMEN:
## SINGLE-HUMPED CAMEL

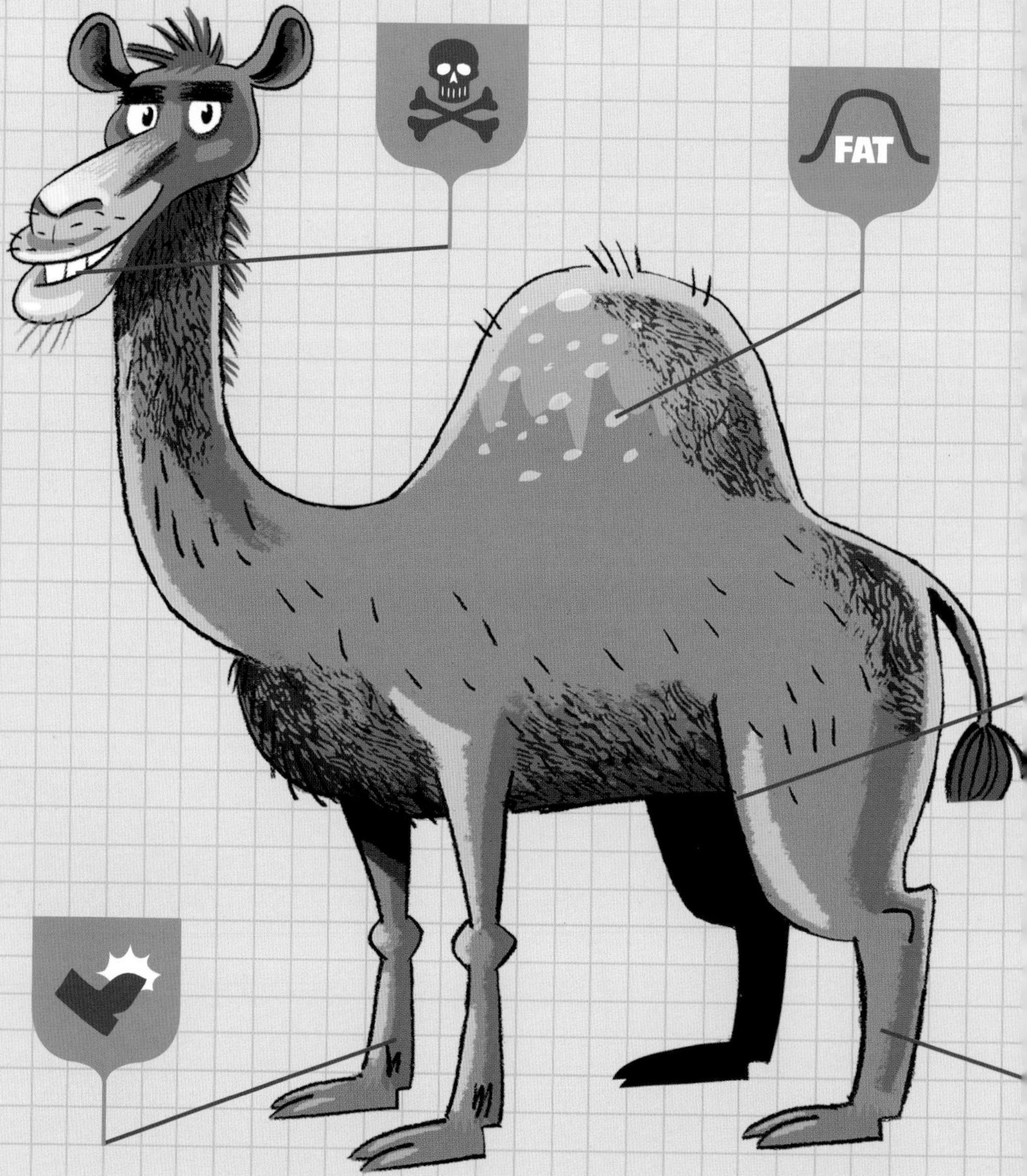
FAT

Camel urine is as thick as syrup, which is just plain gross. As the camel goes without water, the kidneys concentrate the urine, leading to its thickness.

When provoked, a camel will spit a foul-smelling, green fluid from its stomach all over you. At all costs, avoid provoking a camel.

Camels can kick in all four directions with all four legs. Must find a way to turn this skill into trained dancing.

Camels can run up to 65 miles per hour, especially if it is to escape work.

A camel's hump stores fat. The size of the hump changes, depending on the amount of food the camel eats. When running low on food, the camel's body uses the fat stored in the hump, causing it to lean over and droop. How embarrassing!

1

2

3

# *Rudyard Kipling*

## RUDYARD KIPLING
### Founder/Guide

Joseph Rudyard Kipling was born in Bombay, India, on December 30, 1865. He is best known for his short story collections *The Jungle Book*, published in 1894, and *Just So Stories*, published in 1902. He wrote a variety of other short stories, including "Kim" and "The Man Who Would Be King," and many poems. In 1907, he received the Nobel Prize in Literature, becoming the first English-language writer and youngest person to win the award. On January 18, 1936, he died in London at age 70.

# WRITERS

## Sean Tulien

Sean Tulien is a children's book editor from Minnesota. He likes to bike, eat sushi, listen to loud music, and write books like this one.

## Blake A. Hoena

Blake A. Hoena grew up in central Wisconsin. He has written more than fifty books for children, including DC Super Heroes chapter books.

## Martin Powell

Martin Powell has written hundreds of stories, many of which have been published by Disney, Marvel, Tekno Comix, Moonstone Books, and others.

## Louise Simonson

Louise Simonson writes about monsters and superheroes. She's written the award-winning Power Pack series, best-selling X-Men titles, and more.

# ILLUSTRATOR

## Pedro Rodriguez

Pedro Rodriguez studied illustration at the Fine Arts School in Barcelona, Spain. He has worked in design, marketing, and advertising, creating books, logos, animated films, and music videos. Rodriguez lives in Barcelona with his wife, Gemma, and their daughter, Maya.

| | |
|---|---|
| JULIE GASSMAN | editor |
| DONALD LEMKE | managing editor |
| MICHAEL DAHL | editorial director |
| BOB LENTZ | designer & letterer |
| HEATHER KINDSETH | creative director |

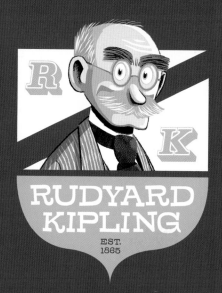

**RUDYARD KIPLING**

EST.
1865

THE MOST TRUSTED NAME
IN JUST SO COMICS.

## capstone

www.capstoneyoungreaders.com

1710 Roe Crest Drive, North Mankato, Minnesota 56003

Cataloging-in-Publication Data is available on the Library of Congress website.
Paperback: 978-1-4342-4880-0

Printed in China.
092012    006936RRDS13